. . . SHE WANTED . . .

Something Else

A Novel by

MEGAN STAFFEL

NORTH POINT PRESS
San Francisco 1987

An earlier version of a portion of this novel was published under the title "The Childhood of Alma Juroe" in the author's *A Length of Wire and Other Stories* in 1983 by Pym-Randall Press, which is gratefully acknowledged.

Copyright © 1987 by Megan Staffel
Printed in the United States of America
Library of Congress Catalogue Card Number: 87-60881
ISBN: 0-86547-293-9

for Jim Randall

. . . I . . .

Rose Ann

$$\cdots \quad \cdots \quad \cdots \quad I \quad \cdots \quad \cdots \quad \cdots$$

It was *1924*, a Tuesday morning in April. The amusement park had just opened for the season, but the midway was empty because all day it had looked like rain. A tall woman in a long, gray coat walked past the merry-go-round. A little boy straggled behind her, and two little girls with braided hair ran in circles around them.

At the end of the midway they stopped in front of the roller coaster. The little girls gave their tickets to the attendant and climbed into the first car. The attendant came over and locked the rail into place across their laps, and because there weren't any other children in line for the ride—or even in sight—on this damp, chilly morning, he went over to the control house. With a grinding of gears, the roller coaster began to move forward. But then it stopped. There were more grinding sounds, and this time the teeth engaged; with a surge of power, the cars began to climb the first wooden hillside.

Rose Ann pulled her hand away from Sybil's and moved to the edge of the seat. She looked over at their mother, who stood on the platform with Russell beside her. Behind them were the bright colors of the empty midway, the rides making crazy profiles against the sky. She gripped the guardrail and looked in front of her at the scaffolding the tiny train was climbing. They reached the top of the hill and with metal wheels squealing on metal tracks, fell downward.

It was the "World's Highest Roller Coaster," guaranteed to make their stomachs jump into their throats or the attendant would gladly refund their money. They began to climb the next hillside, but halfway up the cars slowed to a crawl. Then their car, the first one, tipped over the peak, and they stopped again, looking down the slope they would soon be at the bottom of. When they started to move, Sybil shrieked and burrowed her head into Rose Ann's side so she wouldn't have to see. She was younger, more gullible. If they said her stomach would be in her throat, Sybil would oblige.

They raced halfway up the next hill, and then the cars slowed again. At the top, just as before, they stopped only long enough for the girls to get a good look at the plunge they were about to take. Sybil didn't lift her head from Rose Ann's lap, but Rose Ann sat perfectly still, looking down the track.

On the last and highest incline, the one they called Pike's Peak in the advertisements, there was the same pause as the car was balanced on the apex. To the north, Brooklyn was a frozen arrangement of geometric shapes; to the south, the Atlantic Ocean was untouched open space. Below them, the amusement park was a tangle of color. Rose Ann made Sybil sit up and look at the view. Then, daring herself to do it, she unhooked the guardrail and stood up in the car. She leaned over the side shouting at the top of her voice, "Look at me!" Then again because she wasn't even scared: "Look at me!" From way below, where the danger was blurred by her nearsighted vision, their mother waved back. The gears began to shift, and Sybil whimpered and covered her eyes. Rose Ann sat down, but too roughly, making the car tip sideways. At that moment Sybil happened to shift her weight, and the little wheels locked safely into the track. Rose Ann fastened the guardrail, put her arm around Sybil, and the train moved forward. But it stopped again, to tease them, and then with ferocious speed the two little girls were thrust earthward.

2

In the summer their parents decided to take the children on a vacation. The trunk was packed with each person's allotment of clothing, and the picnic basket was crammed with food and dishes. Their destination was Cape May, New Jersey, the farthest they had ever traveled from their home in Brooklyn.

Wearing his driving cap, Mr. Beech approached the family car. The finicky nature of the automobile made him take every precaution. He inspected the tires, opened the hood, and checked the oil and water. Somewhere halfway they would have to stop for gasoline and check the radiator again. Mr. Beech was worried they wouldn't be able to find a place.

"Everything will be fine," his wife assured him, coming down the driveway with the children. "It will be a safe, lovely trip."

They got on the parkway going south. The engine ticked quietly and the tires were silent on the smooth road surface. Inside, the three children sat together on the backseat. Squeezed between the two girls, Russell was being poked in the ribs. Giggling and squealing, he doubled over to protect himself. But it went on too long. Catching him in a fit of choking, Mrs. Beech turned around.

"That's enough!"

Her tone canceled their humor. "I'm hungry," Sybil said. "When can we stop to eat?"

"You're hungry already?" Their mother looked at her watch.

"I have to go to the bathroom," Russell said.

"Do you mean you want to use the gentlemen's room?"

"Yes."

She murmured to Mr. Beech, "As soon as you see a suitable place, I think we should stop."

At least they had gotten out of New York. Mr. Beech slowed the car down carefully and pulled onto the grass at the side of the highway. When the engine stopped, the insects roared in the quiet.

"Gentlemen's room for you," Mr. Beech said, opening the door.

Russell fell over Sybil and had to be helped down from the running board. Watching him follow their father across the field, rushing on his small legs to keep up, Rose Ann didn't feel any remorse for teasing him. Sybil, her cohort, was helping their mother spread the tablecloth on the grass for a picnic. "Not what I would call an ideal spot," Mrs. Beech was saying.

"Maybe we shouldn't stop here," Sybil said.

"I thought you were the one who was hungry."

Sybil didn't answer. She had been hungry at that particular moment, but now, a moment later, the sensation had passed. But those were the things they never attempted to explain to their mother. She wouldn't have been interested.

Mrs. Beech arranged sandwiches on their plates, and Sybil added chunks of tomato. "I wish we could have stopped somewhere by the ocean," Rose Ann said wistfully.

"Sometimes you can't have everything."

"Me too," Sybil said.

"I suppose you would have preferred the sand too? This is just fine," she said, pulling fruit out of the basket. "I hope you will enjoy yourselves on this vacation rather than spend all of your time complaining. If you complain, there won't be any more vacations."

"We know," Rose Ann said quietly. She took a slice of tomato from one of the plates and popped it in her mouth, wiping the juice off with the back of her hand.

Sybil took a plate and sat down next to Rose Ann.

"Just a minute," Mrs. Beech said. "Where are your manners? Let's wait till Russell and your father get back. They're taking much longer than they should be. I certainly hope nothing's happened."

"Can't I eat? I'm hungry."

"I thought you were the one who wanted to wait for a nicer spot."

Rose Ann stuck another tomato in her mouth and when the juice dripped down her chin she didn't bother to wipe it off. Her mother caught her with the evidence clearly on her face, but she didn't say anything.

"Maybe we should try to find them. I wonder where they could be."

Just then Russell stepped through the bushes, his sailor shirt hanging out of his sailor pants. Their father came next.

"My goodness," Mrs. Beech exclaimed. "I was just beginning to worry."

"We got lost!" Russell said excitedly.

Mr. Beech looked embarrassed.

"Lost? How could you?" They turned to look at the flat, treeless landscape.

"Not really lost," their father said. "You were all sitting down so there was nothing to guide us. I got a little confused, that's all."

"Well, have some lunch," Mrs. Beech said.

When they had cleaned up, they climbed back into the car. Russell sat up front next to their mother, and the two girls sat in the backseat. Sybil was reading a book, and Rose Ann was looking out the window.

"I haven't noticed a gas station yet," Mr. Beech said. "Have you?"

"How's the tank?" their mother asked.

"Well, it's going down," their father said, "but it's not an emergency yet. Not by any means. Just keep a lookout, that's all. And make sure you tell me because I might not see it."

Empty grassland stretched away from the car. Birds circled in the sky, and cows stood motionless beneath an occasional tree.

"Are you sure we're going in the right direction?" Mrs. Beech asked.

"According to the map we are. Pretty soon we should see the ocean."

"*Now* how's the tank?"

"I expect she's getting low." Their father checked the gauge. "Yes sir," he said and turned to his wife. "This is the very thing I was afraid would happen."

"One's bound to come up soon. This road has lots of travelers."

"I haven't seen any other cars the whole time we've been on here," Rose Ann called from the backseat.

"There've been some," Mrs. Beech replied. "But cars aren't what you should be noticing. Keep a lookout for a gas station."

Sybil turned a page in her book. Rose Ann pressed her nose against the window. At last there was a cluster of modest buildings with a rusty pump close to the road. When they pulled in, the dog that was sleeping in the driveway didn't even lift his head, nor did anyone come out of the shacks behind him. "Wouldn't that be something . . . ," their father said, but he got out of the car without finishing the sentence.

When their father returned, a man with blond hair that stood straight up from his forehead, walked behind him. The dog began to bark. The man said, "Quiet, Jeb," and the dog cowered.

Their father talked to the man as he pumped the gas. "We have a long drive ahead of us, and I'd appreciate it if you'd check under the hood."

"Happy to oblige." The man pulled out a bandanna and wiped his neck.

Russell woke up and announced he had to go to the bathroom.

"The gentlemen's room, you mean. Your father can go with you. God knows what it looks like."

After the attendant had checked the car and Russell had been taken care of, they pulled out of the driveway.

"Did you ask him how far it is?"

"I forgot."

"Maybe you should turn around. What if we've missed a turn?"

"There haven't been any turns."

"That's what I'm referring to. Did he fill the tank?"

"Full tank."

"How did everything else check out?"

"Everything's fine," their father said.

"I just wonder how far it is."

"By my guess we have another hour."

They pulled into Cape May exactly an hour later. Pleased with the accuracy of his prediction, their father whistled as he drove down Main Street.

"Now," their mother began, "I want everyone to look out the window for a particular hotel I've always heard about. It's big and white, and it has a porch in front, and it's supposed to be at the very center of everything. Of course, this was years ago, but maybe it hasn't changed."

"We'll do our best," their father said.

"I wonder if we should have called in reservations someplace, just to be safe."

The street was filled with a steady line of cars, and the sidewalk was jammed with people.

"I can't make a quick turn in traffic like this, so we might have to double back. Everybody look out and the first person who sees something holler."

"I'd like to try and find *this* place first. Look for something big and white with a porch. I think the name had the word 'baths' in it. Wouldn't that be something," she said to their father, "if, after all of these years, it still exists?"

When the street ended at the boardwalk, their father had to turn left or right. He looked to their mother. She said, "Well, I suppose if we don't find it one way we can turn around and go back the other way."

Russell woke up and said, "I'm hungry."

Their father turned right.

"When are we going to have dinner?" Sybil asked.

They passed two lower-class guest houses, their porches rickety, their signs faded. Their father slowed, asked, "What do you think?" Their mother said, "It's the kind of place where you'd want to wipe the toilet seat before you sat on it. I don't think we should do it. We'll spend a little more money and find someplace where we're sure it's clean."

When it was clear there would be no more hotels, their father checked front and back for traffic and made a U-turn.

"Just be patient, children," their mother called. "As soon as we find a place to stay, we'll have our dinner. You wouldn't want to end up with no place to sleep tonight, would you?"

"No," Sybil said.

"No," Russell echoed.

Rose Ann peered out the window at a woman who was being pushed along the sidewalk in a wheelchair. She wore a red shawl around her shoulders, and on her head there was a hat with flowers stuck in the band. The elderly man who pushed her wore a hat with flowers, too.

They came to the crossroads and proceeded down the street in the other direction. Just a block from where they had made the first turn, there was an enormous white hotel with balconies and awnings and in the center of a circular drive, a seashell-shaped fountain with a flying fish rising from the water. Out of its mouth hung a wooden flag with the word "OceanView" on it.

"This is it," their mother said.

"It's not called baths," their father said doubtfully.

"It doesn't matter, I know this is the place. Can't you stop?"

Their father pulled into the driveway behind a brand-new, wine-colored Duesenberg. "We can't afford a hotel like this. Look at the kind of cars there are."

"Sometimes it's the place that looks expensive that's the cheapest in the long run. Let me get out and I'll see. Would one of you children like to come with me?"

When Rose Ann volunteered, Mrs. Beech took her comb from her pocketbook and ran it through the snarls in Rose Ann's hair. "Just look at you," she said, "you look like a gypsy."

Hair combed, face stinging from the hasty finger washing, Rose Ann followed her mother through the double doors into the lobby. A fan on the ceiling generated a refreshing breeze. Clusters of palm trees, their leaves fluttering, divided the room into seating areas. Rose Ann's mother marched across the dizzy pattern of an Oriental rug and stopped in front of the reception desk. A man with shiny black hair greeted her. She smiled. Then she said, "My husband and I and my three children, ages four, seven and a half, and nine, have driven here from Brooklyn. We just arrived. Since I have always heard wonderful things about Ocean-View, we thought we'd see if you had any vacancies before trying somewhere else."

The man looked down at the guest book.

Mrs. Beech said, "I know we should have made reservations."

"A family suite is what you'd be needing." He looked at his board of keys. "Number six is available. It has a balcony overlooking the ocean.

Most of our guests request it specially but, by a stroke of sheer luck, it's open. It is yours, madam. And how long will you be staying?" He lifted a golden key from a hook and lay it between them on the counter.

"Can you tell me," Rose Ann's mother asked, "what it would cost?"

He made a triangle with his fingers to support his chin and looked down at her with saintly composure. "A suite for a family of five, with meals in the dining room included, is twenty-one dollars."

"Oh," Mrs. Beech replied. She dropped her arm from the counter. "I'd be very grateful if you'd write that out so I may discuss it with my husband who's waiting outside." As he was writing it, she asked, "Would there be anything less expensive?"

He shook his head. "No, madam, I'm afraid not." Already dismissing them, he handed her the slip of hotel notepaper.

When they got to the car, Rose Ann climbed into the backseat. "We're too poor," she announced.

Mrs. Beech gave the paper to their father. "It's very lovely. And that figure is with meals. That's not so bad."

Their father whistled, started the car.

"I think we should consider it. It might seem like a lot, but with everything included you actually make out better."

"Do you know what they expect just in tips at a place like that?" Their father turned into the street.

"Can't I have something to eat?" Russell asked.

On the next block there was a small white building with a sign on the lawn that said, "Salty Baths." An old man sitting on the porch looked up when the car stopped in front.

"This couldn't be right," Mrs. Beech said.

As their father got out, the man came down the steps. "We're looking for accommodations," their father shouted.

"Don't shout!" their mother hissed out the window. "The whole world can hear you."

"How many you got there?" the man shouted back. He came down the sidewalk and shook their father's hand. "Four plus the wife," their father answered.

The man waved a greeting toward the family. "Six dollars a night for the whole carload."

"Sounds fair," their father said, following the man into the house.

As the children watched, their mother sighed. "Wouldn't it just be our luck? Drive all the way here and end up somewhere no better than home."

"I think it's okay," Rose Ann replied.

"Me, too," Sybil added.

"When can we eat?" Russell asked.

"Won't be long now," Mrs. Beech told him in a tired voice. To Rose Ann she said, "Okay isn't the point. If you're satisfied with okay, then why be alive?"

But it was better than okay. It was good. The children had a room to themselves, and it was clear down at the other end of the hall. Their window looked out on the sidewalk, and the street, and beyond that, to the dunes. Behind the dunes, where they couldn't see it, lay the ocean. Rose Ann pictured a huge wave rising over the sidewalk and flooding the street. It would happen at night when everyone was sleeping. In their dreams they'd hear the sound of water sloshing through the rooms on the first floor. But no one would discover it until morning. Then confusion would take over. Routine and order would disappear, and unexpected liberties would be bestowed on them.

And yet, even without catastrophe, vacation allowed the unusual. For instance, Rose Ann and Sybil were going to sleep in a double bed. Russell was going to sleep on a cot. Mr. Salty Baths, whose real name was such a strange mixture of syllables that the children had been unable to learn it, had pulled the cot out of a closet in their room. After he had opened it, their mother had dusted it off with her handkerchief. Then he had spread a sheet on top of it and put out pillows and towels and light blankets in case the temperature dropped. He had set the cot under the window, but as soon as he left, their mother had moved it to the other side of the room. "Places like these, you can't be too careful," she said, checking the screen to make sure it was securely set into the window. "I don't want you children leaning against this. It's a long hard fall to the sidewalk. Rose Ann, I want your solemn promise that you won't let Russell do any climbing up here. All right?"

"Okay," Rose Ann said.

Mr. and Mrs. Salty Baths invited the family to have dinner with them. Their father said yes, but only if they'd let him pay. Mr. Salty Baths hesitated, but his wife interrupted and said, "Nothing will be turned down. It's been a lean summer."

So, after the required before-dinner washings, the children trooped down the stairs with their mother. Their father was on the porch with Mr. Salty Baths reading the paper. Russell was sent out there, and Mrs. Beech took Rose Ann and Sybil into the kitchen to see if they could be of any help.

Mrs. Salty Baths, a large pink woman with tufts of gray fuzz sticking up from her scalp and a round, shiny face, was standing in the center of the room drinking ice water. There were whiskers on her cheeks. Flesh hung in scallops from her upper arms, and her neck was coiled with creases. Behind the striped wall of her housedress, steam rose from pots on the stove. "My little chickens," she said to the girls, opening her arms to draw them into her. "A nice soda before dinner? How would you like that? Are they allowed?" she asked Mrs. Beech, who nodded yes and then added, "Not too much, it will ruin their appetite."

After the soda they were given the task of setting the dining-room table. Their mother checked that everything was placed correctly and then helped Mrs. Salty Baths dish up the food. When the men were called in from the porch, everyone gathered in the dining room. Mr. Salty Baths sat at the head of the table, and the grown-ups fell into the places around him, the children squeezed together next to their mother.

Russell complained of a stomachache. Mrs. Beech told him to drink some water and eat some bread.

"With lots of butter," Mrs. Salty Baths added, demonstrating as she slathered butter on her own slice. "It coats the stomach so everything slides right through."

Silverware clicking loudly, everyone started to eat. But halfway through the meal, when she determined that the silence had lasted long enough, their mother started a conversation. "Tell me," she began.

Still chewing, Mr. and Mrs. Salty Baths looked in her direction.

"What is the history of your establishment? Have you been in the business very long?"

Mr. Salty Baths laughed. He swallowed and then said, "We're the oldest hotel on the block. Used to be you couldn't stay here without a reservation. We had dining out back," he pointed toward the kitchen, "you can still see it—there's a terrace and used to be, shucks, six, eight rooms that we'd rent out at one time."

"What happened?" Mrs. Beech asked eagerly.

"We got old," Mrs. Salty Baths answered.

"That ain't all," her husband bellowed. "The times changed. The OceanView opened up. The people changed. Weren't families no more. Or at least they didn't come here. They wanted someplace fancy, like the OceanView. All those statues and plants and things, they liked that."

"Used to be," his wife said, "I spent the summer in the kitchen cooking for everybody. Fresh butter, fresh dairy, breakfast, lunch, and dinner. Good home cooking, that's what it was. Old-country cooking. Nobody likes it no more."

Russell helped himself to another piece of bread and butter.

"I suggest you have something along with that," Mrs. Beech said.

"But I like it," he whined.

"Homemade bread, fresh country butter, he knows what's good," Mrs. Salty Baths said. "I bet your stomach feels better now."

He nodded happily.

"Would you like more soda?"

He nodded yes.

"Would you get the boy more soda?" Mrs. Salty Baths said to her husband.

He pushed back his chair.

"He's had enough soda, thank you," their mother said.

"It's good for him," Mrs. Salty Baths exclaimed. "The bubbles eat up all the gas. He'll feel even better. It's in the door," she said to her husband.

Mr. Salty Baths looked at their mother, but their father made a sweeping gesture across the table and in a magnanimous tone proclaimed that they were on vacation and another soda would be just fine.

During coffee, their hosts invited the family to join them in the parlor for their favorite radio program, "The Mystery Hour." Mrs. Beech, who believed that the radio was proper entertainment only if you were confined to the sickbed, said thank you, but they would retire to their rooms to unpack and since they were all very tired, get ready for an early bedtime. Mr. Beech looked at his watch and said, "At six-thirty?" It was then decided that the family should take advantage of the cool summer evening and go for a walk. After face washings and hair combings, the children were ready.

Out of habit, they fell into formation: Rose Ann and Sybil walked in front; Russell was next, and behind him, their mother and father. No one spoke. It was lower class to talk as you were walking. Well-bred people talked in their houses, not outside. Nor did they look down at the sidewalk. It gave you bad posture. Russell kept his hands out of his pockets and to save the soles of his shoes, lifted his feet completely off the ground with each step. No dragging. That was not only hard on the shoes but displayed a disposition for slovenliness. Mr. and Mrs. Beech didn't hold hands, nor did they walk very close. But Mr. Beech smiled. He was happy. They had gotten there without any misfortunes. Russell was happy, too, though he didn't smile. He kept it secret, gloating privately over the fact of two sodas and bread and butter for dinner.

In the front, the family completely out of view and consequently out of their thoughts, Rose Ann and Sybil marched into the evening. No one was ahead of them, only the red clouds at the end of the street and the gaily colored signs and awnings of the shops they passed, marking off the distance. But then the woman with the flowers in her hat appeared from a doorway. The old man pushed her wheelchair onto the sidewalk.

In the sky the red deepened. The edges of the clouds turned fluffy. Sea gulls swooped down from the buildings, calling raucously. In front of them, the woman in the wheelchair laughed. It was a deep, full-bodied sound, and it lasted a long time, the man joining in only at the very end. Long after it had stopped, the air still echoed. Her life must be very wonderful, Rose Ann decided, if something in it was allowed to be so funny.

The girls crossed the street and marched up the steps to the board-walk. At last, there was the ocean, black and loud and powerful. Heads bobbing up and down, a few vigorous swimmers broke the surface. But the ocean swallowed them. When they reappeared, they looked like bits of cork.

"Can I have one?" Russell called out.

Approaching them on the boardwalk was a man selling Italian ice.

"Certainly not," Mrs. Beech called back. "You've had enough for one night, young man."

"What about me?" Sybil asked.

Their mother didn't answer. Everyone looked at their father, who pulled his change purse out of his pocket. As he searched for nickels, Rose Ann wandered back to the stairs they had just passed. She tiptoed down them and stepped onto the beach. Expecting to be stopped at any moment, she went only a few steps, then stood still. A wave gathered far out in the ocean and rolled toward her, growing higher and higher. She ran all the way up to it, kicking off her shoes. With the red sky spread out above her, the black water in front, she galloped through the wet sand. Over the steady roar, she thought she heard her name, but when she turned around, she could see the family still clustered around the vendor. Rose Ann! Rose Ann! The sound of the ocean was deafening. The undertow dragged the ground out from underneath her, and she lost her balance. As she stood up, frothy water pooled at her feet. It was soft and very cold. When the next wave came, she squatted down in the sand, but with water spilling around her, she toppled over. Completely wet, she was no longer cold. As the wave rose even higher, the undertow grew stronger. No more than a scrap of substance, she was dragged away from the shore into the rising, spiraling water. The wave arched above her, and she was twirled around in a cone of darkness. Finally, there were no rules or secrets, and she didn't know enough to be scared of anything. The wave crested, and the force of the falling water pushed her back onto the sand. Struggling to her feet, she saw a man moving across the beach waving his arms. It was her father. She started to run, too, and when they met, he swooped her up to his chest and kissed her all over her face. "Are you all right?" he asked.

She put her arms around his neck.

When they reached her shoes, he got her out of her dress and peeling off his shirt, rubbed her dry with it. Then he buttoned her into it and carried her up to the boardwalk. Russell and Sybil were peering over the railing, eating their ices. Their mother ran up to Rose Ann and kneeled down in front of her, enclosing her in her arms. "My baby," she murmured, "whatever happened?" She kissed Rose Ann's cheeks, felt her forehead, tousled her hair, all the time pressing her against her breast. "Whatever happened, my baby girl?"

Later, when Rose Ann was wrapped in a blanket and sitting against the pillows on the bed in her parent's room, the questions became more specific.

"Whatever possessed you to go down to the beach in the first place? Couldn't you wait until tomorrow when we'd be wearing our bathing suits and going together as a family?"

When Rose Ann was silent, her mother said, "I would like an answer, young lady."

"I don't know," she said.

"And then," her mother went on, "why did you even go near the water? Don't you know how dangerous it is? You could have drowned, do you realize that?"

"Yes," Rose Ann said.

"Then why did you do it?"

She couldn't think of an answer that would please her mother, so with the same certainty she had felt on the beach, she said, "I wanted to."

"Is that so? Well then, there's something that needs to be made very clear. You are not to stay out of my sight for one second until we return to Brooklyn. If I miss you for even a moment, we'll pack everything up and go back home. Before you can say Jack Robinson. Is that clear?"

She was tucked into bed next to Sybil, given a cursory peck on her cheek, and left with instructions to review her behavior before going to sleep. When their mother disappeared, Sybil asked, "What happened?"

"It wasn't too bad," Rose Ann said.

Russell sat up in his cot. "What's going on?"

"Just go back to sleep. Nothing's going on."

He climbed onto their bed, flopping onto his stomach between them.

"No one invited you," Sybil said. He bit her arm. "Stop it, Russell, get away."

Rose Ann shushed them, opening up the covers for Russell to get in. "This is our little baby," she said to Sybil. "We have to burp him and nurse him and tuck him into his bed."

"First a kiss," Sybil whispered, catching on to this new game without further prompting from Rose Ann.

"Get away!" Russell cried, struggling to escape.

"No, you don't, little baby. You stay right here." Rose Ann pinned him down to the mattress, sticking her elbow into his back.

"Ouch!" he cried. "Let go of me."

"Be quiet!" Sybil bent down to kiss him again and this time was able to touch her lips against his cheek. "Sweet baby," she murmured.

"Would the baby like to nurse?" Rose Ann asked, lifting her nightgown over her chest.

Sybil giggled. Russell flopped to the other side.

"Isn't the baby hungry?" Rose Ann asked.

"Maybe he has to go to the bathroom," Sybil suggested.

"Maybe so. You can tell if he does by feeling his thing. Let us feel it," she said to Russell.

"Get out!" he screeched.

Like a crab, Sybil's hand traveled up his pajamas and pinched him on the rear end.

"Not there," Rose Ann said. "In the front."

"But maybe he has to go to the bathroom here," Sybil said grabbing his bottom. "Little boy, do you have to go to the bathroom?" Russell reared up out of the blankets and scurried off their bed. He had almost gotten away when Rose Ann caught his ankle.

"I think he does," she said. "But if we take him down the hallway, we'll get into trouble." She looked around the room, her glance settling on the window. "Do you want to do something very exciting?" she asked her brother.

"Let go of me," he said.

"This might be your only chance to do it."

"Do what?" Sybil asked.

"Come here, I'll whisper it."

Sybil scooted closer and Rose Ann pushed her hair away from her ear and began to whisper. Sybil started to giggle before she had even finished, and Russell, halfway off the bed cried out, "I will not!"

"You don't even know what it is!" Sybil said.

"I'm not doing it."

"It will be fun. Wait till you see." Rose Ann gave Russell's ankle to her sister and got out of bed. She went over to the window and pushed it up as far as she could. Just as it started to fall out, she caught the screen, dropping it to the floor. Sybil hissed, "Be quiet!"

Rose Ann leaned out the window and looked up and down the street. It was completely still. No one walked down the sidewalk, no headlights broke the darkness. She could hear the surf. The coolness that brushed her face could have been the water. "It's a beautiful night," she said, coming back inside.

Russell pulled himself out of Sybil's grasp, but Rose Ann caught his arm. "This will be fun," she said, drawing him next to her. "In the olden days people used to do it all the time."

"Do what?"

"Poop out the window," Sybil shouted, bursting into laughter.

"Shush!"

"I will not," Russell said, struggling to get away.

"We'll be very careful." Rose Ann grabbed his wrists securely. "We'll hold you very carefully so you won't fall down to the sidewalk and crack your head open. You just aim your heinie, and we'll take care of the rest."

"I don't want to," he said, as Sybil started to pull his pajamas down. He resisted all the way to the window, and as they hoisted him up to the sill, one sister on either side, he began to cry.

"He's scared," Sybil said.

"Are you scared?" Rose Ann asked.

He shook his head.

"See, he's not scared."

"He is, Rose Ann. Let's not do it."

"All we have to do is get him to sit the other way and we'll hold onto him. Now, Russell baby, sit so you're looking into the room. We want your heinie sticking out the window."

"I don't have to go to the bathroom."

"The gentlemen's room," Rose Ann corrected.

He put his head down and whimpered.

"Come on, Rose Ann, he's really scared."

"All right," Rose Ann said, pulling him down off the windowsill.

"You don't have to do it. I'll do it and you can see how it's done, and next time, if you have to go to the gentlemen's room in the middle of the night, you'll know what to do and you won't be scared. Now watch," she said. She pulled her nightgown off and, naked, sat down on the cold wood of the sill.

"Be careful!" Sybil cried.

Pushing off from the radiator, she inched out until only her thighs were touching wood. Her bare behind stuck out into the night sky.

In the room, Russell giggled. Sybil warned, "You better bring that thing back in or a bird's going to get you."

But she was out there, exhibiting everything to the entire world. She pictured how it must look from the ground, her two pink cheeks hanging in the darkness. It was wicked and lower class, but she wasn't going to come back in till she was good and ready.

4

Every summer she was sent to a camp in the Adirondack mountains. So there would be money left over for Sybil to go when she was older, her parents could afford to send her for only four weeks. Even so, that was long enough to expose her to athletics. But in three summers of swimming and riding and tennis lessons, Rose Ann hadn't excelled at anything. She didn't have any patience.

During her last summer there, when she was twelve years old, she befriended a boy who also wasn't very good at any of the sports. His name was Eddie, and on three occasions he had convinced Rose Ann to let him kiss her.

The embraces took place under the footbridge that connected the boys' camp to the girls' camp. They would pull apart when footsteps sounded above them, but that only increased the excitement of their secret meetings. Sitting on the bank that sloped down to the stream, they whispered and giggled long past the curfew.

On the last night of the season, when all the other campers were in their cabins, packing their trunks, Rose Ann and Eddie were meeting under the bridge for the last time. Eddie took out his pocketknife and led her back up the slope. On the bridge he selected a spot on one of the posts and began to chisel at it. Rose Ann watched in silence as he steadily picked at the soft wood. Like an old man, he was breathing loudly with the effort. Soon there was a lopsided heart carved into the post. He closed the knife and put it into his pocket. Then he took her hand and led her back under the bridge where they crouched together in the chilly mud. "It stands for us," Eddie whispered, and Rose Ann said, "I know." She was disappointed. If it was going to be where everyone could see it, she wanted her name there, too. What good was a heart if no one knew who it belonged to? But she kept her disappointment to herself and with generous patience allowed him to plant the fourth kiss on her carefully parted lips. When he wanted to give her a fifth one, she told him she had to go back to her cabin to pack.

On departure day the wealthier campers were taken home in cars while everyone else was put on the train. Rose Ann would have liked her parents to drive up in a brand-new Cadillac tourer, but she wasn't one of the lucky ones. Instead, she boarded the train with the rest of the campers and reluctantly joined in the singing and shouting as it pulled away from the country station.

She watched the landscape from her window, the broad Hudson and the cliffs rising above it, and when they were an hour outside of New York, she got up from her seat to walk down the aisle. She walked to the end of her car and pulled the door open to go into the next one. When she was between the doors with the hot air rushing up from the tracks and the loud, naked sound of the train, she stopped. She could see the ground through the opening in the floor. It was a little scary, but she made herself stay there. The train jolted. Panicking, she opened the door to the next car and escaped. The door swung closed behind her and the heat diminished.

Halfway down the aisle, someone called her name. She turned around, and there was Eddie crowded into a seat with two of his buddies. "Where are you going?" he asked.

Since campers were supposed to remain in the center car, they were breaking the rules. Eddie's voice had a note of jealousy because Rose Ann was going farther ahead, and she was brave enough to do it by herself.

"I want to see how long the train is," she answered.

So the four of them began to walk through the train together. They invented a game, rushing through quiet cars with sleeping families just to endure the noise and the rocking in between them. Eddie's companions disappeared, and in the last car he and Rose Ann settled down into an empty seat. There, she allowed him to initiate kiss number five.

Before it was completed, however, she pulled away. "Let's save it until the very last moment, and then it will be more special." She whispered into his ear, "Wait and see."

Rose Ann liked strategies. When she knew what she wanted, she could quickly figure out a plan to get it. A heart on a bridge was useless without her name inside it and furthermore, it gave her a feeling in her stomach of things just melting away, rather than coming to a satisfactory finish. A public farewell with the boy she loved would be a better ending. She could see the dark station, the silver train, the crowd of descending passengers, and there was Eddie enclosing her in a passionate embrace.

As they came into the city, Rose Ann grabbed Eddie's arm and pulled him to the doorway. They watched the familiar landmarks, the muddy Harlem River, and the squat brown buildings. They passed above a street crowded with shoppers, and then suddenly it was dark as the train entered the tunnel. Rose Ann squeezed Eddie's hand, and they watched the darkness until the lights of Grand Central appeared. The platform came into view, first the workmen and then the throngs of people waiting to meet the train. They eased to a stop. The conductor came around to pull down their steps, but with the pressure of her hand, Rose Ann let Eddie know he wasn't to run out. She had already seen the familiar white feathered hat her mother wore in the summer. She had just stepped off the moving stairs and with a busy look on her face, a look that meant she wanted to collect Rose Ann and get back home as soon as she could, she was moving toward them.

Rose Ann pulled Eddie onto the platform, threw her arms around him, and pressed her lips against his. When he recovered from his surprise, he took what he could of the proffered kiss. But as he attempted to return it, Rose Ann let go of his hand and turned around to face her mother. "Mama, I'd like you to meet a friend from camp."

She slapped Rose Ann's face. Then she pulled her away from the little boy who looked at her so timidly. Without saying anything, she marched her across the platform and up the steps to the street.

Russell and Sybil were waiting outside in a taxi. Mrs. Beech opened the door and told Rose Ann to get inside. Her brother and sister moved over so Rose Ann wouldn't sit on them, and Rose Ann began to cry. Her mother disappeared into the station to find a porter.

It was a humid day at the end of July, and the people passing on the sidewalk looked pale and tired. The driver was asleep in his seat with a newspaper spread across his belly. His steady breathing mixed with the sounds of traffic and the bits of conversation they heard as people walked by the cab. Russell asked what was going on, and Sybil told him that Rose Ann was upset. Rose Ann, hunched against the door, was quiet. When her mother returned with a porter, the trunk was tied to the rack on the car. Mrs. Beech settled into the front seat, and as they moved through midtown heading toward Brooklyn, Rose Ann said, "You don't know anything."

Her mother turned around to look at her. "Don't you ever let me catch you doing something like that again."

5

But the admonition that was supposed to create boundaries for her behavior only provided a glimpse into the forbidden beyond. As she grew older, she moved closer to it. It was something she could almost see—a place with a red sky and warm white sand. She saw strange, pointed trees. They stood straight in the air, piercing the sky like needles, their branches making a triangular shape against the flat landscape.

When she pictured this place, she felt she knew other things about it, too. There weren't any sounds; the air was always hot, and as you walked into it, it left the taste of salt on your lips. Thinking about it always made her thirsty.

Once a week on Fridays a woman named Fran Arnet came to their house to iron the laundry. She got there early in the morning and stayed until lunchtime, filling the house with the smell of steam and starch. She sang as she ironed, but always in French. As the iron went back and forth, the number of sheets and shirts and blouses hanging from the lintel over the doorway grew.

Sometimes she took a break in midmorning. She would sit at the table with a cup of coffee and eat the bread and cheese she'd unwrap from a packet she'd brought with her. She was a heavy woman with a strong, masculine face. She cut her bread with a pocketknife, slicing with the blade toward her, like a man.

One Friday she brought her son. He was a thin, graceful-looking boy a year younger than Rose Ann. His name was Emmanuel. For the first hour he helped his mother dampen and roll the clothing. Then he watched as she put the kettle of starch on the stove, opened the ironing board, and got the iron hot. They talked to each other in French, but when Fran began to iron she started to sing and the boy was quiet.

He stood at the screen door and looked into the yard. Rose Ann, who had been sitting on the lawn pretending to read a book, called him over. He came outside, stopping a few feet from her.

"Come here," she said, beckoning him closer. "Don't you speak English?"

Instead of answering, he pulled a peach out of his pocket and took a bite. Then he held it toward her. "Would you like some?"

As she bit into the fruit, she watched him. He had dark, curly hair and olive skin that in the sunlight looked like it was covered with a fine layer of dust. She returned the peach. When he took it, he left a sensation of warmth in the place his fingers had touched her palm. "How come you haven't come out with your mother before?" she asked.

"I usually live with my father. But sometimes in the summer I visit my mother."

"Where do you live with your father?"

"Louisiana."

"Oh," she said.

"It's very hot there. Very different."

The thought of a hot climate made her thirsty. She reached for the peach and took another bite. Then, feeling eyes watching from the dark windows of the house, she led him to the grassy area behind the forsythia bush. In the shade it was cooler.

He touched her lips with his finger.

"Don't ever let me catch you doing something like that again." The angry words meant nothing. As though she hadn't been surprised at all, she touched *his* mouth. He leaned over with his peachy breath and kissed her. She didn't draw away. They did it again. Each time she was less herself, the gangly thirteen-year-old girl with winter-white skin, and more like him, dark and winsome.

The next Friday Emmanuel came again. As before, he helped his mother get ready for the ironing and then, saying something to her in French, slipped out the back door. Rose Ann waited for him at the side of the house. She had an errand to run for her mother, so they set off toward the store together. It was still early in the morning, and since the sun hadn't yet dried the dew, the trees and bushes were fragrant with the smell of damp wood. Squirrels ran along the branches over their heads. The birds called out and Rose Ann said, "It's like a jungle."

Emmanuel sprinted ahead of her, then turned around and skipped backward. She watched him as she walked, his jumps and twists, his quick shy smiles, the glances he gave her from his half-shuttered eyes. His differences pleased her.

Later, when they were crouched behind the hedge that ran around their property, he took off his shirt. As she gazed at his narrow brown chest, he picked up one of her hands and made her feel his nipple. Then he lifted her blouse and touched the breasts that had grown into a woman's size over the winter. When he kissed her this time, his tongue darted in and out of her mouth, teasing her. Then he slid his hand in her pants. She wasn't prepared for him to do that, and she tightened up. But as he touched her, her muscles began to relax. Soon his fingers moved in and out between her legs easily.

She touched him next, grateful at last to explore the peculiar-looking parts she had sometimes glimpsed on her brother. They returned to kissing.

When he suddenly stopped, she looked out, still feeling the red sky beating down on her and tasting the salt on her lips. But as the sensations left her body, the illusion vanished too, and the shrunken bushes and trees, held down by gray summer clouds, took its place. He told her that his mother was probably ready to leave and stood up.

When they reached the kitchen, Fran had already delivered the fresh clothes to Mrs. Beech. They waited as she packed her supplies, shoving them into her bag with an annoyed expression. She gave Emmanuel a sack to tote, and muttering to herself in French, pulled him out the door.

With only a raised hand, he turned around and said good-bye. As Rose Ann watched him go down the sidewalk, she noticed a stickiness between her thighs.

．　．　．　．　．　．　　*6*　　．　．　．　．　．　．

In high school she started to draw. She was good at it because it seemed important to put the things she noticed down on paper. And to get them to look the way she saw them was a challenge. So she filled a drawing book with portraits—herself, her parents, and her sister and brother. The pencil lines were awkward, but the resemblances were there: the wide foreheads, the stubborn chins, and the flat cheeks. Her father was of a different physical type. His face was narrow, his eyes deep, and his mouth small. She made him smile, but to her mother and herself she gave stern expressions.

Sometimes she sat in the backyard and drew whatever she saw in front of her. She colored in the shapes with tempera, learning how to mix the hues to get a shade close to real life. One time she ignored the landscape in front of her and tried to draw the desert. She knew the form of the trees and the contours of the sky and sand by heart. When she filled everything in, the tones were rich and deep.

She was in the habit of leaving her drawing book around the house, and sometimes her mother picked it up and looked through it. Once she called Rose Ann to her side. "What's this?" she asked, pointing to the picture of the imaginary place.

"It's just something I felt like doing," Rose Ann replied. "I was only playing around."

Mrs. Beech closed the book and gave it back. "Everyone knows that the sky isn't red and that real trees don't look like that. Why would you want to pretend they did? It's just being sloppy."

7

The romantic life of an artist attracted her. Renouncing all of the acceptable pursuits to follow such an isolated path seemed noble and dramatic. She did it in a small way when, after she graduated from high school, she applied to an art school in Philadelphia. They accepted her.

"I'm going to pay for this art foolishness for only one reason," her father said to her. "So you can get it out of your system. After that you can either settle down with a husband or pursue a worthwhile career."

During her first year there, she shared a room with her sister, who had been given a scholarship to the university before completing her senior year. Not only that, she was going to study something sensible: history.

Because their rooming house was only a block away from the main north-south highway, they fell asleep to the sounds of traffic. The noise of engines just on the perimeters of her senses, Rose Ann's slumber was fitful. From lack of sleep as well as the obsessions of being a student, she could feel Emmanuel vanishing from the surfaces of her body. The desert vanished, too.

Based on her portfolio, Rose Ann had been accepted into the class taught by a painter named London Quip. He was rumored to be tough on his women students because he believed they should be home having babies unless there was a damned good reason they should be in art school.

On the first day of class, Rose Ann chose a stool in the front of the long, narrow painting studio. She exchanged names with the boy sitting next to her and spoke to him freely because she expected the instructor to show up at any moment and cut them short.

Half an hour later, a small man with a cloth bag slung over his shoulder walked through the door. He hung the bag on the arm of a chair and took off his jacket. The class grew still. He faced them, put his hands in his pockets, and said, "When you get home, I want you to take off all of your clothes. Keep them off until you have to go out tomorrow morning. I want you to feel your naked bodies. I want you to paint with your naked souls, and the best way to find out what that's like is to spend some time in this fine civilization of ours living without any clothes on. If I could do it, I'd assign everyone in here to spend a week at a nudist camp. Now, is there anything you'd like to ask?"

No one spoke.

"Then I'll see you tomorrow," he said. He put his jacket back on, slung the bag over his shoulder, and left the room.

Rose Ann went home and took off everything but her underwear. She explained to Sybil that you couldn't be an artist until you felt comfortable with your naked body. Sybil said she was glad to be in history; she liked to wear clothes. Rose Ann slipped off her bra and started to wash the dishes. She felt a little silly but decided it was a beneficial exercise because an artist had to understand human nature, and human nature grew from the limitations of the physical body. In herself, for instance, though she had full breasts, her legs were thin and her pelvis wasn't round enough. In general, her top was cushiony, her bottom was angular, and she was tall. How this affected her behavior she wasn't sure. She knew only that it wasn't easy for her to show herself naked to anyone. She could reveal the parts, but to show anyone the whole view was difficult.

At their first critique, Quip went through the class and collected all of their drawings. He carried them up to the front of the room and dropped them onto the floor. Then he jumped into the center of the pile, leaving black shoe marks on the top pages. "You're just playing around," he said. "You haven't told me anything yet. When you draw, tell me something! Tell me about your most pathetic self, tell me about your ugly naked body! Talk loud and clear and make me listen. This is garbage," he said looking straight at Rose Ann, "this is nothing."

She went back to their room and took off her clothes again. She draped a blanket over her shoulders and sat cross-legged on her bed, drawing. She didn't speak to Sybil when she came in because the drawing was going well, she was saying something finally, and she didn't want to break the spell. It was about fear. She'd made a landscape of tall, windowless buildings. There was a bird, representing herself, flying between them. Little drops fell from the bird's eyes because it was crying. She worked on it all night, getting her lines ruler-straight, crosshatching to define areas of light and shadow. The next morning she showed Sybil, who said that it was really nice, and then she tucked it into her drawing book to show Quip.

When she took it to him in class, he glanced at it quickly. Then he gave it back to her and moved on to the next student. Later that day he walked to the front of the room and said very softly, "You sweet pampered children, I feel sorry for you. You're so ignorant of life, all you know is melodrama. But let me tell you a secret: Other things go on in life besides weeping and dying. You're going to have to find that out. You're going to have to do some work now. Your plush existence ends right here. Now you're going to find out what work is. A hundred drawings by this time next week. Is there anything you'd like to say?" He scanned their faces for a response, but only one student spoke up. "What shall we draw, Professor Quip?"

"Draw a lemon sitting on a white plate."

It would be easy. She'd show him how she could handle perspective. Her lemon would be so globular he'd be able to feel it bulging from the page. The plate, in comparison, would be chained down by gravity as it sat on the table.

She spent an extra couple of hours working on the lemon skin, making the pores look as realistic as possible. When she was done, she thought it was better than a photograph. She took it to Quip the next day, ostensibly to find out if she was doing the assignment correctly, but really only to give him a chance to see her work without other students around.

She found him in the hallway outside his office. When he didn't recognize her as being from his painting class, she introduced herself and said she wondered if she could just show him a drawing she'd been working on for the assignment. She was waiting for him to answer when he barked out impatiently, "Well, where is it?"

He looked at it for only a moment. Then he said, "Do ninety-nine more and we'll see if you start to get the point of the assignment." With a brusque "Now go back home and do some work," he squeezed past her and went into his office.

She tried to hate him. But in the morning when she chose her clothes she found herself dressing in colors she hoped would catch his attention. At night she'd draw until she was bleary-eyed because he told them that it was only at the extremes of your feelings that you found the patience to create. For days she would go without eating a complete meal, partly because she simply forgot or she had no money, but mostly to find out if hunger produced the kind of work he wanted.

After two months Quip still berated them. He still spoke to them as a collective body; no one yet deserved his singular attention. "You're a faceless, nameless crowd," he said to them. "I haven't noticed that there's an individual among you."

8

The other students were successful in hating him. Three out of ten had dropped out, and the rest worked to spite him. "I'll show that bastard" was the common feeling.

But Rose Ann had surrendered. He was an artist. He could teach her how to become one, too. She put the paint on her canvas with hopefulness. She had magnificent patience because she worked with such an extreme of feeling. She had learned to make her forms understated. The lemon had only a suggested curve, only a suggested texture. Her line whispered. It was so tender she felt teary as she regarded it.

All fall they painted the lemon sitting on a white plate. At Thanksgiving he gave them a new assignment. "We'll move from the minimal to the complex. I want a narrative from you. I want a narrative of essences." On "essences" he pivoted on his heel and looked at them through his glasses. "Distill your experience. Paint it not so I know what the experience is but so I know why you remember it. I want to know why you bother to paint it. Now here it is, so stop chewing gum or looking at me blankly. Try to look intelligent. I want to feel as though my words aren't just hitting a hard surface and sliding down to the ground." He took a long pause and began again. "Tell me your life. Get it down in paint so I can feel it."

It would be this painting that would finally make him notice her. It would tell him to watch *her* because she had something to give.

"Have fifty sketches to show me by Friday."

That afternoon she began to draw. She didn't have any idea of what she was drawing, but she let the process carry her along. At the end of the week she still didn't know what she was doing, but she didn't want to direct her pencil toward something; she wanted, as he said, to let the pencil guide her. She ended up drawing spaces—rooms, hallways, windows, lawns. Or at least that's what they appeared to be.

On Friday everyone tacked their drawings on the wall, and Quip walked past, not stopping at any of them for a longer look. When he got to the end he said, "Yes, all right. This is a beginning. The next step is to create some boundaries, to narrow it down, to get your attention focused. Write about it. Write ten pages about what you'd want to say to me if we were meeting in a bar, just the two of us, and I asked you to talk to me. What would you say? Think about it and then write it down. After that you can start on the painting."

"Anything I'd say to him would only make him laugh at me. What could I possibly tell him about myself?"

"You've always been brave," Sybil said. "You've done courageous things. That's what you should tell him about. It's part of your personality. I'm just the opposite; I'm very careful and very practical, and I'll probably never do anything exciting in my life. You're always having experiences. Tell him about something you've done—something really exciting."

"I can't think of anything."

"Sure you can," Sybil told her.

"Nothing I can think of is really good enough. It has to be something really good."

"What's the most unusual thing that ever happened to you?"

"I don't know," Rose Ann said, thinking of Emmanuel.

That evening when Sybil got back from her classes, Rose Ann was standing in the middle of their room wearing nothing but a sheet. She had pulled her hair back from her forehead and dusted her face with something that made it white. "I am your memory," she whispered, raising her arms and swooping toward her sister. "I am the dream you had last night."

"Come on," Sybil said. "What's going on?"

Rose Ann dropped her pose and sat down on her bed. "I'm going to find out what it's like to be in jail."

"Come on, what are you talking about?"

"I'm going to stand on Broad Street until I get arrested."

"Are you crazy? You could end up anywhere. Anything could happen."

"That's the challenge."

"You don't even have on any underwear. You're going to get yourself in real trouble."

"I don't think so," Rose Ann said. "I know what I'm doing and I know why. I've found the perfect solution. I know how I'm going to write about it and how I'm going to tackle the painting. I can approach it in two ways, symbolically and literally, but first I have to do it."

"You can't," Sybil said. She put her hands on her hips just like their mother did when she was about to deliver a judgment. "You're going to get yourself murdered."

"I'm sure I won't get murdered."

"Or raped, or hit over the head."

"Someone might try but they won't be successful."

"Rose Ann, have some sense, will you? I'm not going to let you go out and get yourself in trouble."

"I want trouble. I want a night in jail. That's the whole point."

"Come on," Sybil said. "I don't have time to argue. I have a lot of work to do tonight, and I'm not going to sit up here and wonder if you're dead or alive."

"That's right, you're not," Rose Ann said, pulling the bottom sheet from her unmade bed. She folded it in half and began to cut a hole in the center. "An unusual experience gives you a new perspective. It makes you realize that what you thought was important really isn't important at all. Danger is a necessary part of life."

"Wait a minute. I have a lot of studying I have to do tonight."

"Then I'll see you in the morning," Rose Ann replied, dropping the sheet and preparing to leave. "And don't worry about me, I'll be all right."

"Wait a minute," Sybil said again. On her face there was the struggle between the desire to believe what she wanted and the fear that her sister might be right. "I'll come on the condition that I can wear my underwear."

The two sheeted figures walked down the back stairway and went out the back door to the alley behind their building. The fall air was damp and chilly. One remarked, "We're going to get pneumonia." The other said, "No, we won't."

They walked single file in the darkness, the sheets lifting in the breeze, exposing their shoes and socks. At Broad Street they waited on the corner for the light to turn green.

They crossed the street and stood by the curb on the other side. Rose Ann spread out her arms and stood still; Sybil stood next to her and did the same. Rose Ann tilted her head back and looked at the sky. Sybil did too, but after some time Rose Ann broke the pose and said, "We shouldn't have worn our shoes. We don't look vagrant enough."

All of a sudden, dream number one began to wave her arms and jump up and down. After a few moments, dream number two did the same. Dream number one opened her mouth and began to wail. She began to fly back and forth like a bird, the sheet whipping around her. Dream number two stood still, wailing and flapping her arms. People were taking notice. Cars were slowing and gray faces turned to look at them. Someone shouted, "You girls loony?" At that, dream number one swooped more vigorously, and dream number two stopped wailing. Dream number one ran up and down, kicking her legs and making frenzied sounds. Each time she kicked, the sheet flew up, exposing her bareness underneath. "Rose Ann!" Sybil hissed, but her sister didn't hear. Dream number two danced in front of dream number one, trying to hide her from traffic. "Hoy-ya, hoy-ya!" dream number one sang out, coming forward. "Hoy-ya, hoy-ya, ho!" She grabbed Sybil's arm, getting her to join in the song. "Hoy-ya, hoy-ya, ho! Hoy-ya, hoy-ya, ho!" Sybil put forth a timid chorus as Rose Ann ran back and forth in front, whipping the sheet around her and chanting with great energy, "I am your dream, I am your soul, hoy-ya-hoy-ya, ho! Here's our man," she hissed. "Put on a good performance." There was a whirling red light in the distance. It approached quickly, the siren getting louder as it came closer. But it kept on going faster, and when it sped past, the pavement echoing from the sound, they saw that it wasn't a police car at all but an ambulance.

Dream number two shouted, "Isn't just being out here an unusual enough event, do we have to get arrested?"

"Hoy-ya, hoy-ya, ho!" dream number one replied. "If nothing happens in ten minutes we'll go back home."

"If we leave now," dream number two said, "I'll be grateful for the rest of my life."

Dream number one turned around and said, "All right, just five more hoy-yas. Then we'll go."

They did five and nothing happened. Feeling a surge of lightness, Rose Ann danced across Broad Street and turned around to wait for the other dream.

They stepped into the alley and ran toward the door. Sybil reached for the handle to fling it open, but it was locked. They knew it would be useless to try the front door because that was locked at ten every night. They could try ringing the bell, but then how would they explain their attire?

"There was smoke up in our room. We woke up smelling smoke, and since we were sure the building was on fire, we didn't take the time to look for our robes, we just pulled a sheet off our bed and wrapped it around ourselves. Then we ran down the back stairway. When we got to the alley, we realized that everything was all right and felt awfully foolish. But when we tried to get back inside, we discovered the door had locked behind us."

"The hole in the sheet, how are we going to explain that?"

"That's simple," Rose Ann said, pulling off her sheet. By the cans of garbage her naked body was strange and beautiful. She bundled the sheet around her shoulders like an enormous scarf and waited for Sybil to do the same.

"Are you sure no one's looking?" her sister asked.

Rose Ann checked behind them. "Go ahead." With the sheet off, Sybil was an angel in the darkness. But then she turned ordinary as she wrapped the sheet around her chest.

They walked out to the main entrance on Broad Street. Rose Ann rang the bell at the side of the ornate, wrought-iron door, pressing it in until she saw a light go on in the hallway. Mrs. Amy, the superintendent, walked toward them in her dressing gown and slippers. She unlocked the door and opened it an inch. "I have never in my life," she said, and then opened it all the way to let them in. ·

It was her best painting. There were floating white shapes at the top and buildings and cars at the bottom. On the side, a scowling face peeked out of a small, narrow opening. On the other side there was a naked woman. She was awkwardly painted, the brushstrokes visible and the line rough and timid.

"I'm tempted to read your story," London told her at the critique. After class he took her aside. "What is your name?" he asked.

9

For the final review before Christmas, London told them he wanted to see all of their work from the first day of the semester on. "I don't want to see just what you think are your best things. I want to be able to look at everything. Questions?"

"I'd have to rent a truck to get all of my work here," one student volunteered.

"Then rent a truck," London said. Passing a sheet around, he added, "Write down the time you appear on the schedule. I will expect you to be prompt."

Rose Ann scribbled the day and time in her drawing book. He had put her in the last slot, on the Friday before vacation.

It was snowing when she woke up. That afternoon as she was getting her work together, it was still snowing. She put the drawings between the canvases and covered them with her raincoat, which was big enough to wrap around everything. Then she made three trips across campus and up to the painting studio. The student before her hadn't finished, so she stacked her work in the hallway outside.

When her turn came, she tacked the drawings up and leaned the paintings against the classroom walls. There wasn't enough room for all of it, so London told her to put the work she liked best against the north-south walls and the work she liked least against the east-west walls and not to bother with the things she felt neutral about. When she had finished, he gave her a nickel and asked her to go down to the cafeteria and get him a black coffee. "Take your time," he said. "I want to look at your work without any distractions."

When she came back she had a coffee for each of them and, because it was already dinnertime, a roll for herself. He beckoned her to the chair in the center of the room, and as she sat down he smiled. He looked so unlike himself she thought something was wrong.

"Rose Ann," he said, "don't ever have a family. Lead a solitary life and paint. If you work at it very hard, you might be very good someday. This is a promising body of work. I can feel you struggling with something. I can feel you trying to break out of confinement, searching for the images that will help you explain what you know." He drank his coffee and threw the empty cup into the trash. "That's all I'm going to say for now. It's been a long day and I'm too tired to talk any more. Also, I want to get home before the snow gets too deep." He put on his hat and coat, and at the doorway he said, "We can talk after vacation. By the way, you'd better get your things out quickly, they'll close the building in half an hour." Then he added, "Have a good Christmas."

She listened to his footsteps go down the hallway. She looked at her paintings. She ate her roll and drank her coffee. Then, because she had more work than she could possibly lug up to her room in half an hour, and because the studio was warm and she was happy, she slumped in her chair and fell asleep.

It had snowed in Brooklyn, but by the time she got home the snow was black and crusty. She felt too preoccupied to spend much time with her family, and she wasn't in the mood to look up her old high school friends. So she spent her vacation going back and forth to the museums and galleries in the city. She took a sketchbook and made notes and drawings. The next semester she wanted to work on portraits. She hoped she'd be able to get her sister to pose.

She also spent a lot of time in bookstores. If she was going to focus on portraits, she wanted to get a better sense of the complexities of a character. She read James's *Portrait of a Lady* and found herself getting excited about the task in front of her. She could do ten paintings of Sybil, each one showing her sister from a different perspective. She began to make preliminary sketches.

A few days after Christmas, she was standing in a Fifth Avenue bookstore looking through the shelves. A man who had been standing behind her suddenly asked, "Aren't you from Brooklyn?"

When she said yes, he seemed excited. "I knew you looked familiar. I'm Teddy Juroe and your name is . . ." He snapped his fingers. "Wait a minute, it's two words, isn't it?"

She blushed when he said that because she had always wanted a simpler name.

"Rose Ann," he said at last. "We met at a picnic last year in Brooklyn. I don't remember where, or when, or what the occasion was, but I know we met there." He looked so pleased with himself she had to smile.

"Listen, I was just going around the corner for a bite to eat. Would you like to join me?"

He looked at her as though she had every right in the world to say no, so she said, "Sure."

They sat at a booth at the back of the restaurant and drank cup after cup of coffee and talked. Or rather he talked and she studied him. He had short blond hair and a square face with a thin, blond mustache. His eyes were green. If she were painting him, she'd put him in an upholstered chair sitting on a lawn with a well-pruned tree in the background. There was something middle class and proprietary about him. She decided that he was one of those men who liked nothing better than to spend a sunny afternoon mowing the grass. He liked order. But there was also something exotic about him. There would be a birdcage hanging from the tree with a strange, florid bird inside it. That would be at the center of the composition, and the greens in the bird would draw attention to the green of his eyes. Thinking of the painting, she remembered that it was the last day she could see a particular show at the Modern. "Do you want to come with me?" she asked.

"I'd like that," he said. "I've never been to that museum before."

As he walked up to pay, she gathered her things. When she picked up her sketchbook, she noticed that her name and address were on the cover, in print big enough for someone standing behind her to read. She didn't think there'd been a picnic last year in Brooklyn.

It seemed to her that there were two choices. She could walk out of the restaurant before he turned around, or she could accuse him to his face and say good-bye. He must have felt her eyes on him as he stood in line at the register because he turned just then and smiled. She decided not to say anything until after the museum. It might be interesting to go with someone who had never been before. After that she would bid him good riddance and stop at a few galleries and then take the subway home.

As they walked to Fifty-third Street, he took her arm. She didn't pull away because it felt all right for him to touch her like that. But what a scamp he was.

Masters of Popular Painting: Modern Primitives of Europe and America. Because it was a weekday, the exhibition wasn't crowded. They started in the American section, pausing in front of each painting for a few moments and then moving on. There were landscapes and portraits and street scenes, all of them awkward and guileless. He probably hated them, although he was successful in looking appreciative. When she saw a landscape of an open field, she caught her breath. Nothing more than a mottled sky meeting the heavily ridged earth, with a farmhouse at the far horizon, it was a study of textures. She looked at it for a long time. He excused himself to go to the men's room. She stayed where she was and studied the painting. Then she moved on to the next one. He probably didn't like the show at all; it wasn't sophisticated enough for him, and it would be tiresome to have to talk to him about it. Even so, she hadn't the least inclination to leave.

The next painting was another rural scene—an outhouse next to a clothesline with hills in the background. The forms were isolated, each stark and clearly defined, even the clothes on the clothesline. It was a point of view she understood. No matter what people did with their lives, there would be this loneliness they would be unable to get away from. He returned and she said, "Are you ready?"

"I've hardly looked at anything," he replied. "Give me another fifteen minutes." He went off to the other side of the room and stopped in front of the only portraits in the show. As he slowly made his way back to her, she watched him. In *her* portrait he would have the same expression on his face. It would be a man surveying the abundance before him and looking pleased with the knowledge that he had been chosen to witness it.

In the elevator he said, "I've always avoided that museum. I thought that historical things were the only things worth looking at." Then he said, "I enjoyed those paintings. I liked the way they made things lie in between pretty and ugly. It forced you to stop for a minute and take a good long look. You didn't just think, oh, that's pretty, and then move on. What did you think?"

She looked up into his wide green eyes and said, "You know something, you never met me before in your life. You just saw my name on my sketchbook." Already she could hear his rebuttal. *I swear to God,* he would say.

"Well, it worked, didn't it? I even went somewhere with you. You've changed my life already. I went into the Museum of Modern Art; I've never done that before. If you don't like it, we don't have to see each other ever again."

"Do you do this kind of thing all the time?"

"Never," he said. "This was a first for me."

As they walked down the street, he had a thoughtful expression on his face. Suddenly he grabbed her arm. "Listen, Rose Ann, I'm going to do the very thing any schlepp would do who just picked up a girl under false pretences. I'm going to try to get her to go out on a date. What would you say? Dinner Saturday at this nice little restaurant?"

It would have been easy to tell him no. But in spite of the opportunity he gave her to refuse him, she knew she would give in to him.

· · · · · *II* · · · · ·

They were sitting across from each other at a small table in a restaurant on the East Side. Empty plates and crumpled napkins lay between them. His face was shadowed in the candlelight, but his voice was clear and strong. He took it for granted that she was curious about him. So he began to tell her his story.

He was older than she was by five years. When he had finished college, he had gone into his father's paper business. That had lasted six months. On the morning he decided to quit, he went into the front office to announce his intentions. What happened next was something he'd never forget. Before he had even opened his mouth, his father said, "I know what you're going to tell me. Good-bye and good luck. I hope you'll find something you'll like. Manufacturing isn't the answer, and I should have been smart and booted you out three months ago. It would have saved me money. Come here, Teddy, and I'll tell you a secret."

He had walked up to the desk, but his father had said impatiently, "Come here, come here." So he had walked behind the desk into the fragrance of his father's after-shave, and his father had taken his face between his hands and whispered, "Do me this favor. Find something where you're out there with the people. You'd be good at public relations. Or get into sales. You have a talent that shouldn't be wasted."

The waiter came over and filled their glasses and when he was gone, Teddy went on with his story. "That afternoon I took myself out to lunch. God, I felt wonderful. Finally to be out from under and to leave on good terms, that was more than I'd expected. I celebrated by going to a good restaurant. It was an Italian place my father used to take me to when I was little. I was sitting by the window and there were two men, fortyish I'd say, at the next table. They were talking about some kind of career, how this particular field was opening up and how someone with the right skills could walk in and land a position with good pay and a long future. They had seen it done again and again, but it was a shame, the one man said, the field wasn't attractive to younger people. The other asked, 'If you have sales potential, what's wrong with it?'

"'No one likes the idea,' the first one answered, 'What is it but selling death?'

"'It's not selling death,' the other said. 'It's selling life to your survivors.'

"'Come on,' the first one replied, 'it's selling death.'

"At that point I realized what they were talking about. I couldn't help myself, so I turned around and said, 'Excuse me, my name is Theodore Juroe, and I think it's selling an investment. I'm interested. Could you tell me where I'd apply?' They gave me the address of the biggest life insurance company in the state and told me who to ask for. I went in for an interview that afternoon. They hired me right away, and I've done it ever since. I'm good at it. I like it tremendously."

"Why?" Rose Ann asked.

Teddy thought about it for a minute before he answered. "Everything we do is a denial of our mortality. We go to the doctor, we visit friends, we have dinner in a restaurant. . . . We function under the illusion that we will always be healthy and, above all, alive. We assume we'll live forever. We can't help it. We know we'll die someday, but it's a piece of information we keep tucked away in the back of our minds. We don't like to bring it out to examine it. Maybe once or twice when someone close to us passes away and we realize that the same thing could happen to us, but once the shock has lifted we forget about it until something else happens to make us remember.

"Do you agree?" He looked at her straight on, his green eyes pleading with her for a response. But suddenly he waved his hands in the air and said, "Never mind. Let me just finish. So . . . because we lock it out of our lives, the idea of death grows terrifying. We run around blindly, trying to escape it, and it only grows more terrible. Then I come along,

Mr. Life Insurance, reminding you of the inevitable, persuading you to prepare for it, allowing you to buy some protection, not *from* it but *for* it. I make you consider the fact of your death; I make you face it. I make you envision your family without you. How will they survive? I give you a chance, if only for a moment, to accept your mortality in a practical way." Flushed with his own oratory, he sipped his wine.

"I like that," she said. "A salesman with a grand spiritual purpose."

"There's other things, too," he added quietly. "I like working with numbers and charts, and I like inquiring into the private affairs of my clients, even if it's only finances and health."

"You just enjoy the power it gives you."

"That's right," he said in a jaunty tone.

The way he looked at her—he was so smug. She pictured herself poking his belly with a pin to deflate him. Instead she said, "Someday you're going to sit for me so I can paint your portrait."

"I'd be happy to," he replied, beaming at her with obvious pleasure.

"That's not what I mean. Someday it will happen because you'll be around." Then, just to startle him, she said, "I think we're going to end up becoming an old married couple, the kind that can't even remember what it was like when they were single."

His face dropped. "I'm not your type. After all, I'm just a salesman and you're an artist. And we're here only because I lied to you the other day in the bookstore."

"But I admire that, don't you know that's why I came out with you tonight? I like someone who tries to get what he wants."

They didn't talk much when he was driving her home. It was cold out, and with the windows closed and the buzz of the heater, the car felt separate from the world outside. When it began to snow, he put on the wipers. They ticked as they went back and forth, scraping the white from the windshield. He was driving slowly because the snow was coming down steadily and the road was turning slick. Since he lived in the opposite direction, she wondered if he was worried about getting home. "I'm sure you can sleep at my house if you don't want to be out in this much longer."

"That's all right, I'll be fine." He turned his attention back to the driving, but the quiet seemed unnatural.

"Is something the matter?"

He didn't reply right away. He shifted in his seat and turned down the heater so there was only a gentle hum. Then he asked, "Were you joking when you said we would get married?"

"Of course I was."

"Then what made you say it?"

"I don't know, the thought just popped into my head."

"But you must have meant it in some way. Should I take it to mean that you want to see me again?"

"I can't. I have to go back to school."

"You're just going to go back to school and forget about this guy who came up with such an ingenious way to meet you?"

Rose Ann smiled. "When I'm at school, I'm completely involved in my work. I honestly don't have time for anything else. I can't even think about other things. I don't mean that I'll forget you, just that I probably won't think about you very much."

"Thanks a lot," he said. Then he asked, "Are you coming home in the summer? Why don't I call you then, see what you're up to?"

"Listen, Teddy, I'm a painter. That's my primary concern. That's what I'm going to do. I'm not like your other girlfriends. I'm not just waiting around for a man to come along and change my life."

"I'm just asking if I can call in the summer. I'm not asking you for anything else."

"I'm sorry," she said. She touched his coat sleeve. "Yes, I guess you can call me."

"Listen, Rose Ann, just tell me the truth, don't worry about protecting my feelings."

And what was the truth, she wondered, as the wiper pushed snow from the windshield. The highway stretched clearly in front of them; then the snow collected again, and the road began to shimmer. You couldn't create a false privacy. No matter how much you might be tempted, it couldn't work. "Call me," she said. "If you remember who I am, I'd like you to call."

"Why do you say that? I'll remember you."

12

When she returned home that summer, she waited for the call. Every time the phone rang she was certain his voice would be at the other end. But when a week had gone by, she decided that he must have found someone else. On the other hand, how could she expect him to know when she'd arrived home?

She asked the operator. There wasn't a listing for Theodore Juroe. She tried another operator and got the same answer. There was a name that sounded like T. Jerry, but again there wasn't a T. Juroe.

For the next few days she wasn't sure what to do with herself. Her plans for the summer had included him. She wanted to start a new series of paintings. They would be small portraits, each one showing him from a different angle. She'd put him under a tree, the birdcage hanging from a branch near his head.

After three weeks when he hadn't called—and surely he would have assumed she was home by then—she started to spend her days in the city, looking at shows. She went back to the same bookstore, but no one said anything to her when she was standing in front of the shelves. She wondered which life insurance company he worked for and looked up "Life Insurance" in the directory. There were too many firms. Then she remembered he'd told her it was the biggest in New York State. She called the company with the largest ad and asked for an agent named Theodore Juroe. "One moment, please," the woman said. Then she got back on and told her there wasn't an agent with that name. "Is there a company that's larger than yours?" Rose Ann asked. The woman said, "This is the largest in New York City." "What about the state?" Rose

Ann asked, but she never got an answer because the woman hung up.

She'd give him another week, and then she'd sit down with the phone book and call all the listings. When you wanted a thing, you went after it. Of course, he might even be married by now.

But three days later the phone rang. Her mother called from downstairs, "Rose Ann, there's a man on the phone who wants to speak to you." She went down into the kitchen to pick it up.

"I'm finding myself in a tight situation and was hoping you might be able to help me out. This is London Quip," the voice said. "Let me explain myself."

He was calling from Maine where he was teaching a painting course at an art school. The problem was this: The assistant he had hired for the summer had gotten herself pregnant. He stopped talking to let her understand the enormous frustration the situation had caused him. "I'm offering the job to you," he continued. She wouldn't be paid much, but she would have her room and board taken care of and would be able to spend the summer painting in a country setting. Her duties would include teaching the class when he had to be away and taking charge of all the details: ordering supplies, arranging for the model, putting together setups, and so on.

"Don't accept the job if you'll have a problem working with me. If you're going to resent being told what to do, then I don't want you. Of course, there'll be the chance to look at your work and talk about it more extensively than we ever did at school. . . . Can you give me an answer in ten minutes?"

She didn't even put the phone down. Looking at her mother, who was watching her, trying to decipher the conversation, she said, "I can give you an answer now. Yes, I'll do it."

"Good. Take the train to a town called Milo. Let us know what time, and there'll be someone from the school to pick you up. You're a good girl, Rose Ann. Thank you."

Three days later she was standing beside the tracks at a station with a sign over the door that said, "Milo." It had been a long, hot ride, and the sudden cool air was refreshing. She had been the only passenger to get off. The conductor had set her trunk on the platform beside her, and with a loud gasp of steam, the train had pulled away.

Fir trees pressed in on all sides of the clearing, filling the air with their sharp scent. The road that ran beside the station was empty. She asked the old man sweeping out the waiting room how far away the art school was.

"It be about ten miles," he said and went back to his sweeping.

"Where does everyone live?" she asked, seeing no houses in sight.

"Hereabouts," he said. After a time he added, "Twenty families is all we have."

She sat on one of the benches to wait, but when it was clear she was in the way of his sweeping she went outside. A convertible had parked by the tracks and a man with sandy hair was climbing out. She walked up to him and said, "I'm Rose Ann. I hope you're here to get me."

"Elton," he told her, extending his hand. He was very tall and wore a long, baggy shirt that made him appear even taller. He hoisted her trunk on his shoulders and stood it up in the backseat. After opening the door for her, he swung himself over the door on the driver's side and started the car.

Town was only a grocery store, a church, and a gas station. They drove along a narrow road with forests on both sides, turned onto another road that looked exactly the same, and then turned into a lane with a sign at the end of it. "Is this it?" she asked.

"Up here a ways," he said.

Without any warning, the forest ended and a lawn appeared. There was a house positioned in the middle of it, and she could see easels on the lawn and people standing behind them looking out at something she couldn't see. "Penobscot School of Art," Elton announced, turning into the circle in front of the house and stopping the car.

She looked at the heavy stone facade, the carving around the windows and the door, the small, bare porch in front. It was so somber she wondered if she'd made the right decision. Elton led her up the steps, telling her that faculty and staff lived in the house and students lived in cabins in the woods. She asked him if he could bring in her trunk so she could start unpacking.

He went back to the car and dragged the trunk up the steps to the porch. He left it there and took her into the house.

When the front door closed behind them, they were enveloped in coolness. The draped and curtained windows, admitting the whiteness of the day but not the brilliance, created an atmosphere of stealth. On the carpeted floors their footsteps were quiet. She stopped to look at a tapestry hanging on the wall beside her. Elton explained that all the furnishings belonged to Mrs. Betock, who had bequeathed the property to the school. "She's still alive, but she doesn't live here anymore, she lives in the South with her sister. There's a caretaker who keeps everything just the way Betock wanted it. You have the daughter's room. She liked the color green. She was sick most of her life so her mother indulged her. She died when she was in her thirties, and it's because of her that the place exists. She was a painter. All these little landscapes," he pointed to a small and ornately framed canvas, "are hers."

Rose Ann peered at it; the fluid colors and the vista of horizon and sky appealed to her. "She was good," she murmured.

"I guess so," Elton replied. "A little too tentative for me. A little too close to Cézanne, if you know what I mean, a little too soft."

Rose Ann looked at him clearly for the first time. She had assumed he was an errand boy, someone just hired for odd jobs, and was startled to see his amused expression. "Then you must be an artist," she said. "I thought you were only . . . " To cover her embarrassment, she offered her hand.

"Only a painter," he finished for her. "At least for the time being. When something else comes along, I might switch. I'm not loyal and I'm certainly not devoted. Quip finds me too loose. But he's a good teacher, and you're lucky he asked you to come. Just don't get pregnant. A second calamity would give him a stroke."

"What do you do here?" she asked. "Are you a student?"

"A student of my pupils. I teach in the mornings, Quipo teaches in the afternoons. By the way," Elton continued, walking toward the stairs, "don't ever let him hear you call him that. He hates nicknames."

In her room, the bedspread, the rug, and the lampshades were green. The walls were tan, and the woodwork was brown. When she parted the drapes, she saw that she was overlooking the lawn. The easels faced her, and in front of them she could see a nude lying against a tree holding what looked like a plaster swan in her arms.

The nude was Mrs. Barney, who was also the cook. The swan *was* plaster, and its beak was broken from years of use. It had been Laura Betock's, and since it appeared in many of her paintings, it had become an image associated with her.

The setup Rose Ann had seen from her window had been something Quip had come up with. Had she looked more closely, she would have seen a single red slipper on Mrs. Barney's foot and a hat with a feather lying on the grass beside her.

"I want fantasy, I want lyricism," Quip told her. "I want these people to be painting their daydreams. It's summer and summer is full of context. It's lustful; it isn't minimal. Winter is the time for lemons on a plate, summer is the time for fullness and mystery. What happened to the model's other slipper? Tell me," he demanded when she didn't reply. "Come on, Rose Ann, take a position on it. What happened to the goddamned slipper?"

It was after dinner and they were sitting on the porch watching the sky. It had been peaceful until he gave her the question. She had been listening with only half an ear, following the sounds of the evening and the occasional noises from inside the house. Only reluctantly did she give her attention to the question, but without thinking about it the answer came. She began to talk, filling in the story as she went along. "She was riding the Ferris wheel," she said. "A carnival had come to the town where she lived, and she had been there all night. Early in the morning, very drunk, she got on the Ferris wheel with a man she had met, someone she liked. It started to go up—they were the only ones riding it—and when the car was at the top, just before it was turned downward, she took off her shoes and stood up. One red slipper dropped down to the pavement, but she was too drunk to notice."

But as she pictured it, she changed her mind. "No, she wasn't drunk, she was perfectly clearheaded. Also, she was by herself. She had wanted to see the sun come up from the top of the Ferris wheel."

"No, it was a roller coaster, that's what it was, and when she stood up she almost lost her balance. But it didn't frighten her, and to prove her steadiness she flung out her arm and dropped her slipper." She turned to look at him and asked, "How's that?"

"That's beautiful," Quip said. "That's provocative, that's brilliant." He took her face between his hands and kissed her on either cheek. "A red slipper lying on the pavement under a Ferris wheel."

"A roller coaster," she said, and then she remembered. She could see her mother and Russell standing way below her, and she could feel the tipping of the car as she stood up. She watched herself wave to them. From the distance of all those years, she felt alarmed by her silly courage.

The next day she arranged her first setup. She took the pillows from the couch in the living room and placed them under the tree. She unhooked a curtain from one of the windows and had Mrs. Barney undress and drape it around her shoulders. She made her lie down on the pillows and gave her a candelabra to hold in her hand. She dragged the hallway mirror out to the lawn and set it against the tree behind Mrs. Barney. Framed by the baroque surroundings, the one full, pink breast and the circle of buttock that were exposed by an opening in the drapery seemed more purely erotic than a completely naked woman. Mrs. Barney moved her elbow to get into a comfortable position, and the curtain opened further, exposing the other breast, the two large red nipples poking from the velvet, like eyes. "I hope you don't mind if I close my eyes?" Mrs. Barney asked. "A snooze would do me wonders."

Rose Ann stepped away to get the full effect. It was good, she thought, but it needed something else. She found the red slipper in the box of props and dangled it from Barney's other hand. For the final touch, she pulled a lily out of the flower garden and set it in front of the mirror.

When Quip came out, he clapped his hands and called, "Another chapter in the woozy life of the maiden Barney. Get to work," he told the students. To Rose Ann he said, "Why don't you start a canvas, too?"

"I don't think I'm ready," she replied.

"You'll die before you're ready. If you aren't working before tomorrow afternoon, I'll find another assistant."

14

As the days passed, she discovered herself thinking about Elton. She was always aware of where he was and what he was doing. He would sit on the porch late into the night, playing cards by himself and sipping from a glass of Scotch. When she went to bed, she could feel him below her window. She would be unable to sleep; the figure on the porch made her restless.

She began to wonder if he was as aware of her. One day he'd sit next to her at dinner and ask her questions about herself; another day he wouldn't speak to her at all. He seemed preoccupied. One night, just as she was falling asleep, she heard him drive away in his car. In her dreams he was wearing the same white sweater he'd worn to dinner that night. He parked in front of her house in Brooklyn and in his long-legged way climbed the steps to her front door. He went up to her bedroom to find her, but she, in the meantime, had gone outside. By the time she woke up, they still hadn't connected.

He wasn't at breakfast the next morning, and at lunch he looked awful. That afternoon she saw him sleeping on the lawn as his students sat in scattered twos and threes and drew the landscape.

After dinner that night, when the others had left and she was talking with Mrs. Barney, he came back and sat down in the empty chair next to her. "That fool Barney went into my room and stole my Scotch. I'm thirty-five years old, and I don't have the vaguest idea what to do with myself if I can't have a drink after dinner."

"Well, you'd better find out," Mrs. Barney said. "I saw you looking half-dead at lunch, and I know what that's from, Elton. I'm not having you ruin yourself in front of my eyes."

"It's not myself, it's my creative spirit. Every once in a while it needs a little watering."

"My ass it does," Barney said, and disappeared into the kitchen.

"We're old friends," he explained to Rose Ann. "I love her, but she's got to stop sneaking into my room." He leaned back in the chair, hands in his pockets. "I'd ask you to join me for a game of cards, but two people should be able to come up with something better to do than cards. It's only good when you're by yourself. And of course without a little booze even that's pathetic."

"Show me around this place," Rose Ann said.

"Haven't you seen everything by now? Where haven't you been?"

"How about the barns? I need to find some more props for my set-ups; maybe there's old farm machinery lying around."

"Maybe so," Elton said, looking at her strangely.

They changed into old clothes and found a couple of flashlights. As they walked along the road behind the house, she felt as though something were going to happen. The knowledge made her so panicky she began to shiver.

"You should have brought a jacket," he said.

"I'll be all right."

She noticed then that he smiled.

In the first barn there was a tractor and nothing else but bags and bags of fertilizer. That was the barn the farmer used. Behind it there was another barn, larger than the first but overgrown with vines. They stepped through the tall grass and came to a side door, pulling it back through the weeds to open it. "When I first came here," Elton said, "they used to keep horses in this barn. Old Mrs. Betock liked to go riding. But the horses were sold that summer. I wonder if all of the tack is still in here. Once it was abandoned, I never came back to investigate."

The inside was cluttered with furniture. There was a car, an old Model T with flat tires and broken windows. Rose Ann peered inside it with her flashlight. Mice had eaten away at the upholstery, and she could hear baby birds squealing from the roof. She turned around to show Elton, but he wasn't behind her anymore. She stood up and looked around. Dust motes hung in the rays of light coming from the window, and the shadowed portions of the barn were too dark to see into. She could feel the interrupted life around her—the hidden bats and mice waiting in the corners and rafters, listening to her movements. "Elton?" His voice when he answered was flat and seemingly close. "I'm in the tack room," he called. "Everything's still here. I'm looking at a hand-tooled leather saddle. There are boots and bridles and riding hats."

Out of the corner of her eye, she saw something move. She turned to catch what for a terrifying instant looked like a person, but it was only a squirrel. Why was she so nervous?

There was a trunk under the window. No one had put a lock on it, and the top opened easily. It was clothing, things made out of velvet and satin that were cold from the damp. She pulled out a woman's dress. With lace around the bodice and cuffs, it was in perfect condition. But holding it up against her, she could tell it was made for a woman thinner and smaller than she was. She folded it neatly and put it back.

Beside the trunk, under a heap of burlap, she could see the corner of a canvas. She pulled off the burlap and uncovered a stack of paintings. Were they Laura's? She turned the first around and saw the house and the lawn and a man standing in the doorway who looked familiar. She pulled out the next canvas, and a young man wearing a white shirt and holding a bright green pear in his hand stared toward the window. His profile, the jagged slope of the nose and the protruding forehead, told her at once who it was. "Elton!" she called. She heard a door close in the dark portion of the barn. He walked out of the shadows, and when he came up to her he put his hand on her shoulder. He whistled as he saw what she had found.

He looked at the portrait for a long time. "They were lovers," he said finally. "Quip almost married her. Something happened, though, and the engagement was called off. I don't know why. I don't think anyone does. But the way he comes back here every summer, you could say he married her after all. He's a mysterious person, that Quip."

She listened as though someone were speaking from a distance. Close up, she was filled with the sensation of having him next to her. She pictured the house, the dark windows that in the daytime reflected the sunlight, the heavy eaves, the high slate roof. She watched herself follow him up the front steps that first day, and once again, felt the coolness spill over her as he opened the door. But she hung back; she couldn't follow him inside so easily this time. He turned around questioningly.

"Would you put your arm around me?" she asked. "I'm cold." With his hand gripping her shoulder, she pressed against him till she could feel the warmth of his skin through his shirt.

He kissed her, pushing his tongue between her teeth so she tasted his breath. She felt his jawbone against her chin, a pressure that was unpleasant. She thought of stopping him as he began to unbutton her shirt. But his hands had opened the buttons so fast she was without defense. He bit at her playfully, touching her breasts. "Wait a minute," she said. He dropped his hands into her pants, and with one against her ass and the other drifting below her belly whispered in her ear, "Does a girl like you like to make love?"

Already he was pulling clothing from the trunk and spreading it beneath them. "I never have," she said.

"Why don't you try it? I'll show you how good it can be."

15

The next morning he was the first to get up from their temporary bed. Hardly looking at her, he stepped into his clothes.

"Where are you going?" she asked, pulling herself up on her elbows.

He zipped his pants. Then he glanced down. "Is that my virgin, or did we chase her away?"

"Your ex-virgin," she said.

He started to move toward the door, but she lunged off their mattress and caught his ankle. "Where are you going? Not even a kiss for the deflowered lady? Who do you think you are? You just come back here and give me a good-morning kiss. Right now, you Elton."

He squatted down next to her, his face long and serious. But when he delivered the kiss, he pressed against her too roughly, his jawbone smashed into her face. When it was over, he touched her forehead briefly. "I'll see you tonight. I have to prepare for my class."

16

They kept it a secret. When everyone was asleep he came to her bed, and he left in the morning only after making sure that the hallway was clear. Wearing a white bathrobe, he would stand at her door and listen before he'd go out. She watched from her bed, waiting for the moment just before he left, when he would turn around and wink at her. It was his only extravagance.

Seeing that tall, spare man standing at her door in his bathrobe, she felt a tenderness for him. She asked him questions, trying to fill in the parts of his life before she knew him. He showed her a picture of himself as a little boy holding the first fish he'd caught. The picture was creased from being carried in his wallet for so many years, but the thick blond hair and the proud expression, yellowed from the age of the photograph, were familiar. She wanted to know everything about him, how old he had been when he first fell in love, what his first sexual experience had been like, what had been his relationship with Mrs. Barney. In return for his history, she was willing to give hers. She wanted to be known as completely as she could. But he never asked her any questions. He seemed satisfied to have her just in the present.

That didn't stop her from searching for the rest of him. He enjoyed talking about his childhood, and it was clear that he missed the little boy who was showing off his fish. But when the questions came closer to the present, he was less eager to talk. When she asked him about Mrs. Barney he said, "Rose Ann, I have a private life." He blurted it out with such an accumulation of feeling that she recoiled. "I'm sorry," he said. "I didn't mean it like that. I only . . ." He spread his hands and looked at her with an embarrassed expression. "I need my privacy," he finished.

"Of course," she replied. "But I have such a strong feeling of wanting to tell you everything, I thought you'd have it, too."

He was silent.

"You goddamned Elton," she said under her breath. "I know why you drink after dinner. It's the perfect companion, isn't it? It doesn't ask questions. It doesn't make you talk." But, from the expression on his face, she knew she had said something she shouldn't have. Afraid of his anger, she put her arms around him and pulled him against her. He kissed her. When they pulled apart, her face felt bruised.

One day she was on the lawn building a setup when Quip came up to her and said, "Rose Ann, when you're finished I want to speak to you." She wondered if he was displeased with the way something had been done. For two days he had been out of town, and, although she had taken over the class, she hadn't been teaching it; the students seemed fine just working on their own. Maybe he had wanted her to take a more active part. Or was he dissatisfied with the setups? She liked to create a crowded environment and then have Mrs. Barney, draped in odd pieces of clothing, stand in the center of it. Perhaps he was getting bored with that situation. Maybe he wanted her to try something different.

She found him in the dining hall sitting over a cup of coffee, writing a letter. When she opened the door, he didn't look in her direction. Something was terribly wrong. Was he going to fire her? Maybe he had found a more promising student in New York. She took the seat opposite him, and he finally looked up. "Rose Ann, I wanted you to come to the Penobscot School of Art to paint, not to fuck around with one of the instructors, not to spend your time diddling with setups, but paint. P-A-I-N-T. I have seen nothing." He picked up his pen and began to write again. "I have work to do," he said. "So leave me alone and go get started. Also—let them draw a nude against a bare landscape for a while, will you?" He looked up. "There's nothing nicer than the naked human form."

At dinner that evening, as Mrs. Barney brought in the platters of food, she'd sneak glances at Rose Ann. Rose Ann, in the meantime, tried to get Elton's attention. He was sitting at the other end of the table pretending not to see her. As he talked to one of his students, she could tell that he felt her watching, but in his stubborn way, he refused to look in her direction. It was just like him; when everybody knew about their affair, he would still keep up the pretense.

After dinner Barney came out of the kitchen and stood to the side nervously as Rose Ann spoke to a student. Wiping her hands on her apron, she stepped up when the student left. "I wonder if you wouldn't mind coming into the kitchen a moment?" Her face turned a bright red, and she smiled uncomfortably. "It'll only be a second, do you have the time?"

Behind the swinging door, Rose Ann found herself in a large room with a black and white linoleum floor. Huge pots hung from the ceiling, and something was simmering on the stove. A mound of sliced tomatoes sat on the counter. Mrs. Barney stopped beside them, gripping the cutting board. Rose Ann pulled up a stool. "What a cheerful room this is," she said.

"There's something I want to talk to you about. I hope you don't mind. We only know each other in a professional way, but I don't know what to do anymore, and there's something I want you to know. It's getting so bad I just can't help it." Mrs. Barney put her hands to her face, and her voice turned shaky. "I'm an old sap," she said, starting to cry.

Rose Ann watched for a moment and then went over and put her arm around the other woman. "There now," she said. "What's the matter?"

"I stink of onions," Mrs. Barney said angrily. "He always used to say I stink of onions."

"Who?" Rose Ann asked.

"Elton Longacre, that's who."

"Why did he care what you smelled like?"

Mrs. Barney began to weep more copiously. Rose Ann squeezed her hand. "There now, you can talk to me."

Finally, the crying fit over, the cook wiped her eyes and blew her nose in her apron. "He made me feel like something you'd keep in the barn," she said bitterly. "I couldn't help it, though. The only man I cared about was Elton. What could he do? He ignored me. He said, Barney, you stink of onions, and then he went his way and I was expected to go mine."

"When was this?" Rose Ann asked gently.

"Last summer," Mrs. Barney said, sniffing between sobs. "If I was young and pretty like you, or if it was a secret what my body looked like, he would pay me attention. I am so lonely for him," she moaned, crying again. "There's no one else who wants to bother. No one cares."

"I care," Rose Ann said, but she knew that wasn't what the other woman wanted.

"If I didn't say a word, no one would notice."

"There now," Rose Ann said, "that's not true at all. So many people like you. You make us all feel at home. When everyone's out there painting you, they do it with fondness. You musn't belittle what you do. You're very important to all of us."

"I know you couldn't manage without me, but that's not what I want. I want *him,*" Mrs. Barney said.

After that it was silent. Rose Ann didn't know what else to say. Finally she asked, "Why did you want to tell me?"

"Because you have him. I wanted you to know how lucky you are. That's all. I just wanted you to know that." She chopped some more on the tomatoes and waited for Rose Ann to speak.

"I'll tell you a secret, but you can't breathe a word of it to anyone."

The other woman put down the knife and looked up. Her eyes were bright from tears.

"Elton Longacre isn't good enough for all of this. Don't be lonely for him; he's not worth it. Elton Longacre isn't a generous man. He'll never be able to give you what you want. He isn't very aware of other people. Do you know what I'm telling you? He's a little boy. The most interesting person to him is himself."

"That's not true," Mrs. Barney said. "He told me I was made of beautiful curves. He showed me some pictures by a certain painter and he told me I looked like them, just as white and beautiful as the women in the pictures."

"I thought he told you you stank of onions."

"That was later," Mrs. Barney said. "Afterwards."

17

That night when he came to her room she sat up in bed and turned on the light. The darkness was soft, and the green of the bedspread was warm. He let his bathrobe drop to the floor and climbed into bed next to her. She moved over to make room for him. "Barney talked to me," she said.

"Oh yeah, what did she say?" Moaning and biting her gently, he kissed her all over her face. He lifted her arms and pulled off her nightgown.

"She said she missed you," Rose Ann whispered.

He moved down her neck, across her shoulders, stopping long enough only to ask, "What did you say back?" He forced her down into the bed and climbed on top of her.

"I told her you weren't worth it."

"You sure about that?" he asked, nuzzling her belly.

"I don't know," she sighed.

There was nothing to do but stretch a canvas and get to work. She set her easel up on the lawn and began to sketch what she saw in front of her. Soon the canvas was covered with penciled lines and the composition began to emerge. There were the lawn and the trees in front of the house, and because the forms were so angular, she sketched in a pond beside the trees, creating tension with the addition of an elliptical shape. She planned to have Mrs. Barney reclining on the banks, cattails growing beside her.

She worked on the canvas all day and by evening had a sense of what she wanted. The next morning Mrs. Barney posed under the tree, and Rose Ann sat with the class and made sketches in charcoal. Mrs. Barney changed positions every twenty minutes, and soon everyone had a stack of drawings.

It felt good to be working again. She didn't stop for dinner but kept on drawing, making mock-ups of the canvas and trying different approaches. That night she had everything spread out in her room; the drawings of Mrs. Barney were on the floor, and the painted sketches were on her bed. She was sitting in the middle when the door opened and Elton came in.

"What's this?" he asked.

He stood at the door in his white bathrobe, waiting for her to pick things up. But she didn't try to clear a path for him. Finally she said, "I've been figuring something out. I think I need to be alone tonight, Elton."

"You should have said something earlier."

"I didn't know earlier."

"But I've been anticipating a night with you, Rose Ann."

"I'm sorry. Surely just one night . . . you can understand, can't you?"

"Of course," he said, his hand on the door handle. He closed it harder than was necessary, and a few seconds later she heard his door bang shut at the other end of the hall.

Not giving it any notice, she went back to her drawings. It was three o'clock before she finally got to bed, but she felt she knew how to proceed with the painting.

The next night when he didn't come to her room, she threw on her sweater over her nightgown and walked down the hall to his room. She knocked and waited, but there wasn't an answer. She turned the knob and opened it, and by the light shining in from the hall, she could tell the bed was empty. Maybe he had gone back to his old habit of sitting on the porch. She tiptoed down the stairs and opened the front door as quietly as she could, but there was no one. She shut it softly and since she was down there, walked back to the kitchen for something to eat. As she washed a piece of fruit, she heard giggling in the next room. It was Mrs. Barney's bedroom, which was just off the kitchen. Without stopping to listen, she knew the other voice, low and suggestive, was Elton's.

19

She finished the painting in a week and took it up to her bedroom to look at later. If she stopped working, she'd only start feeling sorry for herself, so she stretched another canvas and began to draw on it right away. She chose a different spot on the grounds, one where she could work without being disturbed. At first she was painting what she saw in front of her, but again she put in an element that wasn't there. In this case she added furniture. She painted a table and an empty chair with a crumpled dinner napkin on the seat as though someone had just finished eating. She thought of having a nude lie under a tree in the distance but decided it would be too crowded. Nor could she face Mrs. Barney, who had been walking around the school during the last few days looking joyful.

That painting she also took up to her room. Without sitting down to study it first, she stacked it against the wall on top of the other.

She did the third from the porch overlooking the lawn. There were a table and chair again, but a man sat in the chair with his back to the viewer. She painted him from an image in her mind and was relieved that he didn't look at all like Elton. He had a round head and short hair, and from what you could see of his shoulders, it looked like he was wearing a suit. Elton never wore a suit, and even from the back, his head was longer and thinner and his hair certainly wasn't as short.

Elton was arrogant enough to continue to sit with her at meals, and, when Mrs. Barney was bringing in the food, he'd do his best to be as attentive as he could to Rose Ann. She ignored him. He was such a childish man, she could hardly imagine him being a serious painter.

One afternoon she asked Quip. She was on the porch working on the canvas, and Quip had been on his way into the house when he stopped to see what she was doing. Rose Ann put down her brush and said, "Can we talk?" They walked out to the lawn and sat down together.

"Who's the man in the chair?" Quip asked.

She told him she didn't know.

He threw his hands up in the air. "Why do a vague painting, Rose Ann? Why even bother to paint when you've got an ambiguous subject? Decide who it is and give that painting some energy. Make the man be someone you have a response to, and then get that response to work in the painting. You're just wasting your time this way. It's like deciding you'll cross the street but standing at the corner watching traffic. You'll never get to the other side that way. You have to put one foot forward and walk."

"I know who the man is," Rose Ann said softly. "He's someone I know named Teddy Juroe."

"Well, do you love him or hate him?"

"I hardly know him."

"And he's the person you're going to paint? For Christ's sake, Rose Ann, make it Elton and get it over with."

She hadn't expected him to say that. She never thought he paid much attention to what went on between the people around him. "I wouldn't be able to paint if it was Elton. I'd be too angry."

"So what?" Quip shouted. "Do an angry painting. Anger is better than ambiguity. Anger is refreshing. Don't, for God's sake, play it safe with a tepid painting. Face what's going on. Don't run away from it."

"What's going on, London?"

"I shouldn't have to tell you how to use your eyes, girl, do it yourself."

"What kind of painter is Elton?"

"He's a damn good painter. There's a catalogue from one of his shows in the library. Go take a look at it."

She didn't look at the catalogue. She didn't want to see anything of his she might like. Instead, she made some changes in her painting. She turned the chair around so the man sitting in it faced the viewer. It was a man wearing a white bathrobe, holding a glass of whiskey. On his lap there was a pistol. She didn't know why she put it there, but she followed her impulse and painted it in.

She worked on the canvas for two weeks, and when it was done it was thick with layers of paint. The man in the chair was pale and flat, but the landscape around him was rich in color.

When she had finished, she sat in front of it for a long time. There was a world being described there. She knew what the antecedent was, but even so, the image it had been turned into was mysterious to her.

She set the three paintings up in her room, and it was clear to her how powerful the last one was and how timid the first had been. She took the drapes off her window so there would be enough light and then found Quip and asked him to give her a critique.

He came after lunch. Without saying anything, he sat down in front of the paintings and looked. After what seemed like a very long time he turned around. "Rose Ann, I finally know who you are. I can see what you see when you look out of your eyes. I don't want to say any more than that, just keep working." He stood up to leave. She put her arm around him and walked him to the door. As she let him go, she felt her eyes get teary.

Noticing it, he patted her on the back. "You're all right," he said. "Everything is fine. They've been doing it for years. You're not the first, and you won't be the last, and they'll keep on going. They're an old sadomasochistic pair, and you, in the meantime, have become a painter."

"I suppose it goes on every summer," Rose Ann said, pulling away from him. She dried her face. "Can't someone help them?"

"Don't be so naive. Don't be one of those people who think the world should be all love and goodness. There's give and take, push and pull, white and black. Everything has its uses. I was once ready to marry a woman I knew I couldn't make happy. I was terribly depressed when I was with her, but in my melodramatic way, I thought that was just the hardship of love. Thank God the marriage didn't happen. But I became a better painter for it. Do you know why? Because I needed to show myself there was something I could do well. Everything has its uses, it's just that you sometimes don't figure out what they are until later."

"Was that Laura Betock?" Rose Ann asked.

"I guess nothing is a secret any longer." He sat down on the end of the bed and put his hands on his knees. "Well, Elton knew. I guess he was the one who told you."

"No, he didn't, London. He kept your secret. It's just that I found the paintings you hid in the barn."

20

Six years later, when she was living in New York, she did finally see Elton's work. She had a job as a window dresser, and she painted nights and on weekends and saw as many shows as she could. The opening was at a gallery in midtown, and since she lived in the Village, she treated herself to a taxi. As it pulled up to the building, she saw a crowd of people at the entrance. Feeling uneasy about going in, she took her time paying the driver. It had been a long time since she'd seen anyone from the Penobscot School of Art. She didn't know how she would react to Elton, and she wasn't sure if she would even want to talk to him.

She hoped Quip would be there. She hadn't heard from him in a couple of years, and since he hadn't had a show in New York in a long time, she wondered if he was still working.

As the elevator neared the fifth floor, she heard the voices. The doors opened into the gallery, and she walked into a mass of perfumed and well-dressed people. Behind them were the paintings. All she could see were the edges of the canvases, a lot of reds and yellows.

In the center of the room, wearing a white jacket and leaning fashionably on a cane was Elton. Recalling the man who would jump out of his convertible instead of opening the door, she was shocked by how fragile he seemed.

Not wanting to be noticed, she walked around the perimeter of the room, looking at the work. There was a series of nudes lying on a red couch, and it was some time before she realized who the model was. A shy and voluptuous Mrs. Barney peered over tables or from behind plants, and it was clear that, even though she was never in the foreground of the painting, her presence dominated the interiors. She liked the way he put on the paint, leaving the brushstroke visible, building up the colors gradually, and always showing the involvement of the artist. No clean edges or equal spaces anywhere—he didn't try to hide the awkwardness of the human hand.

But the nudes—in each one there was a sense of surprise. Who was that naked woman peering from behind things, and what would it take to give permission for such an erotic creature to come into the foreground?

She saw someone she recognized as a student from Penobscot, but she didn't remember her name, and they only smiled at one another as they passed. Rose Ann approached a wall of pencil drawings. She heard a woman say, "It happened three years ago."

"Was it an accident?" the man beside her asked.

"Depends who you talk to," the woman replied. Then she called out, "Hillary! Come here a minute."

Rose Ann moved out of earshot.

"How do you like it?"

She looked up and saw a round, pink, smiling face. "Mrs. Barney!"

"Mrs. Longacre now, Althea Longacre."

Rose Ann extended her hand, but Mrs. Barney leaned over and gave her a kiss.

"We were married two years ago, right after he recovered. We live up there now. We look after the place in the winter and run the school in the summer. He was ready for it, marriage and everything." Mrs. Barney put a gloved hand up to her shoulder and manipulated a strap under the shiny black material of her dress, grimacing with the effort. Having tucked it into place, she composed her expression. "Has Elton seen you yet? Go up and say hello—he doesn't get around very well these days."

"What happened?"

"Don't tell me you didn't hear nothing about it. Well," Mrs. Barney said, placing her foot forward and resting her hands on her hips, "he shot himself." She waited for Rose Ann to register shock and then went on. "It wasn't an accident neither. But at least he didn't aim anywhere fatal. He just shot at his foot. That laid him up for a couple of months. I don't know what he would of done if I hadn't been there. It put some sense into him, though, because he stopped drinking. Did you see the paintings? He does me well, doesn't he? Go say hello, Rose Ann. He'd like to see you."

Mrs. Barney walked toward the hors d'oeuvre table. Rose Ann continued to look at the work because there were still too many people standing around Elton. When he was finally alone, she walked up to him and said, "I like your paintings very much."

"I was waiting for you to come over. I've been watching you ever since you got here. I knew you'd like them. Most people do. I've been painting well these last few years because I can't run around anymore." He smiled. "I can't get into as much trouble. Come here," he said, beckoning her closer. "I've got a secret to tell you."

She leaned toward his face, and he whispered, "You remember that time in the barn? You're the only virgin I've ever had. I'll never forget you for that. You won't forget me either, will you?"

Instead of giving him the satisfaction of a reply, she walked away. She passed a drawing where Mrs. Barney sat in pastel shadows, and she nodded good-bye to the flesh-and-blood Mrs. Barney, who stood by herself eating a tea sandwich. The elevator opened, and Rose Ann stepped into the hot and crowded interior. It reached the ground floor, and she followed the people out of the building.

There was a taxi unloading at the other end of the street. She had only enough money for a ride halfway back, but she began to run toward it, waving her hand. A small, thin man stepped out, and the cab pulled away. She went in the other direction to get a bus.

"Don't be so blind," a voice behind her called.

Without turning around, she knew who it was. "London Quip!" she cried, and the man walked toward her.

"The only reason I came was to see you," he said peevishly. "I've fallen miserably out of touch with everyone I care about, and there you are running off without even bothering to notice who I am."

They moved under the awning of a building, and he grabbed her hand and said, "How are you doing? Are you painting at all? Students should keep in touch with their teachers, particularly if they're working. Why haven't you done that?"

"I was waiting to hear something from you," she said.

"I've stopped writing letters," Quip told her. "I've stopped answering the phone. All I do now is pay my bills, talk to my students, and think about what I'm going to paint."

"I'm glad to hear you've been working."

"You didn't listen, Rose Ann. I said I was *thinking* about what I was going to paint. I haven't painted anything yet. I haven't touched a canvas in fifteen months." He put his hands in the pockets of his coat and looked across the street. "I'm taking more time to pay attention to what's around me. I reached a point where I wasn't interested in having anybody know how I looked at things. So I stopped painting. It seemed like the logical thing to do. It bruised my ego a little—a painter who doesn't paint—what is he? Well, I can't answer that. But, for the time being, I'm only a watcher and a listener."

They had been standing on the street for a long time. Rose Ann suggested they move to a restaurant, but Quip wanted to say hello to Elton and see the show. "Will you come up with me?" he asked.

She said she couldn't, so they agreed to meet under the awning in half an hour. Rose Ann walked around the block and when the time was up, went back to their meeting place. Quip appeared a few minutes later, and they went uptown to a restaurant he told her he liked. When they were seated, he said, "You put a gun in your painting, do you remember that?"

She didn't know what he was talking about.

"At Penobscot you did a painting of Elton. A very pale man sitting at a table with an exotic landscape behind him? Don't tell me I remember your painting better than you do! There was a gun in the man's lap. That's what I'm referring to. What made you put a gun there?"

She shook her head. She hadn't thought about that painting in years. She remembered the gun, but she couldn't remember why it was there. "I was angry at him, and I wanted to see him hurt himself, I guess. It's hard to say now, since I know what happened. But there always was something about him that seemed dangerous. I think the gun was just an image that occurred to me, so I put it in his lap."

"Well, it proves what I've always believed," Quip said, "that the artist has intuitions that cross all the supposed boundaries. The distinctions we believe in are only a way of organizing the chaos that's around us, but they aren't really there. You know what Elton feels, and I know what you feel. We aren't so separate after all. I can look at Elton, and I can tell that something's changed; the eruption of violence seems to have soothed a ragged nerve. And that ragged nerve is something we know about, isn't it? Now, dear girl, tell me what you're up to."

So she told him what she had been doing, about her job and the place where she lived. She told him the job was temporary, but it paid food and rent and a taxi every once in a while. At the same time, she was looking for a situation where she could have more time to paint. Maybe her skills as a window designer would lead to something else. But she didn't feel anxious about it because the only thing that mattered was what she did in the studio. She'd put an old rug down on her living-room floor, and she painted in there. It had windows on the north, and at night she'd set up lights. She often worked long after midnight, sometimes not stopping until she heard the garbage trucks in the morning. At work the next day it was hard to stay awake, but if she drank enough coffee she could function.

"It sounds good," he said. "Only sleep a little more. It'll help you paint and you'll be happier."

When they walked out of the restaurant, he slipped her a dollar for a taxi and kissed her on the cheek gently.

"Where are you going?" she asked.

"I have to get the train back to Philadelphia. I have a class to teach early in the morning." He squeezed her hand and walked off in the other direction.

She stood where she was and watched till he disappeared.

Happiness. He always said things that surprised her.

21

She was working in the window at the Macy's on Herald Square, tacking up stripes of colored material for their fall coat display. In the past they had always done a scene with trees, but she had decided to make it less specific this year. Strips of red and orange would represent the colors of autumn, a large half-circle would be the harvest moon, and on the horizon, a long jagged shape would suggest the skyline of New York. In the foreground, at the mannequins' feet, there was a black-and-white speckled surface for the concrete of the city. The mannequins were huge against the skyline, but she felt it only emphasized the coats they were wearing.

Since the setup was more complicated than usual, it had taken her longer to fashion all of the elements. It was to have been finished on Sunday, but there she was on Monday morning tacking the last of the stripes onto the sky. She finished by lunchtime and walked down to the employee's lounge for her jacket where she saw a note taped to her locker: There was a form she needed to pick up at the personnel office.

When she went in on her way to lunch, the secretary buzzed the manager. A stocky, middle-aged man came forward and asked her to follow him to his office. He closed the door and offered her a green leather chair on the other side of the desk.

"Miss Beech," he began, "we regret to inform you that we've found your work unsatisfactory."

She looked at him with a shocked expression.

"Let me hasten to reassure you that we recognize your skills. However, we feel you aren't suitable for a job like this. Your setups haven't been appropriate for the general public, and we feel too often they call attention to themselves rather than the clothing." He held a finger up to indicate he had more to say. But she hadn't tried to interrupt him; she could tell from his expression that he wasn't interested in anything she might want to tell him. "However, we are not your typical unfeeling employer. We are prepared to furnish . . ."

"My displays are different," she said, not waiting to hear the rest. "They make people curious enough to stop and look in the windows. When you realize that, you'll wish you'd held onto me." She took her hat and pocketbook and left his office. Looking at no one, she went through the maze of desks in front and found the exit.

The store was filled with lunchtime shoppers, office girls rifling through the merchandise in a bored manner. She had to wait for an empty wedge in the revolving door, and when she got out, the sun blinded her. Not sure what to do, she walked across the street to the park and sat on one of the benches. Her face burned as though someone had slapped her. Deciding she must be hungry, she pulled out her sandwich, ate only half of it, and put the rest in her bag for dinner. Then, telling herself that she was, after all, an artist and that this was only a small incident in her material existence, she spent the rest of the afternoon walking through the Museum of Modern Art.

She painted in her studio that whole first week. She didn't eat much and slept very little, and by Friday was exhausted. On Saturday she slept and did a modest shopping for groceries, and it wasn't until she woke up on Sunday that she began to worry. Even if she didn't spend any money at all over the next two weeks, she wouldn't have enough to pay the rent. But she could get the rent to the landlord two weeks late, which she'd done before, and by four weeks surely she would have found another job. That way she could work in the studio for another week and then spend the week after that looking for a job. In the meantime, something might come her way.

But after the second week she kept on painting. She knew she had to stop, but she'd discovered a rhythm and didn't want to break it. By the time the rent was a week overdue, she had only five dollars and very little food left. Of course, her parents were just across the river in Brooklyn, but she was reluctant to approach them for help, particularly when she hadn't done anything about the situation herself.

The work would make something happen. It had to. She refused to be poor or desperate, and she also refused to be a nine-to-five clerk in a public office. If she kept her attention focused on what she was doing, she would be all right. She had to believe that. She had to close her door, narrow her sights, and let the work take her over.

She set up a still life. It was a simple one: a table covered with a lace cloth and a bowl filled with lemons and pears. Beside the bowl was a pitcher. She drew from it for three days, and then she stretched a canvas.

23

The change came with the pears. She had been up all night. At six in the morning, when the first light of the day turned the living room a clear, clean bluish white, she knew how to get the color of the pears. Sitting in the porcelain bowl, they were red on the edges. They glowed. The lemons next to them were a dense, even yellow, but the pears had patches of red. She mixed the color on her palette, and when she put it on her brush, she knew it would be the right shade—not a defined red but a tentative one, with hints of blue and yellow.

She finished the painting that afternoon and stood at the other end of the room for a long time looking at it. She'd caught the light coming into the windows, the sense of the city beyond them, the possibilities. The lemons were still and heavy, but the pears were alive. On the edge of the one in the foreground, there was a tremor of yellow, a rich tone but a half-hidden line. That was where it lived, the sounds of the early morning, the primitive life behind appearances; it was there at the line where the form gave way to the space around it.

She took the rest of the day off and bought a newspaper. She went to a restaurant down the street for a doughnut and a cup of coffee and opened the paper to the want ads. The waitress forgot to bring the cream, so she went to the counter. The man who was sitting there handed her the pitcher. "Hey," he said, "I know who you are."

He looked exactly the same—cleanly shaved, a neatly pressed suit, and an innocent, boyish expression. It was as though there hadn't been any time since their last encounter. "Teddy Juroe, I still want to do your portrait."

"Don't tell me that. Come on, Rose Ann, forget you're an artist for a second, and tell me you want to see me this Friday for dinner."

24

He took her to an Italian restaurant because he said she looked like she needed a good fattening meal. He wouldn't let her order because he said she'd be too polite to get the right things, so he ordered for both of them. First the waiter brought a bottle of wine, then the antipasto. There was pasta after that, and when they finished the pasta, they had the salad course. The waiter took the salad plates away, wiped the spills from the table, and poured wine in their glasses. Then he brought out the main dish.

Eating took all her attention. Each time one course was finished, she'd be afraid there wouldn't be another. She ate seriously, finishing everything on her plate each time. She couldn't talk, so she was glad he kept the conversation going. She'd eaten so little for so many days that she wanted to give the food all of her attention. When she was done and the last plates were cleared away, she wiped her mouth and said, "I'm sorry. I haven't been much of a dinner companion. Everything was so good I got carried away."

"You were hungry. If you don't have any plans for tomorrow, I'll take you out again."

"For another dinner like this, I would break any plans I might have made."

25

The next day they went to the same restaurant, and he ordered again. She ate more slowly and drank more wine. "I have something to confess," she said. "I've thought of keeping it a secret, but I think I'd like to tell you just so the both of us are aware of something."

Fork in the air he asked, "Aware of what?"

"Do you know what I was going to do that summer when you never called me? I was going to try all of the insurance companies in New York City until I found you."

"Why didn't you just get my number from the phone book?"

"You weren't listed. I think I even tried a couple of operators. There wasn't a single Juroe in all of New York."

"There most certainly was. I've always had a phone, and I've always been listed."

"Well, I couldn't find it, so I tried calling a few insurance companies. I didn't hit the right one, though, and if I hadn't left town that summer, I think I would have sat down with the phone book and tried every life insurance company that was listed. It would have taken me hours." As she was talking, she realized something was becoming obvious, and she wondered how to acknowledge it. She could say, *I wanted to paint you, that's why I needed to find you so badly. I had a portrait already planned, but I just needed you to complete it.*

"Wait a minute, how were you spelling Juroe?"

"G-E-R-E-A-U-X. Isn't that right?"

"No!" he shouted. "J-U-R-O-E!"

"I don't think I even considered spelling it any differently. Isn't that funny, I would have found you if it wasn't for a simple thing like that. By the way, why *didn't* you call me?"

"What summer was that?"

"Let's see, it was the summer I went to Penobscot, so it was thirty-four."

"And it's forty now, so that was six years ago."

"You're stalling," she said.

"A very perceptive young woman." Despite his slicked hair and pressed shirt, he looked ruffled. He sputtered a word or two and then, turning pink at the temples, spread his arms apart and said, "Look, the truth is I decided not to call you. I didn't want to get tangled up with someone who had such a complicated life. I didn't forget you. . . . It's just that I decided . . . Look, it's a difficult thing to admit. . . . I just wanted an easy girlfriend."

"Did you find one?"

"For a while. Her name was Betty." His face was pink all over.

"What's the matter?"

He laughed. "It didn't work out. She wouldn't do anything with me unless we got married. We'd have these long arguments. I'd say, 'But how do you know if you want to marry me unless you find out what I'm like first? I might be a real ape, you never know.' She'd get this stubborn look on her face and say, 'Teddy, I know how I feel.' So my line of argument would run, 'If you know how you feel, then why are you holding back?'

"'It's the principle of the thing,' she'd say.

"'Principle? What does principle mean?'

"Finally she'd say, 'I can't explain it. All I can go by are my feelings.'

"So I'd say, 'Don't your feelings tell you you want to rip my clothes off and make love to me?'

"She'd say very coldly, 'Well, I also know what's right and wrong.'

"So I took what I could get. We would smooch for hours, and I could touch her anywhere above the waist as long as I stayed away from her chest. I learned to make the best of it. Did you ever know, for instance, how erotic it is to caress an elbow?"

She thought it strange that he was telling her these things. How did he know she wasn't another Betty?

When they left the restaurant, he took her arm. They walked back to her apartment building, and at the door she turned around to say good night.

"Aren't you going to invite me up?"

She felt annoyed by the question. He had already made it clear he wanted an easy girlfriend.

"I'm sorry," he said, growing pink again, shoving his hands in his pockets. "I didn't mean to be pushy. Maybe I could take you someplace for coffee, would you feel like that? I just don't want to go back home so soon, that's all."

"Come on, *I'll* make us coffee." But as she took him up the stairs she had second thoughts. Her paintings were all over for him to see, and she'd have to listen to an insurance man on the subject of modern art. He'd ask her well-meaning questions, and that would be unbearable.

She didn't hang up his coat, making it clear, she hoped, that he wouldn't be staying very long. They went into the kitchen, and as she got things ready, she could feel him gazing at everything. Then he wandered into the living room. The still life was up, and the painting of it was on her easel. Out of the corner of her eye, she could see him looking from one to the other.

"Do you remember that show you took me to?" He stood in her doorway, hands pushed against the frame as though he were trying to stretch it. "Your picture reminds me of it. I don't know anything about art, but it just seems . . . oh, I don't know. . . . It's nice, Rose Ann—the way you painted that fruit. I didn't know an ordinary bowl of fruit could be . . . well, how about wise? I think that fruit is very wise."

She could have kissed him. Instead, she handed him a cup of coffee. They stayed in the kitchen talking in hushed tones.

"I always wanted to be unlike anyone else," he said. "I wanted to do something creative—write a fantastic piece of music or build the most beautiful building in the world. Here I am, selling insurance. But I don't feel unlucky. It's just the thing that happened to me, that's all. My desire will have to come out in some other way. Or maybe the fantastic will have to wait for another lifetime. Because I think we get more than one chance. That way, we can afford to go more slowly, make mistakes."

As he spoke, she decided he was nice to look at. There was a freshness about him she liked, as though he had just come a very long way and was arriving at this new place for the first time. She felt excited, as if it were up to her to show him what life was like. That must have been what was happening because, all of a sudden, she was telling him something she hadn't really ever thought about herself, and yet it was something she knew she believed. "Nobody writes fantastic music or builds beautiful buildings. They don't even aspire to it. The ones who are really doing it, the good ones, are never conscious of trying to do something great; they're just doing what their intuition tells them needs to be done. And afterwards only a few will see what the artist wanted them to see. The rest are blind and deaf to it."

"But doesn't that make you want to give up? If so few people are aware of what you're doing, what's the use?"

"Myself," she said, "in the end, that's really who it's for. I can't give up because I can't let it go."

The lights were off in the rest of the apartment, and it felt as though that tiny room were at the center of the earth, a place neither of them really knew anything about. The city was so dark and quiet it had ceased to exist. The only light, the only voices were right there. Everything else that struggled to survive had fallen deep into sleep.

Around midnight he went into the living room to get his hat and coat. Coming back, he said, "You don't have to get up to let me out; I'll find my way."

He didn't realize how still it was out there. He didn't know the city had abandoned them. It was so simple, the two of them alone at the center of the earth talking about their ideas. But he was dressed for the outside, telling her that he would find his way. She didn't want to let him go. So, very gently, she helped him out of his coat.

And then, without even looking, she found the desert. Down at the center of the earth, where they stayed all night and most of the following day, the dark, heavy stillness gave way to the red beach she remembered from so long ago. They had taken their breakfast into the living room. The morning light had destroyed all of the shadows, and as she let her eyes close, she felt the heat and the sand and saw, in the distance, the strange pointed trees. They had gone all night without touching one another, but still she was thirsty and hot. Yet if she got up to get a glass of water, time would start again; it remained the same only as long as she didn't move.

She looked at his sturdy, ordinary body slouched on the sofa beside her, and then she put her hand on his chest.

"I was waiting for one of us to do that," he said.

She stroked up and down, up and down, barely touching him. She was more relaxed than she had ever been in her life, and yet the possibilities of all that could happen kept her body in a wakeful state. He took her hand and stilled it, and as he leaned over, his strange, new breath covering her, the surface of her skin was waiting. Then, as their lips actually met, she felt such a great need she became frantic. It embarrassed her. After the hours of talk and the polite good night when she went into her bedroom and he lay down on her couch—because he had grown up, he didn't want just an easy girlfriend—this neediness seemed all wrong. But she couldn't help herself; at the center of the earth where the sun beat down on her, she couldn't be shy. All the edges of her skin, where her skin broke into the air, were alive. She was hot and thirsty, and as he kissed her all over her face, her neck, her shoulders, she knew there would never be enough. This was all there was. And even when they threw off their clothes there wasn't any more. She had to take what was there now. So she opened her legs and when he was inside her she was still frantic because she couldn't feel him enough, it didn't make enough of a difference. Then everything in the entire world shifted. He and the sky and the sand beneath her gathered into a single point that bore into her, drawing all of her energy into itself, and then suddenly broke open, flooding her with bits and pieces of everything that existed so that she couldn't feel herself any longer.

And then everything it had absorbed began to leave her. The world reassembled itself into the familiar shapes. But she had changed. In all her new roominess, she started to laugh. He began to laugh, too, which made her laugh even harder. And then she began to cry. This was all there was. A thin gray light squeezed into the room, a phone rang in a distant apartment, water ran through the pipes in the walls; even this man who had just made love to her and looked at her with a curious expression because she couldn't stop crying was only a circumstance. This wasn't all that she wanted. There had to be more.

. . . . . 26 . . . . .

They slept with each other every night for two weeks. Usually, they went to his apartment, three huge, barely furnished rooms on the corner of a stately old building in midtown. His bedroom was in the back, away from the noises of the street. There was nothing in it but a bed, so the wallpaper and the molding around the windows were the things she looked at. But even those would disappear as she lost herself when they made love. What had it been like before she knew him? She couldn't remember. In the morning he would get out of bed with his eyes still closed and sleepwalk to the bathroom. When he came back, he would burrow against her, trying to make sleep return. After a few minutes, he'd give up. Then they'd lie on their backs and talk about what they would do that day.

Every morning he made her breakfast. "I always wanted to be a short-order cook," he said. "Those guys are amazing. Ever watch them in a busy restaurant? They have fifteen orders going on the griddle, and they're smoking a cigarette and keeping up a conversation with the person sitting at the counter behind them."

He washed the dishes after breakfast, and then he went into the bathroom to shave. Once, when she followed him there, he hid behind the door. She thought he was hiding behind the shower curtain, so she armed herself with the plunger and leaped toward the bath. But he jumped out from behind her and grabbed her around the waist.

They wrestled together on the bath mat, and in a few minutes he had her pinned underneath him. He lifted her up from the floor and carried her into the living room. "You're just like a little lamb," he said, laying her gently down on the couch, the only piece of furniture in the room.

She had never thought of herself as being a little anything. The diminutive pleased her.

. , . . . *27* . . . . .

It was a Monday morning. When his alarm went off at seven, they buried themselves under the covers. At eight he went into the kitchen to make coffee, and they sat in bed together drinking it. He kissed her shoulders, coaxing her to lie back down. But she held herself rigid, and finally, when he asked her what was wrong, she told him there were two things she needed to do. She had to spend some time in her studio, and she had to find a job. She hadn't paid last month's rent, and there was a pile of bills she didn't have the courage to look at.

He stroked her arm murmuring, "Rosanna, Rosanna."

When she pushed him away, he jumped off the bed and stood at attention facing her. "I agree with you, Rose Ann, this childishness has got to end." He dropped the salute and disappeared into his closet. A moment later he was wearing a tie around his neck and his black going-to-work shoes. "No playing around is allowed. We have to get our lives in order." He pranced in front of her, naked but for the tie and shoes. Then he pulled out a sock and hung it on his penis. "Nothing is to escape scrutiny. There is no rest or luxury allowed." He marched down the hallway and came back wearing a hat and carrying an umbrella. The sock had fallen off.

She went into his closet and found a necktie to put around her waist and a vest to cover her bosom. But she didn't find it as amusing as he did. "Listen, Teddy, I really have to get started on things. I have to get back to my painting, and I have to find a job somewhere. I've got to dig up some money to pay the rent."

"Ask your parents for the rent."

"I guess I'll have to. They don't understand what I'm doing anyway, so it'll only fulfill their expectations. I've got to start looking for work, and I've got to get back to the studio as soon as I find a job."

"Listen, Rose Ann, do something for me, will you?"

"Really, Teddy, I can't play around anymore."

"Just listen, goddamnit."

She looked at him in his hat and necktie. Behind him there was the yellow wall of his kitchen and—the only thing in the apartment that wasn't strictly practical—the rooster clock. He had been in Woolworth's after a terrible day at the office, and it had caught his eye. She looked back at his face and then down at the hard little nipples and the striped necktie hanging between them. "All right, I'm listening."

"Just marry me," he said.

She couldn't. She wasn't that type. Surely he couldn't be serious.

"Marriage has its advantages. Think about it while I make you breakfast."

He stood in front of the refrigerator, taking out what he needed. Bathed in its yellow glow, he looked like a saint from a Renaissance painting. Advantages. Well, if she married him she wouldn't have to find a job. She could paint all day long. She could sleep with him every night. They would always eat dinner together.

But she needed a solitary life. She was an artist. She needed to go to bed thinking about her paintings and wake up thinking about them, and she needed long periods of time to work without any distractions.

He put a plate with eggs and toast in front of her. She broke the perfect yolks and said, "Teddy, I can't."

28

That evening she read the want ads. There was only one listing that looked at all interesting. She circled it: *Florist's Helper. Afternoons.* The next day she called the number. The woman told her to come by the shop so they could meet. "I need a conscientious person," the woman said. "And I want someone I can depend on to be polite."

It was a small shop. The owner herself was small with gray hair twisted on top of her head in a bun. When she introduced herself, Rose Ann didn't catch her name. She asked her to repeat it, and then, when she still didn't hear it, the woman pulled an envelope from the pocket of her apron and taking a black pencil from the table where she wrapped the flowers, slowly printed "Alma Vecchia."

"You must be Italian," Rose Ann said.

"My grandfather was, but I have too much other blood to be much of an Italian." She invited Rose Ann to the back of the shop, and telling her there weren't many customers that late in the day, opened the door to the backyard. It was a small, carefully tended garden, planted with shrubs and fruit trees and flowers that were withered from the cold autumn nights. She beckoned Rose Ann to one of the chairs and a moment later brought out cups of tea. She reached into her pocket and took out the envelope again. "Give me your name and address," she said, passing it to Rose Ann.

Rose Ann wrote the information she wanted and handed it back. "It must be beautiful out here in the summer."

"Is it too chilly for you? We could go inside. I could show you some plants I'm going to put in the ground next spring. I have all kinds of flowering bushes. They're native to a Mediterranean climate, so most of them aren't seen very much in this country. Maybe California," she added, "but not often New York."

"It's fine out here. I'm not cold at all."

But the woman seemed to have forgotten the question. "I don't get to work out here much during the day, but in the warm weather I'm always here in the evenings and on Sunday, of course. My apple tree is doing well this year; did you see all the fruit?"

Rose Ann turned and saw that the little tree was covered with apples. "When will they be ready to eat?"

"Another few weeks if the weather holds."

From the shop they heard the bell over the door announcing a customer.

"You can stay while I wait on them, or you can go if you like. I don't want to keep you. But finish your tea, you shouldn't feel you have to rush off."

Rose Ann smoothed out the skirt she hadn't had time to iron and pulled down the sleeves of a ruffled shirt she hadn't worn since high school. "What about the job?" she asked. "Don't you want to interview me?"

"I should see you tomorrow at two o'clock. Wear work clothes. It's dirty around here."

"Are you giving me the job?" she asked.

"You look like an intelligent girl," the woman replied as though that answered the question.

But it didn't seem like the shop did much business. Maybe she should find something that looked more promising. Standing up, she said, "I should warn you I don't know a thing about plants. I don't even know what anything is called."

Not giving a sign that she had heard, the woman opened the door.

"The only flowers I recognize are tulips and roses."

"Not to worry," Alma answered, finally turning around. "It's very easy. Everything you need to know I will teach you."

29

After the first week she began to take her sketchbook. When there wasn't anything to do, she'd put a bunch of flowers in a cup and draw them. She worked quickly, trying to get the gesture of the blossoms and ignoring the details. She'd been studying the Japanese scrolls at the Metropolitan, going there before she went to work. They reminded her to consider the way shape broke into space. She thought of how air reverberated long after church bells stopped ringing. She wanted that same tension to happen in her drawing as the line cut across the paper.

The little shop did more business than she would have supposed. There was a hospital around the corner, and during visiting hours people were in and out buying bouquets. Then there were the neighborhood customers who'd been coming there for years. They'd buy a bunch of flowers and stand around chatting with Alma.

Rose Ann stayed up front waiting on customers, and Alma stayed in the back cutting and wrapping. It was during the times when no one was in the store that she took out her drawing book.

Alma kept a good stock of the more common flowers—carnations, daisies, roses, and zinnias—but she also had exotic flowers—birds of paradise, snapdragons, and lilies. Those were the ones Rose Ann liked to sketch. Their shapes were more interesting.

"Here's something for you," Alma said once, handing her a bunch of bright pink sweet pea. "I can't sell them because no one buys a vine flower, but they're nice to look at, aren't they?"

Alma often came in with little presents—some muffins she'd made the night before or a new kind of tea she'd brew at their afternoon break. They always stopped work at three o'clock and closed the shop for half an hour. There were few customers then, and Alma said that anyone who really wanted anything would come back. She was firm on this, so even when someone knocked at the door, they stayed in the back room.

She'd been in the flower business all her life. Her first shop had been in a suburb of London. But fifteen years ago, at a time in her life when she needed to do something "really nervy," she sold her business and came to New York. She chose the Village because it was like the section of London she had lived in. She rented the store first and then found an apartment around the corner, which was very handy now because she took care of her father, who was eighty-eight years old and, she said proudly, "still a clear thinker." He had crossed the Atlantic and moved in with her just a few years ago when her mother had died. Alma's eyes grew shiny when she said this and surprised by that sign of lingering grief, Rose Ann murmured, "I'm sorry."

"Nothing to be sorry about. She died peacefully. But you can't help but think how nice it would be if people didn't die."

Rose Ann promptly said, "It would be horrible."

"Realistically, of course, it would be, but don't you sometimes have that wish?"

"No," Rose Ann said unequivocally.

When Alma handed her the sweet pea, she told her it was an old favorite of hers. "We had a fence in our backyard when I was a little girl, and every summer it would be covered with a sweet pea vine. Every summer my mother would tear it out because it's a weed essentially, but that only stimulated its growth because the next summer it would come back fuller than ever. I obeyed my mother's gardening taste, but I think I was always secretly happy to find the sweet pea had returned. That was awful of me, wasn't it?"

"Not at all," Rose Ann said. "I think it was wonderful." She took the sweet pea home and put it in a big pot in the middle of her studio and drew from it for as long as it kept its color. Of all the drawings, she took the one she liked the least to the shop and gave it to Alma. When they were on break, she pulled it out of a paper bag and unrolled it on her lap, all of a sudden feeling embarrassed that she wasn't giving her a very good one. "This is just a quick sketch," she began to say. She looked up and to her horror, Alma's eyes were shiny. "It's not much of anything, Alma, but since you gave me the sweet pea I thought you should have it."

"How lovely it is," Alma crooned, lifting it as though it were fragile. "I shall treasure it always."

"You can't. The paper will turn yellow and crack."

"Then I'll frame it," Alma said. "That's what I'll do. I'll take it to the framer's tomorrow."

"Let me give you a better one to frame."

"Oh, but it's lovely! I know just where I'll hang it, too." She rolled the drawing up again and reverently carried it to the closet in the back of the shop. "It was very thoughtful of you. I am very grateful."

Rose Ann hoped that would be the end of it, but Alma went on. "I don't have many paintings in my home. When I moved here, I had to leave a lot of my dearest possessions behind, and I just haven't found the right things to replace them. My walls are disgracefully bare. I know what I'll do, Rose Ann—I'll invite you over for dinner. That way you can see where I've hung it. It would be so nice if you'd be able to come." She looked at her with such a hopeful expression that all Rose Ann could do was smile and say, "That would be nice."

Teddy called her up in the morning and asked her to have lunch with him. They agreed on a restaurant near his office. She got there first and chose a table in the back.

As he stepped through the door, they waved to one another. She watched him make his way past the tables, taking off his coat as he came toward her. Imagining that he was someone she was meeting for the first time, she tried to see him objectively. Not too tall, shoulders not too wide, he was a nice-looking man. He had honest eyes: playful, inquiring, without judgment.

His breath was cold when he leaned over and kissed her. "How are you?" he asked.

There was such concern in his voice she felt waves of relief spill over her. To be recognized and, even more than that, to be cared for—how lucky. "I'm fine," she said. "I'm paying my bills, I'm eating well, I'm painting, and I'm going to my job. And along with all of the above, my employer has invited me to her house for dinner tonight. I don't really want to go, but being a conscientious employee, I couldn't say no."

He raised his eyebrows. "Want to skip out on it and elope with me?"

She was an artist. She had to live a solitary life. "No, I already told you, I'm not going to get married."

"Are you planning to be single for the rest of your life? That sounds kind of lonely."

"Not particularly," she said. "I plan to do just what I'm doing now—

pay my bills, eat well, and once in a while have lunch with you. I'm not lonely now."

"We'll be good old friends, right?"

"Don't be silly. We'll always be lovers."

"Will we?" he asked. "Forgive me for being so traditional, but someday I'd like to have a family."

"Teddy, you have to understand, I can't be what you want me to be. I'm sorry."

"I am too." He picked up the menu, but then put it down without looking at it. "Can't you let yourself give in to it? Can't you let yourself be content?"

The waitress came to their table and Teddy said, "Give me a sandwich and a cup of coffee."

"What kind of sandwich, sir?"

"Give him the special and give me number seven," Rose Ann said matter-of-factly.

The waitress tucked her pad in her apron pocket and turned away abruptly.

"I want to have you with me every day."

"But you will," she argued. "Not getting married doesn't mean we can't see one another. Teddy, it doesn't mean that I don't love you." She reached for his hand and forced him to look at her. "How can I get you to understand that?"

"Here I was, hoping that after not seeing me for a few weeks you'd have thought about things a little more and changed your mind. I can't face disappointment in the middle of the day like this. We'll have to talk about the weather."

"I'll just go," she said, getting out of her seat.

But he stood up as well. When she started to put on her coat, he helped her with it. Then he put on his coat and took her arm.

The waitress came with their sandwiches, and he said, "Back in a moment" and steered her out through the tables. When they got to the sidewalk he pulled her against him. She leaned into his collar, breathing the familiar cold-weather smell it had. "I'm sorry you can't have what you want. I wish I could just do it."

"You can," he whispered, kissing her forehead.

She pulled away and said, "No, I don't think I can."

That evening she and Alma left the shop together. "This will be fun," Alma said, handing her satchel and umbrella to Rose Ann so she could pull the door closed. "I haven't had a dinner guest in a long time. My father will like having someone new to talk to."

They walked down the street to the liquor store where Alma bought a bottle of wine, and then they went around the corner to a brick apartment house. Alma looked through the mail on the table in the foyer and took Rose Ann up a flight of stairs to a dark hallway. When she opened the door to the apartment, she stood aside so Rose Ann could go in first.

There was a large room with a polished wooden floor, a couch, and a few chairs. Alma took their things to a closet and whispered, "Dad's on the sunporch. He must still be sleeping." Rose Ann followed her through a small, neat bedroom she assumed to be Alma's and then out to a porch filled with plants. Behind a hanging begonia there was a frail little man asleep in a wicker chair. His newspaper had fallen to the floor, and his glasses were pushed up to his forehead. He snored evenly, and his body, but for the rhythm of breathing, was entirely still.

Alma put her finger to her mouth and tiptoed out of the room. When they were in the kitchen she said, "I don't like to disturb him if he's napping. He doesn't sleep well at night. By the way, his name is Charles."

As Charles slept, the two women worked on dinner. Rose Ann set the table, and Alma prepared the food. There was salad, stew, and a special bread she'd ordered from the baker. When everything was ready, they went back to the sunporch. Alma kissed the old man on the top of his head to wake him up.

He opened his eyes and looked straight at Rose Ann. "Is there someone here with us?" he asked Alma.

"Yes, Dad. It's Rose Ann, the one who gave us the drawing."

"So you're an artist," he said, peering at her curiously. He sat forward and reached for a cane that was lying on the floor beside him. "I had a good nap," he said, closing his eyes again.

"Supper's ready, Dad."

"I know. But I'm not a machine. Give me time to get my bearings. There now," he opened his eyes again. "What was I saying?" He found Rose Ann, and settling his light blue eyes on her he said, "I hope flowers aren't the only things you paint."

"I'm sure she paints lots of things, Dad."

"Flowers are the only things my daughter spends her time with, except me of course, although I'm not much of a bother. But sometimes I wish she'd expand her interests." Gripping the cane, he hoisted himself out of the chair. For a few moments he stood uncertainly. Then he reached for Alma's shoulder to steady himself and continued talking. "That isn't to say I don't think she's good at what she does. Look at the plants in this room, they're all the proof you need. But there's a war going on in Europe, and it's only a matter of time before it reaches this continent." He looked at them to gauge the effect of his words. Then he began again. "When the war comes here, all the luxuries we're familiar with, flowers and wine, for instance, will disappear. People don't buy flowers or even pictures of flowers when they're afraid of dying."

"Can we have no more talk of such awful things?" Alma asked, taking his arm. "Come into the kitchen, the food's getting cold."

When they were seated, the table was crowded. Charles held up his glass for a toast. "Good health to us all and happiness and love, particularly love." Alma's eyes were bright with tears as they clicked their glasses.

They helped themselves to the food and began to eat.

"I don't want to scare you women," Charles said, "but an old man sometimes can see things more clearly. Particularly when an old man is about to die."

"You're very healthy, Dad, and you've got many more years ahead of you. Let's not talk about dying, let's talk about life instead." Alma raised her glass for another toast, and Charles and Rose Ann had to as well, although Rose Ann couldn't help but murmur, "But Alma, life includes death."

"That's right," Charles said petulantly, "I should be allowed to talk about it. At eighty-eight years old, I naturally think about dying. Why should I have to keep it a secret?"

"It makes me sad, that's all." Alma's face brightened and in a falsely cheerful voice she said, "I know what, I could get out the photo album, and we could show Rose Ann our pictures of London."

"Couldn't we have more stew instead?" Charles asked, lifting his plate.

While Alma was at the stove, he turned to Rose Ann. "You and I should be very good friends. You weren't bothered by what I said, were you?" When Alma brought his plate back to the table, he winked at Rose Ann.

"The two of you are conspiring against me, I can tell. I bring a dinner guest home, and you both gang up against me." She gave them a barren smile.

Rose Ann tried to mediate. "We've forgotten why I came in the first place. You haven't shown me where you hung my drawing."

"That comes after dinner," Alma said gaily. She got up from the table and took a box down from the top of the refrigerator. "I hope everyone leaves room for dessert."

"What have you got there, Alma?"

"It'll be a surprise, Dad. When you're finished, why don't you and Rose Ann go out to the sunporch, and I'll give you a call when everything's ready."

Rose Ann escorted Charles out of the room and helped him settle down in his chair on the sunporch. She pulled a chair up opposite him and said, "I want to hear more about this war."

"Now, don't tell me that what I was saying came as any surprise."

So Rose Ann told him that with painting and working at Alma's shop, she didn't have time to follow events in Europe. "An artist has to be very particular about what she lets into her studio. Sometimes you just have to close your door and create your own peace if it doesn't exist in the world around you."

But Charles shook his head. "My dear, you can't stay innocent. You can choose to close your door, I'll grant you that, but you can do it only after you know what's going on."

"Then tell me because if you don't keep up with the news every day it gets too complicated to try and follow," Rose Ann said.

"You really don't know, do you? They're trying to get rid of the Jews.

They're pulling them out of their houses and sending them away to work camps. It's happening all over—in Poland, France, Austria—and it'll only be a matter of time before it happens here. Sure, we're an ocean away, but with airplanes and modern ships, what's an ocean?" He leaned back in his chair and spread his hands on his knees. "You Americans are like children. The young boys in England are dying, and the young boys in America are taking their girlfriends to the movies. In the United States everyone wants to stay innocent. But they can't do it for long, that's one thing that's certain."

"So you think they'll come over here?"

He nodded his head gravely. "Hitler will send a telegram in the form of a bomb, and then he'll arrive in person. Why am I the only one who sees it? Why aren't they drafting the young boys now, so they can stop it before it happens?" His voice grew quiet. "Rose Ann, if you choose to be an artist, you have to concern yourself with these things. If you're going to paint flowers, you have to make them as dark and terrible as the world. Otherwise, you're not being honest." Pointing to a table he asked, "Would you get me my cigarettes? If you don't mind, I think I'll have an after-dinner smoke."

Sending out a blue cloud, he leaned back in his chair and closed his eyes. He had the same narrow chin and thin, straight nose as Alma. White hair fell over his forehead, and the hand holding the cigarette was long and delicate like his daughter's.

This was what was important, these small details of the visual world. There was always hardship. But just as light could take the human form and abstract it to a shadow, the painter had to see beyond the particular pain and focus on the generality—the shape, the color, the texture.

What would he say to that if she told him? He would call it an excuse. Maybe it was. She didn't want to think about what was going on in Europe. And, besides, who really knew what was happening? Probably not an old man confined to a small apartment. She would hold on to her peace a little longer.

"I'm ready!" Alma called. Charles didn't open his eyes, so Rose Ann left him where he was and went in the direction of the voice. Alma was standing in the living room lighting candles. There was a vase of flowers in the center of the coffee table and plates and cups set out around it. On the wall, in an imposing gold frame, was her drawing. "My God, Alma, what have you done?"

"Don't you like it?" Alma asked in a frightened voice.

It hadn't been the right thing to say, but she hadn't thought to stop herself. "Well, I feel very flattered. It's very . . . ," she searched for a word but ended with only, "well, it's very beautiful. I think it will look nice in this room, and of course I'm pleased that you're giving it such a good home. Really, I'm very happy about that."

"Good," Alma said. "I was hoping you'd like it. Now let me just cut the cake and pour the coffee, and then I'll get Charles. Did he fall asleep?"

"I think so," Rose Ann said.

"Then I won't wake him. We can have our little celebration all by ourselves. Do you really like the frame?" She handed Rose Ann a plate. "I found it in an antique store, and it seemed such a coincidence that I should have seen a frame on the same day you gave me the drawing. Somehow I just knew it would complement your picture. The carving seems sort of floral, doesn't it?" She sat very straight in her chair, holding the dessert on her knees. "How do you like the cake? I treat myself to it just a few times a year, but I think it's worth waiting for. I know it's a silly indulgence, but just the same, sometimes you need a little something to brighten the spirits, and my spirits were downright soggy the day I bought it. And that was only yesterday—my goodness, doesn't time fly?"

Rose Ann nodded sleepily.

"What did you and Charles talk about in there? May I ask?"

"The war," Rose Ann said.

"His favorite subject. Ever since mother died, he's been attracted to things like that. I guess he felt like mother abandoned him, and now his beloved Europe is trying to do itself in. But it *is* terrible. I think to myself, Alma, you can't afford to worry. You have the good fortune to be in this country now. You have things to attend to. You have your father to take care of and a business to keep going." She chewed her cake indignantly. "But what's the matter with government that they can't stop things like this from happening? It doesn't make sense. We're not children playing in the sandbox. We're adults. We know what it is to suffer. But do we use that knowledge? Of course not. We prefer games. We prefer to bully one another." She took a sip of coffee. "All I can say is thank God the United States of America has the intelligence not to get involved."

When she noticed Rose Ann's plate was empty, she jumped up too quickly to offer her more cake. Her hand knocked her cup, and coffee spilled down her dress. "Drat it!" she cried. "This is my favorite dress. I can never get it straight—hot water for which kind of stains and which ones take cold?"

Rose Ann didn't know either, but she said, "Soak it in hot soapy water and I'm sure it will be fine. Listen, Alma, it was a wonderful dinner and it was wonderful to meet your father. I've had a lovely time, but it's getting late and I should get going."

"You don't have to rush off. I'll take care of my dress later. At least have another piece of cake."

"I really should be on my way."

"You must let me treat you to a taxi. You don't want to be walking this time of night."

"No, it's fine. I do it all the time. I'd like a little fresh air anyway."

Alma helped Rose Ann on with her coat, but before opening the door she said, "You're going to think me so silly, but are you sure the frame's all right?"

"It's very beautiful," Rose Ann said. "It's the perfect frame for that drawing."

Alma looked relieved. "Well, I'm glad you came. I hope we can do it again soon."

The door closed behind her, and Rose Ann was alone on the dark stairway. She ran down the three flights and opened the door to the street cautiously. It was cold and quiet outside. The sidewalk was deserted. She walked down to a cross street. There were men standing in a newspaper shop and others waiting on the corner for a bus. She passed another woman who was walking as quickly as she was with her hands in her pockets and her head down. The night air, black above the buildings and blue around the streetlights, seemed dangerous. When Rose Ann saw a taxi, she put out her hand and flagged it down.

Inside, leaning back on the warm leather seat, listening to the ticking of the meter, she felt safe. Once in her apartment, she put her things away and washed the few dishes in the sink. Then she went to her studio where she sat on the chair and looked at her still life. It was a bunch of flowers sitting in a white vase with three lemons around it.

They were lovely and light and colorful. She wanted it that way. That's what she wanted to paint. That's what she wanted to see when she looked out at the world, and that's what she wanted to paint.

31

The next morning she went out to buy milk and eggs for breakfast. When she came back, she noticed a note taped to her mailbox. She pulled it off and tore open the seal on the envelope. Inside, there was a sheet of cream-colored stationery.

> *Dear Rose Ann,*
> *I wanted to tell you what a lovely time I had with you last night. It was so good of you to come. I hope we can repeat the pleasant occasion sometime soon.*
> *Your friend,*
> *A*

Rose Ann looked at the old-fashioned seal and then tossed the note and envelope into the trash. She went back upstairs.

It was a bright morning. Washed by sun, the walls in her studio were clear of shadow. The arrangement on the table glowed. The lemons looked pearly, and the flowers were translucent with light. She looked out at them as she ate her breakfast. When she was finished, she spread a big sheet of newsprint on the floor and getting down on her hands and knees, began to draw with a thick black crayon.

She could hear Quip whispering over her shoulder, *What do you feel, Rose Ann? What do you really feel?*

She pressed down on the crayon, and her line grew blacker. Suddenly, the spaces between the forms were as important as the forms themselves. *That's not good enough,* he whispered. *Don't be an academic.*

Just show me what you feel. She blackened the objects, and then she blackened the spaces around them. All that was left were a few white lines delineating shape. Knowing that it was a beginning and nothing else, she tacked it up on the wall and started another.

By noontime the light had become harsh, and the room was so bright she saw spots when she went into the kitchen. She made herself a sandwich and ate it standing up, looking at the walls of her studio. They were covered with the morning's work. Each drawing was blacker than the last. In the final ones the solid areas were densely textured, and the white poked through in startling ways. The objects were there, but the viewer had to find them. They couldn't be taken for granted anymore.

Quip hissed in her ear excitedly, *It's not beautiful. It's not easy to look at, but by God, I can hear you!*

That afternoon as she opened the door to the shop, she could see Alma sitting at the table in the back fixing an arrangement. Her hair was falling out of her bun, curling around the collar of her smock, and she had a familiar stoop as she peered down at her work. Just from the way she was sitting there, solitary and content, something suddenly became important. When had she dropped off the note? Had she done it on her way to work that morning, or had she come by last night? Rose Ann pictured that strange, lonely woman standing in her vestibule, trying to tell in the darkness which mailbox was hers.

Alma was surprised by the question. "Last night," she said, "why do you ask?" But her face colored, and to hide it she bent down to her work.

"You had said all of that to me before I left. I heard you and I appreciated it. You didn't have to go to all of the trouble to say it again."

Alma wove a ribbon in and out of the basket. "It wasn't anything, Rose Ann. I just wasn't sleepy. It was only an afterthought. I felt so rewarded after our evening that I wanted to tell you." She looked up with a questioning expression. "It was just an afterthought, that's all. So I scribbled it out on a piece of notepaper and called a taxi. It took twenty minutes from start to finish. Don't be angry, I didn't have any intention of ringing your doorbell. I just popped the note on your mailbox and got back into the taxi." She made a bow, stretched out the loops and then snipped the ribbon. She was working on the baby baskets. That was a girl's. Now she pulled out more flowers and a spool of blue ribbon to make a boy's. She wound the ribbon on her hand and began to weave it through the basket.

Her concentration on that simple task was so complete it tempted Rose Ann to say more. But the point had been made already, so she kept her mouth shut.

Alma put down her work. "Please, Rose Ann, I apologize. Can I get you some tea? You must be cold from your walk. Here, sit down and finish this, and I'll get you something hot to drink."

32

The next week they began to prepare for Thanksgiving. Alma ordered cattails, teasel, and decorative squash, and each day she brought in a different kind of evergreen. She taught Rose Ann how to put it all together in an arrangement, how to make the greens fan out evenly around the centerpiece. While Rose Ann worked in the back, Alma waited on customers. She had been quiet and more accommodating than ever, bringing nuts and dried fruit for their breaks, complimenting Rose Ann on her "fine" designs, and sending her home early. There was a bonus in her paycheck, an extra five dollars that Alma said was a present. The next week, when it appeared again, all Alma said was, "I've given you a raise."

That evening, for the first time, it was dark outside by five o'clock. As they left the shop, Alma asked Rose Ann if she'd join her for "a little pick-me-up at that nice pastry shop."

Rose Ann said she could come for a little while and followed her down the crowded street to a small storefront a few blocks away.

The windows were steamy. There was a bell over the door that rang as they opened it. They hung their coats on the coat tree and walked through the empty shop to a table in the back. Alma handed a menu to Rose Ann. There was an assortment of pastries and finger sandwiches. She could get a tart or a shortcake or a cream roll. Instead, she ordered toast.

Alma said, "They have such wonderful little treats, don't you want to try something more exciting?"

Rose Ann shook her head. "I'm not very hungry."

Alma ordered a French pastry and a cup of English tea and then folded her hands on the table. She looked at Rose Ann. Finally, she smiled. Rose Ann smiled back, but she turned away shortly and took a sip of water.

Alma said, "You feel uncomfortable with me, I know."

Rose Ann looked up in surprise.

"You don't find me interesting. Maybe you don't trust me very much. Also, you wish I'd be more direct. Am I being direct enough now? I've been planning this little meeting all week, practicing what I'd say to you." She bent down. When she looked up again, her eyes were teary. "I feel like my life has changed since we've become friends. Our friendship is very important to me. I don't have many friends, as you may have guessed. In the store, I look forward to the break time when we can talk. You're very different from anyone I've ever known before. I feel in awe of you."

The waitress set their dishes on the table and moved away. Alma sunk her fork into something puffy covered with icing. Cream oozed onto the doily. Scooping it up she said, "There's something so comforting about sweet things. How can you resist them?"

Rose Ann bit into her toast.

Alma licked her fork clean and set it down. "From the first moment I saw you, I knew we would get along. Get along? That's so minimal. But here I am again, being effusive. Silly old lamb. Will you ever forgive me? And now I'm keeping you past dinnertime. You probably need to get home soon, don't you?"

Teddy often came to her apartment when he was through at the office. It was his new plan: short, frequent visits to get her used to the idea of having him around. She had complained that he was using her just for the comforts of an apartment with a few pictures on the wall, but she had given him a key. He was probably there now, waiting for her to return. Well, he would have a little more time to snoop in her rooms. "Why don't we go out for dinner?" Rose Ann suggested.

"I can't," Alma said. "Dad's waiting for his supper. Otherwise, I'd be delighted."

"This is what we'll do," Rose Ann said. "We'll go back to your apartment, make Charles his supper, and then we'll go out."

"You wouldn't mind?" Alma asked.

33

"What an evening this was!" Rose Ann stood in the doorway taking off her coat. Teddy sat at the table in her kitchen with the newspaper in front of him.

"I've been doing charity work. Wait until I tell you." She pulled off her hat and because by nature she was an orderly person, took her hat and coat to the closet. She continued to talk from the bedroom as she changed her clothes. "Some people's lives are so barren," she shouted. "It just makes you sad."

"Have you been working in a soup kitchen?" he called back.

"Of sorts," she replied. She came back wearing old clothes. "That poor woman. All she wants is some closeness with another human being, and the lengths she has to go to to get it!"

"You're talking about Alma, I suppose."

"She took me to a pastry shop tonight essentially for the single reason that she wanted to tell me she liked me. And then she began to worry that she was keeping me too long, so do you know what I did? I did something really good, Teddy. I asked her to have supper with me. We could do it only if we went back to her house and made dinner for her father first. Then we went out. She was so happy. She just talked and talked. Then she stopped talking and just looked at me." Rose Ann paused. "I didn't know what she was going to say. She just looked at me. Finally she said, 'I'm sorry. This must be so boring to you, but I can't help myself.' Then she said, 'I think I'm in love with you.'"

Rose Ann took a sip from Teddy's glass. She asked him how long he had been waiting there and whether or not he had had anything to eat. When he said he hadn't, she opened the door to the refrigerator and took out bread and cheese. She gave him a jar of mustard and a knife and plate.

"Aren't you going to tell me what happened?"

"Nothing happened," she said, sitting down across from him. "Her eyes got all watery as they always do, and I said, 'Thank you.'"

"That's all?"

"When someone is desperate like that, you have to be careful. I don't love her the way she meant when she said it to me, so I couldn't say it back. It wouldn't have been fair. I said thank you, and her eyes stayed teary, and we paid the check, and then we left."

"She must have felt horrible. I think you were being cruel."

"I wasn't at all. I put my arms around her before I left and gave her a kiss. It makes a person feel good when they finally have the chance to say something they've wanted to say for a long time."

"So what's going to happen?"

Rose Ann shrugged her shoulders. "She has no one else in her life to be attracted to, that's all. When I was in high school, we called it a crush."

He finished his bread and cheese and picked up the newspaper again. It seemed so natural to have him there. She thought about coaxing him into the bedroom, but she had intended to work. There was a painting she needed to look at before she went to sleep.

When she walked into the studio, she heard the paper rustle as he turned the page. He hadn't even noticed she'd left. She switched on the light and stood back so she could get a good look at the canvas she'd started. It was another still life, another bowl of fruit sitting on a table draped with a cloth. Looking at it now, she realized she wanted something else. There needed to be some kind of reference to all that existed besides the still life. War? Death? No. She wanted there to be water. Should the table stand on a beach with the ocean behind it? That was too literal. How about on a lawn with a sky in the background? The sky would feel like the sea.

But why all of a sudden did she think of water? She had never paid much attention to it before.

Everything was possible. What if she said, for instance, that water represented change? You couldn't depend on it always being the same because it corresponded to the conditions around it. It could be soft or hard or warm or cold. She, for instance, could be like water. She could allow herself to change as the conditions changed. For instance, what if she turned off the light and went back into the kitchen? He would put down his paper. She would take his hand and just with the pressure of her fingers, let him know what she was thinking. Would they make it to the bedroom? There they'd be in the hallway, half-unbuttoned, tangled together. The sound of their breath, growing louder, would curtain them from all distractions. They'd collapse in front of the door, their urgency the only thing that mattered, and carry the impulse out to its finish, at which point, the same casual thought that had started it would be all that was left them.

She looked at the painting, but it was too difficult to concentrate. There would be water, that much she knew. She wasn't sure, though, how it would appear. Maybe she should take the easy way out, title it *Water,* and let it go at that. She glanced up, aware suddenly of another presence. He was standing in the doorway, watching her.

"Can I stay?" he asked. "Because if you don't want me to, I should get going now."

Was she water, changeable and playful, or was she a hard substance like wood? She wanted to be water.

Thanksgiving was a warm, sunny day. They took the train to Brooklyn. Teddy, who had never met her parents before, brought a bottle of cognac for her father and a bouquet of carnations for her mother. "How are you going to introduce me?" he asked.

"Theodore Juroe," she said.

"But what am I, your boyfriend or your fiancé?"

"You have an ambiguous status. They're just going to have to accept that."

"Her sister met them at the door. As she stared at Teddy, he bowed down and offered her the flowers. "These are for the beautiful women in your family." A blush spread over her cheeks. Then she held out her hand and said, "My name is Sybil."

Her sister was the prettiest in the family, and it had always been nice to show her off. "You take him in to meet everyone, and I'll hang up the coats." As Rose Ann helped Teddy out of his, he gave her a look as though to say, *You coward, so that's how you're going to get out of introducing me.* He followed Sybil to the back of the house, and a moment later Rose Ann could hear her mother's icy hostess voice. Already, she was noticing the quality of his suit and the condition of his shoes. If she decided it was worth it to be gracious to the young man, her tone would become more friendly.

How odd it felt to be back. As Rose Ann opened the hall closet, she was accosted by the smell of wool and mothballs. She found her mother's secret shelf at the back of the closet. There were the hairbrush, the bottle of cologne, and for a quick freshening up before she went out the door, the compact and the lipstick. Rose Ann took out the powder and opened the shiny metal case. She sniffed the dusty smell she would always associate with her mother and taking the piece of lambswool, stood in front of the mirror and dabbed some on her nose. Her mother didn't wear the same color lipstick, but she took some of her mother's perfume and sprayed it on her wrists. Then she put everything back exactly the way it had been. The door clicked shut with the familiar sound.

All the rooms seemed smaller. The stairway wasn't as steep as she remembered. The polished wooden floors that, through her childhood, had so relentlessly transmitted all her clatter, didn't give her the feeling anymore of endless space. And the furniture was ugly—the couch with little velvet cushions, the gilt mirror in the entrance hall, the huge upholstered chair.

When she went into her mother's immaculate kitchen, they didn't hear her come in. Everyone stood around the roasting pan. Teddy was lifting the turkey up while Russell ladled the drippings.

"You're a good team," her mother was saying. She saw Rose Ann just as Sybil, who had been helping Teddy, ran to the sink for a washcloth. Grease had dripped onto his jacket. There was an awkward moment as Teddy reached for the cloth and Sybil started to scrub at the stain. Their hands collided. Sybil handed him the dishrag and backed away.

Russell missed the saucepan, and more grease spilled. Rose Ann's mother said, "Oh, my goodness," in her most passionate tone and pushed them all aside. "Russ, thank you, but that's enough. Teddy, you get out of here, too. Sybil, hand me that plate."

They moved out to the backyard. Rose Ann's father was supposed to be raking leaves, but he was leaning on the rake and looking back at the house. Beside him, there was only a small pile.

"Pleased to meet you," he said, wiping his hands on his trousers. "It's a nice day to get out of the city. I'm glad Rose Ann thought of bringing you along. There's always more food than we can eat, and it's refreshing to have a new face at the table." He grinned. "Tell me, Theodore, what do you do for a living?"

Sybil took his rake, and Rose Ann went off after her. They attacked the corner farthest away from the men, Rose Ann bundling leaves in her arms and dropping them into a pile. She saw her father beckon Teddy into a lawn chair. Then her father walked to the patio and pulled another one into the yard. Soon their heads were bent close together as they talked.

The air smelled smoky. The sun on her face was warm. Leaves spilling out of her arms, Rose Ann took a bundle past Sybil. "Who is he?" Sybil asked.

"He's an old friend," Rose Ann answered. She looked at the two men silhouetted against the sky. The sun made a circle of light around their heads. Her father had his hands on his knees in his characteristic listening pose, and Teddy leaned back with his ankles crossed, hands in his pockets. She couldn't tell what he was thinking. All of a sudden she pictured him lying naked on her bed, wiggling his penis at her. The image made her smile. She considered saying to her sister, "We're lovers," but, remembering her sister's prudishness, she said instead, "He's my fiancé."

Sybil looked pleased. "You haven't told our parents yet, have you?"

"I haven't told anyone. Will you keep it to yourself?" She picked up the leaves she'd dropped and took them over to the pile. When she came back, Sybil asked, "Are you happy?"

She supposed she didn't look very happy if her sister had had to ask. "It's just that I haven't really said yes. I don't even know if we'll actually get married. We'll probably just see each other for a long time. I'm not exactly the type to be a wife."

"Rose Ann, what are you waiting for? He seems so nice; why are you holding back?"

When dinner was ready their mother came to the door and rang the triangle she used to call them with when they were children. She had taken off her apron and freshened her makeup, presumably with the emergency cosmetics in the hall closet. But despite her Sunday dress and her good shoes and stockings, she appeared old. When they were children she used to say, "Wipe those grins off your faces and try to look respectable." She had followed her own advice too well.

She kept a stern bearing as she presided over the carving of the bird; yet she seemed to be pleased. The gravy filled the gravy boat, the potatoes were an even white, and the china and silver gleamed on the table. She tipped the wine decanter over their glasses and offered a toast while they were all still standing. "To the future," she said. "Theodore, may we see you at our table the same time next year and many Thanksgivings after that."

Rose Ann looked at Sybil, but she couldn't have had the chance to tell their mother. Had Teddy said something to her father? Her father raised his glass and in a tipsy voice added, "May our family grow larger by leaps and bounds."

Russell piped in: "May our family grow larger by goldfish and hamsters."

Still holding her glass in the air, Rose Ann said loudly, "I'm hungry. I toast to an end to toasting. Let's eat."

35

"Do you know what I thought you were going to say when you lifted your glass? I thought you were going to tell them that we'd become engaged."

"I considered doing it that way, but I didn't want to make it public so quickly. I haven't even told you, and there I was in the backyard telling Sybil."

"Telling Sybil what?"

"The very thing you've been waiting to hear." She paused. "I've decided I want to get married."

He looked at her, his lips curling into a half-smile. "You should realize that I want lots of children. Can you do it?"

She stared at the darkness outside the window as the train took them back to the city. It was impossible to see anything, not the bridge or the river, only the night pressing against the glass. It was cold. She moved closer to him to get warm. "I'll tell you what," she said. "I'll marry you if we agree to just one child. And that's on the condition that our lives can be arranged so that I'll have time to work in my studio."

"No conditions," Teddy said. "How can you be so deadly practical? What do we know about the future?"

"Nothing," she said. "But still . . ."

"Rose Ann, are you sure you want to get married? Then that's all we know for now. We'll figure the rest out as we go along."

"But how about you?" she asked. "Aren't you making a condition when you tell me you want to have children?"

"But it's not practical. When I say children, we're not talking about something practical. Practical things can be attended to as we go along. What we're talking about now is the body and the blood and the earth. That's what marriage and children are."

"Well, I'd hope that making art also is the body and the blood and the earth. I want to do that, too." Her voice had a whiny tone. She supposed it was tiredness more than anything else.

"All right," he snapped. "Don't relax. Go ahead and try to do everything."

She wondered if she would have to scream if she wanted him to hear her. Why was he so thickheaded? Already the marriage seemed hopeless.

36

On her way to the flower shop, Rose Ann passed a poster in a drugstore urging women to knit for the army and navy. There was a list of things that were needed: gloves, socks, caps, and scarves. Underneath was the slogan, "Give our good boys something handmade." The paper carried war news every day, and a station on the radio broadcast nothing but information on the fighting.

Everyone knew neutrality couldn't last for long. The hostilities were far away, but they were inclusive. Balanced against them, Christmas, with its motto of peace and goodwill, was magic.

At the shop they potted plants and made decorative baskets as fast as they could. There never were enough poinsettias, so they designed arrangements with branches of holly. Working on their breaks and after the store closed, they still couldn't catch up. Alma said that as soon as the Christmas tree vendors hit the streets, things would slow down. But it was only the first week of December, and the trees wouldn't appear for another week.

37

Rose Ann got to the shop early to have lunch with Alma. In all of the rush she hadn't had a chance to tell her about the engagement. She knew that the longer she waited the harder it would get. The older woman was bound to feel abandoned. She would attempt to be glad for Rose Ann, but her face would be pinched with the effort. The easiest thing would be to fling open the door of the shop and say it. She hoped Alma's eyes wouldn't get teary. She didn't want to feel like someone had died.

When she got there, the shop was empty. The register wasn't locked, but Alma wasn't even in the back room. She called. Something was wrong. Then she peered out the back door and saw Alma standing in her garden without her coat. She pulled the door open. The other woman looked up, and Rose Ann said gaily, "I have wonderful news."

"I hope you're not serious," Alma replied, coming closer.

"I am *very* serious. Teddy and I are getting married."

"When?" Alma asked impatiently.

"Maybe after Christmas, we haven't decided."

"Do it this week, before he gets drafted." Then she said, "Don't you know? The Japanese bombed Hawaii."

38

"Fifteen hundred people are killed, millions of dollars' worth of property is damaged, and what does a group of intelligent men and women decide to do about it? They pass a resolution to kill more people and damage more property. They declare war, the idiots. The only person who saw the absurdity of it was Rankin. One person in the three hundred and eighty-nine members of the House! And, when she gave her negative vote, they booed and hissed at her! This is our Congress. This is the body of people who represent us. They behave like they're at a baseball game. There are two teams, and you're with one team or the other; you can't be with both. I don't understand nationalism. I became an American, but only because I wanted to vote. Why should that make me any different from a Japanese? Speaking of which, do you know what they're doing now? They've put the FBI to work. Our boys are out there arresting the Japanese who live in this city and taking them to Ellis Island where they'll be detained like sheep. As though the little woman who lives down the street is an agent for Japan. It makes me sick." She looked up at Rose Ann. Her eyes were shiny. "I can't make any more Christmas decorations," she whispered. "I can't stand the thought of Christmas. I'm going to go home and write a letter to Miss Rankin. If you want to stay and work, go ahead. If not, close the shop." She put on her coat and hat and headed toward the door. Then she came back. "If you close the shop, hang a note on the door: *We mourn the loss of human-*

ity. No, they'll think we're only talking about the men at Pearl Harbor. *We mourn the future losses of humanity.* Would someone understand what we mean by that? *We mourn the proposed sacrifice of human life.* There it is," she said. "I'll see you later."

39

Alma didn't work in the shop anymore. She made Rose Ann manager and spent her time in her apartment writing letters to oppose the war. Not even her father agreed with her position. "There's evil out there," he'd say. "Hitler is killing the Jews. Don't let anyone tell you differently."

Nevertheless, she continued her private protest. She sent long pleas to Roosevelt and Chairman Bloom of the House Foreign Affairs Committee. She walked through the neighborhood, talking to people she met on the street. Her shy demeanor seemed to protect her from harassment. And she was always polite. Holding a white carnation, she'd stop pedestrians by telling them that the recent events in the world frightened her, and she wondered if anyone else was frightened, too. She'd tell them that grown men and women ought to know that peace couldn't be achieved by war, that terror couldn't be stopped by terror.

Most people looked at her in disbelief. Some just walked away. Sometimes, though, they argued with her. "We were attacked," they'd say. "Is America going to tell the world that anyone can just up and attack her?"

"No," she would answer, "but does it make sense to do it to somebody else? Aren't we just increasing the suffering on this globe? Isn't there enough of it already?"

Her father called her naive. "You don't know Hitler, you don't know Mussolini. These people have to be stopped."

To which Alma replied, "I agree, but making war only gives them the power to continue. We're giving them the reason to fight. All we're doing is adding dry wood to the fire."

On most days, Rose Ann closed the shop early and went back to her studio to paint. There was hardly enough business to open it at all. Charles had been right: When people were afraid of dying, they didn't buy flowers.

. . . . . *40* . . . . .

Teddy had given up his apartment and moved in with her. In wartime no one bothered to ask if they were married. He would only be there a few months. He'd enlisted in the army and was scheduled for duty in February.

In January he said, "Well, shall we do it?"

She knew what he was referring to. Did they go along with plans as before, or did they postpone everything? Life had changed so quickly that she didn't know what she felt anymore. She did the things she had always done, keeping faith in the idea that the world wouldn't be chaotic forever. But time had changed; it was so condensed that the future had ceased to be. The present stretched on interminably.

When he said, "Well, shall we do it?," she knew she shouldn't think about it. Thought would make it too complex. She wanted to be like water. She wouldn't ask the unanswerable questions. She wouldn't hold back. She would flow where an opening appeared.

They got dressed for city hall, stopped at the store for flowers, rode the subway downtown. It was over in forty-five minutes. They telephoned their families in the evening and that night fell asleep holding hands. It had been so easy.

4I

Teddy went to a base in South Dakota. After ten months in training, they flew him overseas. In a letter postmarked from Algeria he wrote:

I'm scared most of the time. I'm not a courageous guy. But seeing death and pain around me like this, I know something I didn't know before. I know how precious comfort is. From where I am looking, happiness and love don't exist. Only comfort. That's what I want more than anything else. I want this old body to see me through all this so one day I can close my eyes and feel you asleep in the space beside me. If I could just have that, everything else will come back too.

At night when she fell asleep she'd try to picture him. She'd work on the eyes—get them clear in her mind—then the nose and mouth. His chin was the easiest, and the way the hair curled at the back of his neck. But she could never fit it all together. The face as a whole would never materialize. So she'd start again with the separate parts, teaching herself their shapes. But again it was impossible to make them stick together.

This bothered her. Keeping his image alive in her mind was the only way she knew of protecting him. And she couldn't even do that. What was wrong with her?

In a cruel, self-pitying moment she grilled herself. What she really wanted, she told herself, was for him to die over there. Then she wouldn't be married. Then she'd be able to give all her attention to her work. That was why she couldn't picture him. She just wanted him out of her life so she could have the solitary existence Quip had recommended.

. . . II . . .
Alma

· · · · · · *I* · · · · · ·

It was a gray clapboard house with a garage behind it and a middle-sized lawn between the house and the garage. On the third floor there was a long room with a wall of windows at one end. That would be Rose Ann's studio. There was a master bedroom and a bedroom for the baby. There was a big eat-in kitchen on the first floor.

Standing on the porch, they looked across and up and down the street at all the other houses. It was an old residential neighborhood with well-established trees and neatly kept flower beds. There was an insistence on order, a tribute to family and tradition that appealed to them. Teddy called it security, not quite believing that comfort had actually been returned to him. Rose Ann called it "my new life," seeing before her, not the house across the street, but a shining pool of water. Also, it was convenient. For Teddy it was a short drive to his office in downtown New Haven, and when Rose Ann wanted to go to New York, she could take the train and be there a few hours later.

2

"Once upon a time there was a great big elephant named Oblemagobbles and a very small mouse named Zuchamazuchas who rode on top of the elephant's head. Well one day Oblemagobbles, who was feeling just a tiny bit hungry, thought about the banana trees that stood at the edge of the forest near the lake. When they had been there last week the bananas had still been green. Oblemagobbles had been ready to take them anyway, but Zuchamazuchas had said,"—as Teddy slipped into the mouse's high squeaky voice, the child laughed—"'Green bananas will give you a stomachache. You remember what happened last time. We'll wait a week, dear friend, and then we'll go back.'"

"So Zuchamazuchas directed Oblemagobbles along the forest path until they came to the grove of trees. Oblemagobbles stood underneath them and reached into the branches with his trunk. But these banana trees were so tall, the bananas, which grow at the top of the tree, were too high for him. There they were, peeking through the leaves, fat and yellow and ripe.

"Oblemagobbles stood under those trees and trumpeted with frustration. Now, when an elephant trumpets the entire forest shakes. It makes the birds fly in circles and the monkeys chatter. The walrus who are dozing peacefully in the mud wake up with a start. Poor Zuchamazuchas, sitting on top of Oblemagobbles' head, was thrown up and down with the vibration and had to grab hold of the great animal's ear to keep from falling.

"Oblemagobbles trumpeted again. This time Zuchamazuchas was sent sliding down the elephant's forehead and was stopped, luckily, by the bend in his trunk. The great big elephant tried to reach the bananas again. He was certain they wouldn't fail to drop into reach and when they didn't, a desperate sound rose up from his feet. Zuchamazuchas, hanging onto the elephant's trunk, was thrown up into the air and landed on the ground at the elephant's feet.

"Now that was a dangerous spot. If Oblemagobbles moved, he could easily crush the little mouse. To be squashed under an elephant's feet, particularly when the elephant had been your friend for many years, was a terrible fate. It would be unpleasant for Zuchamazuchas, but it might even be worse for Oblemagobbles who depended on the mouse's supervision to move around in the world of the forest."

Under his hands, Teddy could feel her ribcage. He was aware of her breath moving through the small, warm body.

"'My friend!'" Zuchamazuchas called. Oblemagobbles didn't hear. 'My friend of many years, my very dearest friend!' Still Oblemagobbles didn't hear. 'Watch where you step my friend or you will cause the death of me!'

"But it was all in vain. Zuchamazuchas, as you know, had a very high voice and Oblemagobbles, because he was getting on in years, was just a little bit hard of hearing. He was also getting impatient as the bananas continued to elude him. This impatience caused him to stamp his feet. Each time he set a foot back down, Zuchamazuchas would be afraid.

"He tried to discover a way to escape. First, he hopped up and down on Oblemagobbles' toes but Oblemagobbles didn't pay any attention. Then he bit into the skin around the great animal's toenails but still Oblemagobbles didn't notice. Not giving up, he dragged a stick to Oblemagobbles' foot and with all of his strength hoisted it to his shoulders. Then he ran back a few paces and hurled himself forward, jabbing the stick into the elephant's ankle. He looked up to see if there was a reaction but it was hard to tell. He did it again, this time starting farther away to build momentum. He jabbed the stick into the animal's ankle with what he thought must surely be . . ." Teddy added an edge of terror to his voice . . . "a killing thrust."

The child laughed.

"Sure enough, Oblemagobbles ducked his head and the trunk came down to investigate." Imitating the elephant, Teddy leaned over, sniffing and snorting into her pajamas. She arched back, laughing, and the great big elephant grabbed her in the middle and squeezed tight. "Oblemagobbles recognized the scent of the little mouse and very carefully, brought him back up to the place where he always sat on the elephant's head.

"To be united once again! Zuchamazuchas was so happy he cried. At that very moment, an idea came to him. 'My friend!' he called down the ear in his very high voice. 'I am enormously grateful that you rescued me, and I have an idea that I hope will allow me to return the favor.' He could feel the animal's excitement rippling through his body and knew that he might trumpet again. 'Whatever you do,' he said, 'you have to be very quiet. We're going to . . .'" Teddy began to whisper . . . "'sneak up on those bananas. We're going to take them by surprise. Now here's what we're going to do.'

"He gave the directions as clearly as he could. Then he counted, 'one, two, three, four, five,' and slipped down the elephant's forehead and onto the great long trunk. He scampered along it, finally coming to the end where he found a foothold for himself and sat down. The elephant smelled the mouse and knew it was time to uncurl his trunk and stretch it up into the tree. He did just that but as before, the trunk missed the bananas by just a few inches. But this time, Zuchamazuchas grabbed hold of a branch and pulled himself up to a bunch of bananas. There, he began to work on the stem, gnawing through it little by little with his tiny teeth. It took all afternoon. The elephant waited quietly, munching grass to relieve his terrible hunger. Finally, the bananas came loose and fell to the ground with a soft thud. Because that was the very sound Oblemagobbles had been waiting for, he heard it.

"He moved toward the bananas, his trunk nosing the ripe, fragrant fruit. Peel and all, the elephant popped one into his mouth. As he chewed, pieces of fruit dribbled down his chin."

Now his little girl was slipping off his lap. He pulled her up and tightened his grip around her waist. That made her lay her head against his chest. Then she kicked his shins softly with her bare heels. A sudden, unexplained rhythm.

"Watching from the treetop, hungry himself and very tired, Zuchamazuchas felt very sad. Had Oblemagobbles forgotten about him? The great animal tore off another banana, but as he brought it to his mouth, the banana suddenly dropped to the ground. Zuchamazuchas watched as the trunk rose into the tree. Oblemagobbles had finally remembered.

"Back at the place where he always sat the mouse hopped off the elephant's trunk. There, as though it had been waiting for him, was a big black fly, the kind he liked especially. He ate it in one gulp and then, satisfied, sat down and looked over his friend's head at the green landscape of their forest home.

"Oblemagobbles was chewing his bananas happily. The day closed with an orange sky and a little bit later, the clouds of night moved in. Sitting on top of the elephant's head, the mouse whispered the same song he whispered every evening when they went to sleep:

> 'Let the night sky take us,
> Let the dawn wake us up,
> Let the frogs and the birds sing.'"

Whispering it, Teddy stood up and carried her to bed.

3

They were standing under the fluorescent light in the bathroom. The little girl was standing on the toilet in her underwear, and the woman was standing on the floor beside her. The girl was looking in the mirror, and the woman was holding the girl's eyelid shut and with a small, pointed brush, drawing a black line as thin as it should be. Though she was concentrating, the brush would sometimes slip, and she'd have to wipe the stray mark off with a tissue.

"Hold still," Sybil said, and the little girl, who hadn't moved at all, sucked in her stomach and made herself rigid.

"I'll be finished in a minute," Sybil said, seeing the effect of her words. "You're very good at holding still," she added. "Just one minute longer." She dipped the brush in the bottle of makeup, and the girl felt the wetness against her eyelid. It was a pleasant sensation, and when Sybil stepped back and pronounced the work finished, the girl was disappointed it had to stop. "How do I look?" she asked.

Sybil frowned a little and without much conviction said, "Just like a gypsy. Would you like some lipstick?"

The girl said, "Yes, please."

"All right, now hold still." The child went rigid again, and Sybil said, "Sweetie, you can relax." She had forgotten how calm this child could be. It was unusual for a nine-year-old, and she found it even a little disturbing. Rose Ann used to tell them about leaving Alma in the playpen and going up to her studio and an hour later, remembering her with a pang of guilt and rushing downstairs, only to find her singing to herself contentedly and playing with the figures on her mobile.

People had great hopes for Alma. With Rose Ann for a mother, they said she would surely be a musician or a poet. She would at least do something creative. But with a stubbornness that Sybil secretly approved of, Alma had always stuck to the path of the ordinary. She would have been happiest this Halloween with a costume from the store, but since it wasn't allowed, she had chosen to be a gypsy.

The child pursed her lips, but Sybil said, "No, just keep your mouth relaxed." Her mouth went slack, and pushing the lipstick against it, Sybil felt uneasy with the sudden intimacy. The color went on too thickly, so Sybil asked Alma to smack her lips together. That only smeared it. Sybil scowled and wet another tissue and tried to smooth it out.

"Is it ruined?" Alma asked.

"No, sweetie, it's never ruined. I can always fix it."

"Will I look like a gypsy?"

"You might. Now lift up your head and let me take a look at you." She stepped back to get the full effect. It was odd: There was the quiet, determined face, and the skinny little body in white cotton underwear. "It's better," Sybil said. But the lipstick wasn't right. She took a Kleenex and wiped most of it off. "Now for the powder!" she said gaily. She patted it on gently, and it disappeared into the perfect, milky white skin.

When Alma was born, her skin had been yellow. It was a symptom that her liver wasn't functioning, and they treated it by placing the infant under special lights. They let Rose Ann go back home, but Alma herself stayed at the hospital an extra week, sleeping day and night under the lights. Friends and relatives lined up at the nursery window and peered in at her. She was an ugly baby, thin and yellow, with plastic goggles protecting her eyes and only a few tufts of hair on an otherwise bald head. She looked like an old man. They had called her that, even Alma's mother, who would refer to her fondly as "my little old man."

When Alma finally came home from the hospital, she was the right color but still too thin and serious looking, and the nickname "little old man" stuck with her until, at five months, she started to grow plump. The plumpness lasted as long as she was nursing, but once she was on her own, she grew thin again.

"What else can I do for you?" Sybil asked. She had wiped off the lipstick and applied the powder, and she was ready to give up and go downstairs and have a drink with the grown-ups. "Do you want me to help pick out your clothes? Do you know what gypsies wear?" Her voice had gotten too loud. "Are you satisfied?" she asked more softly.

Alma looked at herself in the mirror. It wasn't a child's glance, ready to find pleasure in whatever it saw, but a self-conscious, critical glance that belonged to someone older. She turned back slowly and said, "Yes, it's nice, thank you Aunt Sybil."

As Sybil helped her down from the toilet, she was glad this child was her sister's and not her own. She was glad she had married a man who didn't want them. "If you need me for something else, just call. I'll be down with your mother."

When the blousy figure of her aunt disappeared, Alma went to her parent's bedroom and opened her mother's closet. Pushing the clothes aside, she scanned the bright colors for a ruffled skirt she remembered her mother once wearing. It was in the back, and when she pulled it from the hanger, the dress next to the skirt fell in a heap on the floor. She closed the closet and went through her mother's top drawer and found the black lacquer box where the earrings were kept. But they were for pierced ears only, and last year on her birthday, when her mother had wanted her to get her ears pierced, she had refused. She left the drawer open and the box on the dresser, picked up the skirt, and went into her room.

Downstairs, Rose Ann carried a tray of fresh drinks to the people gathered on the porch. "I can't believe it's already the end of October," she said. "Didn't the autumn go fast?" The expression on her face, however, implied that things more important than that had happened. And yet season watching could fill Rose Ann with rapture like that; she appeared to experience things more completely than anyone else.

"It's almost winter," someone said, "and do you know what that means? It means that in the afternoon it often gets chilly."

"Are you saying that you're cold?" someone asked.

"You couldn't be cold," Rose Ann said. "It's too beautiful out here. Now tell us, in great detail, all about your weekend in New York." She directed this command to the guest who had complained, and it worked; he forgot his discomfort and began to tell the company about the shows he had seen when he had been in the city.

Upstairs, Alma opened the door to her mother's studio and holding the skirt so it wouldn't trip her, tiptoed up the steps. There was a chest up there where her mother kept the fabrics she used in her still lifes. The silks and cottons were neatly folded and not wanting to get into trouble, she looked at them without touching.

She didn't often go up to the studio by herself. Though Rose Ann hadn't said she wasn't allowed, she hadn't, on the other hand, invited her. So Alma at first knelt in front of the chest and only looked at the stack of colored fabrics. But after looking, she pulled one out from the middle. That made the whole pile collapse. Unfolding it, she draped it around her shoulders. It was definitely too long for a shawl. She tried on others, and some were either too long or too short, and the ones that were the right length were invariably the least exciting. Soon she was sitting in a mass of color and with Rose Ann's large silver shears, was preparing to cut a gauzy pink fabric. The sun slanted through the window onto the floor, and she felt a little dazed by a feeling of well-being or perhaps even happiness. The material cut easily, and Alma rolled the extra piece into a rope and used it on her skirt as a belt. The bigger piece she draped around her shoulders. It was nice; the pink against the orange would be a combination her mother would approve of.

Once when Alma had appeared in the morning dressed in her favorite colors, which were navy, gray, and brown, Rose Ann had wanted to know if someone had died.

"No," Alma had replied cautiously.

"Then why are you in mourning?"

Taking a deep breath Alma had said, "I like it."

"Well, do what you want," her mother said. That had seemed to be the end of it, but then a week later Rose Ann came home with a bright yellow shirt that she gave to Alma as a present.

Alma had said thank you, but she understood its purpose and being as stubborn as Rose Ann, didn't often wear it.

Sometimes Alma went up to the studio when her mother was painting. On a Saturday afternoon when she was bored with private entertainments, she would seek her mother out for company. She would go to the studio door, open it quietly, and start up the steps. At the top she would walk to the window, and as if that were the only reason she had gone up there, peer down at the scene below. But there was nothing new to see on the street. There were the same houses and trees and parked cars as always. No one was out walking, and no one at that moment had even chosen to drive down their block. The floorboards would creak as her mother went from her painting, to the palette, to a point halfway across the room where she'd turn and look at the canvas. The only other sound was the cracking of her mother's gum. Rose Ann liked to chew gum when she painted.

"Alma, sweetie, what is it?"

The tone was exasperated but it wasn't unkind, and Alma took it as an invitation and sat down.

"Honey, I'm working. Can't you find anything to do?"

She shook her head and continued to look out the window. Had she been a different child, she might have let out a sigh at that point or started to whine. But she wasn't, and that meant that her mother was the woman standing in front of the easel, and Rose Ann didn't like children who whined. Also, when Alma was younger, Rose Ann had suggested she call her by her first name and if she could, avoid the word "mommy." "It's an unpleasant term," Rose Ann had said. "It makes me feel like a dish towel."

So now, although all she wanted to do was complain, Alma composed herself and asked, "Rose Ann, who are my friends?"

Her mother told her the five or six names and suggested which ones she might call. "You haven't seen Nancy in a long time; why don't you see if she'd like to come over and do something with you?"

Dutifully, Alma would go downstairs and look up the number. She had friends, people to call up on a long Saturday and ask to come over. That some of them even seemed to like her should have made a difference. But her loneliness was stubborn.

Alma left the material in a pile on the floor, put the scissors back (but not on the table from which they had come), and, hiking up the skirt, tiptoed down the steps. She went to her bedroom and rummaged through her top bureau drawer. A bra was all a gypsy needed to wear with a skirt, so she pulled out the next best thing, which was her bathing suit top. She buckled it onto her chest and pulled it up over her nipples.

But she wasn't sure what to do for shoes. Gypsies went barefoot, but it was too cold to go barefoot, and there was glass on the street. Her rubber boots might be the perfect thing. Gypsies were poor, and they scorned fashion anyway. Rainboots certainly weren't fashionable, and they were the sort of cheap thing a gypsy might buy.

Downstairs, a man named David was telling the people who were now gathered in the living room how he had started to play the piano when he was only four years old. He was Rose Ann's only musician friend, and it was clear he took the position seriously. "The quality of light in my parents' living room gave the instrument a halo. It seemed too precious to touch, which only made me want to touch it more. But this was an antique piano; it dated from the early 1800s and was made by a very famous French piano maker. Needless to say, my mother wouldn't let me near it until I knew how to handle it correctly. So, at my insistence, she sat down at the bench and began to show me the notes. When I touched the ivories, it seemed as though I were touching all that was beautiful and pure in the world. I kept up with it, made my way through several teachers, and by the time I was eleven, I had grown out of Chopin and thought I was ready to tackle Mr. Beethoven."

Sybil crossed her legs and took a sip of her drink. She hoped no one could see the flush she felt drifting across her face from the alcohol. "Didn't you miss not being like everyone else?" she asked. "Didn't your talent keep you isolated?"

"Not at all," David said in a confident manner. "I went through adolescence just like everyone else. I had my loves and torments, my victories and defeats." He gave her a look as if to say, how dare you accuse me of being different.

"Well I feel flattered to have that eleven-year-old in our living room right now," Rose Ann said. "I'm glad you had such perserverance when you were a child. Thank you, it was really a gift for us."

"You embarrass me, Rose Ann," he said, but he beamed with obvious pleasure.

Just then, Sybil saw Alma sneaking down the stairs. "How's the costume?" she called. Alma poked her head into the room, and Sybil said, "Come closer, we can't even see you." She posed at the doorway only long enough for them to make out general things—a skirt that was too big for her, a pair of galoshes, a piece of material hanging from her shoulders—and then she fled.

"What are you?" someone called.

"Can't you tell? She's a gypsy," Sybil said.

"She's a wonderful looking gypsy," Rose Ann added. "She's going to the Halloween parade at her school, and then she'll be home and one of us can take her trick-or-treating."

"I'll go by myself, or I'll go with Daddy," Alma replied, peeking into the room again. Ready to leave, she marched to the front door.

"We hope you win a prize!" Rose Ann called out.

But Rose Ann was lying. Alma knew that her mother didn't believe in classifications or judgments; she didn't even believe in distinctions, and in her still lifes you often couldn't recognize the objects. You had a sense of what they might be, but they were familiar only as memories or as the kinds of things you saw in dreams.

When someone once asked her mother why she didn't make her paintings more realistic, Rose Ann had said it was because she was interested in how people saw things when they were close to dying. "When you die," she said, "you won't see the old separations. Everything will be equal. Nothing will be good or bad any longer—it will simply be. The thousands of soldiers who died in the war must have realized this in their final moment. They must have realized that everything is just like the air. Nothing means anything. Patriotism and democracy are empty terms. Boundaries don't exist, nor do ideas or politics. Everything simply is."

The woman who was questioning her was a reporter from the local newspaper, and she printed the interview in conjunction with an article about a show that included some of Rose Ann's work. But somewhere between the actual interview and the printing of it, Rose Ann's words were changed and she was quoted as saying, "I want to paint air."

Though Alma knew it had been a mistake, it was what she would remember. Her mother wanted to paint air. In her mind, it represented what Rose Ann was always straining toward. Up in her studio, her mother took what you could see and touch and turned it into something abstract. Her father was out of the house most of the day and so as a child she was by herself in the ordinary world of sensations.

On her way to school she passed a goblin, a robot, and a strange creature walking in a cardboard box; was it a washing machine or a TV? There were station wagons full of leering, painted faces. Someone waved at her and she waved back, but she had no idea who it was. When she got to the schoolyard, there were clusters of kids in the satin robes and plastic masks that came from the store. There were witches and monsters and one or two fairies, and everything about them was right. Nancy was a fairy, and she held a wand that sparkled. There was a delicate pink color rubbed into her cheeks and a fake diamond stuck into her neatly coiled hair. "What are you?" Nancy asked, but before Alma could reply she said, "Hey, look at Alma," and everyone turned around. When they began to laugh, Nancy said, "Shut up, you guys, or I'll turn you into frogs."

As they walked toward the gym, they passed the Ukrainian girl, who didn't have a costume at all. "At least you tried," Nancy whispered to Alma, and Alma said, "Thanks a lot." They giggled because no one liked the Ukrainian girl and it was important to make that clear.

Because it was Halloween, the gym teacher was wearing a mask. He jogged toward them, his whistle thumping on his sweatshirt, and told them to find their category and stay there. "Fairies under the basketball net," he said, and looking at Alma, he added, "If your costume doesn't fit into any of the groups, stand with the originals who are by the entrance to the old school." He pointed to a group of strangely costumed people. The Ukrainian girl was in that group, too.

"Is there a place for gypsies?" Alma asked.

"Gypsies by the dressing rooms," he said.

Alma saw a group of girls in long skirts like her own. As she approached, she could see that most of them were from the sixth-grade class. With hoop earrings and scarves wrapped around their hair, they truly looked like gypsies or, at the very least, grown women. When she walked up, a girl named Darlene blew a bubble in her direction, collapsed it, and sucking the pink back into her mouth said, "Alma, this is gypsies."

"That's what I am."

"If you say so." She smiled at her friends and then stepped back to let Alma join them.

The gym teacher jogged over to the red dot in the center of the floor where he always stood as they did their exercises. Putting the whistle to his lips, he gave a short toot. The gym grew quiet, and looking at the mass of costumed children, he began his speech: "Students at Hagedorn Elementary, this is the annual Halloween competition. Make sure you're in the right category"—he surveyed them to see if he could find anyone who was out of place—"and, when you hear your group called, step out six paces, I said *six* paces, not five and not seven. March down to the basketball net, face the judges, try to stand without squirming, and when you hear the whistle, turn around and march back again. March slowly, in beat to the music, and see if you can keep your mouths shut. Do I make myself clear?"

"Yes!" the children shouted in unison.

"Miss Bellows, the record."

Miss Bellows, the reading teacher, walked to the phonograph at the far end of the gym. The first time she put the needle down, it skipped off the record. She got it right the second time, and the only marching song Mel, the gym teacher, ever used filled the air.

"Fair-ees!" Mel called, making his voice go up and down just as he did when they were doing exercises. In a white and pink mass, a flock of fairies stepped forward. They marched down to the end of the gym, some of them waving wands and pirouetting. One girl, who at eleven years old was already an acclaimed ballerina, leapt across the floor on pointe, her arms extended gracefully over her head.

It was the most beautiful sight Alma had ever seen. She looked at her own costume—the rubber boots Rose Ann insisted she wear even if it only looked like rain and the bathing suit that had been her outfit in one summer swim class after another. "Gypsies" was called, and she missed the cue, took two short steps to catch up, but then couldn't find the right rhythm. She tried to walk with a swagger like the other girls, but that only complicated things, and she arrived at the judges' table behind everyone else and had to squeeze in between two of the other girls.

In the tradition of Hagedorn Elementary, the judges at the Halloween pageant were students. There was a representative from each class, and though afterward there would be accusations of favoritism, the fifteen judges surveyed the contestants in a serious manner, making notations on their pads. Alma was opposite Sandy, a third grader she had once seen unzipping his pants for a group of kids behind the one tree in the schoolyard. She had tried to get a better look, but when he saw her elbowing her way into the crowd, he tucked himself in and closed his pants. He watched her now with a sleepy expression, and when the gypsies turned to go back to their places, she could feel his eyes on her back. She was out of step again, and her boots, which she had drawn on hurriedly over her bare feet, made a sucking sound. Halfway across the room, she began to run. But instead of going back to her place, she slipped behind another group and sneaked down the stairs to the dressing rooms. There was an entrance to the schoolyard down there and as she reached the door, she summoned up the vision of the pink ballerina leaping across the terrible wooden gym floor.

Alma pushed, the door opened, and she was released into the bright afternoon. There wasn't a soul in the schoolyard, and even though she was doing something strictly prohibited, traffic passed the gate as though everything were normal. But if she stayed there she would be discovered, and if she walked back home she would arrive too early, and she would feel a little nervous hiding out in the lot that bordered the schoolyard. So she tried the doors on the old building, which was where she had been until third grade, and they too were unlocked. She went up the familiar stairs, which didn't seem as steep now that she was older, and tiptoed along the cool, empty hall to the classroom at the other end. There wasn't anyone in there. She opened the door quietly and slipped inside. It had been her first-grade classroom, and there on the board was the same alphabet exercise they had been taught: A is for Ann, B is for Bobby, C is for Cheryl. They had recited it at the beginning of each school day until, only a week later, they had known the alphabet as well as everyone's name. Only in her year there had been several A's, and they would begin like this: A is for Alma, Ann, and Arlene. B is for Bruce. They would say it in unison as the teacher held up the cards. For a treat, at different times during that year, she'd bring out the cards again, and they'd see how quickly they could run through them.

But it frightened her to realize that it was A is for Ann this year and that it would never be A is for Alma unless there was another first grader with that name.

Without making the decision to do so, she erased the names on the blackboard and put Alma, Ann, and Arlene beside the A and Bruce by the B. She stopped there because she couldn't remember who the C had been. But stepping back to survey her work, she felt scared of being caught and erased those names and put the original ones back. She couldn't remember this C either so taking a guess, she put down Cathy instead of Cheryl.

When she went back to the gym, the prizes were being announced. The ballerina was awarded the blue ribbon. She leapt up to the judge's table, made a deep curtsy, and Miss Bellows pinned the ribbon on her costume.

"And now, young maskers, the fourth annual Halloween competition is finished! School is over!" Mel tooted on his whistle, and a loud roar filled the gym. Alma opened her mouth to scream like everyone else, though she didn't understand the reason for all the excitement. It was only Friday. She would go back home, and Rose Ann would scold her for the mess in the studio, and the weekend would pass and it would be Monday again.

But she screamed anyway, and when she was done, she knew that her face was as red as everyone else's. She had been a failure as a gypsy but, curiously, from the exertion of screaming there was a feeling again, creeping along her nerves, of well-being and perhaps even happiness.

· · · · · · *4* · · · · · ·

There was a sensation, way in the back of her head, of being a stranger. The person she actually was, was quite different from the person she seemed to be. There was a minute scrap of memory, sticking to her brain, of coming from someplace very different. The times she was aware of it, she felt dissatisfied with everything around her. Her parents' behavior bothered her. She would feel frustrated with their determination to be unlike everyone else.

She wanted to lose her separateness. This made her look forward to holidays. They arrived with traditions that told a person what to do and how to feel. Also, they made their house look like all the others. At Christmas, for example, there was a tree in their living room, stockings on the banister, and a string of blinking lights around the door.

The big holidays, like Christmas and Easter, were easy. But with a birthday the specifics were less clear. There were presents, of course, even Rose Ann knew that, but more than presents, when Alma's eleventh birthday arrived, she had desires she wasn't sure she'd be able to explain.

She found her mother in the kitchen the night before and asked her if she remembered what time she'd been born.

"Of course I remember. It was in the evening, maybe around six or seven, or maybe even eight o'clock."

"You don't remember exactly?"

"I'm sorry, sweetie, I don't. If we could find your birth certificate, we could look it up."

"That's all right. It doesn't really matter. I was just curious."

"I guess I don't remember the time because it was such a tremendous experience. . . ."

"Please . . . ," Alma said, recognizing the tone.

But Rose Ann was quick. "You're going to be eleven, and I want to tell you something. You can listen for just a minute. When you were born, it was a glorious moment for both your father and me. When we decided to get married, your father said he wanted to have a child. It sounded like a good idea to me, too. So you see we wanted you. We wanted you very much."

"Rose Ann . . . ," Alma pleaded.

"I had been up all night and finally that morning after a few pushes I felt you come slipping out, a little creature covered with something that looked like cold cream. The doctor lifted you up into the world and put you on my breast. Right away, you started to nurse. I didn't take drugs like alot of other women do. I didn't want to be asleep during the most important moment of both of our lives. And did you know you were the longest baby ever born in that hospital?"

Alma winced at this dubious honor, and Rose Ann said, "There's nothing wrong with hearing about how you were born. It's only biology. It's what human beings were designed to do."

But what was only biology filled Alma with horror. She wished she were a cat or a bird, anything but a human being. They reproduced, too, but at least they did it mindlessly. And even if they remembered what the experience had been like, they didn't speak about it to their offspring.

"You were such a good baby," Rose Ann said, taking a seat at the table next to Alma. "You didn't throw tantrums. You hardly even cried." Her tone softened. "You know something . . . I always thought you were very wise."

"What do you mean?" Alma asked.

"Well, just wise. I don't know how to explain it. And you'll be eleven years old, imagine that." It was just this sort of expression that led Rose Ann into further proclamations, so Alma stood up. Patting her mother on the head to make up for the quick exit, she escaped to her room.

At school there were problems with the Ukrainian girl. Because she was absent two or three days every week, the teacher threatened her with having to repeat sixth grade. This had no effect. Either the Ukrainian girl didn't understand, or else she just wasn't worried.

There was another problem, too. She never brought an absentee note. In fifth grade she had never brought one either, but the teacher hadn't reprimanded her; her foreignness and the suspicion that her parents couldn't write English made the teacher reluctant to subject her to the same rules as the other children.

But Mrs. Sharp, their sixth-grade teacher, administered all rules without discrimination. She was particularly hard on Ulrike, who was large and womanly and came to school dressed in what Mrs. Sharp called costumes. This gave her bad marks in good citizenship. Her blouses were always wrinkled, and her long skirts were garish with embroidery. She wore her hair in braids, and on many days a piece of colored ribbon would be plaited in as well. That was all very well and good, Mrs. Sharp told her, but along with the decorations, she had to carry a clean white handkerchief with her every day.

Ulrike listened to the teacher, but unlike the other students, she never became resentful. Nothing seemed to touch her. She was never prepared with homework and when called on, her responses were minimal. In short, she was simply a shape in the classroom, a shape Mrs. Sharp always seemed to fix her gaze on.

"Bobby, Marianne, Ulrike, and Alma, bring your absentee notes to the front of the room."

Everyone did as she said except Ulrike, who glanced out the window as though her name hadn't been called.

"You were absent yesterday, Ulrike. When you return to school, you must bring a note from a parent. The school cannot consider your absence legal unless you bring a note. Once again you have failed to do this. If, by the end of the year, you have enough unexcused absences, the school is required by law to charge your parents with truancy. Now, no one would want to see that happen, not even you."

Over the loudspeaker the pledge of allegiance came on, but feeling the matter at hand was more important even than that, Mrs. Sharp motioned the class to keep their seats until she was finished.

"If you forget to bring a note the next time you're absent, I will be forced to contact the principal, who will have to contact the board of education, and then, because this is a country where everyone, regardless of their personal likes or dislikes, must by law attend school, I'm afraid truancy proceedings will have to begin. Nothing like that has ever happened at our school before, and it's a shame that one student's carelessness will blemish our good record." She gave them the signal to stand up and, clapping her hand to her chest, led them through the last few lines of the pledge, her voice conspicuous above all of theirs: "and to the republic for which it stands, one nation, under God, indivisible, with liberty and justice for all."

Ulrike was absent the next day, and the day after that, as was her pattern, she came to school. She slipped into the schoolyard just a few minutes before the bell rang and waited by the fence.

It was cold that day, and Alma had to walk against the wind to reach her. "Ulrike!" she called. "Ulrike, come here!"

Ulrike didn't look up.

She pulled a piece of paper from her schoolbook and held it out. "I have an absentee note for you," she called. As Ulrike turned toward her, she waved it up and down.

She came to her side, took the piece of paper, and glanced at it quickly. Then she handed it back.

"Do you think it will work?" Alma asked.

She didn't answer.

"Let me sign your mother's name, and you can at least see if it will work, okay? Can you tell me how to spell your mother's name?"

Ulrike opened her mouth and tonelessly began to spell out a long, foreign word. Alma copied it down. Then she put the letter in an envelope and addressed it to Mrs. Sharp. "Promise you'll give it to her?"

But again Ulrike didn't answer. As she put the note in her pocket, the bell rang and the schoolyard began to empty out. They were almost the last two in the building before the doors closed.

"Ulrike, you were absent again yesterday. Please bring your note to the front of the room."

There was an astonished silence when Ulrike got out of her seat and deposited the note on the teacher's desk. Without showing surprise or even satisfaction, Mrs. Sharp read it. Then she turned to the class and said, "Robert, will you lead us this morning in the pledge of allegiance?"

During afternoon arithmetic, Alma asked to be excused so she could go to the toilet. When she opened the door, she was surprised to find the bathroom empty. She chose the last stall because it was the one farthest away from the entrance, and she could pee without tightening up if someone came in. She locked the door and sat down, and as she was unrolling a handful of toilet paper, she noticed a name written on the wall beside her. It was faint, but when she peered closely she could make it out. With something thin and sharp, someone had scratched "Alma Juro."

As the week went on, there were other things, too: a ribbon tied onto her locker, a piece of candy in her desk one morning.

"Who is he?" Nancy asked. Then she turned to Christine and said, "Hey, look at Alma, she's blushing."

Walking home one day she felt an unfamiliar weight in the pocket of her coat and pulled out a small white box. Though it was taped closed, there was clearly something heavy inside. She tore the tape off and opened the lid and saw a stack of coins. There were five of them, copper colored, with foreign writing on one side and a portrait on the other. She threw the box away and slipped the coins into her pocket.

When Ulrike was absent again, Alma arrived the next day with a note. It was written on Rose Ann's best stationery and sealed in a matching envelope. "You had a cold," Alma told her as she handed the note over. "You spent the day in bed, and you took aspirin every four hours."

"Thank you," Ulrike said and, when the bell rang, they walked to the door together.

6

"What's worse than finding a worm in your apple?"

"What?" Alma asked. She turned around and discovered a face regarding her with unconcealed derision.

"What's worse than finding a worm in your apple?"

"I don't know."

"Come on," the face said, and everything on it grew tremendously expressive. The eyebrows settled into the ridge of the nose, the eyes squeezed shut, and the mouth went wide and thin.

"I don't know this joke," Alma explained.

Though it seemed impossible, the features shifted even more. The eyebrows disappeared entirely, and the mouth indicated such ridicule, she doubted she could possibly be the one it was intended for. On looking around, though, there weren't any other children close enough. "Worse than finding a worm?"

"If you can't guess it, then I give up."

At this the face changed again. It went back to its usual masklike features, and she suddenly knew who it was. "You're Tommy Pyle," she said. He was a grade below her and lived down the block.

"Hey, good for you. Now come on, tell me the answer."

"Worse than finding a worm? A spider?"

"A spider? When do you ever find a spider in an apple?"

"A slug? Worse than finding a worm—finding that your apple's been eaten by someone else, maybe your mother." But she knew this was a lame guess, so she didn't bother even to look at him. "I give up," she said.

"You give up? Boy, you're really out to breakfast. Half a worm, you dummy. The only thing that's worse than finding a worm is finding half a worm." He was red and breathless, but he managed a "get it?" before taking a gulp of air.

"Half a worm," she repeated. "Oh yeah, of course, half a worm, that's funny." She began to laugh, but she knew it wasn't convincing.

"You dodo bird. If you find only half a worm, it's because you've already eaten the other half."

"I know," Alma said, "you don't have to explain."

That was morning recess. At recess in the afternoon, Errol Pyle, the face's older brother, cornered her by the entrance to the girl's bathroom. "Hey, Alma, what country's in your kitchen cabinet?"

His tactics were different. He stood away from his victim and let only his voice make the assault. Alma knew it was another joke, but it had flown by so quickly that she said as kindly as she could, "I didn't hear you."

"I said, what country's in your kitchen cabinet?"

This one seemed perfectly harmless. She knew she'd have to be careful. "You mean there's a country in your kitchen cabinet?"

"That's what I said, isn't it?"

"I just wanted to make sure. Let's see, give me a minute." She looked down at the pitted gray pavement in the schoolyard and then up into the autumn sun and finally centered her gaze on the untroubled landscape of his face. "I give up," she said.

"China," the boy said simply.

"Of course, that's funny."

"No it isn't," the boy said. "It's the dumbest joke there is." He put his hands in his pockets and walked off. Then, at some distance, he turned around and without shouting but loud enough so she was sure to hear, called out, "I save it especially for girls."

She knew the implication. If x was a dumb joke and x was saved for girls . . . But boys, she thought to herself, were even dumber, and besides she didn't care an iota anyway.

She didn't care what anyone thought. At least that's what she reminded herself. But when she was alone the taunts came back to her.

Powerful and irreducible, they let her know who she was. Even if they didn't make sense, when she went over them in private she would worry. Like "fat face." A boy from the Catholic school called her "fat face" whenever he saw her. But she wasn't fat. Or one person speaking to another might say, "That Alma Juroe, she's out to breakfast."

It was the phrase that identified that year. Someone's hasty invention had stuck, and the oddness of it and the extra syllable gave it an added sting. So, "fat face," "out to breakfast," and "dumb girl."

"I hope you don't let it bother you for even a second. You're beautiful and smart, and for someone your age I think you're amazingly attentive and aware. Remember those things when someone calls you a name." Then Rose Ann spread her arms to dramatize the next point. "Embrace whatever it is they say to you, don't shun it, but after you embrace it, pluck it off. Like this," and she plucked something invisible off her sweater. "You embrace it, and by embracing it I mean really hearing it and acknowledging it, and then you get rid of it. It's that simple. It just takes a little practice and a little resolve."

But Rose Ann's advice was never easy to put into action. It involved dignity, and that was difficult when you were cornered in the school-yard and wanted only to melt away. The next time she went to her father. "He called me fat face," she said.

"Say something back to him."

"Like what?"

"Well, what does he look like?"

"I don't know, I never get a good enough look at him. He has red hair, that's all I know for sure."

"Call him asshole," Teddy said.

It worked. Even when the insult was only implied, she would face the antagonist and say softly and very clearly, "You asshole."

And yet, even when she was ready with such a succinct and clear response, school presented terror. For extra protection, Alma loaded her arms with more books than she actually needed and carried them the five blocks between the house and school.

"Do you really have to take all of that with you?" her mother asked. Well, she would be a martyr to the cause of learning—gladly, and without a thought for her own comfort. But after a year she developed bad posture. Her shoulders became rounded and her angel wings stuck out. To compensate for the weight she was carrying, she held her pelvis at a funny angle. She grew swaybacked. None of this was terribly conspicuous; in fact, with her clothes on, no one would have noticed, but one night she was getting into the bathtub, and Teddy saw her before she had a chance to close the door.

"Alma, sweetie, look how you're slouching." Not understanding her embarrassment, he came into the steamy bathroom and tried to adjust her posture. He pressed her shoulder blades into place and pushed on her bottom to align her pelvis, but once he took his hands off, everything went back to the way it had been.

"Well, that's a little better. It's not going to be instant. No change is ever instant, but just try to be aware of how you're standing, all right?" He kissed her on the forehead and then for the first time noticed her discomfort. "Well," he said, backing out, "take your bath. Sorry to intrude."

She heard him go down the steps and knew he would find Rose Ann and tell her about this new situation. So she wasn't surprised when a week later the dance lessons were announced.

At first she was opposed. "If it's anything like sports, I'm not going to do it. And if there are any boys in the class, I'm not going to do it. I hope I won't have to wear a leotard."

"Of course you will," Rose Ann said. "It's a wonderful opportunity. You'll learn a new kind of expression."

"Great," Alma said, "I can't wait to do it."

"You're sounding a little too cute," Rose Ann cautioned. "And a little too spoiled, I might add."

It was a large room with windows at one end and a bench along the wall. The floor was so highly polished it looked like it had never been walked on. They wore tights and leotards, and they moved around the room in clusters, transforming themselves into whatever the teacher commanded. "Be a leaf floating through the sky to the ground. Be a wisp of smoke rising from a chimney."

When they were in class, nothing from the outside world was supposed to disturb them. "As you take off your clothes," the teacher said,

"I want you to take off your concerns and worries, your likes and dislikes, and leave them right there on the bench with your things. There is no one else in here but us, and nothing you have to do but give yourself a chance to be something you aren't."

Her name was Heather, and she wore a fawn-colored leotard and Alma thought she was perfect. She had blonde hair and small, cherubic lips, but her hands were what Alma always watched. They were so delicate they seemed like porcelain, but when she touched you, she left a sensation of heat on your skin.

For Alma it wasn't easy to change into a leaf or a squirrel or a wisp of smoke. She'd start out fine, but then she'd see what someone else was doing, and it would always seem better. She'd try to copy it, and then almost immediately she'd remember how terrible she was at things like that and she'd give up.

Yet she wanted to be able to do it. At home when no one was around, she'd put on her leotard and jump from one piece of furniture to another, imitating the squirrels jumping from tree to tree. She'd become smoke and in languid motions unfold herself up from the floor. For the leaf she'd start at the top of the stairs and drop from step to step, lifting occasionally in currents of wind. It was easier at home where she could use props, but in the bare dance studio there wasn't anything except her imagination. She'd get started on a transformation, but then her attention would falter, and she'd remember who she actually was.

That year winter came early. The first time it turned dark before the end of class, Heather put five candles in the center of the room. "This is darkness," she said. "I'm going to light the candles, and there will be light to chase away the darkness." She struck a match and the room was suddenly filled with huge flickering shapes. "Now each of you is a candle just like the ones I've put here. When the match hits your wick, you'll flare up and provide a light."

She came to each of them and held an invisible match to their heads. It would take a few seconds to catch, and then they'd hear the words, "Be light," and they'd move into the room and glimmer.

"Good," Heather whispered. "But now you've been burning so long that most of the wax has melted, and now all you are is a wick. You are all light now, and you're free to move about. You'll bend in even the slightest breeze, and you'll get smaller and larger according to the currents of air."

The room was still dark, but strange, wavering shapes were tiptoeing about.

"Good," Heather said. "Now all the lights have names, and all the lights have different destinies. When I say your name, the light will become a dream. All right, Alice Adams."

Alice moved out and became a dream. She seemed to be swimming, but it didn't matter if you couldn't tell. The other lights waited, and one by one turned into dreams. Someone was zooming around like an airplane, and someone else was just lying on the floor. Alma watched them for ideas, but it wasn't until she heard the sound of her name that she knew what to do. The dream would be about a dancer, someone who moved so entrancingly her audiences wept when they saw her perform. She passed between the other dreams to the dark windows at the end of the room. There, she moved back and forth, her arms swaying above her head. Then, gathering her long, invisible skirts, she swept forward. There was another dream close by, and Alma reached for her hand and brought her into the magic dance. They sped around the room together, going faster and faster. "Good," Heather said, and she took hold of their hands and steered them across the room. Soon the other dreams joined them, reaching for arms, hands, feet, holding on to whatever was closest. It was motion, hot and dizzy, and they went on and on until at an unknown signal one person broke away. Others followed until finally even Heather left them. From the window she called out, "Daylight is coming, and the dream returns to the dreamer. The dreamer wakes up and becomes her daytime self. She feels light and joyous. She'll take off her leotard and put her clothes back on, and the joyousness will last for a long time. It will persist."

At the door she gave them each a small white candle and told them to let it burn for a little while every night. "When you blow the flame out, feel how the light continues inside you."

When they left the dance studio, the neighborhood was empty and quiet. They walked down Eleventh Street together, but at Oak Lane most of the girls turned off, and only Alma and Alice Adams continued on.

They didn't say anything until Alice's street came up. Then she pulled the candle out of her pocket and said, "I'll have to light it in secret. My father's scared about the house catching fire. We're not even allowed to have any Christmas decorations that plug in."

"How come?"

"When he was a little boy his house burned down. He's never forgotten it." She replaced the candle and turned down her block, and Alma continued into the darkness by herself.

Three weeks later it snowed. It started in the afternoon and kept up with such persistence that businesses and schools closed early. On TV they called it a flurry. They said it was a cold front sweeping across the Great Lakes, and promised clear skies and moderate temperatures the next day.

"It's just moisture," Rose Ann said. "It's not even snow."

But it *was* snow, and though at first it melted when it hit the ground, the front turned in their direction, and it became cold enough for the snow to stick. Then the wind blew and the houses on the north side of their street had drifts up to their first-story windows.

When Alma's father came home, his mustache was hung with icicles, and the kiss he absentmindedly placed on his daughter's cheek was wet and chilly.

"How are the roads?"

"They're fine; you just have to drive carefully."

"You should have come home when it started," Rose Ann said. "This is terrible weather to be out in. People die in this kind of weather."

"They die in any kind of weather. At least in this kind they drive more slowly."

"Well," Rose Ann said and her voice trailed off, a sign that she lacked an immediate answer.

In Alma's family the thrill of any unusual external event quickly wore off, and the old preoccupations came back stronger than before. Teddy went into the kitchen to pour himself a cup of coffee, Rose Ann went up to her studio, and Alma went into the living room for a while, looked outside, and then moved upstairs, too.

She closed the door to her bedroom and pulled a chair up to the window. It was really snow—white light falling from the sky. Under the heavy wetness everything was very still. She could feel her breath move through her body and the cold air on the glass pressing against her skin. Her breath made a white cloud that caused tiny droplets to run down the windowpane, and if she leaned her forehead against the glass, there was an oval shape when she pulled away.

Everything was so quiet that time seemed to have changed. It was so slow that nothing could slip by her attention. For instance, her father was coming up the stairs, and she could hear the pause in each of his steps. When he shut the door to the bathroom, she knew he would be in there for a long time. Rose Ann wouldn't be around either. Alma could hear her moving back and forth across the studio in a regular rhythm that meant she was, as she liked to call it, deeply engrossed.

Alma went downstairs and put on her hat and coat and very quietly opened the front door.

Outside, in the still, flat, white world she was the only moving thing. She twirled around and collapsed in the snow. Getting up and brushing the snow from her pants, she called out, "No school, no school!" Maybe there would never be any more school. At least tomorrow there wouldn't be any, and that in itself was a reason to shout. "No school," she called again, and then she opened her mouth and made the loudest sound she had ever made. It felt good. It was light and dream all around her, but she was sound. She tried a singing voice and then let it move into pure sound. Soon she was shouting more loudly than she had ever shouted before.

Up in the sky a window opened, and Rose Ann leaned out. "What in the world do you think you're doing? Where are your boots and gloves—are you nuts?"

"There won't be school tomorrow," Alma called, but her mother slammed the window down and with angry gestures beckoned her to come back inside.

· · · · · · *7* · · · · · ·

Sometimes she had imaginary conversations. Each time they started casually so that she hardly noticed what she was thinking about, and then they grew more insistent and she would have to put down whatever she was doing and give them her full attention. They only took place when she was by herself, and they never involved another speaker.

Sometimes they could go on for several minutes without an interruption of any kind. When it was herself speaking, she was a patient listener. Even though she knew the outcome of most of the things she told herself, she never grew tired of hearing them again.

When I was little, Alma began, I used to have a nightmare about falling off a cliff.

At the time of this conversation she was twelve. She was sitting in her bedroom staring at the wall behind her desk.

We were driving, she said. Teddy and Rose Ann were in the front seat, and I was in the back. We were in the blue Plymouth station wagon, and in the way back there were blankets and a picnic basket with lunch and dinner.

Rose Ann had planned it. She had found a place on the map where there was a gorge, and she said there would be a waterfall and a beautiful park to picnic in. "You might want to take a bathing suit," she said. "I'm going to take my easel and watercolors."

We started out in the early morning and drove for a long time, and then all of a sudden Rose Ann grabbed Teddy's arm and said, "There it is." My father parked the car, and we all got out and walked to the side of the cliff. It was so pretty. There were little trees covered with flowers. We looked down into the gorge, and the river way down at the bottom was sparkling in the sun. There were bright green birds flying around between the walls. They'd swoop down to the water and then come up again, squawking to one another and making circles in the air. All along the sides of the cliff there were wild bushes. They were just growing out from the rocks.

Teddy and Rose Ann were standing a little ways away from me, and I was looking down at the water, and then the next thing I knew I was falling through the air. I wasn't pushed; I think I just happened to fall on my own. Maybe I tripped on something, or maybe I just jumped.

If I jumped I did it because I didn't feel like I belonged there. I wanted to see what being somewhere else was like. It wasn't nice though, and every time I had the dream I'd wake up crying.

So I kept on having this dream on and off for about a year. I don't know why. Everything was so pretty in the park, but I had to go over to the side of the cliff and find out what it was like to jump off. So I just stepped into the air, and I didn't even close my eyes. That way I saw how everything I had always counted on being in certain places, like the trees and the grass and the sky, wasn't there anymore. There was nothing but this horrible falling that I couldn't stop.

So why are you thinking about it now? she asked herself.

I don't know, she answered, but don't worry.

She turned to the mirror over her dresser and saw her own very white, serious face. She looked at herself directly, without flinching and without making a judgment about what she saw.

8

It was June. The house was bathed in summer colors: The kitchen walls were splashed with the yellow of early evening, and the table, which in the summer they pushed up against the window, was rosy in the declining light. There was a vase of flowers in the middle of the table, and they were thick with liquid color—yellow and red and pink. The plates appeared to glow, and the silverware looked as though it might have just been polished. The truth of the matter was that it hadn't been touched since the day it had been given to them, but the early summer light transformed all the spare realities. It covered the cracks in the walls and made the people sitting at the table look soft and filmy.

Rose Ann nodded toward the flowers and said, "Aren't those flowers wonderfully vibrant?"

"They certainly are," Teddy replied. "Where'd you get them?"

"Finch's," Rose Ann said. "You know, across the street from the liquor store?" She looked up, but it wasn't clear if Teddy understood which place she was referring to.

The window was open and they could hear birds and dogs and the first evening insects. Inside, there were the usual sounds of a family eating dinner.

"How was your day at school?" Rose Ann asked, turning toward Alma.

"Fine," Alma said.

"What did you do?"

"Nothing special."

"How about you?"

"Me?" Teddy asked.

"Did you think I was talking to the wall behind you?"

"I wasn't paying attention," Teddy said.

"Well?" Rose Ann asked. "What was your day like?"

"The usual," Teddy said. "It went fine."

"That's wonderful," Rose Ann said. "Did you go out to lunch with somebody?"

"I ate in the office."

"Whatever for?"

"I didn't feel like going out. I just had coffee and a piece of fruit, nothing much."

"Did you have to give your report?"

"What report?"

"I was talking to your daughter."

"Yes," Alma said. "I was the first to get called on."

"How did it go?"

"Fine."

"Did the class ask you questions?"

"Uh-huh."

"Could you answer them?"

"Un-huh."

"What was your feeling about it afterward?"

She shrugged her shoulders. "I didn't feel worried."

They started eating again, and outside of their window the neighbor's cat began to yowl.

"Oh, yes," Rose Ann said, as though she were answering somebody's question. "It went quite nicely, and I'm so glad you asked because I'd love to tell you about it."

Alma giggled but Rose Ann kept going. "First I had breakfast and then I went up to the studio." She rested her hand under her chin, cocked her head to the side, and in a different voice asked, "What are you working on?" She moved her head to the other side and, just as the cat began to growl, said in her first voice, "Well, I'm working on a new idea."

"Is that so?" the other voice asked.

"Yes, it concerns light," the first voice replied. "I want my paintings to be luminous."

"What exactly do you mean by that?"

Now there were two cats, and the growling had risen to a higher pitch.

"I want them to have a light of their own," Rose Ann went on. "I want the color to suggest luminosity just by richness and texture. I've been looking at Cézanne lately. His landscapes have an energy that I find very appealing. He wasn't painting only what he saw; he was also painting the relationship he felt between his own brush and the lines in nature."

The cats were screaming and hissing. It was a full-fledged fight.

"He didn't separate himself from the external world; that's the difference. He didn't feel alien. It's utterly clear, looking at his pictures, that what he looked out on was tied inextricably to how he saw. Vision and the thing being viewed: There isn't a line dividing it. It's all the same." She looked over to Teddy and in her regular voice asked him if he understood what she was talking about.

"I do," Teddy replied. "I find it fascinating."

"But do you know what I mean? I'm becoming aware of the gestural."

"The gestural?"

Over the screaming, Mrs. Wilkens, who lived next door, shouted, "Stop it! Stop it!" and came down the steps waving a dish towel.

"I'm becoming aware of pure gesture, how the hand with the paintbrush approaches the canvas."

"But what does that have to do with Cézanne?"

"That's what Cézanne was after. When you look at his paintings, you can feel the separate brushstrokes. You can feel the movement of his hand. It's very exciting."

They were growling again. To coax Caspar, her cat, into her house, Mrs. Wilkens clucked and waved and made kissing sounds.

"I can see that it is," Teddy said.

Mrs. Wilkens was successful, and the new quiet was just as dramatic as the fight had been. Rose Ann put down her fork and looked out the window. "What's the matter with the two of you? I make a nice dinner, I buy flowers. We sit down, and nobody says anything. Who am I living with, do you think you could trouble yourselves to answer me that?"

9

When Alma was fourteen her mother was offered a fellowship at the American Academy of Art in Rome. They would provide her with a studio and a small apartment. If she had a family they would make larger accommodations available in an area close to the Academy. For any children there was an American school.

It came as a surprise. Holding the letter, looking shocked and embarrassed, Rose Ann explained to Teddy that she had filled the application out one day almost eight months ago when she had been feeling a little closed in by family life. At this she looked over at Alma to see if she was listening, and Alma, taking the cue, went upstairs. Out of sight, she hung over the railing so she could hear the conversation in the kitchen.

"I'll take the year off," Teddy said. "Life insurance could survive without me, don't you think? Alma could go to the American school."

"I don't know," Rose Ann replied.

"We wouldn't have many expenses over there. So I think we could afford it if I didn't work for a year. And it sounds like your studio would be separate from the apartment, so we wouldn't be under your feet like we are at home."

"I don't know."

"I think this is great. Aren't you excited?"

"I don't know," Rose Ann said again. "It was just an impulse. I certainly never expected to get it. That's why I never even told you. So I don't know if it will work out at all."

"Of course it will. We'll make it work. We'll write and find out what the tuition is at the American school, and we'll get passports and shots, and I could probably just keep my accounts. There's no reason I couldn't do my business from over there."

There was silence. Then, in a voice so low that Alma had to creep down the stairs to hear better, Rose Ann said, "Teddy, I have to tell you something. It's going to be a difficult thing to say so I'm just going to say it. I'm going to do this thing alone. I don't think I'm going to bring you two. I think I have to get away by myself for a little while. It won't be long. Maybe I'll just go for half a year. I think that's what I'm going to do, Teddy, if you could manage all right with Alma."

"All I'm doing is going to a different place for half a year to look at art and draw and paint. That's all. I still love your father, and I will miss the both of you very much."

"Then take us with you."

Rose Ann walked to the bureau and brought over another pile of neatly folded clothing. One by one, she layered her things in the suitcase. "I want to travel as much as I want to, or stay in my studio as much as I want to, and I want to be by myself for a change. I don't want to cook for anyone or clean house or write absentee notes."

"I can do all of that. I'll do anything for you. Why don't you just let us come with you? I'll take care of everything. I'll even do all the shopping."

"Sweetie, it's a foreign country, you don't know the language."

"Neither do you."

"I'm going to take lessons."

"Please, Rose Ann. Never in my whole life will I have another chance like this."

Her mother turned to look at her, her face dark and annoyed. "Your whole life is just beginning, so don't be so sure. Besides, it will be nice, just you and your father here by yourselves."

The word "nice" hung in the air between them as she continued to fold the clothing into her suitcase. Alma was to remember that moment many months later when, in the middle of the ensuing chaos, she heard it again. It meant that you could stand aside from any situation and let your distance give you the freedom to label it any way you wanted. It meant that nothing was absolutely one way or another; depending on your perspective, it changed. But she wouldn't have called the situation "nice." "Nice" implied easy. And even from a distance, if she managed to free herself from the tentacles of circumstance, she couldn't have smoothed it out enough to produce the impression of "easy."

But at the time she didn't know that. So, when Rose Ann announced that the matter was closed and that, if she didn't mind, there would be no more discussion, Alma assumed the old habit of a spoiled, pouting child.

"Besides," Rose Ann said, "there's something more important to talk about anyway. Did it ever occur to you that you might get your first menstrual period while I'm away?"

"I'll know what to do," Alma said.

"It's an important step," Rose Ann replied, turning around with an armful of clothes. She lay them on the bed and sat down next to Alma.

"You're crying again," Alma exclaimed. Over the last few days, Rose Ann's eyes had become teary whenever someone spoke to her.

"Isn't it awful how oblivious we are to time?" Her mother picked up a small paper bag lying on the end of the bed and holding it in her hands went on. "It seems like only yesterday I was changing your diapers."

"Yesterday I was helping you buy a suitcase. I've been out of diapers longer than that."

"You goose," Rose Ann said and put the bag in Alma's lap. "That's a sanitary belt. There's a box of your size napkins in the bathroom closet. I know you know what to do, but it will make me feel better if you have these things. All right?" She picked up Alma's hand and started to cry again. "Maybe I shouldn't go. I should be with you when it happens. It's such an important moment for a young girl. You're going to want me to be there."

"I'll be all right," Alma said firmly.

"Do you know how the belt works? Do you want me to show you?"

"You should finish packing. You're not going to finish in time if you start crying again."

"One more thing," Rose Ann said, wiping her eyes. "I just want you to know that I love you and I'll miss you a lot."

"I know. You don't have to tell me."

"I do have to tell you. But don't you want to tell me that you're going to miss me, too?"

"Yes," Alma said. "I'll miss you a lot."

At four in the morning Rose Ann was in the kitchen frying eggs. Standing at the stove in high heels and her new suit, she already looked as though she no longer lived there. All of yesterday she hadn't cried, and last night at dinner she had been laughing so hard she couldn't stop. The excitement, she had explained, made her feel giddy.

She woke them at four-thirty. Her plane didn't leave New York until noon, but adding some time to get lost, the drive could take as long as three hours. "Get up, kids," she called from the kitchen. "I want to have plenty of time for a nice leisurely breakfast. Teddy, Alma, rise and shine!"

When Alma came downstairs, Rose Ann was sliding the eggs onto their plates. "Is that father of yours on his way? In another minute, everything will be stone cold."

Teddy appeared in his underwear looking as though he were still asleep.

"My sweet husband, there you are." Rose Ann took his face between her hands and gave him a kiss on his nose. He waved her away impatiently. "A little grouchy this morning, aren't we? Grouchy for my farewell breakfast. Sweet husband of mine, have a cup of coffee and try to wake up. Oh!" she exclaimed, "What things I'm going to see! First I'll go to Arezzo, which isn't too far at all from Rome, and look at the Piero della Francescas. What a treat that will be. His use of simple geometric shapes! It's such a straightforward approach to all the complex circumstances we discover in our lives. An egg suspended above a woman's head—that pure, elliptical shape suggesting all the tenderness and compassion you would ever want." From a cleverly disguised pocket in her blouse, Rose Ann pulled out a small lace handkerchief and began to sniff into it noisily.

"Don't cry, for God's sake," Teddy said. "You're looking like you'll never see us again. We're going to be fine, and in six months we'll see each other. Six months goes very fast; just wait and see."

"Not if you're unhappy it doesn't," Rose Ann said.

"You won't be unhappy. You'll be doing the very things you've always wanted to do. It's a rare opportunity, and you shouldn't waste your time feeling unhappy about us. Understand? Now, no more crying. Wipe your eyes and eat your eggs."

At the airport there was a succession of small delays to occupy their attention. It took them a while to find a parking space, and then they lost their way in the terminal. The line at the ticket counter was endless, and Alma held a place for Rose Ann while her parents went to the snack bar for a cup of coffee. While they were gone, Alma pretended that she was the one leaving her family to go to another country. As soon as she arrived she would check into the oldest and most luxurious hotel. She would have her dinner in a lush, beautiful garden where there would be violinists strolling between the tables. After dinner, she would go back to her room and run a bath in the marble tub and have a good soak before going to bed. What wonderful dreams she would dream in her large high-ceilinged room with a balcony. There would be an owl outside hooting into the night. It would be looking for mice, she thought to herself, leaving her daydream to think about something more immediate. There were mice in the garage behind their house, which was where she had been on the day, several months ago, when she had discovered she had begun to menstruate. She had been in the garage looking for her bicycle pump, and feeling something sticky between her legs, she had pulled down her pants to investigate. No one was home, so she simply went up to her room and dug out the supplies she had bought with her friend Nancy two years ago. She washed her pants and flung them into the hamper still wet but without a trace of blood. Then, paraphernalia in place, she put on new clothes and went back outside. That evening she had intended to break the news to Rose Ann, but there hadn't been a chance, and she didn't do it the next day either. When a week had passed, it was too long after it had happened to mention it. She decided to wait until her second period, but her second period came and went, and she didn't bring it up. There was bound to be a speech on what it was like to become a woman, and it was certain to ruin everything. Kept private, the information that she was physically old enough to have a baby was thrilling. When she thought of it at odd moments, it made her feel heroic.

Purchasing the ticket didn't take long, and then the bags were sent off and there was nothing more to do but find the right gate.

"Let's not wait in there," Rose Ann said when they were opposite the lounge for her flight. "It's so dreary." She led them to the end of the hallway where there was a couch in front of a big picture window overlooking the airfield.

"Do you have everything?" Teddy asked nervously.

"I think I do."

"Do you have your money and the address and your phrase book?" Rose Ann nodded.

"And do you know what you'll do once you land in Rome, after you go through customs?"

"I'll find out how to work the pay phones, and then I'll call the American Academy, and I expect they'll just tell me to take a cab. I don't think they would send someone all the way out there to pick me up."

"Now," Teddy said, "you have those pills in case you feel airsick?"

"I never feel airsick. I'm sure I won't need them."

"You don't know. You've never been on an overseas flight before."

"That's true," Rose Ann conceded.

And then once again Teddy told Rose Ann not to worry, that he and Alma would be perfectly all right on their own. Looking tired and a little forlorn, he added, "I want you to have a good time over there. It's a gift they've given you, and you should really use it. Travel as much as you want, and stay in your studio as much as you want, and write us. I think we'll be fine—all of us."

When her flight was called, Rose Ann followed the other passengers outside. At the window, Teddy and Alma watched her go up the stairs and when she disappeared into the plane, tried to decide which seat she was occupying. "It's in the middle," Teddy said. "Maybe she'll wave to us." But they couldn't tell if she was waving or not. After the stairway was pushed to the side, the door was closed. The plane moved forward and then turned toward the runway.

"There she goes," Teddy said, and because they both suddenly felt a little lost, he reached for Alma's hand.

12

With Rose Ann gone, the house was too big for just the two of them. Their movements through the many rooms seemed absurd. Days were long and without the background of Rose Ann's voice, there were noticeable gaps of silence. Teddy appeared a little depressed and to escape from her own feelings, Alma spent a lot of time riding her bicycle around the neighborhood.

When they were in the house, they spent most of their time in the kitchen. The other rooms were too empty, but the kitchen, because it was crowded with appliances, felt all right. As soon as school started again, Alma did her homework there, and Teddy, who never used to bring work back from the office, sat at the table with her, filling out forms and writing reports.

"Do you know something?" Alma asked Teddy one evening. At school they had been reading *Robinson Crusoe,* and the idea of someone finding himself without the usual comforts had seemed familiar. She was Man Friday and her father was Crusoe, and the house that they suddenly had to themselves was the island. "This is an adventure," she said. "I'll be glad when Rose Ann gets back, but right now this is okay."

Teddy didn't answer. He was standing in front of the refrigerator surveying the choices. "I'm going to make myself a tomato sandwich. Do you want one?"

"Yes, please. You really miss her a lot, don't you?"

"Miss your mother? Of course I do."

"Does it make you sad that she's left us?"

"At first it did."

"You're not sad about it now?"

"It's hard to be sad all the time," Teddy said. "Other things have been happening, and there are even entire days when I don't think about the fact that she's not here. I miss her, of course, but we're doing things we wouldn't have had a chance to do if she hadn't gone away. Here we are, eating sandwiches for dinner; that's a new experience, isn't it?"

"Yes it is," Alma said.

13

After the first month they discovered a routine. They'd go their separate ways in the daytime—Alma to school, Teddy to his office—and in the evening they'd meet back home and decide what to make for dinner, or else which restaurant to go to. Alma talked about what went on at school, and sometimes Teddy mentioned what happened at the office, but they never talked about Rose Ann. They read her letters; sometimes they came addressed to them both, but sometimes there'd be a separate one for each of them. Alma kept the ones addressed to her in a shoe box in her closet. She'd take them down to read them over again or just to admire the stack she had.

And then December came and Rose Ann's letters didn't mention a return. In January there were only postcards, and at the end of the month, when the nights left a coating of frost on the windows, a heavy, fat envelope with an Italian postmark appeared in their mailbox.

At the top of the page was the familiar heading:

Academia Americana
Via Angelo Masina 5
Roma

Beneath it, the date, and then the widely spaced lines of her mother's broad, upright script. "I love it here. I feel as though I'm finally alive."

Though it was addressed only to Teddy, Alma had opened it when she came home from school. She didn't read the whole thing, though, because it was clear from the first line that it wasn't intended for her. So she left it on the table and went up to her room.

That evening Teddy knocked on her door and said, "Sweetheart, can I come in?"

She knew he would come in anyway, so she didn't answer.

The room was dark, but instead of turning on the light, he stood in the darkness on the hooked rug Rose Ann had once bought from one of her artist friends.

"Did you read her letter?"

"Not all of it."

"But you read enough to discover that she's staying on?"

"Yes," Alma mumbled.

"Do you know why she's staying on?"

"She likes it better there."

"She's very excited to be there. She has a beautiful studio, and she's studying frescoes, and she feels like she's just in the middle of things. We're doing so well by ourselves, she thought she'd just keep on going. Then she'll stay over the summer and travel with some people she met who are also artists, and at the end of the summer she'll come home. That isn't too far away. It's almost spring, and you know how quickly summer goes by."

Teddy sat beside her on the bed and took her hand. "Did you know your mother was the one who gave you your name? We argued about it before you were born. She wanted to name you after a friend of hers. You've heard her talk about the Alma who owned the flower shop? Well, did she tell you that Alma did some pretty brave things during the war?"

"I know," she said. "You don't have to tell me."

"She was a pacifist at a time when it was very unpopular. But she stuck to her principles, and do you know what finally happened to her?"

"No," Alma said.

"She managed to get a few followers, and the same year that you were born she sold her flower business, which hadn't been doing very well anyway, and moved out West with these few people who believed in the same things she did. They bought some land in the desert and worked it and irrigated it and started a small vegetable farm."

"Is she still there?"

"As far as I know," Teddy said. "She used to write us a letter every Christmas, but then she stopped. Apparently, her farm was successful. . . . So, anyway," he went on, "your mother insisted on giving you this name. I wanted to call you Susan. Just think, you would have an ordinary name like that if your mother hadn't been so stubborn. Would you have preferred it if your name had been Susan?"

She shook her head.

14

Academia Americana
Via Angelo Masina 5
Roma
Feb. 7

My dearest Alma
You wouldn't believe it, but I can now hold a twenty-minute conversation
with the woman in the cheese shop. Not about cheese, that would be easy, but
on religion or politics or paintings. You should hear me! She calls me
Rosanna di Roma, and every time I come into the shop she gives me a
present, some cheese or a box of crackers or a canned sauce she's fond of. To
the unpracticed nose her shop smells like vomit, but to me the aroma is
wonderfully exotic.

Alma was sitting on the toilet smoking a cigarette. She stopped at
"exotic" and spread her legs to drop the ashes. They made a hissing
sound when they hit the water.

In a long gray plume the smoke rose from the glowing end of the
cigarette. Watching it ascend to a point midway above her head where it
suddenly dispersed to nothing, she had an impulse to do something
destructive. It took only a second. The stationery was thin, and just
holding the cigarette next to it, it was soon in flames. She dropped it
quickly into the trash and then, just to see the flames again, ignited
the envelope. The paper turned brown and then black as the little
fire consumed it. "Asshole," Alma muttered and just before the fire

reached her fingers, she dropped the remains of that, too, into the trash. Then she finished the cigarette and flushed the butt down the toilet.

Next to her, in the wastebasket, the letter was igniting the other paper, and there was shortly a smell of burning trash. "Asshole," Alma muttered again, as though her mother was responsible for this problem, too. She put the trash can under the bathtub faucet and let it fill with water. Her mistake, though, was that she left it there.

"What's this?" Teddy asked when he went into the bathroom.

"Nothing," Alma said.

"The hell it is. It smells like something was burning in here. Have you been smoking?"

"No," Alma said.

"If you weren't smoking, then what is the smell from and why is the trash can in the bathtub?"

"I was burning a piece of paper, and when I dropped it into the trash can, the other trash caught on fire."

"What did you think would happen when you dropped it into the trash can?"

"I didn't know it would catch on fire."

"Why didn't you bother to think before you did a stupid thing like that? Am I allowed to ask what piece of paper you were burning?"

"It was a letter from Rose Ann."

"A letter from your mother?"

"She went on and on about a cheese shop."

"That couldn't have been all she talked about."

"In the part I read that was all. I didn't want to hear any more about cheese."

"So you burned it? That really makes sense. Now you'll never know what else she said. You can tell yourself your mother had only written to you about cheese. That gives you a perfectly good right to feel sorry for yourself. Very good. That was a really smart, well-thought-out move. Not to mention throwing something that's still burning into a trash can filled with other flammable material. What's the matter with you? What would have happened if you hadn't been here to put it out?"

"I would have started a fire," Alma said, seeing the fire trucks already and hearing the alarms. She looked up at her father's tired face and down at the trash can with blackened debris floating in the water. She might have burned the house down. All of their possessions would be gone—the kitchen table, her clothes, her mother's paintings. All because of a stupid impulse.

"Come here," Teddy said.

They were standing on the charred remains of what had once been their house, and he was inviting her to an embrace. His face was red because he was angry, and a hug from him was the last thing Alma wanted to have. Nevertheless, there they were, and she found herself walking toward him.

Two days later she was sitting in her room smoking with the window open, and she saw herself do it again. She saw herself lean her cheek against the sweater her father had been wearing that afternoon, and once again felt his heavy, even breathing. He had kissed her on the forehead and brought his arms across her back, and even now, two days later, she could give in to the pure comfort of it.

In her imagination she started writing a letter to her mother. "Dear Rose Ann," she said, "why don't you want to come home?"

15

Academia Americana
Via Angelo Masina 5
Roma
Feb. 20

Things happen that you don't expect. Life continues. Nothing is still, the way it is in a painting. It changes all the time. These changes can sometimes reorder your life in dramatic ways. They upset you and cause you pain. But then, when you can accept them, things get easier. The pain disappears.

What I'm trying to say is that this change not only took you by surprise, it took me by surprise, too. It has caused me just as much turmoil and pain as it's causing you. I wish it was easier. I wish I could just come home and say, here I am! But I can't. There are things I still need to discover, and I can only do that on my own. Bear with me. Be patient.

"I miss you," Alma wrote back. "I'm tired of eating sandwiches."

But, with her mother gone, great freedoms were suddenly available. She developed a habit of foul language. She continued to smoke and gave in to the frequent desire to complain. Rose Ann would have prohibited all of it, and that was certainly part of the reason she allowed herself to indulge.

"Goddamnit," Alma exclaimed one evening when she was at the table doing her homework. "I got a C in geography, and that's not fair."

Teddy, who was sitting across from her, looked up. "It probably wasn't fair. I don't think that teacher likes you."

"She doesn't. She never gives me a good mark on anything."

"She must be a bitch."

"She is."

"She and your mother. No one's good to you and nothing's fair. If the world only recognized your gifts, things would be better."

"You're making fun of me," Alma said.

"I'm not making fun of you, I'm commiserating with you. There's a difference."

"What does commiserating mean?"

"It means that I'm sympathetic to all your complaints."

"Thank you," Alma said. But maybe she *had* only deserved a C on her paper; maybe the teacher was right. She looked at her father sitting across from her with the eternal cup of coffee in front of him and thought again of the question that had been on her mind for the past several weeks. She tested it on herself, and, just before she was about to say it to herself again, she heard her small nervous voice ask it out loud. "Do you think she'll really come back at the end of the summer?"

Teddy looked up from his newspaper. "She'll come back when she's ready to. I don't think she'll be gone much longer."

But then another question, one she hadn't rehearsed at all, popped out after that one. "When she comes back, will she want to live with us again?"

"I think so," Teddy said. "Yes, I think she will."

"But she might not."

"That's true, she might not."

"In that case, what will happen to me?"

"We'll put you in some kind of home. Neither of us would want to take care of you in that case, so we'll probably just enroll you in some kind of institution. Or I guess we could disguise the fact that we no longer wanted you and say that for educational purposes we were sending you to a boarding school on the other side of the country. Or we could just abandon you, we could just leave you here to fend for yourself. You're old enough to be on your own."

"You're teasing me."

"I'm not. I'm letting you see how unreasonable your fears are."

She also began to get breasts. She hoped she would get ones as big as Rose Ann's and wondered what her chances were with her father's addition to her gene pool. As soon as she came home from school, she'd run up to her room to look at her breasts in the mirror. Actually, "tits" was the word she used because that was what they were more than anything else: two small protrusions on her rib cage.

Once in the privacy of her room, she'd turn on the overhead light, lift up her shirt, and survey herself in the mirror on her bedroom door. They were there all right; they were even beginning to make a noticeable slope in her profile. Soon she would buy herself a bra, but not yet. She wanted to keep it secret for a while yet, and a bra would announce it to everyone.

Also, she didn't want to buy just a cupless bra; she wanted to wait till she was ready for the real thing. The Ukrainian girl had had a real one for several years now, and Nancy had begun to wear one, and a few of the other girls in her class had them, too. If all you were good for was a cupless, you might as well wait. She made this decision during a session in front of the mirror. There was no rush, she advised herself, she would have to be patient.

Also, it seemed as though there were certain things you went through before owning such an article. It wasn't something you could have just because you wanted it. Certain things had to be performed. She wondered if kissing was one of them. Was that what the other girls had done? Was that what made them different?

"I've been kissed more times than I can count," Nancy confided to her. "You just hold your breath and wait till it's over. And you have to keep your mouth closed because some of them try to stick their tongues in, and if you have your mouth closed they can't do it. Or at least they can't do it without first asking. If they ask, it's not so bad because then you're prepared. You just hope they don't swish it around for too long."

18

When she came home from school that afternoon, she had intended to go right up to her room and start on the homework that had been piling up over the last few days. But instead, when she got to the house, she put her books down on the back steps and set off for a walk through the neighborhood. The sun was out, and she didn't feel like going in yet. There had been something frightening about the big, empty house. It had looked too dark and still.

The block they lived on was residential, and since it was surrounded on all sides by other blocks with only houses on them, there wasn't much traffic. Dogs roamed the neighborhood freely, and young children wandered about without supervision. Often, a whole street was closed off by kids playing dodge ball.

The houses had interlocking backyards, and while some people had put up fences and others had planted shrubs, a path had been created over the years, and a person could get from one end of the block to the other without walking on the sidewalk. It had been a while since she'd been on the path, but the landmarks never changed much. It went under the tree house in the Turpins' backyard, and then, where she had to squeeze through a hedge, it took her past the hammock. Strung between two half-dead willows, the hammock had been there ever since she could remember. It was moldy and rotten, with only parts of the webbing still intact. They used to take a running jump and land in the center of it just for the excitement of falling through. Someone once had been hurt that way, but she couldn't remember who, or when it had been.

Then there was Mr. Grady's where there was an old truck parked along the boundary line. The game was to lock each other inside it, until one time someone had left Robin Habramovitch in there and forgotten her. When she hadn't come home for supper, her parents had called the police and after that, Grady took off the door.

The path crossed the Steffanellis' yard where there were little trees wrapped in burlap in the winter. The short, stubby forms sticking up from the frozen ground used to scare her. They looked like people without arms or legs, and when she was very young, if she was caught walking back to their house in the dark, she'd have to walk very slowly, her eyes on the trees, so none of them would dare to come after her. If she happened to think of them as she was falling asleep, she'd be awake for hours, staring into the night for any sign of their awful shapes.

At the Yeagers', which was the only run-down house on the block, she walked under the swing set. She could picture Cheryl Yeager pumping the air as she sailed back and forth on her swing. When the family had moved away, they had left the swings behind. The people who had moved in after them never chased anyone away, so the swings became common property. The neighborhood kids played on them all day long, laughing and shouting and filling the air with a creaking sound as the rusty hinges went back and forth on the poles. No one ever came out. One kid said an old man lived there, another said it was two sisters, but Alma had never actually seen anyone. Now, with peeling paint and blank windows, the house seemed disturbing, and Alma walked past it quickly.

Next was the Daytons' where there was a gazebo and a lily pond. They used to sneak to the pond on spring evenings to try and catch frogs. When it looked as though no one were home, they'd sit in the gazebo and play make-believe games. They were serious, complicated dramas about husbands and wives. Alma was usually cast as the husband, and Nancy, with whom she played these games, was usually the wife. Sometimes their characters fought together, and sometimes they seemed to love one another. When they were in love, Alma would have to kiss Nancy on the lips passionately. One time they were down on the floor of the gazebo pretending to be on a bed having sex, and they didn't notice the lights go on in the Daytons' house. The back door opened, and a voice called out nervously, "Who's there?"

They stayed crouched down until they heard the door close, and then, giggling, they tiptoed off.

The path went along the edge of Mrs. Wilkens's property. She had high, impenetrable hedges because she didn't like children or dogs wandering in her yard. She was afraid dogs would attack Caspar, her cat, and children would walk through her flower beds. But there used to be a break in the hedge where they could peek in at the yard. They could see fruit trees, flowers, and, in the middle, a marble birdbath. When Alma was little, it had seemed like the garden in a fairytale; as she passed the hedge, she wondered how it would appear to her now. She found the break in the bushes and knelt down to peer through the opening.

But there was someone sitting right in front of the birdbath, looking straight at her. It was Mrs. Wilkens sitting on an ordinary kitchen chair with her hands folded in her lap and one leg tucked under her so that it looked as though one of her legs were missing.

She wasn't doing anything but sitting, and though she was looking straight ahead, Alma knew she couldn't see her. Mrs. Wilkens's gaze was directed toward the top of the hedge, and her eyes had an unfocused look about them. Was she sitting there because she had been gardening and had suddenly grown tired? But the neatness of her pose made it look deliberate, as though every afternoon she brought her kitchen chair out to the yard and sat on it.

After a while Alma grew tired of kneeling down. Yet she was afraid to leave; what if something was wrong? Mrs. Wilkens looked so peculiar she wondered if maybe she was dead. Or what if she was about to die? Deciding she would wait a little longer, she stayed in her cramped position and watched. But then Mrs. Wilkens stood up and slowly walked back toward the house. When she disappeared, Alma looked at the empty chair, and then she, too, walked on.

The Juroes' was next. She remembered the relief she used to feel when the chimney of their house came into view. She would gallop across the yard and run up to the back door and pull it open. She could picture herself with tangled hair and filthy playclothes, sweaty and hot and pleasantly tired from all her wanderings. But the exhaustion was purely physical because, when she was little, she knew how to find comfort. If her mother wasn't in the kitchen, she'd go to the bottom of the stairs and shout, "Rose Ann!"

At school the next day it was hard to concentrate. Wherever she looked, she could see Mrs. Wilkens staring toward her with the same sad, expressionless face. When she got home, she left her books on the back steps and walked across the yard to the path. At Mrs. Wilkens's property she knelt down to the opening in the hedge and peered through. It was just like before. The chair was in front of the birdbath, and Mrs. Wilkens was sitting with one leg tucked under her and her hands folded in her lap. She was looking toward Alma but with an unseeing expression. This time her lips were moving. Was she talking to herself?

Alma stayed in her crouched position, unable to move. Something fell from Mrs. Wilkens's lap and when she picked it up, Alma saw that it was a string of beads. Had Mrs. Wilkens only been praying? She had seen people praying in church the time she had gone with Nancy. She had liked the singing and the candles, but the kneeling and standing had confused her. She had tried the holy water, learned how to cross herself, and Nancy had shown her what a rosary looked like.

She had assumed those were the things that made prayer work. But maybe it was more simple than that. And if you could do it in your backyard on an ordinary chair, then maybe you could do it anywhere. Maybe you could say anything, too.

As she looked at the chair, she thought to herself that of all the people in the world she would pray for, she would pray for her parents. And if praying only meant whispering about somethings that you wanted, she would like to do that. Before she stood up, she said to herself, "May Rose Ann always love my father. May the three of us be a family forever."

19

The season was changing. The birds that had left for the winter were coming back in noisy, excited flocks. Sometimes they'd settle on the telephone wires and twitter for hours. At the sides of the house, green shoots poked up from the flower beds and the pussy willow she passed every day was covered with soft, gray buds.

Then one morning everything was yellow. The forsythia had bloomed, and someone even brought a sprig to school to give to their teacher, Miss Fitzhugh, during Practical Thinking.

The boy who gave the forsythia to Miss Fitzhugh was named Andrew. He had just moved into the neighborhood, and sometimes as Alma was going to school she'd see him walking ahead of her. She'd been tempted to call out his name and get him to slow down and walk with her, but for one reason or another, she hadn't.

Then one day she did. It just happened. His name slipped out of her mouth before she had time to consider what she was doing. There she was, calling "Andrew," and, because she said it loud enough, he heard her.

"What?" he replied, turning around.

"Slow down," she said.

He waited for her at the end of the block, and as they walked together he told her about the school he had gone to before this one. All the way there they talked. The lawns and houses she had passed a million times were different, and she herself had changed. She felt as though she had expanded outward, so that a little bit of the warm spring air had been included in her body.

Before he moved there, Andrew had lived in the country. He could ride a horse, he said, milk a cow, and slaughter a chicken. He knew how to track a deer and once had shot at one, but it had only been wounded, it didn't die.

"How did you feel about that?"

"Lousy," Andrew said. "He wasn't hurt bad, I followed him a little ways, and I think he was okay."

"Why would you want to kill a deer?"

"I don't know," Andrew said. "But I wanted to."

They were having this conversation behind the garage at her house. He had waited for her after school, and they had walked home together. When they got to her house, she hadn't wanted to go in yet, and she hadn't wanted to sit on the porch in plain view of the whole neighborhood, so they had ended up there. It occurred to her, when she led him through the weeds and they sat down on one of the benches that were being stored back there for the winter, that this was the kind of place where two people could get into trouble. It would have made more sense to invite a boy she hardly knew to sit on the back steps with her. But she had taken him behind the garage, tripping over the ladder someone had thrown back there, to the bench. She had felt like it. And if the bench hadn't been there, they would have sat on the ground.

Because the wood was damp, he took off his jacket and spread it underneath them. Then she saw his arm coming around her shoulders. From the way he pulled her close to him, it was obvious he was experienced. Feeling frightened, she waited, and soon enough his mouth was approaching her own. But there wasn't anything to scare her. Pressed against hers, his lips were softer than anything she had ever touched before. She felt an enormous relief. Here was something that had no resistance. When he pulled away, she asked if they could kiss again.

After the second time, it was clear she didn't need to ask permission. She could simply do it. Each time it was easier, and much later, when she heard her father pull into the driveway, she felt she knew Andrew more completely than she had ever known anyone in her life.

At the same time, he perplexed her. "How could you be the person who shoots a deer and then be the only one who brings flowers to Miss Fitzhugh?"

"What?" he asked.

She repeated the question.

"There's nothing wrong with wanting to shoot a deer," he told her. "You just want to. They're so pretty you just want to get as close as you can to them."

"Then take a pair of binoculars."

"It's not the same thing," he said.

They kissed some more after that, but she was nervous again. Also, it was getting chilly. She could feel him shivering through his sweater. "I have to go in," she said. They stood up and as he put on his jacket Alma noticed that one of the fingers on his right hand was missing. She had noticed something odd about his hand before, but it hadn't seemed important. "You're missing a finger!" she blurted out.

He put his hand back in his pocket and gave her an embarrassed look.

"Could you tell me what happened?" she asked in a gentler voice. "Were you born with it?"

"It was a few years back," he said. "A piece of machinery chewed it up."

"It must have hurt."

"A little." He brought his hand out to show her. "The blade cut across here and here, but they were able to sew this one back on."

"That's awful," Alma said. "Did you ever try to pray that you would have your finger again?"

"They don't grow back if you lose them. Did you think that they did?" He shrugged his shoulders. "It happened, that's all. I'm lucky to have the rest of my hand."

Impressed by his matter-of-factness, she walked back to the house, applying the same common sense to her own situation. When she came into the kitchen, Teddy asked her where she had been.

"Behind the garage kissing Andrew." It happened.

"I'm sorry I asked," he said. "Who is Andrew?"

"A boy in my class."

"Well, before you do anything else with him, wait until your mother comes home."

"I'm only in ninth grade. I'm not going to get pregnant. It just turns out that he's a very interesting person."

"Why are you telling me this?" Teddy asked. "Why doesn't someone your age want to keep their first kiss a secret?"

"Because it's not my first kiss," she lied.

"Well, whichever kiss it is, number one or number two . . ." He was standing in front of the icebox and pulled some celery out of a bag on the bottom shelf.

"What are we having for dinner."

"Carrots and celery."

"With what?"

"I'm not sure yet. We'll figure it out. Alma," he said, "is your strategy to make me feel worried so that I'll tell Rose Ann and then Rose Ann will come home? If you're going to kiss a boy, kiss him because you want to and not for any other reason. And then don't tell me about it, please. Kissing is private." He walked to the sink and turned on the water to wash the celery. She dropped her books on the kitchen table and went upstairs. She shut her door and sat on her bed. She didn't even feel like lifting her blouse to look at herself in the mirror; she didn't move. She sat and looked at the wall over her desk.

They kissed a lot after that. When Andrew's face was close to her own, she noticed the corner of his mouth. When she was looking at his hand, she noticed the scar where his finger used to be. It gave her pleasure to look at both of these places. The spot on his mouth seemed gentle, and the place on his hand seemed strong. When she looked there, it wasn't hard to imagine him stalking a deer. She would picture him walking barefoot through the forest wearing just a loincloth, and then she'd see him standing in a clearing listening for the sounds of an animal. He was exotic.

"If you tell me what it's like being a boy, I'll tell you what it's like being a girl."

"What?"

"Couldn't you try to describe it?" she asked.

"What?"

In the shade his pupils were large and black, and his hair, which was rumpled, stood up around his face like feathers. He was a rare bird. She needed to get a close look at him, or she might never have another chance. She pulled her blouse out of her pants and lifted it over her face.

"I see them," he said. "But they're not very big, are they?" He put his hands on her breasts gently, as though he were touching something sacred.

The next time she tried a different tactic. "Will you let me take a look?"

"What?"

She pointed to the place where his penis was supposed to be.

"Later," he said. "I have to go home."

"Why can't you show me now?"

"I can't," he said, and he turned bright red.

One time she took his hand and put it on her nipple, and as they were kissing, his tongue pushed in between her teeth and touched her own tongue. His hand stayed on her nipple, and it was squeezing it, but the other one had started pushing at his pants. She saw him reach inside his fly and pull something out through layers of cloth. For a while it was hidden under his sweater, but then he moved the sweater and said, "Look."

Once when Alma came into the house after making out, there was someone in the kitchen with her father. She was introduced as Gloria, and Alma later found out that she sold life insurance in the same office where her father worked.

Gloria was remarkable. She was taller than Teddy, and she had long blonde hair that was piled haphazardly on top of her head and fastened with pins that she was always securing. She did this without a mirror. She simply took the loose pin out of her hair and stuck it back in, without appearing to worry about how it looked.

When Gloria was there, Alma and Teddy had a lot to talk about. Gloria listened to them with the attentiveness of an entire spellbound audience, and often Alma would say things she hadn't realized she had been thinking about. She learned about herself when she was talking with Gloria. Also, Gloria seemed to know a lot of things and what was perplexing or considered wrong, she seemed to accept.

For instance, about Rose Ann's year away from home, Gloria said, "She did something she knew she wanted to do. I call that being a responsible adult." About Rose Ann's frequent silences, she said, "She wanted a vacation from her family. Let her have one. If you feel like speaking to her, then *you* sit down and write her a letter." About life insurance, she said, "I wanted a job I could do anywhere in the United States, that I wouldn't have to think about on my days off, and that would give me enough money and time to travel." About what went on between boys and girls who were Alma's age, Gloria said, "Well, Alma, this is just the beginning."

It always shocked Alma when she noticed that Gloria wasn't beautiful. She wasn't busty like Rose Ann and yet she was bigger and awkward looking. She had gray, far apart eyes, and her nose was long and bony. Also, she was too thin. She dressed in a plain way, without perfume or jewelry. And she didn't embarrass people or exaggerate things or try to be dramatic.

Once, when they were alone, Alma asked Teddy, "Are you going to want to divorce Rose Ann and marry Gloria?"

"No," Teddy said. "Rose Ann is my wife; Gloria is my friend."

"But don't you love Gloria?"

"My feelings for Gloria are none of your business."

Andrew often took his penis out of his pants now, and she had even touched it. She was surprised that it was as warm and soft as it was, and touching it made it seem less terrible. It was only a part of his body, she reasoned, not unlike his elbow. She tried to imagine what Gloria would do if she were ever asked to touch something like that, and since Gloria was always so self-assured, Alma assumed she wouldn't decline. That's what I call taking responsibility, she'd say. That's what I'd call seeing an act through to its finish.

But then something else happened. They were behind the garage, and things had progressed a little further. He was squeezing her nipple, she was touching his penis, and all of a sudden he was pushing against her.

He looked like he was about to cry. He grabbed his penis out of her hand and closed his eyes. It was larger than she had ever seen it, but when he let it go, it was small again. Then he opened his eyes and looked at her sheepishly.

"I'm sorry," he said. "I couldn't help it." He wiped the tip with his obligatory ninth-grade handkerchief and tucked himself back in his pants. "I'm really sorry," he said again, "I didn't mean it to happen." Suddenly he looked very sleepy and to get him to notice her again, she asked him to tell her what it was like.

"What?"

"What do you think I mean?"

"I can't tell you that," he said.

"Why not?"

"Because it can't be explained to a girl. And even if it could, you wouldn't understand anyway."

· · · · · 20 · · · · · ·

"Alma," Miss Fitzhugh said, "if Ruby has two fifty-pound bags of potatoes, and Mary buys a third of them, and Nancy buys a quarter, how many pounds does each of them have?"

On Wednesday afternoon between two and three o'clock they did word problems in Practical Thinking. They were exercises not only in math but also in vocabulary comprehension and common sense. As the year went on, they grew progressively harder, but Fitzhugh had given her the first one for that day, and that one was always easiest. Alma had the numbers down on her pad. All she had to do was add and subtract, and when she had the answer her voice sailed over the small, regular waves of background sounds. "Mary has thirty-three pounds, Nancy has twenty-five, and Ruby has forty-two."

"Now," Miss Fitzhugh went on, "if Ruby wants to keep 12 percent of the potatoes she has left and sell the rest to the next customer for 2.7 cents per half a pound, which is 2.5 cents less than the price she sold them for to her first customers, how much money will Ruby have made?"

Miss Fitzhugh put down her book and with a benevolent expression peered down the row at Alma. "Do the figuring in your notebook, and when you have the answer, write it on the board. While you're working on this problem, the rest of us will be doing problem number one on page thirty-seven."

The light coming in through the windows was golden. Everything was benign; everything was at rest. The geraniums on the desk were a deep green, and the cracked plaster walls were glowing. The faces around her seemed sculptured. The light settled on the different planes: the plane of someone's cheek, the plane of someone else's desk. The shoulders of the person in front of her sloped gently under the faded checks of his shirt. The air was buoyant, and it kept her floating. She didn't know the answer to this or anything else that might be confusing, but she wasn't helpless. There was a direction for her to move toward, a goal. She couldn't say what it was, but she could feel the certainty of it spreading across her chest. There was an entrance. There was an entrance to everything, and none of the exits were barred. Even now someone was tapping her knee. She looked around, and Buddy Diamond, who sat behind her, placed a finger on his lips and pressed something toward her under the desk. It was a very small piece of folded paper. She opened it on her lap, and conscious of Miss Fitzhugh's patient glances from the front of the room, looked down.

But it was only a number, nothing else—no decimal point, no dollar sign, just the numbers eight, zero, two and no name. Was it eight hundred and two or eight dollars and two cents?

She threw the paper far into the recess of her desk, pushed her chair back, and walked across the gray linoleum squares to the blackboard. First the chalk squeaked, and then it slipped mysteriously out of her hand. Conscious of the many faces beating into her back, she picked it up, drew a dollar sign, and deciding it must be eight dollars, wrote eight, decimal point, zero, two.

"Very good," Miss Fitzhugh said happily. "Now, Buddy, if Vincent has five ladders and two of them are twenty feet long and the others are thirty-three feet long, and the house he is going to paint is three stories high, the first story being fifteen feet, the next story being thirteen feet, and the third being half the height of the first . . ."

"Thank you," Alma said.

"You're welcome," Andrew replied. He looked pleased. But then his face turned crimson, and sending her a glance from his dark, wide-open eyes, he peered down at the pavement.

"Wasn't it you who sent me the answer for that problem? That problem we did in class today, wasn't it you?"

"I can't do those," he said. "It wasn't me."

They were standing at the edge of the schoolyard watching the hundreds of people pouring out through the doors. Among all of those anonymous faces there was someone who had come to her rescue. It pleased her that it had been done so secretly. Had it been Buddy Diamond? It would have been easiest for him, since he sat behind her and he was good at math. He was probably the best in the class.

Since it was early Friday dismissal, there was a lot of fighting and yelling in the schoolyard. Most people had made plans for the rest of the afternoon. Andrew was going to play baseball; Nancy, who she didn't like much anymore anyway, had to babysit; and there was nothing for Alma to do but go home. Maybe she could catch up with Buddy Diamond, except that he was probably playing baseball, too. "Diamond's on your team isn't he?"

"He's the shortstop," Andrew said glumly. "Listen, Alma, could you come here a second?" Without waiting, he pulled her around the corner of the fence. Then he blocked her view of the schoolyard and cupping his hand over his mouth began to whisper something.

"What?" Someone two feet away was calling someone else a queer. It was the kind of thing Diamond was always saying. "Let me see what's going on," Alma said, trying to get Andrew to move aside.

He grabbed her arms. "Will you listen to me for a second? I have to tell you something." His face was as contorted as it had been behind the garage. "Alma, I think about you. Did you hear what I said? I THINK ABOUT YOU ALL THE TIME."

"Andrew . . . ," someone called. "Aren't you coming?"

He released her arms and gave her a desperate look, and then he walked off. As she watched him, she heard him say it again. She counted it out. Eight syllables even—nothing left over. A complete statement. The pure pleasure of seven measly words. "Andrew!" she called. He turned around and she waved.

On the way home in the yellow light, the branches cut long, thin shapes against the sky. Maybe Teddy would be home early. He didn't know it was early dismissal, but maybe he would feel like taking the afternoon off and going somewhere with her. If they went downtown, maybe he would be in the mood to let her buy something.

Gloria's car was in the driveway, which was a good sign. Maybe the three of them could do something. She opened the back door and left her books and jacket on the table. The house was quiet. Though Teddy's briefcase was sitting by the refrigerator, she didn't hear any voices. Picking a banana from the fruit bowl, she headed out of the kitchen. Her father called it ambulatory mastication, this habit they shared of walking at the same time they were eating. He usually did it with a cup of coffee, and she liked to do it when she was having a snack. Bananas were a perfect mobile food because they were self-contained and left no crumbs.

In the middle of that merry observation she walked into the living room. Because they were standing at the dark end, she didn't see them at first. But then the shadow moved, and she was staring at the shape they made before understanding what it was. At first she thought it must be another man, so strange was it to see her father embracing another woman. His eyes were closed, and there was an expression of perfect happiness on his face. Gloria was moaning softly. They were rocking back and forth, her father's hands on Gloria's behind, stroking it. His knees were locked around her leg, her fingers moving up and down his back.

Alma turned to leave, but Gloria looked up and saw her. "Your daughter's home," she whispered.

"I want you to understand," her father said, pouring them each a cup of coffee. He grasped the back of a chair and looked into space. "Besides being thinking creatures, we're also part animals. We enjoy touching each other and things like that."

As if Gloria wasn't there, she said, "I thought you said she was just a friend."

"She is and that's why we were doing what we were doing. Sometimes very good friends like to kiss one another. When you're older and when you've found someone that you care about very much the way I care about your mother, this won't seem so confusing. I'm sorry you walked in on us, but I want to reassure you that nothing was going on that you have to worry about."

"I'm not worried."

"Good. I'm glad to hear that." He patted Alma's head. "Well," he said cheerfully, "this is all a part of growing up, isn't it?"

She knew he wanted her to give a sign that she had forgiven him. But to look at anyone was impossible, much less attempt a smile. So she took her jacket and walked out the door.

Thick with the chatter of lawn mowers, the air carried her across the backyard to the path. She stooped down at the opening in the hedge and saw Mrs. Wilkens on her hands and knees weeding her garden. She couldn't help but picture her sitting on the chair praying. Then, as she remembered the little prayer she had said for her family, tears came to her eyes. She turned around to look at their house. The windows were black shapes reflecting the sun; she couldn't even tell if Teddy was still in the kitchen. Fuck him, she thought.

She walked back to the garage. Creeping behind it, she decided to sit on the bench for a while. The sky above her was white, the clouds thin and flat. Nothing moved. She wondered how her father could be so stupid. Didn't it mean anything to him that he was married? She heard the kitchen door slam and then the sudden roar of an engine. Peering around the corner, she saw Gloria's car backing onto the street. Let him worry, she thought to herself. Let him think something had happened to her. She wasn't going home yet.

She rang Andrew's doorbell. A dog barked and some moments later his mother, with the same preoccupied look that she always had, opened the door. "Yes?" she asked distractedly before noticing who it was.

As Alma saw the food stains on her apron and smelled the aroma of cooking behind her, a hatred for this tiny woman and her ordinary household made her unable to speak at first. "Is Andrew home?" she finally asked.

"Andrew's playing baseball; wasn't he there? I'm sure he told me that's what he was doing. Oh, dear," she said, wiping her forehead with the back of her hand. "Don't tell me you went to the field and didn't see him."

"No," Alma said. "I haven't been there yet." Without saying good-bye, she turned around and walked down the steps.

The baseball diamond was across the street from the church. Andrew was in the outfield, his red shirt a spot of color against the dirt. He waved and jogged toward her.

"Hi," she said. "How's the game?"

"I think we're losing. Nothing much is happening. What's going on?"

She shrugged. "Want to do something with me?" she asked.

"Like what?"

"I don't know. Maybe go somewhere for dinner?"

"Where do you want to go?"

That he would want specifics annoyed her. "I just thought we'd never done that before and maybe it would be nice. Could you get some money?"

"How much?"

"I don't know. Do you want to do it?"

"What?"

"Go out to dinner. What did you think I meant?"

A new batter came to the mound. Andrew picked up his glove and said, "I have to go. Just wait for me, will you?"

She lay back on the grass. The sun warmed her face. The shouts from the field, puncturing the tight fabric of the afternoon, were inconsequential. Her father had fallen in love with Gloria, and he and Rose Ann would get divorced. She covered her eyes. There was yelling on the field, an argument about the rules. First there was one voice and then two or three others joined in. "Shut up!" someone bellowed. "Go soak your head in a pail of water." Get a hold of yourself, she thought. Maybe nothing would come of it. But the way they were standing there, their bodies fit together like they belonged. "See ya later," someone called. Like they were in love. "Hey, Alma," Andrew shouted. "Game's over." She sat up, saw him in the distance loping toward her. His shirt blew out like a flag, a warning hoisted against the flat white sky. She remembered her mother's words as she had packed her suitcase. "Nice," she had said. But it wasn't nice, living with just her father. Her face felt large and swollen. Her body felt completely hollow.

When she let herself in that night she heard the television on in the living room. That made everything seem even stranger; her father never watched TV. Just so he'd know she was home, she turned on the faucet for a glass of water. "You're back," he said, peeking around the door.

"Yes," she replied, daring him to say anything else.

"I was a little worried. You could have called."

She only looked at him, and then she turned around and went upstairs.

The next morning, after she was sure he had left, she went into his room and sprayed some of Rose Ann's perfume on her wrists. She opened the first drawer of Rose Ann's bureau and touched the neatly folded scarves. The drawers underneath were mostly empty, but opening this one, it was hard to believe her mother was gone.

Downstairs, he had left her a pot of oatmeal on the stove, coffee in the coffeepot, and as though she were a guest and wouldn't know where things were kept, he had put a bowl and cup out on the table. Also, there was a napkin with a message written in pencil.

"How about a movie tonight?" it said.

She could see his hands on Gloria's back, kneading the cloth of her dress. They slipped down to her behind, and Gloria moaned and crushed her hip against him. Their mouths were pressed together, moving against each other, opened wide. She was running her hands up and down his back. Then she saw Alma.

Screw the oatmeal. She poured herself some coffee and had a cigarette. The phone rang.

"It's me," Gloria said. "Let's talk. I'll pick you up in ten minutes and we'll go somewhere."

"I was going to do something else."

"Really? Is it something that can wait? This is pretty important. I know how upset you are. Give me a chance."

"What would we do?"

"Anything," Gloria said. "Whatever you want."

"I really can't. I have plans with Andrew."

"That's not good enough. I'll pick you up in ten minutes and we'll go downtown. Will you be waiting outside?"

"I guess so," Alma said. She hung up the phone, finished her cigarette, and used it to light the next. She combed her hair. She glanced at herself in the mirror but didn't make an appraisal. How she looked didn't matter. She lit a third cigarette. Then she heard Gloria turn down the street, her car roaring and bucking. She had inherited it from a younger brother and besides the special muffler, it was jacked up in back and had stripes along the side and fancy hubcaps. Also, it was a wreck. Teddy refused to ride in it, but she had always wanted to see what it would be like.

Gloria pulled up just as Alma stepped outside. "What are we going to do?" she asked, opening the door.

"I thought we could walk around, get some lunch, and in the meantime we could talk. How does that sound?"

"I just had breakfast," Alma said, lighting up.

On the radio a woman was telling them about spectacular buys at Carpet City. Her insinuating tone spilled over the dusty seats and invaded the grainy texture of the windshield. Alma wished she had remembered to bring sunglasses; the heat coming in through the glass and striking her arms made her feel unprotected. She watched the smoke drive the glare away and, as they started down the street, announced that she hoped they would take the expressway.

But Gloria had a strange way of getting there, making a turn every other block and pulling them deeper into the neighborhood. They went down blocks Alma hadn't been on in years and then suddenly, dwarfing the squat houses, towering over the sloping roofs, were the huge, concrete risers for the expressway. Gloria pulled onto the entrance ramp, came around the curve, and moved into traffic. Her hair was down and the wind was gently pulling it out of the window. She grabbed it back and stuck it under her shirt, but the wind worked it out again. She held it in her hand for a while and then asked Alma to look for a rubber band in the glove compartment. They crossed to the middle lane, a slow car was in front of them, and Gloria moved into the left.

There wasn't a rubber band in the glove compartment, or at least she couldn't find one with all the crap that was stuffed in there. Gloria was passing the car on their right and had her blinker on to switch back into the middle. Alma slammed the glove compartment shut, thinking that she didn't just have to sit there and submit to whatever the two of them concocted. It was obvious that Teddy had put Gloria up to this, and it wouldn't work. How dare she pretend to be her friend. Nor was Gloria her mother, and there was, above all, nothing they needed to talk about.

"You didn't see one in there?"

"No," Alma said. Now they were back in the slow lane, going a meager forty-five miles an hour. "Can't you go any faster?" she asked.

After that there wasn't any talking. Gloria pressed on the accelerator, and the car jumped forward. Alma watched the speedometer and smoked her cigarette. She could see Gloria's profile: her eyes following the road, her mouth unmoving, tightly closed. They were dropping down into the shopping district. The road pushed them toward the buildings and then, at the last moment, swung them over the river where a flock of gulls was circling the water. One broke away from the group, dipped down over a wave, and flew up again. They were going seventy-five. The music coming from the radio was covered by the sound of the car, and all Alma was aware of was a wispy, ineffective rhythm. Since the exit they wanted was coming up, Gloria crossed into the next lane. She still hadn't slowed down, and the exit was just beyond the hood but two lanes over. The big, loud car moved across the dividing line and streaked onto the ramp, taking the curve at a dangerous speed and hardly slowing at all until they got to the light.

Suddenly it was very quiet. Alma realized she'd been gripping the door handle. Gloria took her hands off the wheel and wiped them on her pants. "You shouldn't make people perform for you," she said. "It's spoiled and ugly and stupid, and I thought you were smarter than that."

"Maybe," Alma said. But she wasn't the one who needed to be chastened. "You can't tell me anything."

"What's that supposed to mean?"

"You're not so smart yourself."

"Do you want to explain that?"

"I'm talking about a couple of things. For instance, you didn't *have* to drive as fast as you did. For instance, my father is married and my mother is coming home soon. They'll get back together, so what's going to happen to you?"

"I don't know," Gloria said quietly. "I can't predict the future."

She turned down a side street and pulled into a parking lot. Opening the door, she told the attendant they'd be gone most of the afternoon. "Are you coming?" she asked, ducking back into the car. Alma opened the door on her side and got out. She followed Gloria down the street, keeping her eye on the green dress as it moved in and out of the crowds.

Afraid of losing her, Alma quickened her pace. But Gloria had tricked her. She stepped out of a doorway as Alma went past. "Caught you," she said, taking her arm. Her grip was light and cool; Alma slipped out easily.

"Are we going to go on like this all day long?" she asked.

"Maybe," Alma said. She sounded like the spoiled child Rose Ann always hated.

"I think not," Gloria replied. She flung her hair over her shoulder and walked briskly ahead. Her dress was ugly and out of fashion and rumpled as though she'd been wearing it for days. Yesterday, it had melted into the room so easily that Alma hadn't seen them at first. They had done it, of course. Probably more than once. She tried to imagine them in a bed together naked. What if Gloria got pregnant? There wouldn't be any question then that Teddy would leave Rose Ann. Maybe Gloria was trying to get pregnant so that would happen. She was probably tired of living alone.

She'd stopped in front of a department store window. Alma considered crossing the street, but then how would she get home? She didn't know which bus to take. Seeing nothing else to do, she stopped at the same window. It was a group of women playing golf. Posed in alluring postures, they wore starched white shirts and very short shorts. Only one was swinging a club, the rest were watching.

"They have a nice restaurant in here. Are you hungry?"

They passed through the revolving doors into the coolness of the store. Gloria led her past hats and cosmetics, and at shoes they got on the escalator. Alma looked down at the spots of color, the shapes of people milling about below them, and then finally at the blonde hairs on Gloria's arm where it lay on the railing in front of Alma's. She couldn't understand how someone could fall in love with this woman. She didn't fit in. Certainly not in a department store—she was so obviously unconcerned with fashion. Maybe she was enormously sexy. Maybe she knew all kinds of sexy tricks. Or maybe it was just that she was more accommodating than Rose Ann.

The restaurant was crowded. Women were talking to one another, looking at the menu, laughing and gesturing. There was a steady buzz, a community of female voices. They found seats by the window looking out on the river. When the waitress came, Gloria asked Alma if she'd like a beer. Though she would have loved to have one, she said no, water was fine. They ordered their sandwiches and the waitress left. Alma glanced out the window.

"What frightened you about finding us like that?" Gloria asked.

"I wasn't frightened."

"It must have been shocking to see your father kiss someone besides your mother. I'm sorry you happened to see it. But your father and I want to make it very clear to you that, although it might have seemed like something of great significance, it wasn't. Teddy is a wonderful friend to me. I like him very much. In fact, he's probably the best friend I've had in a long time. But I would never do anything to threaten his relationship with your mother. I'm looking forward to meeting Rose Ann when she comes home. I think I'll like her."

Alma took a sip of water.

"Does anything I'm saying make you feel a little bit better? Would you say something back to me? You're so quiet I have no idea what you're thinking." Gloria poured some beer into Alma's coffee cup, but Alma didn't touch it. "Talk to me," Gloria said.

"I can't." She looked her adversary full in the face.

"Why not?" Gloria asked softly. "I don't understand."

"Because you're my father's lover."

"Haven't you heard any of the things I just said to you?"

"Yes," Alma replied. "I heard them all."

Their sandwiches came. They ate them carefully. When they were finished, Gloria paid the bill and they left. Walking back to the car they didn't say anything. The radio played all the way home. There was a song she liked, but she braced herself against the rhythm, didn't give in. When they pulled into the driveway, Gloria put her hand on Alma's knee to restrain her. She said, "You could save yourself all of this torment if you'd allow yourself to believe me."

"I'll think about it," Alma replied, opening the door.

She did think about it. It occurred to her that it might after all be true. And if it wasn't true, what could she do about it anyway? It shouldn't matter to her one way or the other. It was her father's life.

When Teddy came home she knew right away that he'd already

spoken to Gloria. By the way he walked from the car to the back door, she could tell he was thinking about it. When he opened the door, he said, "There you are." Then he put down his briefcase and went to the coffeepot. "I understand the afternoon didn't go so well," he said, pouring himself a cup. "Maybe this is just one of those things that takes a little time. Your parents' private lives aren't a subject that's open for discussion so I'm not willing to hash it out with you, but what I *can* tell you is that there is nothing going on that you need to worry about. When Rose Ann gets back, life will return to normal."

"I hope so," she said and went up to her room.

21

She decided to tell Rose Ann. There she was in Europe, painting and going to museums and feeling pretty lonely, and here he was lovey-dovey with Gloria. Right in the middle of the afternoon, the door wide open. At least it would make Rose Ann return. Would she warn Teddy that she was coming, or would she suddenly descend when they were right in the middle of it? Caught in the act, ha! ha! She would be furious.

As far as Alma could remember, there had been only one time when Rose Ann had been really angry. It had been directed toward Teddy, so Alma hadn't seen the whole of it. But the edges she'd been allowed to glimpse were startling. She had watched from the hallway. Rose Ann was standing in the bedroom, naked but for a pair of panties, sweeping her hand across the dresser and letting the bottles fly. She didn't say anything; she just put her hands on her hips and with a terrible look on her face, listened to the glass crash to the floor. Her father got up and shut the door. Later he came out and said, "Your mother had her feelings hurt because of something I did. But she's calmed down now. Do you want to come in and say hello to her?"

The room had reeked of perfume. Rose Ann was picking pieces of glass out of the puddles. Walking up to her, the smell was so overwhelming Alma had to sneeze. Rose Ann asked Teddy to get her the mop and broom. When he was gone, she took Alma's hand. "I didn't mean to scare you, but every once in a while it's good practice to let yourself feel what you really feel, even if it means destroying things.

Once you allow yourself to do that, the anger goes away. It's like magic."

That hadn't comforted Alma particularly, but Rose Ann had gone back to the mess, saying she had to get it cleaned up before someone cut themselves. She came out later dressed in a black shirt and black pants with a wide red sash wrapped around her waist.

"You look like a toreador," Teddy had said.

"I feel like one," she replied.

The perfume had inhabited their house all week long. They burned incense and opened windows, and that helped.

If she discovered him with Gloria, she would want a divorce. It wasn't her nature just to let things pass. She liked to be in the center directing the action. Upheaval didn't scare her.

So maybe she shouldn't tell Rose Ann—at least not directly. She would have to write to her as though she knew nothing, maintaining peace, tranquility, and her parents' marriage. She would be her father's accomplice.

"If Marianne had twenty-three pies and 25 percent were blueberry and 13 percent were apple and the rest were pumpkin, how many of each kind did she have? While Ulrike is figuring out the solution, I'd like the rest of you to be working on problem three on page thirty-nine."

But Ulrike was at the board already, writing the answer in thick, bold numbers. She put the chalk down and without looking at anyone walked back to her seat.

After class Alma waited for her in the bathroom. She watched the door of the last stall where Ulrike had disappeared. Finally there was a flush, and then there was a long rustling of clothes, and after some fumbling with the latch, it opened. Ulrike began to walk past, but Alma put out her hand and stopped her. "I didn't know you were so good at math. You were the one who sent me the answer in class last time, weren't you?"

Ulrike shrugged.

"Thank you. I had no idea it had been you."

"You're good at letters, this is what I'm good at." She tossed her hair over her shoulder and looked at Alma clearly. "We could be a help to each other," she said.

23

They were behind the garage. As he was kissing her, she imagined that she was an older woman. Andrew was her secret lover. Both of them had families so they had to meet at odd times in secret places. If either of their spouses found out, there would be big trouble. He might lose his job, and she would surely get kicked out of the house. She should never have allowed it to start in the first place, but since it had, she couldn't stop.

Alma put her arms around Andrew's back, gripping him tightly. She imagined it a thicker, wider back like her father's. She made a sound of passion. "Mmmmm . . ."

"What?" Andrew asked, pulling away.

That destroyed it. She closed her eyes, whispered, "I didn't say anything," and tried to get the fantasy going again. He obliged by pulling her against him and smashing his mouth against hers.

24

Dear Rose Ann,

I have a boyfriend. His name is Andrew and he has red hair and plays baseball and before he moved here, he used to live in the country. I am becoming better friends with the Ukrainian girl. Dad and I are doing fine. A lot of times Gloria comes over and cooks dinner with us. She's Dad's new friend. She works in his office and drives a beat-up old car that used to be used for racing. It was her brother's and he gave it to her. Dad won't ride in it, he says it's too loud and will ruin his reputation in the neighborhood. I wish you could come home now.

I love you,
Alma

· · · · · *25* · · · · ·

Academia Americana
Via Angelo Masina 5
Roma
May 17

Alma my dearest,
I am sitting on the balcony of a friend's apartment and watching the people on the street below me. So much has happened to both of us, and yet it seems like only yesterday when I left.

I will be very pleased to meet your boyfriend. It's wonderful at your age to experiment with sex, but it's something you can't do with your eyes closed. As with everything else in life, you must be aware. But I trust you and am pleased by your news.

By the way, are you certain you haven't started to menstruate? Watch for a little brown stain in your underpants. That's all it might be in the beginning. Don't hesitate to write me if you have any questions. (About this or anything else.)

Right now, the woman who runs the flower stand directly underneath the apartment has begun to sing. What a lovely country this is. My friend tells me that she sings every evening when the sun goes down.

Thinking of you with love and fondness,
Rose Ann

26

Teddy decided to hire a housekeeper. They were good at putting things away and straightening the few rooms they lived in, but no one had done any heavy cleaning since Rose Ann had left. The carpet in the living room hadn't been vacuumed in eight months, and the kitchen floor hadn't been washed. Alma had never seen her mother do those things either, but that was because Rose Ann generally did her cleaning at night. She didn't like to waste daylight on something that could be done just as easily at another time. She didn't like to paint under artificial light, but she could wash dishes and mop a floor.

"Her name is Mrs. Blair," Teddy told her the next day as they were fixing dinner. "She's a Negro and she's in her forties, and she seems very nice. She's going to come here tomorrow afternoon just to see what she'll need to do and I'm leaving it up to you to show her where things are kept. I have to get tires put on the car, and I don't think I'll get back until dinnertime. So I'm counting on you to remember to come straight home when school lets out. She'll probably get here a few minutes before you do, and I don't want her to have a long wait."

"All right," Alma said. She set a hard-boiled egg in the egg slicer and guillotined it with a swift, downward stroke. Dinner was going to be hard-boiled eggs and carrot and celery strips. She threw the vegetables in a bowl and put it in the center of the table. Half of the sliced eggs she slid onto her plate, half onto her father's. "Does Mrs. Blair have a family?"

"She has six grown children who no longer live at home and two little adopted boys she calls her volunteers."

"Volunteers?"

"You'll have to ask her about it. You'll get a better story from her than you would from me."

At school the next day she was imagining what her conversation with their new housekeeper might be like when the social studies teacher called on her to summarize the research she had been doing for the final report of the year. "Before you begin," he said, "let me remind your classmates that while Alma is talking it should be silent in here. Now, Alma, would you be kind enough to proceed? First tell us what your subject is, and when you speak, speak loudly and clearly. All right, Alma, go ahead." He turned to the blackboard and wrote "Juroe" and put a dash beside it.

She wondered what would happen if she simply refused. What if it was in her power to stop all forward motion? Minutes, even seconds couldn't accumulate; lives would come to a standstill. The fly buzzing on her desktop would suddenly be quiet. She felt everyone looking at her. Just as curious as they were to know what she was going to say, she opened her mouth. Words came out of it. "My subject is Bechuanaland in Africa."

He wrote "Bechuanaland" beside the dash.

"I have researched the imports and exports and what kind of government that country has."

"You'll have to speak more loudly," he said, turning around. "The people in the back of the room can't possibly hear you."

She cleared her throat and more words sailed out. "I have also looked into what the capital city is and the names of the other major cities and told about the population."

"And what did you find out about the population?"

Finally sense intervened. She said, "My notes are at home, Mr. Rupp."

"What are they doing at home, watching your favorite program on TV?" The class tittered. "If you have done the research you were assigned, you should have no trouble recalling some of the more interesting data you found. Am I correct?"

She nodded unhappily.

"And did you do it?"

She nodded again.

"Then there's no reason to hesitate."

She cleared her throat. "Well," she said, surprised that time hadn't moved any faster. They were all still there. "It's mostly Negroes. There isn't a big population." She paused, trying to dream up another bit of information. "They're poor and they don't have modern transportation."

"And what do they export and import?"

"They export bananas." Bananas grew in hot countries, didn't they? Africa was hot. Also, they had gotten her in a mess once before, now maybe they'd save her.

He wrote "bananas" under "Bechuanaland." "And what do they import?"

"Tires," she said softly, choosing the first word that came to her mind.

"You'll have to speak more clearly, Alma. Did you say tires?"

"Yes," she replied.

"But I thought just a moment ago you told us that they didn't have modern transportation."

She blushed. "They have buses, Mr. Rupp, they just don't have cars."

"All right, Alma, I will accept that. But if they have to import tires, it would seem probable that they would import other parts for their buses as well. It would seem likely, in fact, that they would import the entire bus."

She came to. Her body quivered with alertness. She was ready; nothing would daunt her. And she knew his tricks: He baited you with what appeared to be common sense so that those people who hadn't done the work and weren't convinced themselves by what they were saying would surrender to his argument. Once they did that, he would reveal the true fact, which was always the thing, just a moment before, he had forced you to deny. So, although it might make sense that they were importing the entire bus, the true fact, Alma reasoned to herself, was that they just imported the tires. You had to stand up for your original statement. "It's a cottage industry," she blurted out, seizing a term the class had recently learned.

"Does that mean they manufacture buses in their cottages?"

"Yes," Alma said. "One cottage is responsible for the engine, one for the fenders, one for the steering wheel . . ."

"I see," Mr. Rupp said, smoothing back his short, black hair, "and the only things they are unable to fabricate in their living rooms are the tires."

Alma nodded yes.

"But isn't the manufacture of buses a rather greasy, sloppy industry to take place in a person's home?"

"Yes," Alma agreed, "that's why they do it in their backyards. A cottage industry doesn't mean actually in the home. The men make the buses in the backyards, and the women do other things in the house."

"I see. And where do the men get the raw materials for the manufacture of these buses?"

"They get delivered," Alma replied, seeing an old army truck stopping along a dusty road and thin Negro men coming out of broken-down shacks to greet it. "They get metal and tools and things, and instruction sheets about how to put it together."

"And one cottage makes the steering wheel and one cottage makes the fender. . . . Surely they need more than an instruction sheet to tell them about that."

"There's an inspector," she added hastily and at the same time saw another thin Negro man, this one wearing a uniform, walking through the backyards.

"I see," Mr. Rupp replied. He sounded almost agreeable. "But I'm afraid I find it hard to believe that in a poor, undeveloped country like Bechuanaland, there would be the necessary industrial know-how for the manufacture of buses."

"There are industrial supervisors," Alma said, staring at the sprinkling of dandruff on his sloping shoulders. "They're Africans who studied in car factories in the United States. They supervise the production. They're above the inspector, and if the inspector thinks something is wrong, they'll come and look it over." She saw a small, dapper black man in a neatly pressed suit walking along the road swinging a briefcase. The workers liked him because he gave them American cigarettes and bottles of American after-shave. Out of respect they called him "boss," but they'd tell him jokes and play cards with him.

"I see," Mr. Rupp replied. "But leaving this aspect of your subject for a moment, I'm curious to know what the other industries are in Bechuanaland." He wrote industries on the board and put a dash beside it.

"It's mostly bananas."

"Buses and bananas, there's nothing else?"

"If I had my notes maybe there's something else."

"Do you recall from your reading any mention of diamond mines?"

Most people would say yes to a question like that, but Alma knew from experience that Mr. Rupp asked it only because the answer was no. So she pretended to be thinking for a second and then said she might be mistaken but she didn't really recall anything about diamond mines. If he asked about the major cities, Alma would be trapped, but cities escaped Rupp's attention and instead, he made another attack on buses, this time sneaking up from behind and taking her by surprise.

"And yet, even with a supervisor trained in the United States, it is entirely unbelievable that a country like Bechuanaland is able to manufacture such a complex piece of machinery as a bus. I'm afraid that what we have been listening to here is a rather long-winded story that had its beginnings in Alma Juroe's girlish imagination rather than in a reference book." His small black eyes settled on Alma's face, and his tone changed. "Unless you're able to bring the source from which you've taken your information, you will receive an F in preliminary research. I suspect you haven't opened a single book, and I would advise you and the other bumps on the log around you to get cracking and shake a leg, each and every one of you."

Alma spoke up. "But everything I said is true. Only I can't bring you the source because the source isn't a book."

Mr. Rupp looked at her in disbelief. "What is it then?" he asked evenly.

Catching a glimpse of the huge proportions of her lie and understanding how one lie pulled her into the next one before she even realized it, she panicked. "It's a lady I know named Mrs. Blair." She stopped, hoping the one half-truth would miraculously purge her.

But Rupp persisted. "Who, pray tell, is Mrs. Blair?"

"A Negro woman who cleans our house," Alma replied easily.

"And what is her connection to Bechuanaland?"

Realizing that all was lost, she listened to the story rush out of her mouth. Mrs. Blair, she told the class, had a cousin named Bobby who lived in Bechuanaland and had recently become an inspector for the motorized bus industry. His sector was the southern plains region, she said, trying to recall from the map whether the terrain was flat or mountainous.

"That's quite fascinating, Alma Juroe, and you're very right, you wouldn't be able to bring your source to school. However, because truth is the goal of all of our pursuits, please have one of your parents send a note confirming the existence of Mrs. Blair and also her cousin Bobby. Perhaps Mrs. Blair could add her signature as well."

Alma nodded hopefully because to appear defeated would be an admission of guilt. But she was too tired to do any arduous pretending, so she opened her desk and ducked her head to look for something. Only when Mr. Rupp went on to the next subject did she feel safe enough to close the lid and face the front of the room.

They finished the day on the other side of the building in Mr. Hawkins's algebra class. The letters and numbers that covered the blackboard in increasing density soothed her as the hour progressed. Here was something beyond morality. It was nothing more than symbols, and the things being symbolized could be lies or oranges, their nature didn't alter the functions.

She was too numb to follow the lesson, but since she had been singled out once that day, she figured she was safe. Mr. Hawkins's midriff jiggled under a wrinkled shirt as he added new letters to the board, and his shoes squeaked when he walked to his desk to survey the class. During that last month of school, Ulrike had become his favorite student, and when no one else volunteered an answer, he'd nod at her and she'd go to the board and finish the equation. Her long braid would swing back and forth as she wrote. Then she'd go back to her seat, and Mr. Hawkins would explain to the class what she had done.

"If you take x to the seventh power and multiply it by y to the fifth power, this is what you come up with. Now let me break it down into small steps so you can see how we arrive at that solution." He turned his back again and the scratching of his chalk filled the room.

Dust hung in the air. A cobweb stretched across the bottom of the windowsill, and the sun glimmered on the strands. Every moment the sun was farther west. Although the earth kept on turning and would never stop, she knew what she really was: a stationary particle forever fixed in the chalky classroom. The sun warming her face made her drowsy, and relinquishing the last obligation for attentiveness, she closed her eyes.

But the bell rang and the crowd pushed her down the stairs, and once her feet touched the macadam of the schoolyard, Andrew grabbed her arm. "You haven't got a housekeeper," he said.

"Yes, we do." And because she couldn't reconcile herself to the idea that she had lied with such appalling thoroughness, she told him that everything she had said was true.

"What?"

"Everything." She shrugged her shoulders and was about to walk away when he pulled her closer. "Everything?" he whispered.

Her stomach rippled nervously. To prove to herself that she could do whatever she wanted, she took his face between her hands and kissed him squarely on the lips. Then, because that wasn't enough, she slipped her tongue between his teeth and touched the warm, wet insides of his mouth. In the bright daylight, in full view of anyone who cared to watch, the dark cavity of his mouth seemed frightening. It was wetter than her own, and its taste was strong. She let go of him abruptly and said she needed a drink of water.

"What?" he asked, looking startled.

"I have to get a drink of water," she said firmly and before he could answer, began to walk toward the fountain. But there was a line, so she went to the girl's bathroom and drank from the sink. When she came out he was waiting for her with his hands in his pockets and a curious expression on his face.

"All of that was really true?" he asked.

"Of course," she said. "Would I make up a story like that?" She walked toward the street, and Andrew called, "Hey, Alma, wait for me, will you?"

She stopped and watched him come toward her. "What's going on?" he asked.

"I have to get home to let in our housekeeper. She's probably there already. I have to get going."

"All right, I just want to walk with you."

"Sorry."

"What's going on? All of a sudden you disappear."

"Andrew, please could I walk home by myself? I'll see you in school tomorrow. I'm just tired, that's all. Please?"

He looked hurt, but he turned around without saying anything else, and she began to walk in the other direction.

The blocks disappeared quickly, and no time at all had passed before she reached her house. She was thirsty again and since there wasn't anyone on the front porch and there wasn't a strange car in the driveway, she did something she wasn't supposed to do. She turned the water on at the side of the house and drank from the end of the hose. But shutting it off and coming around to the back door, she saw a large black woman sitting on the kitchen steps. She was fanning herself and watching Alma approach.

"That K bus got me here sooner than it was supposed to. I've had lots of time to snoop around. I peeked into all them windows, and I can see why you folks want some cleaning done." She looked Alma in the eyes and asked, "Where's your mama gone?"

"She's in Europe studying art."

"She couldn't take y'all with her?"

"She didn't want to," Alma replied.

"Y'all must be one troublesome bunch to get left behind like that!" Mrs. Blair let out a sudden laugh and then closed her mouth. "I suppose I'm speaking to Mr. Juroe's daughter? You know who I am?" When she put down her fan and and stood up, she was the tallest woman Alma had ever seen. "Your daddy told you I was Mrs. Blair because that's what I told him, but Sal is my real name and everyone I know calls me that." She held out a warm, calloused hand and gripped Alma tightly.

In the house, Alma took her down to the basement and showed her the cleaning supplies. Then she took her through the rooms on the first floor and moved upstairs. At the last door in the second-floor hallway, Alma paused. "My mother's a painter," she said, "and up there's her studio."

"She's a painter? Well, child, you didn't tell me that. Come on, show me her pictures."

Alma opened the door and started up the steps with Sal close behind her. She had an uneasy feeling, taking someone she hardly knew into Rose Ann's studio. Though most of the paintings were in storage racks, there was a small still life hanging on the wall with an apple, a lemon, and an empty bowl. They were sitting on a wooden table against a background of dark blue.

Mrs. Blair stood in front of it and said softly, "She sure sees the shadows."

The rest of the studio was empty, with only the easel in the center of the room and a jar of old paintbrushes sitting on one of the windowsills.

"This must be the smell of paint," Mrs. Blair remarked as she looked around. "It really stays on in a room doesn't it?"

When they returned to the kitchen, she asked Alma if she could trouble her to make them a cup of tea. "I like a nice cup of something hot even in the summertime. Then we can sit on the back steps, and at a quarter past five I'll walk down to my bus. Once I'm gone you should come back in and wash them dishes. You can't make dinner in a kitchen that's a mess like this."

Out on the steps Mrs. Blair propped her elbows on her knees and sipped the hot tea. Alma gazed out toward the garage and, attempting to sound as though she were asking something that had only just popped into her mind, she said, "Have you ever heard of Bechuanaland?"

"What's that, something you've been studying in school?"

"It's a country in Africa."

"I never heard of it. Where's it located?"

"I'm not sure," Alma said.

"So what did you want to know?"

"I was wondering if maybe you knew anyone who lived there."

"In Africa?" Sal slapped her knees and snorted. "Child, every person I know lives in this city right here. Africa is too far back for anyone to remember, much less have relatives over at. All we have in common with those folks over there is the color of our skin, and no matter what anyone might tell you, that don't amount to much."

"I guess you're right," Alma finished lamely. "Only I have to do a report on it, and for the preliminary research I have to collect as much information as I can, so I just thought I'd ask."

"Well, there's no harm in that. Only I don't want you jumping to no conclusions just because my skin's a shade darker than yours." She paused and glanced at her watch. "Well, I'll see y'all next Tuesday, I gotta go get that K bus." She gave her cup to Alma and stood up. Then, picking up her satchel, she started down the path.

But Alma called, "Wait, there's something I meant to ask you!"

"Save it for Tuesday or I'll miss my bus."

"Couldn't I walk with you?"

"Sure, child, but Lord, what is it you want to know?"

Since Mrs. Blair was so touchy about Africa, Alma couldn't possibly ask her to write a note. That left Teddy, and with him she'd have to lead up to her subject gradually. In order to do that, she figured she needed to find something out about the volunteers. They would probably start out by talking about Sal, and Teddy would want to know if Alma had asked her who the volunteers were.

"The volunteers?" Sal said. "You sure are a funny girl. Now why can't that question wait till Tuesday? You don't want to go back and do them dishes like I told you. That's why." Nevertheless, she took her fan out of her satchel and began to walk more slowly. "The volunteers are Nelson and Clarence. They're brothers but they're very different." Her voice softened. "I call them volunteers because my children are all old and gone away from home, and I was ready to become a regular old maid living alone in an empty house. Well, one day I go to the supermarket to buy just a few things, and it was cold out and there in the parking lot was this cart with two little boys sitting in it with nothing more than summer shirts on. It was way over in the corner of the lot, and I go over to them and I say, 'Where's your mama?' They was about one year and three years then, and they just looked at me, they didn't say nothing. Well, there was no one around, and I feel how cold their skin is so I know they been there a long time. So I give them my bag to hold, and I wheel them back to the store. I go up to the guard and I say, somebody left their children behind, and all manner of things start happening. The manager comes out and the police come out, and before long it's agreed that they'll go to the county home until their parents can be located. Well, no one knew what their name was so the parents was never found, and no one ever contacted the supermarket asking about their kids, so I decided that since it appeared they wasn't wanted, I would adopt them myself. They have me fill out all manner of forms and applications, and not until four months later do I get to take them home. I give them first names and I give them my last name, and five years has gone by and they go to school now. You see why I call them volunteers? They didn't come out of my own body, but I got them just the same. My big children like them, and they fill the house up real nice."

"Do you have a husband?" Alma asked cautiously.

Sal fanned herself vigorously and said, "You full of all manner of questions. Didn't nobody tell you not to bother yourself about other people's private business? Since you asked it, I'll answer it, but this is the last one, I'll tell you that! Well, Mr. Blair never bothered himself to come around none. It wasn't my fault; he had himself a fancy for another lady." She stopped fanning and looked at Alma. "Now you go home and wash them dishes. I've jabbered with you long enough."

27

Back in the house, alone with the mess in the kitchen, she wrestled with the unfamiliar sensation of her body. It was hard to believe that just that morning when she was getting out of bed, she was still the old Alma Juroe. Even walking through the doorway of her homeroom at school, she was her old self. But something had happened during social studies, and she had changed. She hadn't felt it at the moment it was happening, but afterward she had been aware of something that was different. She wished she could forget everything and find her old body again. Because now there was a part of herself she couldn't feel, as though she had swallowed more air than she had space to hold, as if her skin had swollen outward to contain it all.

28

"How did it go?"

"How did what go?"

"Mrs. Blair. Did you remember to come home early?"

"I came home right after school, but her bus got her here sooner than it was supposed to, and she was already waiting for me at the back door."

"Did you show her where things are kept?"

"I took her through the entire house, and then we sat on the steps outside and had a cup of tea. I asked her about the volunteers, and she told me all about them."

"Sounds like you had a pleasant afternoon."

"Not really," Alma replied. "I got in trouble at school."

Teddy opened the door of the refrigerator and stood in front of it for a few minutes without saying anything. Then he opened the cupboard above the sink and surveyed the cans and boxes.

"Maybe we should have scrambled eggs," Alma offered.

"I'm tired of eggs. We might have to make ourselves a real dinner."

"Why don't we just go out, then?"

"Why go out when there's a perfectly good chicken in the freezer?"

"But that's been there for ages," she said, "and besides it's frozen. We couldn't have it tonight."

"Oh yes we could." Teddy turned the water on full force, and soon the sink was filled with steam. He took the chicken out of the freezer and set it on the counter. Then he pulled off the plastic wrapping and immersed the big orange bird in the hot bath. "We'll let it sit for a few minutes to thaw out, and in the meantime you can finish your story."

Don't you know what could happen? she wanted to ask her father. *Don't you know that everything could dissolve? Why don't you open your eyes for once? Why don't you think of somebody besides yourself?* "I never saw Rose Ann do it like that."

"Your mother wouldn't know about a last-minute tactic like this. She's too well organized. Wait till you taste it. It will be the tenderest chicken you ever sank your teeth into. We'll make some of Theodore Juroe's famous pineapple chicken sauce, and we'll cook up some rice, and we'll have us a treat." When she didn't respond, he added in his indefatigably humorous voice, "I bet you didn't know your father was the chicken-cooking king of the 1947 poultry bake-off."

"Come on," she said. "This is going to take forever and I'm hungry."

"The first rule for any gourmet cook is patience. Now . . ." He pulled down a can of pineapple and a box of rice and took out pots and bowls and a can opener. "First we open the pineapple and pour it into a bowl. Then we add a little oil and honey and whatever spices appeal to us. Cinnamon might be good, don't you think?" He searched through the spices for cinnamon and sprinkled a generous amount over the pineapple. "The next step is to pour it into the Waring blender so we'll get a nice thick sauce. Right?" He poured the pineapple mix into the blender and turned it on high. Then he looked at Alma. "Do you know what you could be doing? You could be melting some butter in a frying pan. Now I'll test the chicken with a fork like so. . . ." He plunged a fork into the chicken's side, but it didn't penetrate. "Needs more time," he announced. "Just a few more minutes."

Alma's butter was frying to a deep charcoal in the pan and on another burner, the rice was in a pot ready to be turned on. "That chicken's hard as a rock," she said. "We're not going to be able to eat until midnight."

"Are you doubting your father? Taste this pineapple sauce. Come on, taste it."

Alma looked in his eyes warily and took the spoon he offered her. Oh, she doubted him all right. The sauce, even at the first contact it made with her tongue, would clearly overpower any food it touched; thick and sweet and laced with cinnamon, it would smother the chicken in a sticky goo. But he didn't deserve the truth. So she said, "It's okay," and then added, "but I still don't think that chicken's going to thaw."

"Well, what does hot water do to ice?"

"It melts it."

"All right. I thought you wanted to tell me about your day at school."

"But chicken and ice aren't the same thing."

"They're both cold and that's all that matters." He looked at her and said, "Don't worry. Tell me about school."

"Well," Alma began, trying for a tone of indignation, "Mr. Rupp was asking us about the research we'd been doing on these reports we have to write, and I raised my hand and he asked me what I had found out so far. I was ready to tell him all about it, but he kept on interrupting to ask me to talk louder. Then he asked me about something, and I was confused at that point, and I thought he was asking me about this other thing. But he was asking me something else, so when I gave the answer he got mad. I didn't know why he was mad, so when he asked me again I gave him the same answer. I thought he was asking me about Negroes who are in this country now who originally came from Africa. So I happened to mention Mrs. Blair, but it turned out that that wasn't what he was asking at all. He wanted to know what kind of people lived over there, and he thought I was trying to tell him that this person I knew lived in Africa. So he wanted to know who this person was and how did I know her." When the butter began to smoke Alma turned off the flame. "Anyway, he began to doubt everything I was saying, and tomorrow I have to show him a note from you that says I know somebody named Mrs. Blair and that Mrs. Blair is our housekeeper"—she stirred the butter idly with a fork—"and that she has a cousin who lives in Africa."

"I'm confused," Teddy said.

"The whole thing was a mistake, and he thought I was trying to say something that I wasn't saying at all. If you could just write me a note, he won't give me an F in preliminary research."

Teddy walked to the sink and poked the chicken with a fork. "It's ready," he said. "Now if you'll put the oven on five hundred, we'll get this bird cooking." He lifted it out of the water, set it down on the counter, and began to pat it dry with a towel.

"You don't cook chicken at five hundred. You cook it at three-fifty."

"Do you want to eat at midnight? A fast-cooked bird keeps its juices better. You wait and see." He set the chicken in a pan and began to baste it with Alma's butter. Then he sprinkled paprika and pepper over it and with a flourish, slid it into the oven.

"It's not preheated yet," Alma said.

"It doesn't have to be, the chicken will cook just the same." He put the basting brush in a bowl of sauce and set it on top of the stove. "Now," he said, clapping his hands, "how's the rice? Let's put the rice on, and in a short while we're going to have us a real dinner!"

Pretending that it might all work out, that she would fit into her body again, that her father knew how to manage this family she belonged to and could even cook a chicken, she lit the burner under the rice and put the lid on the pot. "Will you write it?"

"Write what, sweetie pie?"

"Write me that note."

"I don't understand why the note is required. Does everyone have to bring in a note?"

"It's just me," Alma explained.

"But why, sweetie—that's what I don't understand."

"He thought I was lying, that's why."

"Well, were you?"

"Well," she said, "I was saying one thing, and he thought I was saying something else."

"But what made you think Mrs. Blair had a cousin in Africa?"

"I don't know."

"Well, unless you can do a better job of explaining, I won't even consider writing a note. I still don't understand how this cousin suddenly appeared."

"He wanted to know who had lived there, so I thought of Mrs. Blair's cousin."

"But you hadn't even met Mrs. Blair at that point, so what on earth were you talking about?"

"I don't know," Alma replied. "Something came over me, I guess it's because I've been upset the last few days. . . ." As she said this she felt a tightening in her face, a symptom of ready tears. She didn't give in to them, though, and went on with her story. "I don't know exactly what happened. He kept on asking me questions, and I answered them as best as I could, but then he made me repeat everything louder and I got confused. I'd say something and he'd take it the wrong way. I just kept on saying these things that popped into my head, and then I don't know exactly what happened."

"You know perfectly well what happened. You were making up a story to save your skin and appease poor Mr. Rupp."

"What else could I do?" Alma asked, her voice rising. "What would you do if you were hounded by a teacher like that?"

"What I would have done isn't the question. I probably would have tried the same thing you did, and I'm sure I would have failed at it just as miserably. You should have told him you weren't prepared to answer any questions, and that would have been that."

"You don't know Mr. Rupp."

"But I know you and I'm surprised that you don't seem to know yourself any better. Let me baste this chicken, and then I'll tell you something."

"You don't need to tell me anything. The whole thing was a mistake, I know that, but it happened and I need a note, that's all."

Teddy pulled the pan out of the stove and brushed the yellow sauce over the bird. Then he slid the pan back in and closed the oven door. "You're not good at lying, Alma Juroe. Neither am I. We're too transparent."

Alma threw the empty pineapple can into the trash. If he wasn't good at lying, then why did he keep on lying about Gloria?

He raised his voice. "When I'm telling you something, I'd appreciate it if you'd do me the courtesy of listening. We can't get away with it, that's all. Some people can pull it off; others can't. We belong to the latter species."

"So that means you're going to let me get an F?"

"It'll be an F you deserve. That's all I can say."

"But don't you care about my grades?" She felt puffy and swollen. Her face was red and hot, and her legs were numb.

"Not enough to write you this note."

"I don't believe you're telling me that."

"Believe it." And, to prove there was nothing more to say, he poured himself a cup of coffee and sat down at the table to read the paper.

She didn't feel like going up to her room, but she couldn't stay in the kitchen any longer. So she went out the back door and stood on the lawn. The trees looked larger in the twilight than they did in the daytime, and the garage looked farther away. In the sky there was nothing but the vaporous shapes of the clouds and above them, the watery edge of a hidden moon. So far away from where she stood, it made her feel her isolation more acutely. She crossed the lawn to the garage and sat on the bench behind it.

Asshole, she thought to herself. Fucking asshole. Her hot, swollen face felt even tighter. Seeing the little girl sitting by herself on the bench in the nighttime, she felt sorry for her. With tears sliding down her cheeks, dropping onto her arm, she nestled into her misery; in that, there was comfort. Noticing her two white hands resting on her knees, she was struck by their uselessness. Nothing they could do would solve anything. She was completely powerless. And with her mother in Europe she was completely alone.

Later, after she had dried her face, she walked back to the house. When she went in, Teddy looked up. "It's almost done. You must be starving."

"I just want to tell you something," she said quietly. "When school's out," her voice cracked as tears threatened to appear again, "when school's out I'm going to fly to Italy to be with Rose Ann."

"Why?"

"Because I hate it here." She began to cry. "I want my mother, I want her to come home."

"Why?" he asked again.

"Because you're fucking up." At this she began to wail, feeling the sound draw all the air out of her body. Choking on her sobs, she managed to say, "I'm going to lose everything I have. All because of you."

"Why?"

"Because you've fallen in love with Gloria."

"Now we're getting somewhere," Teddy said.

Her body had returned. She was just as she had always been: small and thin with familiar sensations skimming along her bones.

"First of all," her father said, "yes, you could at any moment lose everything you have. On your way to Italy, finally escaping the tyranny of your father, the plane could crash. Or the house could go up in flames, and you and I could die in our sleep. We could be driving somewhere, and another car could go through a red light and smash into us. Nothing you have is secure. Anything could happen at any time. And if life is this fragile, love is even more risky. Rose Ann could be won over by a tall, dark-eyed Italian and never come back except to see you. It's unlikely but it's entirely possible. I could meet a woman I find infinitely more exciting than Rose Ann and ask for a divorce. That also is unlikely but entirely possible. Or maybe something less dramatic would occur. What if one of us decided that we preferred living alone to living with the other? Then we'd each have you only part of the time. That too could happen. If people tried to protect themselves from all the possible dangers, they wouldn't do anything. They wouldn't go anywhere and they wouldn't love anyone. Love is not dependable. But, from where we are at this moment in time—at this exact place and at this exact instant—I can say to you in all honesty that I haven't yet met a woman I love more than Rose Ann, that I look forward to having her back, and that the ties that this feeling has created between the three of us will hold . . . Did you hear what I just told you? Will you remember it? He reached for her hand and reluctantly, she gave it to him. "Now, shall we take care of a small piece of business?"

"What?" she asked warily.

"Get me some stationery and we'll see what your note should say. All right?"

She brought him the box from Rose Ann's desk and they sat down at the table together. "Dear Mr. Rupp," he scribbled at the top of the paper. "We do have a housekeeper named Mrs. Blair. And Mrs. Blair and Alma were one day talking about Africa because Alma was curious to know . . ."

"If she knew anyone in Bechuanaland."

"If she knew anyone in Bechuanaland," Teddy wrote. "Mrs. Blair, unfortunately, did not and I'm afraid that in a moment of panic my daughter led you to believe otherwise. She is sorry?"

"I guess so," Alma replied.

"She isn't even sure that she's sorry."

"You can't say that!"

"Then how about, I doubt if she'll ever do it again. That should satisfy him. Sincerely . . ." The pen made the automatic loops and slants and he signed his name.

29

School ended two weeks later. On the first day of summer vacation, Sal went through the house and opened all the windows. "How can y'all stand these stuffy rooms?" She told Alma to go outside and pick some flowers.

They had only dandelions in their yard, so Alma crept through the opening in the hedge and stole some marigolds from Mrs. Wilkens's flower bed. Sal arranged them in a jar and placed them in the center of the kitchen table.

"Now y'all have a pleasant room to eat in. Why couldn't you have done this for your father? There's plenty of things growing out there, why don't you bring something in every once in a while?" She picked up her broom and still muttering, started sweeping the floor. "Some people don't know how to make their life pleasant. They just got to wait around for someone else to do it for them. Get out of my way now," she said, going after Alma. "Go do something useful."

When Andrew stopped by that afternoon, he wanted to know if Alma would go fishing with him. "I've got two poles and a bunch of worms. Ever been fishing before?" He gave her a sly look as she shook her head. "All it is is an excuse to be outside doing nothing. You didn't have any other plans, did you?"

The bus let them off at the outhouses by the park's entrance. Andrew slung the poles over his shoulder and reached for her hand. The lake was at the bottom of the hill, a long gray shape under the sun.

"What kind of fish can you catch in there?" she asked, watching the light that shivered at the edge of the water.

"Walleye, trout—all kinds. Even catfish."

"Can you eat them?"

"What else would you do with them?"

"I don't know. Throw them back."

"Throw them back? You're not going to feel like throwing them back when you've waited hours and hours to catch them."

"Do you know how to clean a fish?"

"Sure I do," he said. "I can clean a fish in five minutes flat—I know because I once won a contest."

The beach was full of sunbathers. People were shouting to one another, and music was blaring from a radio. There was a volleyball game in progress. A dog that seemed to belong to no one barked when the ball hit the sand and growled ferociously at anyone who tried to get it.

On the other side of the beach, they found the road again. It took them toward the uninhabited part of the lake. There they found a path that took them into the woods.

"The thing about fishing," Andrew said, "is that it has to be quiet. You can't do it where there are other people around. You want to find a place where it's just you and the fish. Maybe there can be another fisherman, but that's all."

Walking through moss and leaves, climbing over a fallen tree, it felt as though they were being admitted to a secret place. The lake was in front of them, a shiny darkness under the afternoon sun. It was entirely empty, entirely still. Along the shoreline, there was a large, flat rock poking out of the water. When they sat down on it, they couldn't see the beach or hear the radio or the people.

"Do you come here a lot?" Alma asked.

"I came here once in the spring. It was still cold. I didn't catch but one little fish."

"Did you eat it?"

"Sure I did. I roasted it right there over a fire. Tasted good, too. Best little fish I ever had."

He showed her how to use the rod and then, with his back to her, skewered a worm on the hook. When he handed it to her, she knew she shouldn't say anything about the fate of the worm. "Reel her in every once in a while and see if the bait's still there."

They fished on opposite sides of the rock. They didn't talk because he said it was important to be quiet, but she kept sneaking glances in his direction. Once she caught him peeing into the water. Twice she reeled in her line, but the worm was still there.

She practiced holding her rod very still. Listening to the sounds around her, she felt alert to even the tiniest disturbance. She felt as though, by way of her fishing line, she were connected to all the life that existed around the rock. Then she felt a tug. It took her by surprise. She jerked the rod up and sure enough, there was resistance. "Andrew!" she called. He saw her rod bending at a crazy angle and rushed to her side. "Here, take it!" she said, trying to pass it to him.

"Hold on tight. Steady her. Now bring it up slowly." The rod was jumping up and down as the fish fought the hook. With all the movement, it was hard to reel in the line. "Couldn't we just let it go?"

"You have to bring it up first."

"Couldn't you do it for me?"

"Alma!" he shouted. "Pay attention!"

The fish was out of the water, a long silver fish leaping wildly on the line. It twisted and flopped in the air, trying to free itself. Suddenly she knew what to do; it wasn't mysterious any longer. She reeled in slowly and steadily so the fish wouldn't cut its mouth. Very carefully, she lowered it to the rock so Andrew could release the hook. "Be gentle," she said. "I don't want him to get hurt."

Struggling to hold the fish still, Andrew pulled out the hook. He tossed the fish in a bucket of water, and they watched it flop around. "That's a good size," he said to Alma. "There'll be a nice bit of meat on him. He'll be real tasty, I bet."

She breathed the fishy smell, looked down into his golden eyes, saw the smooth snout, the delicate pink of his mouth. She touched him with her finger. He was as soft as moss. "He's pretty," she said.

"He'll be even prettier in a frying pan."

They sat down and watched him together. He was so beautiful she couldn't see how anyone would want to eat him. "Look at his tail! Look how he's trying to turn around!" Surely Andrew couldn't fail to appreciate a live fish. But he wasn't paying attention. He was giving her a doleful stare, and then he was leaning over the bucket to kiss her.

It seemed to her that kissing was a good bit like fishing. It couldn't be rushed, you had to have patience. Also, you had to concentrate on it; you couldn't be occupied with other things. You just waited and then, unmistakably, it would happen. Just as though there'd been a tug on your line, the pace would change all of a sudden. Things would begin to move quickly; you'd feel different. Even if you hadn't felt much like kissing at the beginning, you began to feel like doing it more. Pretty soon you wouldn't want to quit. Hours could go by. Important things could be taking place around you, and you wouldn't notice.

This time, though, they stopped before any of that could happen. "I want to fish some more," Andrew said, pulling away from her. "One measly fish for the two of us isn't very much. Let's see if I can get one, too." He hooked a worm on his line and went to Alma's spot on the rock.

She stayed where she was. She didn't want to cause any trouble for the other fish. She lay on her back and let the sun warm her. But there were noises coming from the bucket. The fish was butting its head against the sides of the pail. She leaned over and petted it with her finger. She could feel the panic rippling through his body and could imagine how frantic he must be. Touching him probably only increased his fear so she stopped. Very quietly, watching Andrew to make sure he didn't turn around, she lifted the bucket and carried it off the rock. Ducking behind the trees for cover, she walked along the shore. At what looked like the kind of shady spot a fish might like, she squatted down and tipped the bucket over. The fish floated into the muddy water and then flipped its tail and disappeared.

She walked back with the empty bucket. Just as she was about to set it down, Andrew saw her.

"What are you doing?" he asked.

"I let him go."

"What?"

"I let the fish go."

"What did you do that for?"

"I wanted to," she said.

"That's a stupid thing to want to do."

"I don't like to eat fish."

"What about me? Maybe I do, didn't you think of that?"

"Listen, I caught him so, if I wanted to, I could let him go."

"Who showed you how to catch a fish? Whose fishing equipment did you have? Whose idea was it in the first place?"

"I still wanted to let him go. I didn't want him to die."

"There are plenty of fish, Alma. One less fish isn't going to make any difference, not even to God."

"I don't believe in God," she said. "I just didn't want him to suffer any more."

"Fish can't suffer, they don't feel anything."

"You can believe that if you want to, but I don't. I'm glad I did what I did, and I'd do it again."

"I guess I can't ever take you fishing."

"I guess not," she replied. It was the first time they had ever argued about something. But she knew she would never give in. It was exhilarating to be so certain about something.

"Well, what do you want to do now?" he asked. "If I catch a fish, you'll just let it go. The bus doesn't come for another two hours so there's no use walking back. Who wants to wait by the outhouse?"

"We'll think of something," she said. It was a rare opportunity to find themselves in such a private spot. She was sure they wouldn't waste it.

But he was still angry. He sat where he was and ignored her. She lay down on her stomach and looked at the bits of mica glittering in the sun. There were creases all over the surface of the rock, as though it had been several smaller rocks at one time that, over the centuries, had grown together. But could a rock grow? Probably not. The creases were made by the wind and water wearing down the surface. But why not the whole surface, why just a thin line?

Andrew apparently had forgiven her enough to move beside her. Lazily, he ran his finger up her arm, giving her goose bumps. She could feel his breath filling the space between them, knew he was staring at her. She closed her eyes. His finger moved across her shoulders and up her neck. Then, he leaned over her and blew warm air under her blouse.

Such attentions made her sleepy. She kept her eyes closed, waiting for the tug on her line. But she couldn't concentrate. She was thinking about the fish. Such a slippery, dark creature—what right had they to bring it into the daylight? Let it stay where it belonged; let it remain mysterious.

He lay down beside her. When she turned toward him, she was surprised to discover that familiar old Andrew was just as strange as the fish. She touched his mouth tentatively, as though she were touching something she had never seen before. It began to move as she was touching it. "Don't say anything," she whispered. "Just be quiet."

They lay face to face and watched one another for a long time. At such close range he was a strange specimen. *Human boy,* the caption would read, *circa 1960.* She supposed she looked the same to him. Her nose probably seemed as complex as the stars.

When they boarded the bus they were the only passengers. They took seats on opposite sides of the aisle and looked out of their separate windows. But, as they pulled up to the next stop, Andrew turned toward her. Loud enough to drown out the engine he said, "I can't believe you threw a perfectly good fish back in the water."

It pleased her that he didn't understand.

When Alma returned, Mrs. Blair was sitting in the kitchen drinking a cup of tea. The marigolds were in the middle of the table, a braided placemat under the vase. A bronze figurine that Rose Ann kept in the living room was arranged on the placemat, too. There was a bowl filled with peaches on the counter, and she had hung a painting of Rose Ann's next to the window. "Where did you find that?" Alma asked.

"Just sitting up there in your mama's painting racks not doing anybody no good. That's a nice little picture, I says to myself, seeing it out the corner of my eye when I passing. It should be someplace the family can see it. This bare spot always bothered me so I hung it there."

It was an old one of Rose Ann's, from the period when the objects in her still lifes were suspended in what looked like a primeval sludge. All the colors were mixed with brown, and the paint was layered on thickly.

Shape melted into shape; there weren't any true edges. There were only hints of identifiable objects so although there seemed to be oranges, the oranges were eaten up by the space around them, and the bowl they sat in was barely perceptible.

Her mother used to have it in their bedroom. Alma could remember looking at it as she lay on the bed and watched her mother get dressed. It was a ritual. When Rose Ann had an occasion to dress for, she did it with great care. First, she sat on the bed and put on her stockings. She'd lay out a brassiere and go to the closet to pick out her dress. Then she'd choose her jewelry. She'd slip on the clothing and ask Alma to fasten the necklace. It would be a heavy silver piece that covered her mother's chest like armor. "How does it look?" her mother would ask. Alma would step back to get a better view but turning around to peer at herself in the mirror, Rose Ann always decided for herself. "Come on, pumpkin," she'd finally say, spraying on more perfume to make sure she was adequately scented. "Let's go find your father."

30

Teddy was standing in the backyard. Gloria was walking toward him. From where Alma was watching, she could see Gloria's face. It was vacant. There wasn't an expression at all as she was listening to something Teddy was telling her. Her hair was white in the sunlight, and her blue dress was the same color as the sky. There were little clouds along the hemline. Suddenly, she bent forward, her knee coming up to her chest, her hand moving to her shoulder, her other hand opening against the sky, and on her face, wide and happy, a smile. Teddy must have said something funny.

Alma opened the back door. They turned. Teddy stopped in midsentence, and Gloria froze her expression. "What are you guys doing?" Alma asked.

"Just shooting the breeze," her father said. "Why, what are you doing?"

"Oh, I don't know." She kicked at the gravel in the driveway.

"What do you say we all hop in the car and go out for a drive?" Teddy said this looking from Gloria to Alma and then back to Gloria.

"Okay," Alma replied. Excursions had been their pattern of late. She would ride in the backseat, Teddy and Gloria up front. It meant they didn't have to struggle until Teddy stopped for lunch. Then, sitting in a restaurant face to face, they created conversation.

· · · · · 3I · · · · · ·

She woke up in the middle of the night. Something was different. Coming back into her room after going to the bathroom, she tripped over a shoe. The sound startled her. She tried to wrap the quiet around her again as she got into bed. But now there were voices. She walked to the window and tried to see down into the yard. The night was too black. But even though they were talking quietly, she knew who it was. What time was it? Her stomach tightened when she saw the orange face of her clock. Four in the morning was too late for him to be with Gloria.

In bed again, she couldn't get warm. The voices continued with hardly a modulation in tone, just an even background of talk, sometimes in Teddy's pitch, sometimes in Gloria's. She drew the covers around her. Ten after four. Finding the right spot on the pillow, she nestled into it. But she was wide awake; she couldn't sleep. And what she was thinking about was probably as dangerous as whatever it was they were doing out there.

Rose Ann still didn't know she had started to menstruate. She might be wondering if there was something wrong with her. Or, better still, she might begin to suspect that Alma had had intercourse and gotten herself pregnant. In either case, she would want to come home and take Alma to the doctor. Right away, if she thought she was pregnant. She'd have to arrange for Alma to go to one of those homes for unmarried mothers or try and con some doctor into doing one of those operations.

Outside, her father coughed. It was almost four-thirty. Should she make her mother worry about all of that? It would be kinder than letting her come home at the end of the summer to find her husband hopelessly in love with a woman who looked at him with a vacant face when he was talking to her, who dressed like the sky, who listened to him without judgment and then smiled because he had said something funny. She wasn't preoccupied, she wasn't rushing off to her studio, she wasn't talking about her paintings at dinner. She listened to what he said, empty of other thoughts, completely vacant.

The next day she woke up early. She had breakfast with Teddy and, after he left for work, went off to the library. Under "Reproduction, Mammalian," there wasn't much to choose from. She found a book called *Congratulations, You're Pregnant* and managed to check it out despite the librarian's wary glance. When she got home, she took it up to her room and spent all morning reading it.

By noontime she knew about swollen breasts, nausea, and the overactive bladder. She slipped the book under her mattress and went down to the kitchen to start a letter to Rose Ann.

In the first draft she began by mentioning Andrew. But with pregnancy symptoms thrown in on top of that, it would seem too obvious. Better leave it a little vague, let Rose Ann do a little guesswork and come to her own conclusions. Alma copied the final draft onto a piece of airmail stationery, making the writing sloppy so it would look as though the letter had been jotted down quickly.

Dear Rose Ann,

Do you realize I'm going to be fifteen soon? I wish you could be here to help us celebrate my birthday. Dad's going to take me to whatever movie I want to see and then we'll go out for dinner. I just hope I feel better by then. It seems like every five minutes I have to go to the bathroom. Then, yesterday morning I had to throw up when I got out of bed. I just made it to the toilet in time. I don't know what it was, probably the dinner we had the night before. Or maybe it's the cold that was going around at school. Everyone in our class had it.

Dad's doing fine. School is finally out. Gloria still comes over sometimes. I miss you.

Love,
Alma

32

"Why do you want her back so badly?" Andrew asked. "Don't you like not having her to boss you around?"

But Andrew didn't know her mother. Rose Ann didn't boss you; she gave you choices. She let you decide what you wanted to do. Of course, she made it clear which choice was the right one, and naturally she pressured you a little to go in that direction, but she didn't make you. The final decision was entirely your own. Concerning the present situation, what would Rose Ann want her to do?

Sitting in their backyard, watching Andrew go into their house, she asked herself this question. She imagined Rose Ann on the subject of their long separation. "Strange things sometimes happen, things you don't expect. You have to accept the situation as it is rather than force your desires on it. Just be patient."

She pictured her mother standing in the kitchen, a figure dark and complicated like the forms in her paintings. Seeing Gloria with her sunlight hair standing next to her, she decided that Rose Ann was wrong. Some things you didn't accept. Some things you had to fight for.

Andrew returned with tangerines, the spots of orange making bright circles against his shirt. He began to toss them in the air. Missing one, he leaned over gracefully to pick it up from the grass. He pulled another tangerine from his pocket and began to juggle. But he didn't know how to juggle, and one by one they dropped from his hands.

When they finally got to eat them, they were juicy from all the bouncing around. The peels were scattered under their feet, scraps of color in the bare dirt. They spit the seeds out noisily. Andrew wanted to play who-can-shoot-the-seeds-farther, but she wasn't in the mood. She was thinking about the letter. It would be two or three weeks at least before it reached Rose Ann. Already it had been a week. In another week then, Rose Ann might be wondering if she should fly home.

"When you meet my mother," she cautioned Andrew, "the most important thing is to talk to her just like you would talk to anyone else. If you call her Mrs. Juroe and act real polite, she won't like you. You've got to pretend she's just a friend of yours and call her Rose Ann."

Andrew lay back on the ground. He stretched his arms over his head and pushed up on his pelvis till he was doing a perfect back bend. "I'm bored," he said, coming back down. "The best thing to do on a day like today is go fishing. But that doesn't work with you." He turned over on his stomach and began to do push-ups. "You want to bet I can't do fifty?"

"I bet you can't do fifty," she said automatically. "I'm bored, too," she announced. But that was what summer vacation was, day after day of boredom. You had to invent an activity to keep you busy. One summer she had read all the books in the Young Adult section in the library. Another summer she had tried to build a tree house. Last summer she took long bike rides. This summer she would wait for her mother to return. But that was too passive. She would get exhausted from inactivity. Surely she could find something to keep herself busy.

Yet when she imagined it, it always happened dramatically. Passion was supposed to get it started, not lack of anything better to do. Still, who was to say how something was supposed to take place? Maybe this was all there was. Maybe nothing was going to happen; maybe old Andrew was the one after all. And they weren't even anywhere romantic, like the woods. And it was even daylight.

But, as she looked at him, she forgot they were only behind the garage. She looked at the place on his back where his shirt had ridden up to expose his skin. And seeing the elastic on his underwear where it showed just above the waist of his pants, she wanted to pretend she hadn't been thinking those thoughts at all. Because there was too much she'd have to give up. And what if there was nothing to replace it—what would she be? Better not try to find out. Numbness was far better than fear. But then he turned over. She knew he had been thinking about the same thing because when he leaned toward her there was a different expectation in his movements. She realized she didn't know him at all. Or at least he wasn't who she had thought he had been. When they kissed, his mouth was tight. Fuck . . . the word itself was tight. Follicle . . . fallopian . . . the picture of the uterus. She pulled away and sat up. Surprised by the interruption, he looked at her oddly.

"You have to wait," she said, aware that she was talking very slowly. "You can't get me pregnant," she explained, her voice small and flat in the sunlight.

He sat up and pulled his wallet from his pants. From the billfold he took out a small cellophane package. Tearing off the wrapper, he held up the rubber disk.

"How long have you been carrying that around for?" Though she had never seen one before, she knew what it was.

"I don't know," he said. "Maybe a year." He slipped the condom in his pocket. Then he put his arm around her, pulled her close.

She felt his breath as he fiddled with the collar on her blouse. Thoughts of all kinds ran around in her head. Why did he get it in the first place? And how did he get it—did he actually buy it himself? That he was a boy and thought of being prepared with things like that—she wondered if he had more than one. There was danger. When an egg popped out of the ovary, a minnow could tag it. Life could duplicate itself. "Come on," she said, as his hand slid against her skin.

He coaxed her down to the ground with him and then unbuttoned her shirt. She didn't want him to do that, but she couldn't stop him. Or didn't try. He only looked at her, though; he didn't touch her. Yet he had seen her chest a million times before. She thought of Rose Ann, wondered if she would see through her scheme. Although she might be a little suspicious, she would probably want to come home just to make sure. Once she was home and discovered what was going on, she would undoubtedly feel grateful for the pregnancy scare. She needn't even find out that Alma had made it up. He got on top of her. She could tell he was nervous. Then he pressed his face against hers, forcing her mouth open. She let him kiss her. Then, because she couldn't just lie there, she decided to kiss him back. The sun touched his hair, framing him in a circle of light. Everything got very quiet. The sky was pressing down on her; the coarse dry grass was pressing up. She could feel the coiled energy inside the earth making everything grow and change. She never wanted to stop. But suddenly he did. He unzipped his pants, then he unzipped hers, and they both stood up to get them off. She knew she was ugly standing stark naked in the outdoors. He looked too white and with his penis pointing to the east like an arrow, a little foolish.

They stood together. She imagined they were two fish meeting each other in the lake. But she was the only one who could transform. He stayed a minnow, but she could become a host. With his eyes closed, he pulled her against him. She closed her eyes, too, pretending she was the housewife secretly meeting her lover. His penis butted between her legs. Andrew unrolled the condom. "You aren't scared, are you?"

She shook her head. Then she asked him if he was, realizing of course, that he wouldn't be, that for him it was a different thing altogether.

"What?" he asked.

"Scared."

"Sure I am. I've never done this before."

They lay down in the grass. He couldn't find the right place at first, and then the opening seemed to be too small, so he smeared some spit on and it went in better. She was glad he didn't say anything. She didn't want to have to acknowledge what they were doing. Puffy and red in the face, he began to pump up and down furiously. A moment later, he was sprawled across her, his belly slippery with sweat. When his penis slid out, she was relieved.

"Where you been?" Mrs. Blair asked when Alma came into the kitchen. "I been waiting for you to show yourself. I been sitting here waiting for you a long time because this afternoon I was up there in your room changing your sheets, which I gotta do every week as you should know, and a particular book couldn't help but escape my attention." Her mouth tightened when she placed the book on the table. "You getting your period every month like you s'posed to? That boy been fooling around with you?"

"No," Alma said, growing red in the face but shaking her head.

"You telling me the truth, girl? Because that is *trouble*, with your mama gone and your daddy wandering around with his head in the clouds. It not be the time for something like this to happen. What's that boy think he doing, fooling around like that for? Why he's no better than the boys in my neighborhood. All good for nothings, no regard for nothing, just trying to get as much as they can . . . and you only being a child," Mrs. Blair continued in a shrill voice.

"I'm not pregnant," Alma said.

"You sure now?"

"No way I could be."

"Well, I'm glad to hear it. You sure now? What's this book doing under your bed then?"

"I got it out of the library. I was just curious and I just wanted to read it."

"Well, you sure gave me a scare. I been sitting here thinking what you ever gonna do with your mama gone and a situation come up like this. But you mind now. Don't you let that boy do nothing. Because let me tell you something girl, and you listen to me good. Anything you give them they want more. Give them a kiss and they want to have sex with you and that's no lie. And you just not old enough."

Alma tried not to smile but couldn't help herself.

Mrs. Blair looked at her suspiciously. "You make him behave, Alma Juroe. It's your life he's playing around with. Now how about a cup of tea? I missed my bus and it be an hour and a half till the next one."

They heard Teddy's car in the driveway. The door slammed shut and they watched him cross the yard. He came into the kitchen, put his briefcase down on the chair, said hello, and then, walking to the coffeepot, asked if there was any left.

"Don't touch that poison myself," Sal said. "Don't know how your stomach can take it."

"Doesn't hurt me a bit," Teddy replied. He looked at his watch. "Tell you what, I have to run into town on an errand. You and I can catch some dinner," he said to Alma, "and Mrs. Blair, we can take you home."

"That's real kind of you, Mr. Juroe, because, as it so happens, I just missed that K bus."

Because she was a nervous passenger, Mrs. Blair insisted on sitting in the backseat. She gave directions to Teddy and issued cautions when she thought it was necessary. "Now you take this curve nice and slow, Mr. Juroe, because you never know when some maniac gets it into his head to fly through at eighty miles an hour." She took them to a part of the city Alma had never been to before. The houses were dilapidated; the corner stores were boarded up. Teddy slowed down for a stop sign. "This where the drug addicts hang out so you look around you real careful. Some of them so out of their heads they just walk into the street like they never seen no car before in their life." There was trash blowing along the curb, broken-down cars sitting in puddles of glass. Men stood on the corners, not paying attention to the children dashing up and down the sidewalks. Once Teddy had to slam on the brakes because a child suddenly ran in front of them. Mrs. Blair leaned out of the window and called, "You almost got yourself killed. Watch out where you going." The little girl stopped in her tracks, looked at the unfamiliar car, and then waved when she saw Mrs. Blair. As they drove through the section she proudly called "my neighborhood," Sal was waving to everyone they passed. On a block where the houses faced the tall stone wall of "the factory," she directed Teddy to slow down. They pulled up in front of a small wooden duplex. There was an old couch on the porch with a little boy of seven or eight sitting on it. "That be my Clarence, my oldest." When Mrs. Blair eased herself out of the car, the little boy came down the steps toward her. Teddy and Alma came around to meet him, and Mrs. Blair said, "Shake their hands, Clarence; this be my employer." She turned to Teddy. "Come on in and you can meet my Nelson."

"We can't stay long," Teddy told her.

"You can stay long enough to meet my family, Mr. Juroe." She led them through the front door and into a dark living room. The TV was on in the corner. A child sat in front of it, watching it so intently he didn't hear them come in. "Nelson!" Sal called. "Somebody's here wants to meet you. Turn that TV off and stand up."

"This is my youngest," Mrs. Blair said, putting her arm across his shoulder. "Nelson, this is Alma and Mr. Juroe." He shook their hands and then went back to stand by Sal. "Did you go to Eleanor's today like you s'posed to?" He shook his head. "Your brother?" He shook his head again. "You spooking me, boy?" He nodded yes. Whereupon she pulled him against her and gave him a squeeze. "You been at Eleanor's?" she asked Clarence when he came in.

"Yes, ma'am," he said. "Had beans for lunch." He moved behind a chair and peeked at Alma.

"Let me pour us a glass of wine, and you can sit a minute."

"We can't," Teddy said. "We should get going."

"Stay for twenty minutes and we'll have a drop of my cousin's home-made wine together. It's nice and sweet. Now this be an occasion, Mr. Juroe. I'm always coming to your house, you can stay a little bit in mine. You can meet my boarder, Mr. Samuel Lem. He just getting up now 'cause he has a night job over at the factory. Now sit," she said, beckoning him into a chair, "and Alma, you come with me into the kitchen."

The kitchen was a shed off the back of the house, but the boards were painted white, and there was plumbing and electricity. Mrs. Blair took three wineglasses from a cupboard and pulled a bottle of wine out from behind a pail that was under the sink. Putting a finger to her lips, she said, "I have to keep it hid." She poured red wine into two of the glasses and grape juice, which she diluted with water to make it the same color, into the third. "This for the grown-ups. Get me three glasses over there, and I'll pour juice for you kids."

When Alma carried the tray into the living room, there was a thin, light-skinned man talking to Teddy. He was dressed in a three-piece suit made from cheap, shiny material. As Alma set the tray on the table, he started to cough. Pulling a neatly pressed handkerchief from his breast pocket, he covered his mouth. "Excuse me," he whispered. After slipping the handkerchief into his pants pocket, he clasped his hands between his legs in the manner of a man not used to sitting in a parlor and talking. Alma handed him the glass, and his glance rested for a moment on her face. "You sure you have the right one now?" As he took the glass from her, his sleeve rode up, revealing a large gold wristwatch and a smooth, hairless arm.

"She thinks it hurts my pride if anyone knows I only drink grape juice. Wine doesn't agree with me, or more properly, it agrees with me too well." His voice was crisp and soft, and he spoke carefully, without any accent at all. "I spent my entire life running away from my love of liquor. I lived out of a suitcase. Sometimes it was cardboard, sometimes it was first-quality leather, depending on my circumstances. Then I came here. But you know as well as I do that a way of life is hard to change." He began to chuckle, then he cleared his throat and went on. "I kept that suitcase under my bed—it was a fine black leather one—in case I got the urge, so to speak. But Sal knew it was there, and one day when I was out she took it away. I've never seen it since. You can be sure there were times when I've wanted it, but there wasn't a suitcase in this entire house. I considered taking a paper bag, I was that desperate, but even when I was spending my days on the streets, only half alive from all the liquor I was consuming, I'd never carried my possessions in a paper bag. A five-dollar suitcase I wasn't too proud for, but not a paper bag. So I stayed put. And, like you have to, I figured out ways to be happy. Drinking was something I couldn't do anymore."

"Was it your work that made you travel in the first place?" Teddy asked.

But Mrs. Blair came in and answered for him. "His habits made him travel. But now he stays here and behaves himself."

"Well, you're in good hands if she takes care of you the way she takes care of us," Teddy told him.

"I just know how to keep him in line."

"That she does," Mr. Lem replied. "That she does. Speaking of which, it occurs to me I never told you, Sal, that they're moving my position on the line to foreman. That's how I stay put," he explained to Teddy, "they give me what they call incentives."

"Congratulations, honey!" Mrs. Blair reached for his hand and held it in her own, saying, "That's the best news I swear I heard in a long time."

Mr. Lem ignored her touch and continued to speak to Teddy. "I don't have anything to argue with. They treat me satisfactorily. Of course, I go in the blackest part of the night when the entire Eastern Seaboard is fast asleep, and that cuts me off from society, but maybe conditions will change. Maybe if I just hold on a little longer, a position will become available in the daytime."

"I'm hoping," Mrs. Blair said gently, placing his hand back on his knee.

Sitting next to Clarence and Nelson on the sofa, Alma felt her arm prickling at the place where it brushed against Clarence's. Her whole being was tense because of it, and she knew that Clarence felt it too. But suddenly Nelson flopped down on Clarence, causing him to collapse onto Alma's lap. That made the three of them laugh. Nelson tickled Clarence but his real target was Alma, and he quickly climbed behind Clarence to attack her. Alma tickled him back and he squealed with joyfulness. Mr. Lem chuckled, exposing large white teeth. Mrs. Blair said, "Nelson, you behave yourself," but Nelson continued to squeal as he nudged Clarence and Alma. No one tried to stop him; no one wanted to. Mr. Lem turned in his chair as though to study them. Teddy sipped his wine. Alma remembered the moment, that afternoon, when she was standing in the grass behind the garage and pulling down her pants. This was the secret in the body, Alma thought, picturing Andrew again, his face puffy and red, his eyes squeezed shut. This room, this tall black woman, the light-skinned man, the two little boys, and herself—this was the secret in the body. Even beyond them, in the streets and the cars and the small dilapidated houses—everyone was pulling off their pants to find the secret. Then she remembered her father and Gloria, and an ache spread across her chest.

· · · · · 33 · · · · ·

Teddy wanted to take Alma to a movie for her birthday. Alma didn't want to see a movie at all, much less the one he was interested in. She told him he didn't have to do anything special. She didn't feel much like celebrating anyway.

When she told him that, he looked hurt. "How about I take you to a nice restaurant downtown for dinner?"

But they never had anything to talk about, and the prospect of sitting across from each other through a long meal wasn't pleasant. "Let's just eat here. Maybe we could invite Gloria."

He looked at her in surprise. "I thought Gloria would be the last person you'd want to have. How about Andrew?"

Andrew was out of the question. She couldn't have someone she had fucked with eat at the same table with her father. "He's supposed to stay home tonight. He's grounded. Why can't we invite Gloria?"

She heard him on the phone in the hallway. "Glory? Listen, I know what we decided, but something's come up. It's Alma's birthday . . . ." He lowered his voice after that, and there were only phrases of sound until his "good, see you soon" before he hung up.

That evening Gloria arrived with groceries. Her present to Alma would be the meal she'd prepare for the birthday dinner. She set the ingredients out on the table, put on an apron, and went to work. She sliced some vegetables, threw them into a pot, and added wine and water and soy sauce.

"Do you want some help?" Alma asked.

"Get me two eggs, milk, and butter."

Alma took them out of the refrigerator. In the meantime, Teddy poured wine into Rose Ann's best long-stemmed wineglasses. "Just a minute," he said when Alma took a sip. "I have a toast." He waited for Gloria to stop what she was doing and then cleared his throat.

"We've found ourselves in peculiar circumstances, Alma and I. Just the two of us living together for all of this time, we've experienced things that fathers and daughters don't often have the chance to share. Embarrassing things, things I wouldn't want to go through again. There have been uncomfortable times, and there will most likely be more. In fact, I've often wished I had married a more predictable woman, or at least one who wouldn't just up and go off to Europe like Rose Ann, someone who would stay here and protect me from my child. Because that's the heart of it. In most households, fathers are the part-time parent. They're protected from the turmoil. The mother cleans the spills, wipes the tears, and listens to all the worries. She grooms the children before sending them off to the father. Without the grooming, things are rougher, more ragged. As a result I know my fifteen-year-old daughter better than I would otherwise. I know who she is. Or do I? At least I know her well enough to know that I don't know her at all. That is to say, she isn't a child anymore. That's happened just recently. One day I came into the kitchen, and there she was: This young woman who turned around to say hello to me was my daughter. How could that be? Realizing that I had known her from her earliest beginnings, I felt proud. Fifteen years ago, right about now, my daughter cried out for the first time. Now look at her."

They clapped hands. Gloria hooted and cheered but the kitchen felt thin with just their three bodies. There was too much noise. Teddy's speech, Gloria's enthusiasm—everyone was trying too hard.

But it didn't really matter because time had moved on. Gloria was back at the table cutting vegetables. Teddy was at the sink washing dishes. Everything thinned out like this when you got older. The things you thought were important turned out to be ordinary. Nothing was special the way you thought it would be. Fucking was ordinary. Birthdays were ordinary. Even husbands playing around. She watched her father leaning toward Gloria as she whispered something in his ear.

Was Teddy a good person? Whatever she told him made him throw his head back and laugh. But he laughed only once and then returned to the sink. Gloria bent over the table mixing something in a bowl. Her hair was down this time, one long braid that fell over her shoulder.

"Do you know what he said to me?" she asked, and even before she gave the punch line, Teddy started to smile. She dipped her finger in the bowl for a taste and with her finger still in her mouth, looked toward Alma. "There you are," she said. "It's gloomy when you turn fifteen, I know. Come and help me, I need someone to stir this."

The phone rang in the hallway. They all looked up but no one made a move to get it. Finally Alma went to answer. "Hello?"

"I'm doing something very extravagant," the voice said. "I'm calling my sweet daughter on her birthday."

"Rose Ann, where are you?"

"I'm in a little balcony apartment in Trastevere. It has one big room that I eat and sleep and paint in. It's in the old Jewish ghetto of Rome, very poor but very picturesque. I'll be here for the summer because I had to give up my studio at the academy. My dear child, how are you?"

"I'm fine. We're making dinner."

"I wish I could be there so I could give you a long birthday embrace instead of a birthday phone call. I miss you terribly. I've been thinking about you so much I decided I just had to talk to you, whatever the cost. My dear child, happy fifteenth birthday. What are you and daddy making for dinner?"

"And Gloria. She's here, too. I've told you about Gloria."

But Rose Ann wasn't interested in the subject of Teddy's female friend. Instead she said, "Listen, there's something we need to discuss. I was a little concerned when I got your letter. Are you certain you haven't had any sign of blood in your pants? I'm a little concerned that you haven't started to menstruate. Some women develop more slowly than others, and surely that might be all it is. Are you sure there hasn't been any sign of it at all? Alma? Are you there?"

"I think so."

"What do you mean, you think that you have it?"

"I don't think so."

"Are you saying that you *have* started to menstruate or that you haven't?"

"I'm not."

"You're not what?"

"I'm not menstruating yet."

"Uh-huh. Well, how are you feeling, sweetheart? Did that nausea you were telling me about go away?"

"Sort of."

"What do you mean? Do you still get it sometimes?"

"In the mornings, mostly when I get up."

"That's happening pretty regularly?"

"Pretty much."

"And do you still have to urinate as much?"

"What?"

"Do you have to go to the . . . This isn't a very good connection, is it? I asked you if you still had to go to the bathroom a lot. You wrote me that you'd been going to the bathroom to pee a lot. Is that still happening?"

"I think so."

"What do you mean?"

"I've been having to pee at night."

"Maybe you're drinking too much before you go to bed; could that be it?"

"Maybe. Sometimes I have a cup of coffee."

"I bet that's it. How about during the daytime? Are you drinking a lot of coffee during the daytime?"

"Not any more than usual."

"Anything else different that you notice? Any more symptoms?"

"Why?" Alma asked. "Do you think I have something terrible?"

"I'm just concerned," Rose Ann said. "Tell me anything that's different in the way you feel. I'm trying to get a complete picture. Then we'll know if there's any reason to be worried, right?"

All of a sudden the connection improved, and her mother's voice flew into her ear with such volume and clarity they could have been face to face. The voice that had encircled her person forever now hovered in her ear, strong and warm. "This isn't a symptom," Alma said. "It's just sort of a funny thing. My tits are bigger and they hurt. What do you think that is, Rose Ann?"

"A woman's bosoms respond that way to several things. It could be that you're finally getting your period. How's your appetite?"

"It's good. I'm always hungry."

"You sound like you're pregnant, could that be possible?"

She had forgotten this about Rose Ann. Her mother never waited for the right opportunity; she always spoke. "What?" Alma asked.

Rose Ann repeated the question.

"I can hardly hear you," Alma shouted.

"Who is it?" Teddy called from the kitchen. Alma put her hand over the mouthpiece. "It's Rose Ann, but I can hardly hear her." Teddy's chair scraped on the floor. "Mom?" she shouted. "Are you still there? I can't hear anything," she said to Teddy as he came through the door. "Bye!" she called into the mouthpiece, and before he could reach her, hung up the phone.

"What's the rush? I would at least have liked to try. You two were jabbering for a long time, what happened?"

"I don't know," Alma said. "All of a sudden everything got fuzzy."

"Well, how's she doing?"

"Fine," Alma said. "They moved her into a new apartment."

34

She pulled *Congratulations, You're Pregnant* out from under her mattress and left it on her table where her father could see it if he happened to glance in her room. Was that being too obvious? On second thought, she opened her top drawer and stuck the book in there so part of it would poke out. Hidden, but not quite. That was more believable, a hint that Teddy could accidentally stumble on.

At dinner his face was relaxed. Clearly, Rose Ann hadn't contacted him, and he hadn't yet found the book. Her poor father, walking right into her trap. But he deserved it. He had represented a world that didn't exist. It wasn't benevolent; it was filled with false doorways, quick turns, hallways that ended abruptly. So let him sweat a little; it was only fair.

That night, when she pulled the covers down on her bed, she found a little box lying on her sheet. It was tied with a rubber band, and her full name, Alma Juroe, was written on the lid in pencil. When she opened it a piece of paper folded into a tiny square fell out. It was covered with lines of careful script:

Dear Alma,
I know you are a good girl. But just in case something happened I am sending this remedy my friend in my neighborhood told me. The Negroes she come from say it guaranteed to make a girl miscarry. This be a secret between you and me.
Your friend,
Sal

There was a list of ingredients—cayenne, molasses, Epsom salts—and underneath were instructions about the exact temperature of the bath-water and how long you had to sit in it.

Alma folded the paper along the crease lines, put it into the box, and put the rubber band back on. Then she stuck the box under the mattress. Feeling like the princess who slept on top of the pea, she closed her eyes and tried to go to sleep.

. . . III . . .
Teddy

Academia Americana
Via Angelo Masina 5
Roma
Sept. 12

Dear Teddy,
Dear husband of mine, my sweetheart. It's lonely without you. I have made a friend, a lovely woman, also a painter, an American, who I often have dinner with. But my body is stiff with loneliness. At least I am painting. That goes well. I am relearning color here. All is so vivid—the sky, the rooftops, the crazy silhouettes of the churches. You wouldn't believe the sky. I always thought they were just being dramatic, but the skies of Tintoretto and Titian, they really exist. Such a spectrum of yellows!

This is what I'm here for, I tell myself. And still I can't help but think about what I'm missing at home. So I'm in two places at once. I'll have to learn how not to do that.

Just a note. All my most passionate love,
Rose Ann

Academia Americana
Via Angelo Masina 5
Roma
Oct. 28

Teddy my dearest,
I woke up very early this morning and went out for a walk. There were only the birds, and the fruit and vegetable vendors setting up their stalls. Be-

hind the Romanesque church on the corner, a dawn unlike anything I've ever seen. The colors were taut and hard, not watery like at home.

But I've almost forgotten. You won't guess who I ran into at a restaurant last night. London Quip. He was sitting by himself, looking very much older. When our group sat down at the table across from him, he turned to see who it was. I guess it was the English. I was so happy to see him. So I excused myself from my party and spent the evening with him. We walked all over the city and talked about everything. He'll come to my studio tomorrow to look at my paintings and then he's going to take me around to his favorite spots in the city.

I'll let you know what he has to say about my work.

My dearest, stay well, Always thinking of you and Alma,
                                                      Rose Ann

                                                      Academia Americana
                                                      Via Angelo Masina 5
                                                      Roma
                                                      Oct. 30

Teddy—

The paintings are too small, too pinched, too neurotic. I'm holding something in, protecting something that I'm afraid will get harmed. They're frightened paintings. I could be painting in a prison somewhere, rather than in a studio with a dramatic view of the river and the seven hills of the city. What I must do is unlock myself. Face what I'm frightened of so it won't be a secret any longer. If it's a secret then it has the power to control me.

I think that what I'm afraid of is that if I really start to paint here I won't want to come back home. I won't want to be a mother or a wife. I won't want to live in the suburbs, shop at the supermarket, and do all of those things I was so accustomed to. Real painters don't do that. All real painters do is paint.

I know that's ridiculous but there it is. So I gave myself a prescription: ten large canvases, landscapes, worked on quickly, not labored over.

Quip has gone to Africa. He said he wanted to live somewhere where there wasn't such a thing as the self-conscious artist alone in his studio trying to *produce something called art. He wants to find out what it's like to work on a project as a community. He says he is tired of the individual and all his deceptions. He wants to see active, egoless creation.*

In the meantime, I am left to struggle.

Rose Ann

Home
Nov. 11

Dear Rose Ann,
Out of chaos, chaos reigns. Out of calm, calm persists. I'm afraid we are party to the former. Very infrequently does the latter live at our house. And yet we are fine.

And you? I'm sorry your meeting with Quip was so disappointing. But you're stubborn so you'll figure it out. You are a wife, a mother, it won't disappear. Don't worry. You also are a very fine painter. That too, won't disappear. At different points, one part of your life will take precedence over the other. That's all. You're there to paint. Give yourself permission to do it.

Love,
Teddy

. . . . . . *I* . . . . . .

As he passed his daughter's bedroom, light broke across the hallway. With eastern windows, her room filled with sun in the early morning. He stepped in. It was safe—he had heard her leave hours ago. Plans with Andrew, she said. To do what? He couldn't remember. Fishing, perhaps?

The bed was all light. Clothes spilled from the furniture, dissolved into light on the floor. He looked at her desk, not touching anything, not even reading the titles of the books lying about, only breathing disorder. He couldn't handle the clothes or pick up the bottle of perfume or any of the bits of pocket litter that lined her bureau: quarters and pennies, a book of matches, a squashed pack of cigarettes, a rubber band. Her top drawer was open, and a book poked out, binding side up so he saw what it said. Underwear thrown around it, brassieres and underpants tangled together. To look further, to feel her fifteen-year-old daughter body, he opened the drawer. The book opened and a diagram of the uterus with a fetus inside it made him stop. *Congratulations, You're Pregnant.* Homework for school? But school was out. He closed the drawer, book inside it.

Slob, he thought, as he looked around. She was a slob; her room was a mess. He sat on the bed and breathed in the unkemptness, the youngness and girlness of it. He lay back on the bed, looked up at the spot on the ceiling that she must look at every morning when she woke up. Who would ever have guessed it? That he was here, that this was what had happened in his life. The sun touched his forehead. They were lambs, all of them, Rose Ann, Alma, himself, all little animals munching grass together, keeping each other warm. Except that now it was Gloria and not Rose Ann.

He watched his thoughts topple into the groove. He liked thinking about her, liked it so much he hadn't the desire anymore to fight it. She was the longest woman he had ever been with, longer than Rose Ann, who was a good height herself. There was no end to her. Slim and tight with muscle, she was a tomboy woman. She'd trap him underneath her, pinning him down with her legs. He couldn't complain. It was a nice place to be, those long legs clenching him.

She was not beautiful. Nor was Rose Ann. He didn't like beautiful women: too complete, too perfect, as though they could exist without you. Why bother with them? He didn't. Of course, he hadn't ever had much opportunity.

Not that they were ugly. Just that they changed. In some lights they were too plain, in others they were astonishingly handsome. Rose Ann standing in the bedroom, bosoms loose, trying on a necklace. She was beautiful then. Gloria leaning over the sink, her hair undone.

When he was in her kitchen that time, it had smelled of baking. Breads and little cakes, just out of the oven, were cooling on the table. He sat over them, drinking coffee, watching this woman methodically work through a stack of dirty dishes. There was abundance in everything about her—the head of hair, the frame of her body, the baking, the cooking, the generous amount of time she had for him. And when they were naked, it was only the two of them: there was nothing else, nothing even to name or point to, nothing to distract them at all. It was pure sensation—irrational, illogical, renewing.

For her it was the same way too, because she had said to him, "How will we ever stop?"

That happened the day after he had been watching her in her kitchen. She had come to his house after dinner, when Alma had already gone up to her room. Hearing a tap on the back door, he had opened it and found her on the steps. "We have to talk," she said in a brittle tone, moving past him to stand awkwardly in the middle of the room.

He kissed her, merely as a greeting, but she'd pressed herself into it. It would have gone on, too, reached the point of no control, but he pulled back, remembering that Alma wasn't asleep yet. "We don't want to get carried away," he said.

"Oh, don't we?" she replied, her voice shrill.

He put his fingers to his mouth to shush her and ushered her toward the table. "Sit down," he commanded.

She sat.

"Let me get you a cup of coffee."

She shook her head. "Just a glass of milk."

He poured her a glass and delivered it, thinking how peculiar it was to be in love with someone who had such different tastes than he did.

She took a sip of milk and then looked up. In a level voice she said, "You want to know why I'm here. I've been thinking about what's going to happen, and I have a question. It's a serious question so you have to give me an honest answer. Are you ready?"

He nodded just as gravely as she looked at him.

"How are we going to stop?"

Right away he knew what she was referring to. They could speak in shorthand. All lovers, he supposed, developed that ability. But just to have more time, he asked, "What do you mean?"

"When Rose Ann comes home, what will happen?"

And of course, he'd wondered the same thing himself. But he'd pushed the thought away by thinking it would all work out. And because he was willing to be cowardly, it postponed the question.

"Tell me what you're thinking," she said.

So he told her that he didn't know how to answer her, that he couldn't predict the future, that he wasn't even sure that he wanted to. That was when she stood up from the table and slammed down her glass. He smiled at that, he couldn't help it—imagine being dramatic with a glass of milk.

"You're a child," she said, seeing his grimace and misinterpreting. "Not even a child! I've gotten mixed up with a baby boy. What an idiot you are!" Her voice was getting louder.

"Please, let's talk outside," he whispered, because he was afraid Alma would hear them.

Outside, in the darkness, her face was shadowed. To make sure she was really there, to hear her, he asked, "Why am I an idiot?"

"You tell me you can't predict the future. Well, only an idiot would think you had to wait to find out about the future. As though you had no choices, as though you couldn't decide anything on your own!"

"I'm sorry," he said. "I just wasn't thinking."

"Then think, Theodore." Her tone was icy. "Think, and then let me know what you've decided."

He expected her to get into her car and drive away at that point. But she walked closer and in a more friendly voice said, "I'll tell you what I've decided. Maybe that will help you."

"I have a better idea. Why don't we come to a decision together?"

"If that's what you'd like."

She was calm now. The panic had been subdued, and he could feel her relax into the still night air. They sat on the back steps next to one another and talked the whole thing through. And yet, it could have been real estate they were discussing. Those were the kinds of words they used—plan, choice, alternative. When she asked him if he would leave Rose Ann to be with her, he said, "Right now, that's not an option." She was there beside him, the warmth of her skin radiating against him, and those were the words he chose. And she seemed to have expected him to say that because all she responded with was "So long as I know." They talked some more and the decision they came to was that it had to end. She was the one who said it first. And it was easy for him to agree because he was an idiot. He would do anything, say anything, because when he was with her he was sick with love. Even when he pushed her car out of the driveway and listened to her engine explode the silence down the street, he didn't feel abandoned. He knew it would be a long time, if ever, before he could be with her again, but the fullness of her presence hadn't left him yet.

The emptiness came the next morning and stayed with him all week long. He wanted to go to her, more than he had wanted to do anything that he could remember, but he didn't. And then at the end of the week it was Alma's birthday, and how he had rejoiced when she had asked for Gloria. Of course, he suggested alternatives. But, happily, Alma was determined. So he went to the phone and called her. "Listen, I know what we decided. . . ." It all started again, her flesh, her wonderful legs gripping him. He had never been with a woman who was strong like that.

Enough to leave Rose Ann? More than Rose Ann? That was the question. Did he love her that much? He did, he did, but he didn't know if he wanted to break things off with Rose Ann. He loved Rose Ann, too. Despite her selfishness and all her strange determinations, he was always excited to hear her voice. And there she was in her studio on the other side of the ocean, painting the river and the seven hills. It took some courage to want a woman like that.

And where was he? Sniffing in his daughter's bedroom, a parent on the prowl, looking for something. What evidence was he in search of?

Only light, he said. I came in for the light.

Did you find it?

A pure white light, yes, thank you.

The last time he was with her he had tried to be as clear as he could. "Listen, I'll leave you when Rose Ann comes home. We both know that. But let's have each other up until then. Don't let's try to protect ourselves. Anything else, but let's not do that."

"We have to. You don't know how much it's going to hurt. Me especially, because at least you'll have Rose Ann." Later she said, "You're right, we can't. That's not what life's about."

What life was about was something he didn't have words for. You felt what you felt, you did what you needed to do according to how you felt, and you were kind.

But he wasn't being kind. Like a dog who got in the way, she would be abandoned. She would be angry at herself for starting something with a married man, and she would be angry at him for taking her up on it. She might hate him eventually, and what a strange turn that would be. Because he would still love her: her hair, her skin, her eyelashes.

"We have till the end of the summer," he told her.

She looked at him with that bare-throated look and said "All right."

Time to move on. The light was changing. As morning approached noon, the white was replaced by yellow.

But he felt a lump in her mattress as he sat up. Because he remembered hiding things there when he was a boy, he put his hand underneath it. Nothing. Just as he decided there was nothing, he touched something. He pulled out a small box tied with a rubber band. It looked like the kind of box a ring came in. Were things getting that serious between her and Andrew? Too sacred an object for a father to handle, he returned it to the same spot.

· · · · · · *2* · · · · · ·

The next day it rained. He woke to the sound of water running through gutters. His first thought was about the downspout on the west side. It was clogged with leaves. He had meant to clean it last fall but forgot. Or didn't forget, just couldn't find the ladder. He didn't want to climb out of a window or shimmy up the tree and get onto the roof that way; he was a ladder man, but the ladder had mysteriously disappeared. If he didn't have to go to work, he might try to find it.

It rained most of the day. The tree outside his window at the office dripped with water. The sounds of the typewriters punctuated the rain. Along with voices and footsteps, the morning was all percussion. He was aware of Gloria next door, could feel the slide of her nylons as she crossed her legs under the desk.

More than Rose Ann? Did he love her that much? He loved them both.

Outside, a bird landed on the ledge of his window, flapped its wings frantically, and then flew away. He thought of coffee. A cup to celebrate the hour. Surrounded by tapping, he stood up. He should waltz to the coffee machine, across the perfect black-and-white linoleum squares. The fluorescents buzzed and the other electrical fixtures added to the tremble he could feel in the air.

Coming back, an artist at no spills, he peeked into her doorway. All golden hair, all legs. His woman of the limbs looked at him. She waved, holding her hand in the air only momentarily. It made him think of something. The memory came tapping into consciousness, and he was sixteen years old again. He had just learned to drive. He was out in the country, going along a road with a field on one side and a row of houses on the other. They were built on an embankment, all alike. Each had a garage, a porch, and a steep driveway. Approaching, he could see children playing in a front yard. They climbed into the car parked at the top of their driveway and as he came closer the car started to roll backward. They must have released the brake. It came toward him, gaining speed. He swerved into the ditch, and just as the other car rolled in front of his hood, he stopped. Then he leaned on the horn because someone was coming in the other direction.

After that he had understood everything: love, desire, want. He had *wanted* to stop in time. And he didn't really have enough time to stop so he swerved, hoping it would work. The parents pulled the kids from the car and carried them, screaming, up the steps to the house. The father came back a few minutes later. He walked to Teddy's window and peered inside, didn't even extend his hand, just looked.

"God bless you," he said. The man's voice shook with emotion. "Someone else might not have been able to save them."

Teddy nodded. What could he say: It was something I wanted to do? It had to work? But he said nothing and then started the engine. As he passed, the father held his hand up, one man standing alone in the road and signaling another man as their ways parted forever.

Gloria's hand up as he passed her door—a woman signaling her lover? No, not at the office. It was more of a stop sign: Don't let my private life follow me here. Go away.

He walked back to his desk, sometimes stepping on the lines that separated the squares of linoleum, sometimes planting his foot smack in the middle. The rain beat on the windows. Rivulets of water ran down the glass.

· · · · · · 3 · · · · · ·

Who am I?

You're married to Rose Ann. You have a daughter named Alma. You live in a comfortable house. You sell insurance. You even used to enjoy your job.

Then what's happened?

You fell in love with Gloria, and she isn't part of it. She's not allowed. You can't have all that you have and have her as well.

Why not?

4

He wanted to go to a movie. He wanted to go to one of the older theaters downtown where there was enough legroom between the seats and the walls and the seats themselves were covered in velvet. It would be womb-like and the outside world would seem far away. It didn't matter what was playing. They could get some popcorn and give themselves up to the darkness. He hoped Alma would be willing to go; he didn't like going by himself.

He found her at home, sitting in the kitchen, reading a book. *Congratulations, You're Pregnant?* No, something else. "What are you reading?"

Instead of answering she showed him the cover: *The Practical Fisherman.*

"You're getting serious, aren't you?"

"Not really. It just gives me and Andrew something to do. It's kind of interesting. We look at them for a while and then throw them back. The other day we caught a bullhead. It's bright red, did you know that?"

She went back to her reading, but he knew she was only peering at the page, waiting for something to say to him.

"I was thinking of going to a movie. Want to come?" There, he'd popped the question.

"Which one?"

He found the paper, opened it to the amusements page. They bent over the table together, elbows touching. He was in love with his daughter. Gloria, Rose Ann, Alma: his three women. Did he love Alma the best? But what kind of fool wanted a hierarchy? Three loves, all very different. With Gloria it was lust, and with Rose Ann it was something steadier than lust. Did that mean he loved Rose Ann more than Gloria? Yes, he did. For Alma it was love like breathing; he couldn't put a quality to it. It was the steadiest and the most dependable.

He hoped she would find something she wanted to see. How to plead with your daughter—please come with me to a movie because if I sit in a theater by myself I am no different from the other men who wandered in for a bit of the life they were missing.

"There's nothing good," she said.

"You're sure?" He scanned the ads for the theaters he liked. A musical at the Lyell, a comedy at the Moravia, and something he didn't know anything about at the Littleton. That was the best one. It had plush, wine-colored seats and an enormous black-tiled men's room. He dialed the number, asked the woman what the movie was about.

"It's a story about World War II," she said. "Not recommended for children."

"How about a fifteen-year-old?"

"It's up to you, sir. I wouldn't take mine."

Judging from the ad, the comedy at the Moravia was about a man who loved dogs. That might be just the thing. "Heartwarming," it said. "Old-fashioned. Romantic." Just what he wanted. "How about this?"

She made a face. "That's the best one there is?"

He nodded.

"Can we make it?" she asked, looking at the kitchen clock.

5

The first time he stopped there, her kitchen had smelled of oranges. It was just before Christmas, so he assumed it was holiday baking. He decided she was the kind of woman who liked to have special breads on hand for unexpected guests, people like him.

It was orange pudding, she said. She'd been making it all day yesterday.

What was orange pudding? He'd never heard of such a thing.

She smiled. "You get some oranges. . . ." She lifted her hands to her hair and took out a hairpin. A strand fell over her shoulders.

But he wasn't going to make it; he didn't want a recipe; he just wanted to know what it was.

"That's what I'm about to tell you," she said. She took out another hairpin, and the whole mass of hair spilled down. "You pop them into a pot of water and boil them for hours and hours. That makes your house fragrant. I boiled those oranges all day yesterday and all night. Then this morning I took them and mashed them to a pulp, added some other ingredients, and put it in the refrigerator. In a few hours it will be pudding."

She opened her icebox and he saw a big white bowl sitting on the top shelf with bags of things pushed in helter-skelter around it. He could tell hers was the kind of refrigerator that would have nothing identifiable in it. Rose Ann kept a refrigerator like that. Everything eventually became something, but only after hours of preparation. In the meantime, if you were hungry for something fast and easy, there was nothing to eat. He'd complain but Rose Ann would say, "I'm not that kind of cook. I don't believe in instant food."

"But couldn't you keep just a stock of cheese?"

"There's carrots and peanut butter," she'd say. "Won't that do?"

This woman, too, would have nothing in there that was immediate. If a person were hungry at eleven o'clock at night, they'd have to wait while she whipped something up. He didn't want that. What was he talking about? He hadn't been offered. Her pins were out, her hair was undone, and she had closed the door to the refrigerator. "Are you having a party or something? All that orange pudding, what's it for?"

"Me and you."

"Oh, don't count on me. I have to be going. Alma just got home from school and will probably be wondering where I am."

She began to unbutton her blouse.

It was then that he noticed that her kitchen floor was carpeted. That was odd. She was the type to have bare wooden floors in her house. He didn't puzzle over it too long, though, because he was interested to notice that she wore nothing under her blouse. Am I being seduced? He asked it out loud.

She stopped halfway, only a crescent of breast revealed. Pushing her hair from her face, not in a coquettish manner but in a businesslike way she said, "Are you willing?"

He had never been one to analyze. He believed things were simple, that life consisted of what you wanted and what you didn't want. If you followed that, you'd have access to all that you needed. The plain and simple came first; the subtleties came later. If he phrased things in terms of what he wanted, then he always knew what to do. That was his method. What he wanted at that moment was not to get home but to see the rest of her breast.

They threw their clothes on the floor and lay down right in the kitchen. That made it easy, later, to serve the pudding. She just hopped up and dished out two bowls, and they sat on the floor and ate it.

"How is it?" she asked.

He couldn't answer. He couldn't taste yet. He was too loaded with sensation to distinguish something as insignificant as dessert.

. . . . *6* . . . .

He pulled into the parking lot. One smooth action: tires kissing the curb, door swinging open, man stepping out. A medium-sized man with the normal middle-aged roll at the waist. Shoes striking the pavement, legs making diagonal bars of shadow, he stepped onto the sidewalk. From the train of shopping carts he wrenched one free and fell in behind an elderly woman as the door swung open. It smelled of fruit and sawdust. Even with air-conditioning, the water fountain, the astonishing length and number of aisles, modernization couldn't wipe out the odors he had associated with the grocery store since boyhood.

They needed the usual things—eggs, cheese, milk, and bread, plus whatever else leapt out at him. He started on the left side of the store with dairy. Most people, he noticed, started on the right.

As he pulled out a package, five or six other cheeses fell to the floor. He bent down to pick them up, but the one he wanted slipped from his grasp too. Coming down the aisle there was a little boy in sneakers. They looked at one another. "See what I did?" Teddy asked.

"Why did you want to do that?"

"It was an accident," Teddy replied.

The tall, sinewy woman about to turn the corner, legs ending in wooden sandals that clopped on the floor and caught his attention when he first walked in, was the boy's mother. "Donny!" she called.

Donny ran up to her breathlessly. "Look at all the cheese that man dropped!"

They turned the corner and he was alone. He picked everything up, put it all back but the one he wanted, which he threw into the cart.

Down a ways he found milk, then eggs. He opened the carton and checked for cracks, which was something he had once seen another shopper do. Now he did it, too. A professional. And yet, he never found any, even though he did a thorough job of it, rocking each egg to find any sticking. He thought about the fact that despite the handling and moving and the egg's terrible fragility, the shell didn't break. Was it a mysterious force that locked the shell around the white, the white around the yolk so that even with rough treatment the shell didn't shatter? Or was it the miracle of the container instead?

Moving past chucks and shoulder and rib eye, he stopped at hamburger. Two hamburgers grilled in the broiler. He picked up the leanest and dropped it in.

Was this the supermarket Rose Ann came to? He wondered. Even though she did all the routines everyone else did—laundry, shopping, dry cleaners—she never talked about it. She did it so secretly you never knew if she had been out half the day on errands or not. Was she ashamed of it? Was that why she kept so quiet?

He, on the other hand, rather enjoyed it. Probably the only man in the entire supermarket, he took his time, moving in an orderly fashion from one side of the store to the other, slowing only at the food that appealed to him. Noodles, for instance. Green or white; or wide, narrow, or very narrow; or straight or curly. How did you decide? What he did was try to picture it on the table covered with sauce. There, it was narrow. What about the sauce? Well, it was red.

Approaching the checkout, he scanned the lanes for the one male clerk who worked at the registers. A believer in the principle of classification, he always organized Teddy's purchases before he rang them up, putting dairy together, vegetables together, meat together, and so on.

Teddy put his items on the roller in just the way he pulled them out of the cart. When it was his turn, the clerk glanced over, said, "Hi there, the wife sent you shopping again?"

He didn't know how to answer. Watching the man's long hairy arms shuffle the products into their correct order he said, "No, I live alone."

He lied just in case the man lived alone too—just to give him company if he needed it.

"Yup," the clerk said, his hand moving across the roller for the next item. "Makes you learn, don't it?"

Teddy reached in his back pocket for his wallet, handed over a bill, which the man snapped and lay on top of the drawer. After the passage of change between them, they each filled a bag. Teddy hoisted them into the cart. Setting out for the door, he lifted his hand in a farewell gesture. The man only nodded back.

Driving home he was struck by the system of grids, the black streets sliced by the line running down the center, the white pavement, the right-angle corners. They went about their lives in a village erected on graph paper. They worried and laughed and made love all within squares. And if you were age forty-nine and felt your life was worth the spectacular sum of a hundred thousand dollars, how much did you pay? He went six columns across, kept his finger there, and brought the other hand down fifteen spaces. There, that was the figure, thirty-seven dollars and fifty cents.

He pulled up to the line and stopped for a light. Then he put the blinker on to signal a right turn. But what if you went, say, the three columns across but, instead of bringing the other hand down fifteen spaces, what if you swept a curve and landed off the chart completely? That would be freedom.

Could you do it that way? You couldn't, he told himself, steering the car around the corner, following the lines.

7

He would tell her. He would say it like this, simple and no excuses: "Rose Ann, while you were away I met a woman. We would fuck till our bodies melted, till our shins shivered, till my socks ran off. We would fuck till my cock withered. We fucked everywhere, on her kitchen floor, in my car, in our living room one day when Alma found us, though we weren't fucking then, we were just working up to it.

"You were away, Rose Ann. I was lonely. I think she's wiser for having seen what she did. Not that she saw much, not enough so she'd know what was going on. Yes, we talked about it, and no, she didn't seem upset. Gloria went out with her the next day, and they talked about it some more." But he shouldn't say her name. She should remain anonymous, his long-haired, long-limbed woman of excess. "I have been fucked, Rose Ann, like I've never been fucked in my life. I never knew such fucking was possible.

"And as if that wasn't enough, but it was, believe me, it emptied me of all desire, there were blow jobs, too. Something at which she's an expert, and she likes to do, and she even swallows. There wasn't a division of bodies. The cock was hers, the cunt was mine. There was no feeling of 'Now I will do her,' 'Now I will move onto him.' It was all the same."

He would say something like that, more or less. At any rate he would tell her. He didn't believe in secrets. He had always told her everything, and he had no desire to change habits now. Of course, he had never had sex with another woman before, but that didn't mean he should lie to her. He couldn't sleep in the same bed with her if he couldn't tell her the truth.

Besides, Alma knew. She might have already leaked it to Rose Ann or at least intimated that something was going on. He couldn't expect his daughter to be underhanded for him.

He lived within lines and rules and boundaries. He couldn't pretend they didn't exist.

8

It was a misty morning. He stood at the back door and looked into the yard. He stepped into the grass, then walked across the lawn experimentally, trying out the breeze, the temperature, the smells. Dew soaked his shoes and the bottoms of his trousers. Still, he didn't turn around and go back inside. It was too quiet in the kitchen. Alma was asleep and the house was heavy with her slumber.

He wanted to get started on some projects, so he'd just wait until the sun dried things out. He sat on the steps and drank his coffee.

They were odd jobs, nothing terribly important. His thought was that if he started on them now, he'd be done in a month and a half when Rose Ann came back. Clean out the gutters was number one, plant some flowers in the pots out front was number two. . . . He couldn't think what number three was at the moment, but come September there'd be at least a semblance of domestic order.

A cardinal flew down to the grass and hopped around a bit before going off again. He stared at Teddy, his small unblinking eye sizing him up, a male eying the competition. Teddy put down his coffee cup. Where was that ladder? Not paying attention to the squelch of his shoes in the grass, he went off in search of it.

At ten o'clock, when the sun was high and the grass was dry, he found it. He had forgotten about the things he'd stored behind the garage. Someone obviously had been back there because the bench to the picnic table had been moved out and the ladder had been tossed to the side. He grasped it in the middle and started to walk off when he noticed something hanging from the end. A piece of plastic, or that's what he might have thought had he been someone else. But this old scavenger of love relics knew what it was. They used to hunt for them under the grandstand. Even at seven years old they knew what they were used for, and with each sticky balloon they became accomplices to the act they tried to imagine. They'd take them to a particular tree and hide them in a knothole in the trunk. They called it the dingdong tree. One summer the tradition was that whenever you were outside you saved your piss until you reached it. Then you sprayed the trunk, creating millions of black ribbons to watch trickle down.

He was the dingdong king. He could pee longer than anyone else, and he also found the most rubbers. Forty years later he still had the knack. As soon as he caught a faraway glimpse, he had known what it was. He also knew on whom it had been used.

She didn't wake until noon. When he came into the house, his sleepy, nonvirginal daughter was sitting at the table in her nightgown, smoking a cigarette. He offered to fry her some eggs. How could he say anything? She did what she wanted, and what she wanted was her own business. Why should he intrude? She sat on the chair with one leg tucked under her, the other swinging back and forth. Her feet were bare.

He stuck two slices of toast in the toaster, took out the butter. When he was in high school the girls used to paint their toenails. They didn't fuck their boyfriends; they wouldn't have risked their reputations.

He broke her eggs in the butter and a few minutes later when the edges had turned just a little crispy, flipped them expertly so the yolks stayed whole. He slid them onto her plate, added the toast, and delivered her breakfast with a fork and jam. "I bet you didn't know that I always wanted to be a short-order cook," he announced.

She didn't reply. Hair dripping over her neck, she bent to the table. She lifted the fork to her mouth and chewed, took a bite of toast, chewed some more. A taxi stopped in the driveway. The driver walked around to the trunk and took out a suitcase. He opened the passenger door, and a woman wearing a turban stepped onto the gravel. The sun gleamed on her earrings. She paid the driver, then turned around, and hands shielding the glare from her eyes, looked at the house.

They sat there without moving, looking back at her. Then Alma ran to the back door and flung it open.

"My little girl!" the woman called. They threw their arms around each other, and when they drew apart they both were crying. They walked into the kitchen holding hands. Teddy stood up.

"I'm home," Rose Ann said.

"I see that," he said, smiling foolishly. "What made you come back so early?" But he didn't go up to her, he made her walk across the room to *him*. It was only right; she had been the one who'd left. She walked into his arms, and with hands accustomed to someone else, he hugged her.

"It feels good to be back. I didn't mean to surprise you, but whenever I called no one was home."

His face reddened. "I've been out and about. I'm sorry."

As she looked around, she noticed the painting. "That's an old one, whatever made you bring that back down?"

Alma said that Mrs. Blair, the new housekeeper they had told her about, had hung it there. She turned to Teddy with an appeal for help, and in the silence he could feel the great space between the three of them. "We have a lot of talking to do," he said in what sounded to him like a ridiculously official voice. "Why don't you sit down? You must be tired."

As though she were a guest, she did as he bid her. She unwrapped the scarf from her head, and her foreignness vanished into the room. It was the old Rose Ann. She had a different haircut, but that was only incidental. She looked the same. "Would you like a cup of coffee?" he asked.

"Are you really offering me some of that vile American coffee?" She turned to the window and exclaimed to the view she had stared at for a good many years of her life, "What I would do for a cappuccino right now!"

Ignoring her, Teddy got up and poured himself a cup. There would be this posturing for a while. It would be annoying to listen to, but they'd have to put up with it until she became inured again to life in the suburbs.

"All right," she said.

He looked at her without understanding.

"I'll take some coffee."

Alma hopped up to pour her a cup, and when she delivered it, Rose Ann gave her a kiss on her cheek. "You've gotten prettier," she said. "You're not the child you were when I left."

That's correct, he thought. The princess of behind-the-garage passions with Andrew was not a child any longer.

"I'm becoming a fisherman," Alma said proudly.

Rose Ann raised her eyebrows, a mannerism he hadn't seen before, but instead of answering the comment she said, "What I'd like for us to do, my daughter, is go off somewhere tomorrow, the two of us, just us women out on the town. Teddy might have to take us because I don't know if I can remember how to drive a car. . . ."

"Of course you can," he said. "The minute you get behind the wheel, it'll all come back."

She dropped the pretense quickly. "I guess you're right. Once an American, always an American. Then Alma and I will have a date." She took a sip of coffee and made a face.

That afternoon Rose Ann called the shipper about her trunks, Alma called the airport about the rest of her bags, and Teddy sat at the table and wrote a grocery list. Burdened with the unwillingness to know what he was feeling, this simple task was all he could manage. He hoped it wasn't too obvious, and to appear to be engaged, he offered comments every once in a while.

As far as keeping all but the most practical considerations out of his head, he was successful. But it took work, and at least one stray thought leaked through the barrier. He recalled a time when he was thirteen years old, wearing a pair of swim trunks that were too small for him, and attempting to hide his erection.

In the evening they were in the bedroom getting ready for sleep. Rose Ann spread a nightgown across the bed and was standing beside it, taking off her underwear. Her bra unhooked, the familiar bosoms tumbled out. Then she pulled off her panties and naked, walked to the closet to hang up her dress. She had a flat, pinched behind. It was too white, almost pathetic. He thought of Gloria's tanned melon cheeks and how nice it had been to squeeze them. "You never did say why you came home early. Did you just want to come back, or did that trip you were going to take with your friends not work out?"

She turned away from the closet. "I wanted to take Alma to the gynecologist. She said she'd been throwing up. Did you know that? I was worried she might be pregnant."

He remembered the book in her drawer. Of course, it all made sense. Why couldn't he have put it together?

"From what she told me, she has the classic symptoms. How has she seemed to you? Has she been out of sorts lately?"

He didn't know. He had hardly been home. His thoughts had been too tangled to have observed much anyway.

"What's this Andrew like?"

"A smart-ass kid, full of yes-sirs and thank-yous, but I always had the feeling he couldn't be trusted." No man could be. But this was only a pint size. How dare he? A primitive anger made him hot. "She's only fifteen years old," he said out loud, but the fact didn't offer any protection. "I thought they were using rubbers anyway."

Rose Ann looked at him in surprise. What kind of father was privy to his daughter's birth-control practices?

"I found one behind the garage," he explained. "Today when I went out there I just happened to see it."

"That doesn't mean anything. That could have been from five years ago."

But he could tell the difference. This one had been fresh.

"So . . . ," she said after a pause. "I hope it's just a false alarm."

They looked at one another. He wondered why she didn't seem more upset. Still naked, she was sitting on the end of the bed. She might as well get it all at once, he decided, a complete welcome-home present. He grabbed the nightgown and dropped it into her lap. Then in a tone much calmer than he was feeling, he said, "Put this on. There's something I want to talk to you about."

She didn't put it on. Of course, it was Rose Ann. Why couldn't she simply do something you wanted her to do? Since she had challenged him, he made himself look at her body. But he didn't feel any of the old sympathy, and it was easy to conjure up the numbness he needed to talk.

"Something happened while you were away. I felt kind of lonely. I wasn't out looking for anything to happen. It would have been fine just me and Alma."

"You don't have to tell me, Teddy. In fact, I'd rather you didn't. We've both had tremendous adjustments to make and I know they're bound to create some confusion. Look at me, I had a new culture to learn as well as a new independence. We need time to settle in a bit. Then we can talk. Right now, the thought of all the places I've been in just one day . . ."

She pulled down the covers on the bed, put on the nightgown. She never liked to sleep naked; she said it made her feel cold. It was always a contest then to uncover her. He'd slip under the blankets and seduce her out of her clothing. This time what he did as he got into bed was ask her a question. "So did you finally get Quip to fall in love with you? Is that what happened over there?"

"I only saw Quip two times and then he went to Africa. He's not interested in me in the least. I don't think he's interested in women."

When she said "women" she took his hand. "Some things have stayed the same," she said, guiding him under the blanket, under her nightgown, between her legs. He was dismayed to feel his cock grow hard. He combed her with his fingers and she put her knees up and spread herself more. His whole body quickened with expectation. It thought she was Gloria. The hair that fell over the pillow was long and yellow; the pelvis that humped up and down with the motion of his hand was wider; the feet that began to churn the sheets at the end of the bed were a size ten, not a seven and a half narrow. He stroked and jiggled her, keeping it going until finally, when she sat on top of him, waiting for him to move, his body discovered the deception. This wasn't his cowgirl. This wasn't his slave driver. This wasn't the woman who galloped him into the ground till the mattress was soaked. This was Rose Ann. *Let's try something new. This time, why don't you fuck me?* All he needed to do was ask. But his prick wasn't going to wait.

When it slipped out, she said, "I think we lost something." Not giving him even a moment to feel stupid, she kissed him and gracefully climbed off. "We must be rushing things," she said, holding his tiny penis. "Let's wait until we're more accustomed to being together."

9

All through the day he felt at his trousers. Never in his whole life had that ever happened. His problem had always been the opposite. It's just a little complication, he assured himself. You've got to be straight with her. Once that's over with, everything will be back to working order.

Because they used to be good together. He could remember, before they had Alma, whole days spent screwing in her apartment. When they would finally go out, usually to get a drink before they went back for dinner, the world would have an unreal quality. He would feel so drained he would be shaky, and if he got close to someone, he was sure they could smell the scent of sex on his clothes. They'd go back to her apartment, make a late dinner, and fall into bed exhausted. But they wouldn't sleep, at least not at first. Because their bodies acted like magnets, and once the pull started to work, nothing would keep them apart. Although he remembered there were times, even then, that when he started to turn toward her, something in him would want to hold back. That tiny reservation stayed with him even as he started to kiss her. And when the kissing turned into a hunger, that tiny reservation was still there, hidden at the base of his spine where he could feel it. So that as he took her into his arms and felt the tension just waiting to be released, felt how she needed him before she could ever be restful again, realized that his was the final, controlling power, the black spot of doubt that had been holding him back would vanish. But only then. Every time it would take him that long.

After that it would be easy. Giving himself up to her smell, he would bury his head into all of her cracks and creases without any hesitation. Laboring over the bend in her knee, her elbow, under her arm, he would tease her until he could stand it no longer.

At the end, after he had slipped out and recovered himself, giddy and stupid from relief, they would laugh.

But remembering it now it occurred to him that with Gloria he had never wanted to hold back like that. There were no reservations with her. He wasn't afraid she would consume him. Or was it only that he was older, or didn't think about having children? Or was it that he loved Gloria without any fear, unlike the way he loved Rose Ann?

They wouldn't return till late afternoon, so he went into the kitchen to call her. He poured himself a cup of coffee and sat by the phone.

But maybe the days with Rose Ann were over. Maybe he'd never be able to desire her again. Not with Gloria out there distracting him. He dialed the seven perfect digits and after her crisp hello he said, "It's me. Something's happened. Rose Ann came back yesterday morning." She asked a question. He said, "She didn't mean to surprise me. She said she tried to warn me, but you know how it's been, I was never home. Listen, I don't want to stop seeing you." He closed his eyes to hold the feeling in. "I want you. Can I come over one last time?"

"I'll be home tomorrow morning."

He put the phone in the receiver and looked at it, a strange black, inanimate shape. Sometime later he picked himself up and went out the back door. He walked to the garage for the ladder. Activity, he thought to himself. Clean those gutters. Destroy the birds' nests, scrape out the leaves. Activity to distract the soul. He'd do the back first. That was the most accessible.

He climbed to the top and then remembered that he needed gloves and rags and a small, stiff brush. Where in God's name had Mrs. Blair put things like that?

He climbed down, went to the garage, and looked around. Nothing. He went into the house and tried the cellar. Apparently she had been doing some arranging down there. Cans of different kinds of cleaning fluid sparkled on the shelves over the sink. Rags were folded neatly on the table, and buckets and brooms were lined up by the washing machine. She had hung things on the wall—a hammer, work gloves, a trouble light. He took down the gloves and, collecting all that he needed, went back upstairs.

It was hot. He leaned the ladder against the roof and started up. On the roof, it was hotter. He tiptoed along the edge, crouched down, and peered at the lawn. He was fine, just one story high, standing on a flat roof. Obviously, a man who knew what he was doing. He'd figure the routine out with this one so when he worked on the upper runs it would go quickly.

He should have brought a trash bag to catch all the junk. Instead, he threw everything down to the ground; he'd just rake it up later. When he was finished he climbed back down and took a moment to figure out the best way to reach the other gutters. He needed a bucket to carry his tools in and a plastic bag. He also needed to take a leak. He stopped in the kitchen and got a cup of coffee. Then he walked around to the side of the house. He'd have to prop the ladder there and work on the gutter from the ladder. That would be a lot of climbing and moving of the ladder, but he couldn't see any other way to do it. The roof was just too steep. Unless . . . He took a sip of coffee, finished the rest, and set the cup in the grass. Unless he was able to sit on the peak and get at the gutters with a long-handled broom. Tidy Teddy, errant father straddling the roof for Sunday's pleasure. He didn't see why it couldn't be done; it would certainly make the work go faster.

He made a trip down to the cellar for a broom. Walking back, he noticed how high the roof peak was. He had always been uneasy with heights, but on the other hand, he had always believed that making yourself do something you were scared of doing was the only way to find out that few things in the world could harm you.

He leaned the ladder against the roof and started up. On the top rung he wondered how he would ever make it to the peak, but he answered his own question as he stepped off the ladder and slowly crawled up the incline. Teddy the homemaker on top of the house. He began to sweep the west gutter with his broom. When he needed to reach farther, he just humped along the peak. A strange cowboy. He wondered that other people didn't clean their gutters out this way. Once you got used to the perspective, it wasn't so bad. And it probably wasn't any less safe than the traditional method. When he reached the chimney, he grabbed it with one hand and tried to swing himself around it. As he did so, he realized that in the last two hours he hadn't thought about the situation even once. Maybe it would all work out. He would just be one of those men who arranged his life around two women. What was he thinking of? What kind of arrogant bastard even considered a thing like that?

Anything was allowed. Nor did it matter how pathetic a human being he was. Such care as he had never received in his life was given to him now. Soft breathing above him, the quiet of absolute concentration, and on his skin, a warm cloth tingling the forgotten nerves. Such tenderness he'd never had, not since he'd been a baby. He opened his mouth but it was easier to send his thoughts silently to the mute face above him: I love you. All my pores ingesting the air of this room are thankful. My lovely, lovely human being, don't ever leave me.

There were voices next. They were in the room but not close to him. Someone was there whom he knew. Rose Ann! He opened his mouth but it didn't seem as though anything came out. Why was he unable to speak? He wanted to cry.

There was the sound of footsteps. He closed his eyes and saw a huge polished dance floor. Around it there was a park with small, dark trees. It was twilight and the air was filled with birds. Arranged on tiers on the stage, the orchestra began to play. It was the kind of music he never listened to: bold and fast with lots of horns. They were melodies somebody else might have remembered from their adolescence. He had never been much of a dancer, and yet there he was, standing in the center of the dance floor wearing long white scarves and swaying back and forth to the music. Searching for encouragement, he looked at the men in the orchestra, all of them in black tuxedos. As they played their instruments, they glanced outward with empty stares. He began to panic. But the music coaxed him to take little steps, free himself of his silly fears. He moved forward two steps, backward two steps, calming himself. Then he saw Rose Ann. She was in the park, calling him. He beckoned her onto the dance floor, but she stayed where she was in the shadows. Trying to pick out her shape as she walked between the trees, he was filled with a terrible longing.

He opened his eyes. The room was bright with sun, and Rose Ann was sitting on the chair beside his bed, looking at him calmly. Right away he began to accuse her. She never stayed put. She kept on disappearing. What was he supposed to do? But she looked at him so kindly he knew she hadn't heard. So who were you fucking in Europe? he shouted. Thin and shaky, his voice hit the air.

She said very patiently, "You're in the hospital. Alma and I found you on the ground. You're all right. We're going to take care of you."

"Like hell you are." Still shaky but louder. The effort exhausted him. He tried to cover his face with his hands so he could cry, but he couldn't get his arms to move.

"You're a lucky man. You could have been killed falling from a roof that high. But you only had a pretty serious knock on the head and two hairline fractures, one in your pelvis, one in your collarbone. That's all. The doctors were amazed."

That isn't all, he thought to himself. Just wait till you hear what I have to tell you. He opened his mouth to say it, but his eyes slammed shut, and she was far away again, a dark figure moving between the trees.

The next time he woke she was looking out the window. He tried to lift himself up in the bed but his legs wouldn't move. "I have to talk to you," he said.

She turned around, saw him regarding her and asked, "Teddy dear, how do you feel?"

As the music started up again he moved forward. There was a change in rhythm, and he twirled around experimentally. All was fine, perfectly fine. He made what felt like a graceful sweep across the floor, found that the orchestra wasn't laughing, and gaining courage, twirled around and around in his glorious space. There were no barriers, no edges anywhere! He leapt and hopped and danced himself crazy. The gentlemen in the orchestra looked out with steady faces, and the music surrounded his movements deftly. "That isn't all!" he shouted gleefully.

"All of what, sweetheart? Were you dreaming?"

"I've discovered what it is to really fuck someone." Her face came into focus above him. He could see the lines under her eyes, the tiny hairs around her tightly drawn mouth. She wasn't beautiful. She never had been.

"Do you know where you are, Teddy?" Her voice was soft, thick with concern.

He knew all right. "We fucked. We sucked and we fucked. We ate orange pudding." He would tell about using her belly for a bowl. Why dirty any dishes? Since this struck him as being terribly funny, he began to laugh. But he stopped himself, noticing that her mouth hadn't moved. She should understand that under the surface of all serious things there was a layer of playfulness. Oh, her jitterbug snatch!

"I love her," he said as clearly as he could. "Her name is Gloria." But then he remembered. He might be free, but edges and barriers still existed for her. "I don't know her name. It's not Gloria, don't think that I said that."

Next to him, her face was the color of the walls, and she stared outward with the same unyielding expression the orchestra had. He looked into the forest, saw her shadowed figure walking away from him. "You can't leave us like that!" he shouted from the dance floor. "We're a family!" The word stopped all of the music. In the silence he was aware of his chest swelling with feeling. He wanted to cry, but when he tried to cover his face with his hands he discovered again that he couldn't. She had disappeared. "I love her!" he shouted, staring into the empty park.

· · · · · *II* · · · · ·

A woman leaned over the bed. Her braid fell between them, the hairs brushing his cheek. She tossed it over her shoulder and leaned in closer. He sunk his face against her breast gratefully. The closeness of her skin soothed all his senses, and he felt happier than he had ever been before in his life.

· · · · · *12* · · · · ·

When he was bored he tried new steps. This one, for instance, was something that he remembered was popular in high school. The orchestra played the old tune, and he slid into the routine he had never been able to do, a fast marching one-step with arms flapping up and down. Now there wasn't an audience to appreciate it, but he didn't care.

A nurse came in and pulling down the sheet, brushed his arm with alcohol. He whirled to a stop breathlessly. When the needle invaded his skin, he didn't feel any pain. She kept it in and put on another tube. But she was awkward at it, couldn't get the new one to draw, and had to take it off and try again. From his elbow to his chin, he was burning.

13

It was late. He had woken from a dream. The hallway was quiet. All he heard was snoring and the muffled sound of a TV. Someone else was awake then. They kept the night away with the light of the television.

Darkness closed in. There was a great weight on his lungs. Take me, he thought to himself. I've been serving you all my life. I'm ready. Just get it over with. But the pressure lifted. It was like the war when he would wait for death and it never happened. He prepared himself for giving up everything he had, but during the one close flash, it was the guy next to him who got the mortar and not him at all. As he watched him go, saw the body get ripped to nothing in seconds, so much of himself was there in that spot it was strange to discover he was alive when the noise stopped.

14

When he opened his eyes, someone he didn't recognize was sitting in the chair by the bed. She was reading. As he tried to get a better look at her, she turned his way. Her face was blurred at the edges. Even so, he could tell she was very beautiful. Light shimmered on the edges of her skin, and when she moved her arm, she left traces of light in the air. She put the book down on his night table and then, noticing the pitcher of water, poured some into a glass and offered it to him.

He took it but when he tried to drink, the water only dribbled down his chin. She leaned him forward and put another pillow behind his back so he was in more of a sitting position. Her touch was so lovely he didn't want her to stop. But she went back to her chair and with hands tucked in her lap, looked at him.

"How did someone like you get here?"

"Rose Ann dropped me off."

"Do you know Rose Ann then? Would you give her a message?"

"Daddy, don't you know who I am? I'm your daughter, Alma."

It was still too painful to move his arms, so he couldn't knock any sense into his sleepy head. "My sweetheart, I'm sorry, I'm sorry." He concentrated on getting his thoughts into language. He couldn't be a fool with her. "You looked like an angel. You should have seen the light. I thought I was in the war, and when the bomb hit, I dreamed I died. There's something I want to tell you. It's very important. Can you come here?" She came to the bed and he was able to find her fingers, closing his hand around their warm, strong life. "I love you," he said, feeling his eyes brim with tears. "Will you tell Rose Ann that I love her too?"

15

A cart rattled to a stop outside his door. A nurse with a horsey face approached with a needle. He hoped she would be more accomplished than the last one. In one swift motion, she pulled the tourniquet from her pocket and tied it around his arm.

"No more needles," he said in a strong voice.

She looked down at him for the first time. "We're just going to take a little blood, Mr. Juroe. It'll be over before you know it, and then you won't be disturbed again."

But it seemed to him that this had been happening for days. There must be pints and pints of his blood somewhere in the bowels of the hospital. "What do you use all that blood for?" He couldn't let it continue; they were sapping his strength. "Don't fucking take any more blood!"

"Just calm down," she said, pulling his arm toward her.

"You goddamn leeches! Get away from me!"

She jabbed the needle into his vein, and the rich color rose to the top of the test tube. "Now that wasn't so bad," she said as she untied the tourniquet. She pressed the cotton against the spot, gripping his arm firmly. Then she released it to his care so she could mark her sample and pack her tools.

· · · · · *16* · · · · ·

When he came home after the war he wanted to have a child. After seeing so many people die, he wanted to give someone life.

Rose Ann had hesitated. "Don't you want to wait a little, get back on your feet, get settled? Why do we need to rush into this? Let's just take our time, Teddy, please. I'm just in the middle of a good working period, and I'd like to be able to go on without thinking about having a baby just yet. Could we do that? I just need to approach it more slowly. It's a big step, especially for me."

All he wanted was to give something back that had been taken away. So much had been taken away. They had been so cruel he wanted now to be kind. And love. He wanted to climb on top of this woman and lose himself. When she took out her diaphragm, he wanted to grab it from her, throw it out the window. The sight of her lying on the bed with her legs spread to insert it made him hate her. Why did she think you could take away so much and not give anything back?

One night when they were in the kitchen, cleaning up after dinner, he tried to tell her. She was at the refrigerator, putting the food away. He was wiping the table. "You don't want to have a child," he said.

She turned around, looking bothered.

"When you married me you knew you didn't want one, but you couldn't admit it. Now what you're doing is stalling, hoping I'll change my mind. You have no intention of ever telling me the truth because you can't even face it yourself. You don't want to put anything out for anybody else. All you're interested in is your own success as an artist,

you own self-advancement. I want to end this marriage right now. I can
see that nothing will ever happen with you. You're stuck; you're just
saying the same thing over and over again: *Rose Ann is an artist. Rose Ann is
an artist.* That's all you're saying. You're not moving forward, finding
out about the rest of it. *Rose Ann is an artist. Rose Ann is an artist.* It's getting
boring. You could try painting other things. Rose Ann is a woman, for
instance. Rose Ann is a woman who likes to have babies. She's a sexy
woman giving this man a place to be. Because I'll tell you something,
Rose Ann, and I want you to forget yourself long enough to listen. This
man feels a little crazy coming back here. He thinks he might have killed
some people over there."

She put her arms around him, and he started to cry. She rocked him
back and forth, murmuring to him softly. He didn't pay attention to
what she was saying; he was bidding the fear and anger and the terrible
guilt to come out because this would be the only chance he'd ever have.
A long time passed and he was still sobbing; she was still rocking and
talking to him. He could have stayed there forever. Words and touch.
This was the reason behind everything in the world. It was the beginning.

But after a while enough of the pain eased that he began to hear her.
"This is a sexy woman who thinks she wants to have a child."

That was what she was saying. He couldn't believe it. He started to
cry some more, finding the guilt went even deeper. When it was over,
his insides ached. He was so light he could feel his breath moving up
through his rib cage. She was still rocking him, saying softly under her
breath, "Here is a creator woman who wants to be fucked."

But he didn't want her to say it just because she'd been pressured into
it. So he told her, "You have a choice. What do you want to do?"

"Everything," she replied.

He thought it was the same day but he wasn't sure. He wasn't holding cotton to his arm anymore so maybe more time had passed than he'd been aware of. To the woman sitting in the visitor's chair he asked the question that had been on his mind when he went to sleep. "Why am I still here?"

It was Gloria. She put down her book and came over to the side of the bed. He wanted her to touch him, brush back his hair as a mother would for a sick child. But she only took his hand, squeezed it in hers, then put it down on the sheet. Under his back, the mattress felt damp. He'd been lying in the same position for so long there was a depression underneath him. And his back ached.

"They're observing you," she said. "You had a lot of bleeding in the brain, and your fractures have to heal."

"How long have I been here?"

"Three weeks."

"How much longer will they keep me?"

She shrugged. "You'll have to ask the doctor."

But she had to help him because he didn't know who his doctor was. There had been only women in his room. Should he assume his doctor was one of them? He wasn't sure. She was only a few inches away from the bed, but she didn't make a move to touch him. He could see creases around her mouth, a pimple on her chin. He knew there were tiny blonde hairs along her upper lip, but she wasn't standing close enough for him to see them. He wanted her to sit on the bed, wrap him in her arms, and tell him everything would be all right. But she wasn't going to do it. She was going to insist he be an adult, make him lie there separate from her, and ask questions when something was bothering him. All right then. He could do it. Look what he knew already. He'd been there three weeks. They were checking him for seizures. He was slipping around the dance floor twirling his rags. But the clothes he wore were only lengths of hospital sheets and not the scarves he had first imagined. The space, so exhilarating in the beginning, now just appeared to be empty.

He waited for visiting hours the next day, and when Gloria poked her head in the door, he said in his normal voice, "Hi, I feel much better."

She came up to the bed and looked him over. "You really *are* better, aren't you?"

"Is my doctor a woman?"

She frowned for a moment, then shook her head. "I don't think so. I've never met him but I just assumed . . ."

"I've got to talk to him. I want to know what's going on."

"We'll call a nurse," Gloria said and before he could stop her, she pressed the call button.

It was a young girl who appeared in the doorway. She had on the right clothing—the white dress and the thick shoes—but she couldn't have been more than fifteen. "You look like my daughter. How old are you?"

"Can I do anything for you?" she asked.

He could only mumble, "You couldn't be any more than seventeen."

"Didn't you have a question, Teddy?"

"I did," he replied. He turned to Gloria, but not understanding his dilemma, she only smiled at him. He had to search for it in his own befuddled mind. Finally, with both women watching, he remembered what it was. "Where's the doctor?" he asked. He said very slowly, "I want to know what's happening to me. I want to talk to the doctor, and I want to talk to Rose Ann and Alma."

The nurse looked at Gloria questioningly, and Gloria said, "I'll contact his family; you need to get the doctor."

When the girl went out, Gloria stayed in the chair. She looked ill at ease, but he was too tired to try to figure out why. All he wanted was to lay his head against her breast, feel her arms around him. He was exhausted from trying to be an adult. Couldn't she see that? But it didn't look like she would come over, and he was afraid to ask. He was too old for such childish comforts.

Yet he couldn't move any longer. He kept stumbling over the sheets like a fool. Everyone was laughing at him. No, they weren't. No one else was there. He was an adult now, and he was completely alone. Where was Alma? "I want to see my wife and my daughter. Would you call them?"

Gloria picked up the phone by his bed and dialed a number. He watched her face as the phone rang. Her lips were locked; the pimple was only a scab now; her eyes were focused on something private. He wondered if she were impatient to leave. When she was about to hang up, he motioned her to wait a little longer. Maybe they had been outside and were just running into the hallway to answer it.

She put the receiver back in the cradle. "Teddy, I have to go. I'm sure a nurse will call them for you. Would you like me to ask one to do that?"

He would like her to sit on the bed next to him and hold his hand. But she was packing her things, not even looking at him. "Could you write the number on a piece of paper so I could dial it myself?"

"Don't tell me you forgot your own phone number!" She left a piece of paper on his night table, kissed his cheek, and disappeared.

He tried to reach the phone from the bed, but it hurt to hold his arm out that far. Deciding not to ring for a nurse, he grabbed the rail and dropped his feet to the ground. He knew he could stand because he'd done it before. It was just a matter of sitting on the side of the bed with his hands flat on the mattress, and pushing on his wrists. Easy. He pulled himself along the railing till he was opposite the chair. Willing his bottom down, he plunged into the cushion. Seated, with the phone in his lap, there was a new view of the room. How much more interesting everything was. All his nerves alert, he gazed out over the furniture.

OR–7–1523. Maybe Rose Ann was waiting at home for him, filling the upstairs rooms with the smell of oil paint as she worked in her studio. When Alma came back from school, she'd go down to the kitchen to make dinner. Except Alma wasn't in school, it was summertime.

No one answered. He put the phone to his ear and waited. When there was something you wanted, you had to be patient. They came in with his dinner tray, and he motioned them to leave it on his bed. Putting the receiver down, he reached for the cup on the tray and managed to position it without any spills. In his lap, the phone rang on. He sipped coffee and looked out the window. Just wait, he counseled himself. He watched the room fill with red light as the sun went down. Then he listened to the nighthawks circling the building. It occurred to him that for the first time he was there, really there. And he was lucky, just as she had said he was. His mind was clear now. He knew what he wanted.

Sometime later they came back for the tray. He woke up when the cart stopped outside his door. A woman so large the green hospital suit barely covered her came into his room.

"What's the matter, sweetie pie? Not hungry this evening? Nothing you like?" She clucked her tongue as she picked up his dishes. "You didn't even taste nothing. Feeling all right?"

"Can I have more coffee?"

"You ain't had no dinner, what you want coffee for? Now how 'bout this piece of berry pie? We'll make a deal. If you eat this pie, I'll get you some coffee."

She handed him a paper plate and a plastic fork. He had to shift the phone to grab it, and she said, "Whatcha doing with the phone off the hook? Must be someone you don't want to be home for, right?"

He took a bite of the pie and let the sweetness sit in his mouth. It was disagreeable to him, so as soon as she disappeared, he spit it out.

He was tempted to lean back and close his eyes. Trying to stay awake, he stared at the metal closet across from him. What was inside it? Towels? Hospital gowns? Maybe his clothes were hanging there. He tried to remember what he'd been wearing. Then he tried to remember why he'd gone up to the roof. It had something to do with its being Sunday. But he couldn't imagine what.

He allowed himself a catnap, just a minute or two to rest his eyes. The next thing he heard was a voice close to his ear. It was the night nurse.

"Two A.M.," she said, "Time for you to get some proper sleep."

She helped him to the bathroom and then brought him over to his bed. After pulling the sheet up around him she leaned over. Two strangers in the middle of the night, one giving the other comfort—it would have made sense if she had kissed his forehead. But she only switched the light off on the other side of his bed and then straightened up. "Sweet dreams," she said, laying her hand on his cheek and then, too soon, taking it off.

After his morning medicine, but before they came for his blood, he got himself out of bed and again made the journey to the chair by the phone. OR–7–1523. He knew what he wanted. He only had to wait till someone would hear him. The ringing stopped and he put the receiver firmly against his ear. "Rose Ann?"

"She isn't here. I'll take down your number and have them call you back."

"Who am I speaking to?"

"This is the housekeeper."

He couldn't remember her name so he said, "Is that so? What do you call yourself?"

Immediately suspicious, the voice said, "None of your business what I calls myself. If you leave your name and telephone number, Mr. Juroe will get back to you."

"This *is* Mr. Juroe."

He could hear her chuckle. "You been pulling my leg. Now what you up to?"

"I'm at the hospital. Could you tell me where Rose Ann is?"

"You're still at the hospital? What you doing there? Nothing bad, I hope."

"Everything's fine. Only I want to talk to my wife."

There was a pause. Then she said, "Well, she went to Philadelphia. Didn't you know that? There was this note here for you that says when you come home from the hospital they would call you because she and Alma went to Philadelphia. Doesn't say what for. Now what you doing at the hospital, and when did your wife come back?"

"Please," he said, "I have to find them. Would you help me, Mrs. . . ."

"Why, Mr. Juroe, my name is Sal."

"Thank you." He closed his eyes. "Now, please, did they leave a phone number?"

"Take me a minute. I be upstairs and the note be down in the hallway by the phone. You just hold on and I'll run on down there and see if they left you a number."

But before she could have reached the stairs, the nurse with the needle bustled in. "I need you to hang up and get into bed, Mr. Juroe."

He looked at her, didn't move.

"Just tell your party you'll call back. Not the end of the world. This'll be over in three seconds if you do like I say." She tried to take the phone out of his hand, but he wouldn't let go. "I'll have to call an orderly, Mr. Juroe."

"Get out," he whispered.

"You'll call your friends back in five minutes—nothing so terrible about that." She pulled the plug from the wall and draped it over the night table victoriously. He let her lead him to the bed and gave up his arm for blood.

She was considerate enough to plug the phone in before she left. As soon as her white shape vanished from his doorway, he got back into the chair, put the phone in his lap, and dialed. There was a busy signal. He hung up, looked at the closet, the gray metal surface stretching across his vision like a wall, and tried to figure out why Rose Ann went to Philadelphia.

For breakfast there was a different attendant. He was able to get two cups of coffee without having to make any deals. She took his tray away, not noticing that he hadn't touched his food. With the cup balanced on the arm of the chair, he tried again. OR–7–1523. Still busy. He waited fifteen minutes, dialed again. Now there wasn't an answer. Where was she? He hung up, dialed again. It rang and rang. He hung the phone over his arm so it was close enough to hear and slouched down in his chair to wait it out. When they came with his lunch, he told them he wanted only coffee. They gave him a refill without any questions and left him alone.

When you knew what you wanted, you only had to be patient. But by the afternoon he had to get out of the chair. The therapist had suggested he practice his walking so he reached for the walker she had left in the room. Hesitant, cautious, he went out the doorway. But nothing was hurting so he went up the hall and then back down. Up and back, from the elevators to the stairs. An ambulatory man. He passed the nurses' station and one called, "You're doing great! Tomorrow we'll try you on a cane!"

This kind of progress was easy. It was the other that would take some work. And maybe it was all very simple. Maybe Sal had only been in the basement washing the clothes. Or washing the basement. Or vacuuming the entire house. Or maybe he had simply imagined her voice and she hadn't been there at all.

Back in the chair, he dialed again. But it only rang. On and on. She had been vacuuming. And when she had finished that, she had decided to go outside and wash the clapboard on the porch. Because she was a steady worker, she'd come in only when she was about to leave to go home. He'd catch her then.

When he could hear the dinner cart at the end of the hall he knew it was close to five. He still wasn't hungry. Food was unimportant now that he knew what he had to do. He dialed, waited, hung up, and dialed again. Suddenly there was a busy signal. Just to savor the sound, he kept it to his ear until the cart drew close to his door. Then he put the receiver back in the cradle. Help was near, just an engagement of the wires creating a temporary setback. She was there after all. She had just been too busy to answer.

He put the phone to his ear again, took a sip of the coffee left over from lunch, and dialed. This time it rang. He pictured her turning away from the dishes she'd just started washing and picking up the phone with soapy hands. Or, since it was taking so long, stopping to dry them on the kitchen towel. He would wait. Even if she were just shutting the back door to walk down to the bus stop, he would wait long enough for her to unlock it and answer the phone.

"Hello? Mr. Juroe?"

He looked up.

"There's something wrong with this family. You're here in the hospital, and your wife's in Philadelphia. Y'all need a manager. Now what you in the hospital for? You sounded a little confused on the telephone, but you look pretty good to me." Mrs. Blair came to the side of the bed and picked up the arm they got all the blood from. He winced as she pressed the needle bruise. "You're pale." She put the back of her hand to his forehead. "No fever, though. Now what's going on?"

"Where have you been?" he asked. "I've been trying the house all day."

"Why Mr. Juroe, I was only there long enough to call around to the hospitals to find out where you was located. Then I took the bus home, and waited till my kids got back from school. Then I took two buses to get here. It wasn't but more than half an hour that I was at your house. Now what's going on?"

"I fell off the roof. I've been here for three weeks, or so they tell me."

"Fell off the roof? Lordy, Mr. Juroe, what you doing up there? I had no idea it was anything so serious. The note just said, when you come home from the hospital, like you was just there for an afternoon. I figured you'd come home long ago and what with Alma in Philadelphia with her mother, you was just living at the office mostly, or I thought maybe you was living somewheres else." She winked. "It ain't *my* business to poke my nose into my employer's affairs. I just figured I would clean the house till someone told me to stop 'cause there's always more cleaning you can do, even in a place that nobody's been messing up. Or, I says to myself, maybe he's just been keeping things nice and tidy."

Tidy Teddy, home on a Sunday, making good. What had he been making good? "Rose Ann came back early, and I need to talk to her. Did you get the number?"

"Congratulations, Mr. Juroe. You must be so happy. Anything the matter for her to come back so early and then take Alma with her to Philadelphia? Everything's fine with Alma?"

Then he remembered that she was pregnant. His fifteen-year-old daughter had gotten herself pregnant. Were they in Philadelphia getting an abortion? That must have been why they left so suddenly. She had just expected him to figure it out. But why Philadelphia? He would have thought New York. The crazy circumstances of all of their lives. He remembered now. Tidy Teddy cleaning out the gutters, a guilty cowboy straddling the roof. "I have to talk to them," he said. His pregnant daughter, his unpredictable wife. It took courage to love a woman like that.

"They didn't leave no number, Mr. Juroe. It just said they would call you when you got out of the hospital."

An attendant brought in his dinner. It was the fat one again. "Leave it there," he said, pointing to the bed table, "and please, would you bring me more coffee?"

"You can have all the coffee you want if you eat your dinner." She smiled briefly at Mrs. Blair and waddled out.

"Let's see what they give you. Some nice asparagus spears!" She lifted the lid from another dish. "A hamburg with melted cheese and a mushroom sauce! All these dinners been so good?" She spread the napkin in his lap and swung the table over his legs. "Here's some juice. You drink that first, it prepares the digestion."

He did as she said because it was a relief finally to give up. Rose Ann had disappeared again, and this time she had taken his daughter. Mrs. Blair sat on the end of the bed and watched him.

"I'm sorry they didn't leave you no number. Seems to me they ought to have done that. But maybe they didn't know what the number was. So maybe she intends to call, like she says."

He looked at her brown, weathered face and thought to himself, here was someone who took care of other people. Look how she'd taken in those two abandoned children.

He ate all of his food and then put down his fork. The fat lady brought him some coffee and took away his tray. He looked at the metal closet, thought to himself, *I was wearing my old clothes because I was up there cleaning the gutters. I slipped from the peak of the roof, and when they came home they found me on the ground.* She followed his gaze but he caught her glance on its way back to his face. "Please, Mrs. Blair, I need your help."

· · · · · *18* · · · · · ·

The first thing she did was call the nurse. When the nurse came, she demanded that her employer be allowed to see his doctor.

The nurse said that the head nurse was acquainted with the case and would be more than happy to answer any questions.

Mrs. Blair told her to send in the head nurse, and when the head nurse appeared she introduced herself as Mr. Juroe's cleaning woman. She said she didn't know anything about hospital procedure, but since her employer had been there for almost a month, she wondered if he might be able to see the doctor in charge of his case. Her employer's family was away, and her employer himself was still weak from his injury so she was the only one to help him while he was there. Would they be able to schedule a conference with his doctor tomorrow?

The head nurse said she would talk to the resident and most likely he would be able to help them.

Mrs. Blair said she wasn't familiar with a hospital as modern as that one and imagined that things must be very different from the old-fashioned hospital she was used to, but her employer didn't even know who his doctor was and wasn't that a terrible shame? A person didn't get well if he didn't trust the person that was taking care of him.

The head nurse said that the resident was highly qualified. The doctor, who had checked in on Mr. Juroe every day during the first two weeks, always delegated routine care to the resident when the danger period was over. If he hadn't been in to see Mr. Juroe it was because the charts indicated that he was progressing satisfactorily. The resident, they could be confident, had been monitoring the case very closely.

They would be grateful, Mrs. Blair said, if the next time the doctor was available the head nurse would ask him to step into her employer's room. In the meantime, of course, they would see the resident; she was sure the resident was a very knowledgeable person. She thanked the head nurse for her time and added that seeing as she was in charge of all the other nurses and all the patients, she must be very busy attending to many important matters. Realizing that, they were grateful for her attention in this matter and they would trust whatever she or the resident might recommend. The nurse left with a pleased expression.

Mrs. Blair turned to Teddy and said, "Sometimes it's handy if you know how to Uncle Tom."

19

A week later he was out. Gloria picked him up in her hot rod and took him back to his house. The first thing he did was flush the pills down the toilet upstairs. He left the cane the therapist had sent home with him behind the door and walked down the steps slowly, holding on to the banister.

Gloria was sitting at the table when he came into the kitchen. She didn't even notice he was walking on his own. "I thought I would sneak out while you were up there. But, stupid person that I am, I didn't do it."

He realized she wouldn't look at him because she was about to cry. To comfort her, he reached for her hand.

She pulled away. "I don't want you to touch me. I'm going to stand up and go out the door. All right, Teddy? If you don't want me to do that, you have to say something. I'm willing to wait for you if you want to leave Rose Ann, but if you don't intend to do that, I'm going to drive to the office and request a transfer. Are you following me? In two weeks I could be living in another city. You'll never see me again."

"I'm tired," he said, sitting down in the chair across from her. "I just got out of the hospital. Please don't ask me to make a decision like that."

But it didn't matter to her that he was in no condition. He could see that she hadn't even heard him. She got to her feet and started toward the door. But she stopped halfway and said, "Can I kiss you?" She came back across the room and bent down to embrace him. As she pressed her mouth against his, he could have given in to it. She was waiting for some kind of signal. But he kept his lips loose, the kiss uncommitted. They could have been relatives saying good-bye at the train station.

When she stood up he couldn't get out of his chair. He was exhausted. Also, he didn't want her to think he was going to stop her. He knew what he wanted and it was very simple. Things would be more difficult for her.

He didn't even watch as she went out the door. He heard her start the car and back down the driveway. Her muffler rumbled all the way down the street, but then she turned the corner and the house grew quiet.

What did you do when the woman you had been the most intimate with took herself out of your life? He made his way into the next room and lay down on the couch. He didn't wake up until the next morning.

· · · · · 20 · · · · ·

He got up with a start. Had he smelled coffee? But the house was as empty of scent as a tomb. He must have dreamt it.

He found his shoes. He tucked in his shirt. He wondered if they knew at the office what had happened to him. Might be worth a call.

He was in the hallway, dialing the number, before he realized that he was getting around without even thinking about walking.

"Mutual Life, may I help you?"

"This is Teddy," he said to her cheery voice.

"Mr. Juroe!" she exclaimed. "How are you doing?"

"Well, I'm getting around. But I suspect it will be another couple of weeks before I'm back at the office. By the way, did my wife ever contact you when I was in the hospital?"

"No, Mr. Juroe. We were worried sick. Gloria filled us in of course but there were a few days there when we just didn't know . . ."

As her voice trailed off he pictured the front desk with the slats of the venetian blind reflected on the wall behind it. He remembered what it had been like there, the air prickled with bits of conversation, the sun distancing all the outposts so the walk from his office to the woman in front was an expedition. He'd float past thickets of sound, arrive, say what he needed to say, and float back.

"You were too sick of course to do anything about it."

"I wasn't really sick, I was just a little foggy. When I fell, I got a terrific bang on the head. It made me disoriented, like I had never really woken from a dream." To the question about his present state he replied that he was doing fine and that yes, his wife was back from Italy to take care of him. As he hung up he pictured the other secretary walking to the desk to get the news. He could imagine their excited whispers. "He didn't know that his wife hadn't called us? Can you imagine? Maybe she never came home."

He passed down the length of the office and stood at Gloria's door. He pictured her sitting at her desk, bending over her papers, tendrils of hair curling down her neck. If she was talking to a client did she make him desire her? Would she cross her legs or let her fingers drift over the base of her neck as she looked in his eyes? He didn't know how she acted with other men.

Sitting down at the kitchen table, he put his head in his hands. Where in Philadelphia was Rose Ann?

21

An hour later he called her sister Sybil. Then he called her artist friends, but no one even knew Rose Ann had been back in the country. He got the number of the art school from Philadelphia Information, and when the secretary answered, he took a breath and said, "This is Theodore Juroe." He cast about for his next line, letting his voice sink to his belly so it would sound calm. "I wonder if you would be able to help me. My name is Theodore Juroe."

"Uh-huh," she said. "I got you."

Her rejoinder confused him. So he asked the easiest question he could think of. "I wonder if I could speak to Mr. London Quip, the painting instructor?"

"He's in Africa. Okay?"

"That's fine," he said, perplexed by this as well. Why did she want his opinion of Quip's choice of countries?

"He'll be back in September. If you're a student, you can talk to Leonard."

"No, thank you," he said. "I'm not a student," and then, because he could sense her impatience, he said, "Thank you very much," and hung up.

He went to the window and stood there for a few moments, looking outside. It was surprising that the day was so sunny, the sky so blue and perfect. If there was only some coffee. He boiled water, made himself some tea. Then he dialed the train station. If he could get to the station in half an hour, he could be in Philadelphia by three o'clock. But he didn't know if he had any money. He couldn't remember. And just to be safe, he'd need to have a lot. It might take longer than an afternoon to find her. Then where would he stay? If he had money, he could stay anywhere. He went to the desk and took out his bankbook. First the bank, then the train station. He needed keys to drive the car. But the car wasn't in the driveway. She must have taken it to Philadelphia. Of course, Alma would be sleepy after her abortion. She could sleep in the backseat as Rose Ann drove her home. But they might have been in Philadelphia two weeks already, and the operation had probably been done some time ago.

He called a taxi, went outside to wait for it. Standing in the sun, he was overcome by a feeling of expectation. Light, buoyant, he stepped into the balmy air. He looked down the lawn toward the garage. The trees made interesting shapes against the sky, and he was reminded of the park that had surrounded the dance floor. He stepped forward, turned around, stepped back. Perfectly balanced, a creature of harmony. A cab turned into the driveway, pulled to a stop on the gravel. Teddy told the driver he needed to get to the train station by twelve o'clock, but he had to stop at the bank first. "Can we do it?"

Instead of answering, the driver started the car.

The bank was empty. Six tellers watched him, their faces immobile, their expressions yielding nothing. He was reminded of the men in the orchestra.

"Do you play an instrument?" he asked the woman in the middle, the one he went up to. He saw her hand move to her buzzer, and the guard at the front door walked toward them.

"Just a question," Teddy said.

She gave him a professional smile. He took out his bankbook, asked for a withdrawal slip. Pen poised over the line, he thought about the amount of money he wanted to take out. He might not find her in a single afternoon. So he wrote the first three digits of his account number—that would be more than enough—and handed her his book. "In small bills, please."

She nodded only slightly. With such a perfect, expressionless face, he thought it a shame she wasn't playing any music. As she counted the money in front of him, he watched the movement of her hands. He couldn't concentrate on the numbers. When she passed the bills under the grate, he discovered he didn't have his wallet. "Thank you very much," he said, stuffing the roll into his pocket.

As the taxi sped down the streets, he counted the money. Six hundred and thirty-seven dollars in tens and twenties. He stuck two hundred dollars in three of his pockets and the thirty-seven in the pocket where he normally kept his change.

"Five to twelve," the driver said, pulling up in front of a huge Roman temple that stood by itself in the rubble of downtown rehabilitation. Teddy ran into the station, his feeling of expectation made grander by the distances the building contained. Diving through layers of sound, some of it close to his ear, some of it far away, and some of it so magnified it didn't seem to come from a place at all, he found the stairway for his train and just a moment before they closed the silver doors, ran on board.

22

He had expected to see her right away. He had expected sympathy to draw them together. But pushing past the crowds on the sidewalk, he realized his foolishness. From the train station, he had wandered into the shopping district. Men and women, dressed correctly, walked briskly past him. He slowed down. He was tired. He had just gotten out of the hospital. And it had all been a mistake. Those times with Gloria—how did he know anything like this would happen? *I'm innocent*, he wanted to say. But they only stared at him, their eyes settling on his clothes. He looked down, saw the torn, bloody shirt, the pants stained with roof tar. Of course, they were the clothes he had been wearing when he arrived at the hospital. And it was what they had sent him home in because nobody had thought to bring any others. How could he have left the house in such sorry shape? *I only fell in love*, he wanted to say, *but, really, I'm one of you—Christ, I sell insurance.*

Coming to a busy street, he stopped at a newspaper stand. When he pulled out a ten-dollar bill, the man asked him to do him a favor and find something smaller. "Look, I just got out of the hospital," Teddy said. "This is the first thing I've bought in four years." He heard the mistake but he didn't bother to correct himself. It didn't matter. And it might have been years, the simplest things were so tremendously difficult.

"All right, all right." A newspaper under his arm, the man began counting out change.

At the end of the street there was a large municipal building. Going throught the portal, he found a courtyard. People were sitting on the low stone wall around the flower bed. He sat down next to them, opened the paper to Arts and Entertainment. Maybe there was an opening she would go to or an alumni reunion at her old school. There was a new show at the museum. Maybe she'd be interested enought to see it.

He asked directions, found out he could walk there. On the other side of City Hall, the vista opened. There were long avenues planted with trees, a traffic circle with fountains and flowers, and a walkway leading to an enormous yellow building he assumed to be the museum. Over his head there were flags. And under the trees there were benches where a person as tired and confused as he was might sit down, get their bearings. But he didn't sit because time was crucial; the museum might be about to close. There wasn't anyone he could ask, so he plodded onward. But then he realized that the building was farther away than he had at first imagined. And if he got there and the place was closed he wouldn't have the energy to walk all the way back.

Beside him, traffic pulled up to a light. A woman sat at the wheel of an enormous black car. "Do you have the time?" He pointed to his wrist, mouthing the words, but behind her closed window she looked straight ahead. "Do you have the time?" he called to the man in the car behind her. "Ten after five," the man called back.

It would be closed. But he walked a little further down the line of cars just in case they were there, just to give Alma a chance to see him. He waited for the air to deliver the sound of her voice, and when it didn't, he turned and walked back to City Hall.

If it was five o'clock, he ought to be hungry. But all he wanted was a cup of coffee. Where would Rose Ann go to eat, where would she be staying? She couldn't have stayed at a hotel all this time; she must have been at a friend's house. Teddy had never paid much attention to all the names she'd bring up, most of them people connected in some way to art. If he could just find one of those familiar names, he'd have something to start with. At City Hall he turned in a new direction. He came to a restaurant, opened the door, and found a place at the counter under the warm yellow lights. Across from him, there was a young man with his daughter on the next stool. The trusting glance she gave her father—it could have been Alma when she was that age. How silly this game of hide-and-seek. Why couldn't she simply walk out of the shadows and say, "I'm here." "Coffee, please," he told the waitress.

When she set it before him, he asked her if she knew where the art galleries were. She put her hand on the counter, thought a moment. Then she turned around and asked the other customers. Did anyone know where the art galleries were? The man with the daughter said Walnut: Walnut near Rittenhouse Square.

On Walnut he saw the car. Brown, square-shaped, a crumpled fender— it had to be theirs. Even from a distance he could see her feet smashed against the window, hear the muffled sounds from under the blanket they tented over themselves in case anyone happened to peek in. They had been nuts to do it in the backseat, two human beings their size. And in the parking lot of their office building, and over lunch when people were going in and out. But he had always parked at least an acre away from the entrance, and it was extremely unlikely that anyone they knew would get into the cars on either side. She would go there first, and then he, and they would leave in the same manner. Because they couldn't help themselves. They had been giddy and stupid like a couple of teens.

Four new tires, a Connecticut license—it was his sexmobile. The doors were locked but peering inside, he saw a sweater lying on the backseat. All golden hair, all legs. But it had stopped, and he was relieved. You couldn't be giddy and stupid all your life. Why not? He would just have to show Rose Ann.

He walked down the sidewalk expecting her to burst from any doorway. When he reached the galleries, he looked for one she might have mentioned. Perhaps there was an opening. He noticed a lighted window on a top floor with people passing back and forth in front of it. Could she be there? He ran across the street and into the building. On the top floor, he walked into a large room. The walls were hung with huge, three-dimensional paintings. Springs and tubing leaping off the canvas, swirls of fluorescent colors—it was nothing he would have wanted to look at more closely. But she would have been able to explain them. She would have given them a place in the world, a reason for existing. He walked into the next room. More paintings, same artist. Even from a distance they made him uncomfortable. A pretty Chinese woman came forward, eyes settling on Teddy's clothes.

"Excuse me," she said, taking his arm, "but this is a private opening. You have to have an invitation."

"My wife has it," Teddy explained. "In fact, I was just looking for her."

"Then you can come back when you find her," she said, taking his elbow and guiding him toward the door.

"No, really," he said. "She's right around here somewhere. Rose Ann Juroe, you must know her. She's a painter. She went to school here, studied with Quip. You must know Quip." He spoke fast, looking her in the eyes.

"Are you sure she was coming to this gallery? There's another opening down the street. Why don't you check there?"

There was pressure on his elbow again, surprisingly firm for a woman so small. They came to the elevator, and for a moment he thought of resisting. What if she was just coming out of the bathroom, or what if there was another room where she was standing quietly, looking at the show? But the pressure pushed him forward when the doors opened, and he was trapped inside, sinking downward.

He went to all the other galleries, but the buildings were locked. It was then that he realized she must have been lying just to get rid of him. Why was he such a fool?

At least he had the car. If nothing else he could stay there until they appeared. They had probably gone to dinner. So they would be coming back soon. Or maybe dinner and then a movie. In any case, he would wait for them. Waiting was easy enough.

But when he returned to the spot, the car was gone. He walked down a few more blocks just to make sure—it wasn't there.

At Rittenhouse Square he found a hotel. To get a room for the night, he had to give up a quarter of the contents of one of his pockets. Standing in the marble lobby, catching views of himself in the gold-flecked mirrors, he was obedient to their requests. Nor did he blame them for wanting the bill paid in advance. He was a man without luggage or even a wallet. And as exhausted as he was, he could remember neither his

phone number nor his address. So on the form they gave him, he left the
lines below his name blank.

When the bellboy closed the door behind him, he crossed the dim,
quiet room, and dropped onto the enormous bed.

23

The next morning the voices of the chambermaids woke him. It felt like it was late. He pulled the curtains open, looked out the window. Rain. The puzzle of streets and buildings made him feel hopeless. Just the density of downtown Philadelphia would keep her hidden.

Out on the sidewalk he looked for her face under the umbrellas. Cars splashed water at his pant legs. A bus, coming up to the curb, displaced gallons onto his feet. He passed a department store, noticed the number of people stepping out of the revolving door, and went inside.

It was a huge, cavernous space. Sound pressed against his temples. As he put up a hand to brush back his dripping hair, an ache ran through his collarbone. The dampness was irritating his fracture. At the center of the great hall, he found a directory. Maybe she, too, had come in out of the rain and, to kill some time, had gone to the fourth floor, to Women's Town and Country. He retraced her path, riding the escalator upward. Then, looking down at the figures moving about on the ground level, he saw her. She was with Alma, standing at the perfume counter. Over their heads, a big plastic bottle of Chanel swung back and forth in the breeze. And just in front, white letters zigzagging through pink waves, a banner said *beachwear*. He leaned over the railing and shouted her name. Distance swallowed the sound. Still, he tried again. But he knew she couldn't hear. He ran up to the next floor and around the landing to the down side. He couldn't see perfumes, couldn't watch where they went next. Pushing past the people in front of him, he ran down the steps to the ground floor. He dashed around to the other side, spotted the Chanel bottle and wound in and out of merchandise to the perfume counter. They were still there. "Rose Ann!" he cried. She looked up, curious and suspicious at once. The noise of the busy department store stopped and in the long, uninterrupted glance between them he knew only that this present, the tiny overlapping of circumstance that he had been hoping for, was finally there. His chest tightened. The days and days of thought when he had lain in bed in the hospital rose into memory. She walked down the aisle toward him and stopped a foot or two away.

"I'm a mess," he said, letting the tears run down his face.

They took a taxi back to the place where they had been staying. Alma, his beautiful, gentle daughter, the angel that had been at his bedside, sat next to him, holding his hand. Rose Ann sat beside the driver, not once turning around. When they pulled up before a row house, Teddy wondered if they had arrived at the wrong address. It wasn't the way he had pictured it. Not an old Philadelphia homestead at all.

Did he want a cup of coffee, she asked as she led him into the kitchen.

He sat down at the table, looked around at the grimy counter. "What's the deal here?"

"We're taking care of things while they're away."

"Who?" he asked.

But all she said was, "Friends, it's not important."

Alma came in, said she'd love to go to that movie down the street she'd always wanted to see. Would they mind if she disappeared for a couple of hours? "Because anyway," she said, clutching her umbrella, not daring to look at either of them, "I know you want to talk. Bye!" she called from the front door. "Nice to see you two together!"

"So," he said when the house was quiet, "did she have an abortion?"

Rose Ann laughed. "She wasn't pregnant. It was all a ploy to get me to come home. Very clever. She just wanted me to come back. She missed me. That's all. She said she would never go that far with Andrew; neither of them were old enough." She stopped talking. But then she broke into her silence. "By the way, I resent the hell out of this. Who do you think you are chasing after me? What gives you the right? And don't say Alma because I could tell you a thing or two about parental responsibility." Her dark, steady eyes reflected the lights of the kitchen. He couldn't see into them, couldn't find any focus on him in their depths.

"I've been looking for you," he said. "For two days I've walked all over this city."

"And you found me. Good for you. But let me tell you something. It's over with. You're on your own."

"What's going on?"

She didn't answer. In the window behind her, he noticed that the rain was letting up. Against the gray sky there was a single black tree. Here, in this small airless room, the outside world was far away. At this point in his life to be so dependent on the details of an unknown person's existence—the torn calendar hanging on the refrigerator, the paint peeling on the cabinets—who knows how long he might be stuck there. "Listen, something happened when you were away. I fell in love with another woman. I didn't intend for anything like that to happen, but it did. It would have been fine, just me and Alma waiting for you to get back. But then this woman appeared. And then when things got kind of serious, she asked me to choose, you or her. That was when I realized I wanted to be with you. I couldn't choose her. So now she's moved somewhere else. I don't even know where." Across from him her face was still. His voice went on: "Listen, I've been with a woman who is completely different. I've learned new things."

She sputtered, slapped her thigh. "You can spare me the details. Those I have heard ad nauseam."

He looked at her blankly.

"The last time I saw you you were reporting on how delightful it was to screw this woman who we might as well call by name. No, excuse me, not screw. Fuck was the word you used. That you hadn't known what it was to fuck a woman before. You were very clear on that. What you and Gloria did was what the word fuck really meant. You went on to tell me how it had been different from what you and I, poor deluded souls that we were, had been satisfied with."

"In the hospital?"

"Yes, in the hospital."

"I guess it all spilled out."

"Yes, I guess it did. Maybe there's more. At any rate, it was certainly all I cared to hear about."

"I was out of my head. I didn't know what I was saying."

"But it all actually happened. And it sounds like she had quite a repertoire. On the floor, in the car . . . sex in the bedroom must be dull by comparison. And she makes orange pudding?" Her face was so taut he thought it would crack. "And she licks it off all of your most interesting places? Just go back to her. Don't waste your time here with me."

"I never would have told you all of that. Not if I had known what I was doing."

"The orange pudding, her jitterbug snatch, her I don't know what else—I didn't listen."

"I'm sorry." He began to cry. "I love you and I want to live with you again."

"I'm sorry, too," Rose Ann said. "Because I'm leaving you. You're on your own." She leaned back in the chair, hands behind her head, victorious. "Finally, after all of these years, I'll be in my studio painting. Full time. No interruptions . . . Alma will probably decide to stay with me and that would be fine. I can take care of just the two of us, but I can't run a family. Not if I'm going to be an artist. It's taken me a long time, but I've finally understood that."

"What's the matter with you?"

"Nothing's the matter. I've finally come to my senses." She looked at his flushed, tear-streaked face.

"I wasn't myself!" he cried. "When you go through a trauma your mind just spills whatever it's been collecting. I was out of control. I'm sorry."

"Don't apologize."

"Really, I'm sorry that you were the one who had to listen."

"I'm sorry, I'm sorry. I'm sorry, I'm sorry. You sound pathetic." She turned away, picked a pear out of the fruit bowl and with a small, bone-handled knife, began to peel it. Under her hands, the skin came off in one long piece. Until it broke. She let it fall to the table and started again. There was a tiny sound that the knife made as it pulled against the firm pulp of the fruit. It was terrible in their silence, a small grating sound that filled the room.

"You took our daughter and disappeared when I was helpless."

Her hands stopped. She put the pear down. "Even though I could still hear all of that trash you threw out at me, declaring your love for her the first day I was there and then treating me to a description of your sexual performances on the second—even though I could still hear all of that—I called that hospital every morning to find out how you were. The day they released you I just happened to miss, and by the time I tried you at home you had already left. And I'll tell you something else. This mission of yours is going to fail. Because tomorrow morning Alma and I will drop you off at the train station."

"Look, let's get something clear." He pushed the chair back, stood up. "I wasn't going to keep any secrets. I wanted to tell you about her. I trusted you to be able to understand. You can't just leave us and expect everything to tick away smoothly. You're part of the routine and when you pull out . . ." He had walked to the doorway and was turning around when he realized he was explaining it all wrong. Her face, swallowed by the angles of the room, small and pinched and dark . . . He had wanted her to go to Rome. She should always have the chance to do something like that, to extend herself. She shouldn't have stayed home to keep the order. It was just that . . .

"I know all about your good intentions. The first night I was home you started to tell me. And I knew already! Alma certainly hinted . . ." She paused, picked up the pear. "The fact remains, I've made my decision."

When she started to peel it again, he pulled it out of her hands and threw it into the sink. The hollow thud, as it landed, stopped them both. "I get it," he said quietly. "I can screw someone else, that doesn't bother you, I just can't fall in love. In fact, I bet it would tickle you if I screwed someone else and found them not as exciting as you. If I reported that, it would make you feel good, wouldn't it? Rose Ann the Terrific!"

"Stop it!" she screamed. "I've had enough! Just get out of here!"

He stood in the doorway, refusing to move.

"Get on the train and go back to New Haven, or wherever you came from."

"I can't. I'm tired. We met in a bookstore. I picked you up."

"That's beside the point," she said.

"We have a daughter. She's fifteen. There are a lot of things we've been through."

"And?" she said, standing up too, putting her hands on her hips, facing him.

"I'm not ready to give it all up."

"Oh no?" She went to the sink and washed his coffee cup.

"I want you to sit down. I've been in the hospital for four weeks. I need to talk."

Impatient with him, she looked up.

"That time after the war? You remember. I was thinking about it in the hospital. When I finally told you what I was feeling, you held onto me for hours and hours." Her hands holding his head against her chest, against her blouse . . . "What you gave me then, and I can tell you exactly what it was, was forgiveness. I'm not asking for that right now—you can't ask for it anyway, but I want to talk to you. I feel like I'm going crazy."

"I don't doubt it." she said, turning away from the sink. "But what you need is a good analyst. I can't be the one you come to. Not anymore." Drying the cup, she put it back in the cabinet.

Then her arm came down, her fingers gripped the counter, her pelvis pushed against the sink. Yet he could read her thoughts even in her back. With shoulders hunched up like that she wasn't feeling so sure of herself either. The room was hot. Their bodies drank up all the air. Well she could relax; he was too tired. "Where can I go to lie down? Because I can't stand this anymore. I need to close my eyes and then I'll get out of here."

She sighed, pushed her chair back under the table. He assumed he was supposed to follow her when she went into the living room and then up the dark, narrow stairway to the second floor. "You can lie down in here," she said, walking down the hall. The door was stuck so she pushed it with her knee and it flung open. Light broke into the gloom. He walked into someone's studio, the windows spilling the brilliance of an after-rain sky onto the floor. In the old days, it would have been peace.

At one end of the room there was a small bed made up like a couch and at the other, a table with brushes and paint next to an easel. In the middle, he saw a setup for a still life. It was hers. He recognized the material draped over the crate. It was the same style as before, a bowl filled with fruit, an empty pitcher. After the river and the hills of Rome, the Italian skies, she was still doing these things? Had that been the problem all along, that she was unwilling to give up control?

She walked to the couch, pulled down the cover, found a pillow. "This will have to do," she said, turning around.

He started to shiver. He couldn't stop.

She told him to get undressed, that she'd hang his wet clothes on the line outside to dry. "You'll be okay," she said.

Her tone, he noticed, was crisp and practical.

"I can pull the shades if you want it darker. Do you want me to do that?" She walked to the first window.

"I don't want that!" he shouted, leaping up from the bed. "Don't pull the shade down! Don't hang up my clothes! Leave me alone if you're really going to leave me! Just get out of here!"

She started to go.

"And don't take me to the train. I can get there myself." He was in his underwear and socks, standing in the middle of the room. "Why do you have to do it?" he asked.

"I have to, Teddy," was all she said. She was leaning against the door, one hand on the knob, the other, open, against her dress. Anxious to flee, she could have been downstairs already.

"Make me understand. Because it feels all wrong to me."

"To me it feels right. In fact, I've never been so sure . . ."

He kicked the still life. The pitcher fell onto the floor noisily, the bowl smashed, the oranges rolled.

"I'm a passionate woman!" she yelled. "And if that hasn't been good enough . . ."

He shot an orange into the corner of the room. It hit the molding and bounced back.

She screamed at him. "Get out of here! Coming into this house, demanding me back . . . It's over with! I'm not going to do this anymore! I'm not stupid."

"Be stupid!" he shouted.

The quiet was thick. Starting way down in the pit of his stomach, breath was traveling up to his ribs. She was watching from the corner of the room. "You asshole," he whispered. He wanted to take her face between his hands, show her there was no reason, anymore, to be jealous or hurt or angry. Instead, he picked up the material and lay it down over the crate. Then he placed the pitcher on top of it and got on his knees to gather the oranges. He would do this much and then he would lie down, and then maybe in the evening or the next morning he would leave. But as he was going after the last orange she spoke. "Don't bother. It was a boring still life." He was on his hands and knees, about to grab the orange, and her voice, as calm as though they were best friends in the middle of a long discussion, went on: "I can't do still lifes anymore. I'm not even interested in landscapes. What I want to start doing is the figure."

He stood up, and without any decision from him, his legs started to take him toward her.

"You've really done it. You really know how to muck things up. And you're the last person to be calling me an asshole, I hope you realize that."

"I know," he whispered. He was. He was getting closer, but he wasn't sure if she would accept him.

As if she'd heard something outside, she turned toward the window. "What?"

"You idiot," she said. She turned back to him and when his eyes caught hers, the hollows of her cheeks collapsed and before she had a chance to stop it, her face broke into a grin.

"What's that about?"

"I'm thinking," was all she said.

He didn't know if that meant that he could smile too.

"Do you remember the time we left before the food came?"

"What are you talking about?"

"Years and years ago . . . that restaurant in Manhattan . . . when I was working at the flower shop. We met over lunch and I told you I didn't want to get married? And you couldn't bear the thought of it so you started to leave? And I followed you out?"

Design by David Bullen
Typeset in Mergenthaler Fournier
by Harrington-Young
Printed by Maple-Vail
on acid-free paper